Christmas Wishes for the Railway Girls

Maisie Thomas was born and brought up in Manchester, which provides the location for her Railway Girls novels. She loves writing stories with strong female characters, set in times when women needed determination and vision to make their mark. The Railway Girls series is inspired by her great-aunt Jessie, who worked as a railway clerk during the First World War.

Maisie now lives on the beautiful North Wales coast with her railway enthusiast husband, Kevin, and their two rescue cats. They often enjoy holidays chugging up and down the UK's heritage steam railways.

Also by Maisie Thomas

The Railway Girls
Secrets of the Railway Girls
The Railway Girls in Love
Christmas with the Railway Girls
Hope for the Railway Girls
A Christmas Miracle for the Railway Girls
Courage of the Railway Girls

Christmas Wishes for the Railway Girls

MAISIE THOMAS

PENGUIN BOOKS

PENGUIN BOOKS

UK | USA | Canada | Ireland | Australia
India | New Zealand | South Africa

Penguin Books is part of the Penguin Random House group
of companies whose addresses can be found at global.
penguinrandomhouse.com

Penguin
Random House
UK

Published in Penguin Books 2023
001

Typeset in 10.4/15 pt Palatino LT Pro
by Integra Software Services Pvt. Ltd, Pondicherry

Printed and bound in Great Britain by Clays Ltd, Elcograf S.p.A.

The authorised representative in the EEA is Penguin Random House
Ireland, Morrison Chambers, 32 Nassau Street, Dublin D02 YH68

A CIP catalogue record for this book is available from the British
Library

ISBN: 978–1–804–94221–5

www.greenpenguin.co.uk

To Helen and James Odling
18 February 2023

And to their proud parents,
Simon and Geraldine Shires
and
Nigel and Deirdre Odling

Christmas Wishes
for the
Railway Girls

Chapter One

July 1943

Alison kept looking at herself in the dressing table's triple mirror as she got ready to go out for the evening with Joel. The midnight-blue dress suited her, not just in colour but in style, with its fitted bodice and the gently flared skirt that would swing beautifully when she danced – not a wide swing, but one that was muted and discreet, in keeping with the current fashion, not to mention the strict regulations concerning clothes, above all the rule that decreed that no fabric should be wasted on unnecessary details such as pleats, turn-ups or fullness.

The midnight blue was a formal evening gown and had originally belonged to her sister Lydia, but Alison had suggested a swap.

'My apricot for your blue,' she'd said. 'I haven't worn the apricot for ages.'

'But it's a lovely dress,' said Lydia, fingering the material. She was obviously tempted.

'I know, but it has . . . unpleasant associations, you might say. I last wore it on the night that Paul met Katie. I've never worn it since.'

'Oh, Alison.' Lydia lifted her hand from the apricot dress and laid it tenderly on Alison's arm. 'But it's not as though you haven't found happiness elsewhere. Joel adores you.'

'I know, but I still have no desire to wear the dress I was wearing when my old boyfriend met the girl he later told me was the love of his life.' A little shudder rippled through Alison's shoulders. Oh, the hopes she had entertained on that fateful occasion! 'So, will you swap dresses?' she asked Lydia in a bright and breezy voice. 'You wouldn't be superstitious about the apricot dress bringing bad luck?'

'No.' Lydia smiled. 'I've always admired it, actually.'

'Hmm.' Alison pressed her lips together, trying to look stern when really she was smothering a smile. 'I seem to remember you "admiring" a lot of my clothes when we both lived at home – yes, and helping yourself to them.'

That made Lydia laugh and her blue eyes twinkled. 'It's what sisters are for.'

Now Alison admired her reflection. Lydia's old midnight blue went well with her colouring. She had chosen the apricot because it was an unusual colour, but she could see now that it was more flattering to Lydia's fair hair than it ever had been to her own brown hair and eyes. Her gaze swept across the triple mirrors. There was a long mirror inset into one of the wardrobe doors too.

She took a moment to look with pleasure around the bedroom she had recently moved into. To start with, when she had come to live in the house in Wilton Close, she had been given what used to be the box room, a small room with a ceiling that sloped down to about four feet from the floor. There had been space for a narrow bed pushed into the corner, plus a cupboard and a chest of drawers. That might have sounded poky, but dear Mrs Cooper, who looked after them all so well, had made the room as comfortable as she could, keeping it spotless and popping sachets of dried lavender into the drawers, as well as making sure there was a hot-water bottle between the sheets all through the colder months.

After Mabel's wedding at the end of June, Alison had moved into the big bedroom with Margaret, taking over what had been Mabel's share of the space. Dear Mabel had been an important part of their friendship group, but now that she was married to Harry she had moved down south to live with him near Bomber Command. Mr and Mrs Morgan, whose house this was and who had decamped to North Wales for the duration, had slept in single beds, each with its own little bedside cupboard. The girls shared the dressing table and the wardrobe. There was even a fireplace, though fuel shortages meant that they only had the coal for the downstairs fires these days, and precious little at that. Thank goodness for summertime. Last winter had been hard and the coming winter wouldn't be any easier. In fact, it was certain to be worse.

Alison had never met the Morgans, but she was grateful to them for going to North Wales. Because of that, Cordelia had been able to recommend Mrs Cooper to them as a housekeeper who would take good care of the house in their absence and not kick up a fuss about being required to hand it back to them after the war. As well as looking after her lodgers, Mrs Cooper ran a little cleaning business called Magic Mop. It was possible for her to be out of the house earning a bit of money partly because Mrs Grayson, another lodger, had taken over the kitchen. Mrs Grayson, though never formally trained, was an expert cook and she found great satisfaction in providing tasty, nutritious meals for the household. Sometimes Alison got her to write down a recipe for her to take to Mum, and she knew that Mrs Grayson also sent recipes to Margaret's sister, Anna, in Shropshire. Now she was also sending recipes to Mabel.

Satisfied that the midnight-blue dress suited her, and feeling far lovelier than she had ever felt in the apricot, Alison turned her attention to her dark hair. She knew herself to be good-looking in a fresh-faced kind of way. 'Natural and unaffected' was how Mabel had once described her looks and Alison liked to remind herself of that sometimes. She had good hair, she knew that. When it was properly curled and styled, it hung a short way past her shoulders. Like many girls, she wore it in a simple pageboy cut that was easy to style away from her face. She curled her fringe too and wore it flicked back.

Alison had always enjoyed dressing up to go out and she loved looking her best. When she had been Paul's girlfriend, she'd wanted to look her best for him. It was different with Joel. *Everything* was different with Joel. Yes, she wanted to look pretty for him, but she wanted to look her best for herself too. She had submerged herself in being Paul's other half. Much as she loved Joel, she would never submerge herself like that again.

Her pulse quickened at the thought of being with him very soon. People liked him because of his cheerful nature, but he had a serious side too and Alison was sure his patients must find him both kind and reassuring. As for herself, well, the way his blue eyes softened when he looked at her practically made her bones melt.

Venetia, Joel's attractive, clever, graceful sister, had done her level best to get rid of Alison in the early days of their relationship in favour of an old girlfriend she had wanted Joel to get back together with, but Joel hadn't wavered in his devotion to Alison, even though they hadn't known one another all that long at that point. Joel's steadfastness had been exactly what Alison had needed after the way Paul had treated her. She had devoted herself to Paul heart and soul for a number of years – and then had come the occasion when she had worn the apricot dress.

It had been at a dance organised by Cordelia to raise funds for War Weapons Week, held in the glamorous ballroom at the Claremont Hotel. Alison had worked herself up to expect a proposal – just as she had so many times before. She felt ashamed of herself now when she recalled how desperate she had been for Paul to go down on one knee. She had planned it a thousand times in her head, but Paul had never proposed. She had told herself he was biding his time, and maybe he had been, but then Katie had come along and . . . well, he hadn't felt the need to bide his time before popping the question to her. On top of being devastated by heartbreak, Alison had tasted bitter humiliation.

But that was all very much in the past. Alison had met Dr Joel Maitland and loved every moment of being with him. The heart that Paul had shattered had been pieced back together again, though it wasn't the same heart it used to be. Gone was the girl who had thought of nothing but marriage.

She was happier now with Joel than she had ever been with Paul. With him, all she had ever thought about was getting a ring on her finger and buying fish knives and a cut-glass fruit bowl ready for when they got married. She'd been all set to live with Paul's mother, the two Mrs Dunaways doting on the man they both loved. Alison had built up to every anticipated proposal with anxious elation and then felt crushed every time it had failed to materialise.

That had been the old Alison. The new Alison could only shake her head in wonder. She had grown up a lot since then, not just through her experience of heartbreak but also because she had an interesting job that she loved. The old Alison had seen work as something to be got through until her 'real' life started, when she became a housewife and mother. Even when war had broken out and women were needed in the workplace as never before, that had still been the way she had perceived the clerical post she'd been allocated on the railways.

But after Paul dumped her, she had been given a new post.

Miss Emery, the assistant welfare supervisor with responsibility for women and girls on the railway, had sent for her.

'As the war continues,' Miss Emery had told her, 'we'll need more and more women, the most experienced and capable of whom will find themselves being promoted through the ranks.' Then she had astounded Alison by adding seriously, 'You are just such a capable girl, Miss Lambert.'

As well as being astounded, Alison had felt resentful, because what she had wanted more than anything was to get back together with Paul, not to be offered a new job, but she couldn't help feeling intrigued when Miss Emery went on to explain what lay ahead.

'I'd like to prepare you for a responsible role – not in the offices, but on the railway itself. To do this, I'd arrange for you to gain a variety of knowledge and experience, which will not only help to prepare you personally for what follows, but will also make it appear to other people that you are suitable for a post higher up. What do you think?'

That had been back in the second half of 1941, coming up for two whole years ago, and Alison was no closer to finding out the nature of the special job she was building up to. Her discreet hints seeking information had been ignored and the one or two outright questions she had dared to pose had been met by a coolly raised eyebrow and a murmur of, 'Really, Miss Lambert, you know better than to ask.'

Nevertheless, Alison loved going to work and was proud to feel she was playing her part in the war effort. She had gained experience in a variety of roles over the past couple of years. Every so often, Miss Emery would place her into a new environment for a time – the marshalling yard, a signal box, the various workshops – so she could be taught how everything worked. Her arrival was greeted with varying degrees of enthusiasm. Upon being informed that she was there to gain experience, her new colleagues either welcomed her and did all they could to teach her the ropes or else they resented the suggestion that their jobs could be learned so quickly. Moreover, even all this time into the war, there were still men who didn't like the idea of a woman in any position other than the lowliest. Most chaps were courteous and helpful, but there would always be those who chose not to be.

Although Alison had hated this new role to start with because she had been so ground down by heartbreak, she had gradually come to realise that work was more than a way of filling in the time before marriage. It was interesting and worthwhile in itself, something that had been a revelation to her. This knowledge had changed the way she viewed herself, increasing her self-respect. She could even be grateful that she hadn't had the chance to marry Paul, because that would have robbed her of the opportunity to become this new person, who was so much more than a housewife-in-waiting.

The old Alison had been well and truly left behind . . . or had she? Mabel's wedding had stirred up all kinds of feelings. Being happy for Mabel had set Alison thinking about herself and Joel. Joel was deeply in love with her. Right from the start, he had made it clear that, after having a string of girlfriends, this was a serious relationship and he was in no doubt that Alison was the right girl for him. Thus far, Alison had been more than content to have a handsome, devoted boyfriend to spend her spare time with. Was it now time for more? Or was she just in love with the idea of it because of Mabel's wedding?

Chapter Two

Alison walked into the crowded buffet at Victoria Station to meet her friends. It was one of those occasions when they could all manage to be here – well, except for Joan, of course. Her life was based around her home now that she was a wife and mother. Alison had known that the others would all be here this evening because of their system of leaving messages in a notebook that Mrs Jessop, who was in charge of the buffet, kept under the counter for them. Sometimes Mrs Jessop joked that with all the shortages, not just of provisions but also of crockery and cutlery, their little notebook was the only thing that was always present.

As Alison queued up for her tea, she looked around the room for her friends. Yes, there they were, all squeezed together around a single table, sharing seats so as not to deprive any neighbouring tables. Seeing Alison, Emily waved to her, which made the others look round and smile across the room through the wisps of tobacco smoke.

Alison felt a rush of affection for them all. She spared a moment to be grateful to Miss Emery too. As well as entrusting Alison with the job that was building up to goodness knew what, Miss Emery had also provided her with these dear friends who meant so much to her. Way back on their very first day together on the railways, Miss Emery had issued them with a piece of advice.

'Be friends with one another – regardless of age or background or anything else that would normally come between you. You'll be women in a man's world and some of the men, I regret to say, aren't keen on your being here. If you can turn to one another for support, it will help you all.'

How right she had been – and not just because of being women in a man's world. The friendships that had been forged in the early days of their working on the railways would last a lifetime. Alison knew that in her bones. Look at Dot and Cordelia. They were the best possible example of female friendship. Never mind that they hailed from different social classes, which before the war would have kept them rigidly apart. As Dot had cheerfully pointed out more than once, before the war the only way she and Cordelia would have met would have been if she had been engaged as Cordelia's charwoman – and that certainly wouldn't have resulted in any kind of friendship.

Cordelia, with her calm civility, her neatly styled ash-blonde hair and the pearl earrings she always wore, was every inch the middle-class wife of a well-to-do solicitor. Working-class Dot had bright hazel eyes that missed nothing and her blunt common sense was matched by a warm and generous heart. Dot, the mother of two serving soldiers, always referred to the younger members of their group as her 'daughters for the duration'.

Alison's gaze travelled over those 'daughters' now. Emily was actually Cordelia's daughter, and the newest member of their group. With her heart-shaped face, blue eyes and dark, naturally wavy hair, she was a pretty girl. Alison felt deep sympathy for her because Emily had been badly let down by her boyfriend before Christmas last year. As well as feeling compassion for Emily, she also felt admiration, aware that the younger girl, still only seventeen, had coped with her own unhappiness much better than Alison had coped when it had happened to her. Alison dearly hoped that Emily would meet a new boy, one who would stick with her for keeps, unlike Raymond.

Next to Emily was Persephone, leaning across to share a private word with Dot. A moment later, both of them laughed and sat back, smiling. After years of yearning after Forbes Winterton, who was friends with her brothers, Persephone had fallen for Matt Franklin. The Honourable Persephone Trehearn-Hobbs and a railway fireman! There had been some unpleasantness caused by a snippet in a society gossip column, but Persephone and Matt had come through the storm and were still seeing one another. Good for them.

Sharing a chair with Persephone was Colette. Of all of them, she surely must have been through the most. Sweet-natured, quietly spoken Colette had been married to – was still married to, for that matter – a cunning man who had fooled everyone into believing him to be the best husband in the world when really he controlled Colette's every move and she had lived in fear of how he would behave every time they went home and shut the front door behind them. Finally, he had beaten poor Colette black and blue and she'd ended up in hospital. To everyone's amazement, Tony had been permitted by the magistrate to join the army instead of

11

serve a prison sentence, but at least Colette was safe now and rebuilding her life.

Margaret was the only one of them to have no romantic history. Alison couldn't understand why, because she was a pretty girl with lovely dark hair and she had a kind-hearted personality. She had courage too, as Alison had discovered on the night Joan's baby had been born right here in Victoria Station during an air raid. Alison and Margaret had climbed up onto the station canopy to deal with incendiaries, but really it had been Margaret who'd been responsible for that, with Alison simply tagging along, buoyed by Margaret's gritty determination. Alison was glad to be sharing a bedroom with her now and hoped to get to know her more closely. Alison smiled to herself. Maybe Joel could provide a fellow doctor. It would be lovely to see Margaret with a boyfriend.

When Alison reached the counter, she exchanged a few words with Mrs Jessop, using the teaspoon that was tied to a small block of wood to stir her tea. That was the not so subtle way in which Mrs Jessop made sure her spoon didn't get 'lost' in these days of acute shortages.

Carrying her tea carefully, Alison made her way across the buffet towards her friends. It still felt odd not seeing Mabel there with them.

The others broke off from what they were talking about to say hello and make her welcome, then they returned to the subject of the invasion of Sicily, which had started the previous weekend.

'Sicily is being defended by the Germans and the Italian Sixth Army,' said Emily. 'I saw it on the Pathé newsreel when

I went to the pictures with my friend Lucy. Do you think Sicily will fall quickly?' she asked hopefully.

'Don't hold your breath, chick,' Dot advised her. 'It'll probably drag on for several weeks. That's how it happens. There's a battle or some such and the bigwigs say how crucial it is and you think "Oh, good," but then whatever it is drags on and on. Hark at me, putting a dampener on things. I don't mean to.'

'It's not like you, Dot,' said Persephone, a note of concern in her voice.

'I think it's just put me in mind of El Alamein. It felt like Reg and me waited for ever and a day to hear that our lads were all right.' Dot sighed. 'That was the best part of a year ago.'

There was a moment's silence around the table. Alison knew the others were thinking the same thing she was. What a long time the war had lasted and how much longer would it go on?

'On a happier note,' said Marga[...] 'I had a letter from Anna.'

Alison smiled. She always liked hearing about Margaret's sister. At the same time, she [...] ll aware of her own luck in having Lydia nearby. The w[...] separated Margaret and her much-loved older sister because Anna had been in the family way back in 1939 and so had been part of the mass evacuation that had sent schoolchildren and mothers-to-b[...] to places of safety.

'How is she?' asked Cordelia. 'And the twins?'

'They're all fine, thank you,' said Margaret with a smile. 'Do you remember how Anna started ba[...]ng for some of the ladies she cleans for, using recipes from Mrs Grayson?'

'Is she still doing that?' asked Colette.

Margaret nodded. 'She now bakes for other ladies too. She doesn't earn much for doing it, but she enjoys it. She says that Mrs Grayson's sultana pudding is going down a storm in Bridgnorth and Hampton Loade.'

'It's good that she's keeping busy,' said Cordelia.

'One of her ladies gave her an old shirt that she cut down to make a little dress for Anne-Marie. She said there was enough fabric left to make a pair of knickers, but she can't find elastic in the shops at any price.'

'She's not the only one,' Dot remarked. 'There was a fella on the market t'other day selling old flour sacks and women were buying them to make boys' shorts and cushion covers.'

'We're all making do,' Cordelia said in a resigned voice. 'With towels and tea towels on ration, we're all hanging on to old linen we'd have replaced without a thought before the war.'

Persephone leaned forward. 'I know this is going to sound really shallow, but have you seen the price of hats? A decent hat that would have set you back a guinea before the war now costs about eight pounds.'

'It's not shallow at all,' said Colette, 'or if it is, I'm shallow too. You used to be able to get a good coat and skirt for four-teen guineas before the war, but now that would cost forty pounds. Forty!'

'Mabel wanted a pretty nightdress for her honeymoon,' said Margaret. 'Before the war – twenty-five shillings, some-thing like that. These days – a tenner.'

'Poor Mabel,' breathed Alison.

'Her mother sent her some rather lovely silk rayon and Joan made a nightie for her,' said Margaret.

'We should just be grateful for Utility,' said Colette.

Well, yes, folk probably were grateful, because it meant that ordinary items were available and you didn't have to pay the vastly inflated wartime prices for non-Utility. All kinds of things were available in Utility – clothes, furniture, carpets, household items, all of them basic and entirely functional in design.

Dot laughed. 'My sister Minnie got herself some Utility cups and was most indignant to find they didn't have handles.'

'Wot, no handles?' quipped Emily, quoting the now famous cartoon character Chad, who was always pictured peering over a wall, his long nose hanging in front of the bricks. The familiar refrain of 'Wot, no oranges?', 'Wot, no petrol?' and so forth was a humorous way of mentioning shortages.

The others laughed in a moment of pure camaraderie. It didn't matter how bad things got. Friendship and determination would see them through. Alison was reminded of the words on the memorial to the men of the old Lancashire and Yorkshire Railway who had given their lives in the Great War.

Unity, strength, courage, sacrifice.

Chapter Three

Alongside two other girls, Margaret worked at cleaning the loco. She was armed with a scraper for the wheels and her own bundle of thick rags. It was a heavy job. The tender had to be cleaned as well as the loco – and then there were the wheels. Thick deposits had to be scraped out fully before the wheels could be thoroughly cleaned and dried. It was essential for them to be done properly because the wheeltappers would then come along to test for cracks. Margaret always thought of Mabel when she did the wheels, because Mabel's late and much-loved grandad had been a wheeltapper.

Margaret took a moment to stretch her back and roll her neck. She wore a boiler suit in the cold months, but at this time of year she was more comfortable in a pair of heavy-duty dungarees with a shirt underneath, its sleeves rolled up above her elbows. Her brown hair was tucked away inside a turban, but it was impossible to keep her skin safe from the thick grease, oil and filth. You were always supposed to be able to recognise munitions girls who worked with a certain type of powder because their skin went yellow. Well, the same went for engine cleaners. They hadn't a hope of having truly clean nails again until after the war. Even when Margaret thought she'd washed everything off her skin, somehow there were always marks left on her pillowcase. Mrs Cooper took it in

16

her stride and whenever Margaret had spent a shift on wheels or undercarriages, she always laid a cloth across Margaret's pillow. Mabel used to call it 'the sacrificial cloth'.

So, yes, Margaret's war work was filthy and often back-breaking – but, oh, the pride it engendered. There was nothing more satisfying or inspiring than seeing one of 'her' locos getting up steam, ready to pull its load. Mad as it might sound, Margaret had grown to love the railway engines. She even felt compassion for those that, if this had been peace-time, would have retired by now. Instead, like the old folk who had returned to work to do their bit for their country, they were working past their true retirement date.

When it was time to stop for a cuppa, all the girls and women stepped away from their work gratefully. Margaret noticed her chum Sally sitting on her own on the edge of the platform, feet dangling. She went to sit beside her. Sally seemed lost in thought. When Margaret dropped down by her side, Sally gave a little gasp and her blue eyes widened.

Margaret laughed. 'Sorry. Did I make you jump?'

It took Sally a moment to smile back. Her face looked ser-ious in repose, but when she smiled she looked quite lovely. She was a slender girl, but she was agile and strong, both of which were important for the kind of work they did. She had stamina too, which was an essential quality. Margaret liked her. She was good fun. Not in a life-and-soul-of-the-party kind of way, which wouldn't have suited Margaret, but she had a sense of humour and was a good sport.

Sally had been born on the day the Great War ended, so she was heading towards her twenty-fifth birthday. She was from Whaley Bridge, where her parents still lived, but

17

Sally had got digs in Levenshulme, which was much closer to work.

The two of them sometimes went to the pictures together. They had seen Bette Davis in *Now, Voyager* not long before Mabel's wedding, but come to think of it, they hadn't been since then.

'D'you fancy going to the flicks one evening?' Margaret suggested. 'If you fancy a musical, *Hello, Frisco, Hello* is on, or there's *Sherlock Holmes in Washington*. You like Basil Rathbone, don't you?'

'Actually, would you mind if I said no? I'm . . . well, I've been feeling tired lately.'

'Are you all right?' Margaret asked, concerned. Then she asked the question her late mother always used to ask. 'Are you sickening for something?' Margaret had never been completely sure precisely what this meant, but quoting Mum was a way of showing she cared.

'I'm fine,' said Sally. 'We're all tired these days, aren't we? I think it's just caught up with me, that's all.'

'If you're sure,' said Margaret. 'You don't look your usual self.'

'The oil and grease are making me feel a bit icky. It's nothing.'

'Maybe you just need a good night's sleep.'

Sally smiled at her. 'Thanks, Nurse Margaret.'

Soon it was time to get back to work. If loco cleaning had involved any lighter duties, Margaret might have asked their supervisor to go easy on Sally for a day or two, but engine cleaning was hard work, full stop, and everyone was always glad to reach the end of their shift.

Later, Margaret said goodbye to Sally and her other colleagues and headed for home. Her body ached, not so much because of the physical effort her job demanded, but because she longed for a hot soak in a deep bath, preferably one with bubbles and a delicious scent, but the regulation five inches of water was as much as anyone got these days, together with a sliver of rationed soap to keep you company.

At home, Margaret had a strip-wash, the water in the basin quickly turning black and needing to be refreshed. When she'd dried herself, she pulled on her dressing gown and returned to the bedroom that Alison now shared with her. She truly liked Alison, but she could never forget what lay between them. Not that Alison had any idea of it. And Alison's ignorance was what made it all the more difficult for Margaret to let go. She ought to be accustomed to keeping the secret by this time, but there were occasions when it burst to the forefront of her mind. The day she had helped Alison move from the box room to the bedroom had been just such an occasion and the secret had been bubbling away ever since.

Well, it wouldn't carry on being like that, Margaret was certain. Give it time and sharing with Alison would feel perfectly normal and comfortable . . . and the secret would subside and leave Margaret alone. That was what she wanted more than anything – for the memory of her own old relationship with Alison's boyfriend to fade away and vanish from her mind. Alison knew that Margaret and Joel had gone out with one another for a time at the beginning of the war, but that was all she knew. She didn't know that Margaret had adored Joel back then. Mind you, nor had Joel been aware of the extent of Margaret's feelings for him. She had worshipped the ground he walked on – wasn't that the expression?

Most important of all, Alison didn't have the first idea that Margaret and Joel's relationship had led to a pregnancy. At the time it had happened, back in 1940, Margaret had firmly believed that Joel, having succeeded in getting her into bed, had then scarpered, no doubt chuckling with glee. It wasn't until the spring of last year, 1942, that Margaret had learned that his disappearance hadn't been through his own choice. At the same time, Joel had been deeply shocked to hear of Margaret's pregnancy, which had ended in a painful and frightening miscarriage.

Together, the two of them had decided to tell Alison only that they had been out together a few times, and nothing more than that. It had seemed best that way. Alison was spared a difficult truth – and Margaret got to keep her shameful secret.

Chapter Four

'My two boys,' said Joan, her heart melting like wax at the sight of her darling husband and the little son they both adored playing peek-a-boo, something that fourteen-month-old Max never failed to find hilariously funny. Bob was endlessly patient and would spend any amount of time with his son.

Gran had once ventured to say that bathing the baby was the mother's job, not the father's.

'Oh aye?' Bob had turned to look at her, his face and his voice nothing but pleasant. 'Did your son never give his babies their bath?'

'Of course not,' said Gran.

'Then he missed out on one of life's delights,' said Bob. 'I want to spend every moment I can with Max. I give thanks every day that I'm in a reserved occupation and can watch my son grow up. Think of all those men in the services who are missing out on their children's young years. Only I want to do more than just see Max grow up. I want to be a part of every aspect of it.'

'Says the man who's never changed a nappy,' Joan remarked.

Bob grinned. 'Well, there are limits.'

Since they had moved into Gran's house in Torbay Road, the house where Joan and her late sister Letitia had grown up, Joan's love for Bob had increased, no   ause he was such a wonderful father but also becau of the polite, cheerful way he behaved towards Gran, something that had deepened Joan's respect and admiration for him too. Joan and Gran had had a difficult relationship for a long time and the wall between them had for a time seemed insurmountable. Not only that, but Joan had had no intention of attempting to scale it. But life had moved on when the long-held secret that had driven them apart had unexpectedly thrown them back together and they'd had to join forces to keep the secret safe from the rest of the world. It was after that had happened that Joan had felt able to return to live under Gran's roof. She and Bob had needed somewhere bigger because of Max being on the way. Moreover, Joan had seen that maybe Gran – the domineering, judgemental, grim woman who had brought her up so strictly – was no longer as strong as she used to be.

They had divided the house. Gran's bedroom had been moved into the old dining room and she now lived downstairs while Joan and Bob had the upstairs, using Gran's former bedroom as their sitting room. They all shared the kitchen and the bathroom. It had turned out to be a good arrangement, a mixture of support and privacy, reliance and independence.

Now Bob left off the game of peek-a-boo to glance over his shoulder at Joan. 'Two boys?' he asked. 'Shouldn't that be three? Brizo! Come here, old chap.' As the dog bounded towards him, Bob slung an arm around him at the same time as turning back to Max. 'We've got Mummy outnumbered, haven't we, eh? The three Hubble boys.'

Joan laughed. 'Well, the three Hubble boys had better get a move on or we'll be late for tea.'

They were going for Sunday tea to Bob's folks in Stretford. Dennis and Bernice Hubble adored being grandparents to Max, who also had three aunties to coo over him – Bob's sisters, Maureen, Petal and Glad. For Max to have a loving wider family meant the world to Joan, whose only relatives as she grew up had been Gran and Letitia. But it wasn't just because of Max that she loved and appreciated her in-laws. It was also because of the way they had welcomed her into their family with open arms.

'No such thing as in-laws in this house,' Mum had said. Mum – that was what Joan called Bob's mother, and his father was Dad. After growing up without parents, it was wonderful to feel she now had a mother and father. Some people said you couldn't miss what you'd never had, but it wasn't true. As a child, Joan had always longed for the love that could only come from parents.

How lucky she was. She had Bob and Max. They were privileged to have a comfortable home with more space than many enjoyed in these days of bombed-out families. And she had her fun-loving Hubble family. In spite of the war, her life felt perfect.

Well, except for one thing . . .

Sunday tea at the Hubbles' was always a pleasure. Bob and Joan had brought with them a carpet bag containing the things Max would need to stay there. Mum and Dad, who worked on the railways, had both got tomorrow as their day off, so when Joan and Bob went home this evening, Max was going to stay behind to spend tonight and Monday with his doting grandparents.

Bob laughed. 'Some day off it'll be. He'll run you ragged.'

'I can't think of anything better,' said Dad, bouncing Max on his knee and making neighing noises.

'It'll be a day off for you an' all, Joan,' Mum said to her. 'I know how much he means to you, but you'll enjoy having a day all to yourself.'

Joan smiled back but didn't say anything. The back of her throat seemed to close over as frustration bubbled up inside her. As it happened, she wasn't going to get a day off. Like many young mums all over the country, she minded other people's children so that those mothers could go out to do war work. Joan would spend tomorrow taking care of the two little ones she was responsible for. Sometimes she got really fed up with it. She wanted to go back to her old line of work. She used to love her job on the railways.

She had been a porter at Victoria Station. Mostly, her job had been to assist passengers by trundling their luggage to wherever they needed it to be taken – Left Luggage, the taxi rank or another platform. At other times, when a train arrived containing consignments of food or other things, she would ferry crates from the platform to the stores. Or she might have to help load heavy packages of salvaged paper destined for the paper mill. Oh, there had been all kinds of jobs to do! Her favourite, though, had always been working with the public. Pushing suitcases around on a sack trolley might not sound like much to some people, but Joan had found it interesting and satisfying and no two days had ever been the same.

As well as loving her job, she had also enjoyed spending time with the friends she had made. They had all been put into different jobs, but they had consciously built up a solid friendship by making sure they met up regularly in the buffet. In time, that had expanded into other areas of their lives. Joan smiled at the memory of the various tea parties they had enjoyed. They were experts when it came to celebrating a special occasion with a tea party. And it wasn't just the railway girls who were friends. Their group had grown to include Mrs Cooper and Mrs Grayson; Joan had lived with them in Wilton Close before she got married. And there were the husbands and boyfriends – and Miss Brown and Mrs Mitchell from Darley Court, a nearby mansion that provided rooms for meetings and training sessions for the various local civil defence organisations. Joan had made a point of inviting Margaret's widowed father to the tea party they'd had for Max's first birthday, because Margaret and Mr Darrell had had a big falling-out in the early days of the war and had only reconciled their differences last year. Joan knew all about falling out with your closest family and she'd wanted to support Margaret and Mr Darrell in their restored relationship.

Joan held in a sigh of nostalgia. The railways had given her so much. She still saw her friends, of course, and they felt more important to her than ever, especially now that dear old Mabel had upped sticks and headed off to pastures new.

Before she left Manchester, Mabel had set up a nursery in Chorlton only five minutes' walk from where Joan and Bob lived. Demand for places was high and the available ones were filling up quickly.

Joan adored Max, but she knew that mothers weren't supposed to want to leave their children. Was it wrong of her to dream of going back to work?

Chapter Five

Margaret led the way upstairs. Joan had come round to Wilton Close. Before the war, she had worked as a sewing machinist at Ingleby's, where she had made clothes for those customers who could afford it and altered clothes to fit for those who purchased ready-mades. Mrs Cooper, who worked in the WVS's clothes exchange, had alerted Margaret to the presence on one of the rails of a beautifully tailored pre-war dress in a rich, creamy hue that was almost but not quite pale yellow, patterned with splodges of rosy-brown. It was a lovely garment and Margaret had fallen for it right away. She didn't have much in the way of good clothes, her family home having taken a direct hit early on in the war.

The dress was too big and, being a few years pre-war, too long, but Joan had kindly offered to alter it for her. The two of them had originally met because they had both worked at Ingleby's, though Margaret's job had been on the shop floor. It was really when they'd been assigned to fire-watching duty together that they had started to get to know one another.

Margaret opened her bedroom door and waved Joan inside.

Joan smiled as she looked around. 'My old home,' she said, a note of affection in her voice. 'Here.' Placing her shopping bag on Margaret's bed, she withdrew the neatly folded dress and held it up by its shoulders.

Margaret inhaled a breath of pure pleasure. The round neck was topstitched, as were the patch pockets. The sleeves, which fell to halfway between shoulder and elbow, were slightly flared – but not so much as to look unpatriotic in these days of stringent regulations. As well as taking in the bodice, Joan had shortened the skirt.

'And I've used some of the leftover fabric to make a tie belt so you can chop and change between that and the leather belt it came with. The rest I'll use for making needlecases and pincushions for the WVS to put in their next sale of work.'

'That's a good idea,' said Margaret. 'Thank you for the dress and the belt. You're so clever.' She smiled. 'Much as I loved my job at Ingleby's, I can't help thinking that yours has served you better in the long term.'

'Try on the dress before you say that,' Joan chuckled.

Margaret did so, standing in front of the long mirror in the wardrobe door to admire the effect.

'The cream and that browny shade go well with your colouring,' Joan commented.

Margaret was pleased to see that they did. Did they even lend a bit of richness to what she had always thought of as her very ordinary brown hair and hazel eyes? Her brother and sister both had fair hair and blue eyes. As the youngest, she had always looked up to them and had the feeling that they were better-looking, with more attractive colouring.

'I'll tell you what would go nicely with that dress when it gets chilly,' said Joan. 'That jumper Anna knitted for you.'

'Yes, you're right.'

It was another reason to be pleased with her new dress. Anna had knitted a sweater for her out of russet-coloured wool into which she'd been obliged to add a 'patriotic' cream stripe because she hadn't been able to get her hands on all the russet she needed. Opening one of her drawers in the chest of drawers, Margaret took out the jumper and slipped it over her head.

'Oh, that's perfect. And it means I'll be able to wear the dress all year round. Wait – it needs one thing more.'

From her drawer in the dressing-table, Margaret removed the necklace her friends had given her in the spring of last year. It was a little silver 'W' on a dainty chain. They hadn't been able to find an M for Margaret or a T for Thomas, her late mother's maiden name which she had adopted by deed poll, so they had got her a W for William in honour of her beloved brother. It had been of deep emotional significance because at the time William had been missing in action. To the profound relief of Margaret, Dad and Anna, he had later been accounted for. Thanks to a stint in a field hospital, he had returned to his duty.

The necklace was one of two equally precious pieces of jewellery, the other being Mum's engagement ring, a narrow gold band, worn thin, with a row of five little diamonds. Dad had given Mum's wedding and engagement rings to Anna because she was the older daughter, but last spring Anna had sent the engagement ring to Margaret. Both the ring and the 'W' necklace were unspeakably important to her.

Joan smiled understandingly as Margaret put on the necklace. 'Anna's jumper and William's necklace. Now that really is perfect.'

After a few moments Margaret removed the jumper and gazed at the reflection of herself wearing the dress. 'Again – thank you,' she said, turning to Joan.

'My pleasure.'

'You'll always have a job to fall back on, won't you?' Margaret remarked and was surprised to see Joan's expression change. 'Have I said the wrong thing?'

'No, of course not.' Joan pressed her lips together for a second, then appeared to make up her mind. 'Can I tell you something?'

Sitting on Margaret's bed, Joan held out a hand. Margaret went to her, taking her hand as she sat beside her. The mattress dipped slightly.

'What is it?' Margaret asked.

'I would dearly love to return to work.'

'You are working,' Margaret pointed out. 'You're childminding. We're always hearing that that's proper war work, because it releases mothers to work in the factories and so forth.'

'I know. I understand that. But . . . I've realised it isn't the right thing for me.'

'I thought you loved looking after Max,' Margaret said, surprise making the words pop out before she had a chance to consider them.

'I did. I do. Max means the world to me. You know that. I loved every minute when it was just him and me at home, but it isn't just him and me now. I look after two other little ones and they're quite a handful.'

'It's your war work,' Margaret said quietly. What was Joan building up to?

'And I understand how important it is. Mothers have to be supported so they can go to work with an easy mind.' Although Joan's voice was soft, it nevertheless held a note of urgency. 'But I dream of going back to the railways. I was so happy there. And wanting that doesn't mean I love Max any less.'

'Of course it doesn't,' Margaret assured her. 'No one who knows you would ever think that. Is that what you're intending to do? Go back to the railways?'

'I've been thinking about it for a good while. I talked to Mabel about it.'

'Times have changed,' said Margaret. 'The war has changed everything. It's normal now for married women to go out to work. It's normal for mothers too. The country doesn't have a choice.'

'Do you remember Cordelia telling us right back when we first met – no, wait a minute. Of course you don't. It was before you joined us. She said something like, "It's horrible to be at war, but seize every opportunity that comes your way." Returning to work would be a big opportunity for me. In peacetime, the only mothers who go out to work are poor women or widows. And – and it isn't just what Cordelia said. I keep remembering something Letitia told me.'

'What was that?' asked Margaret.

'I don't want you to think badly of her, but she said she was enjoying the war. She adored working at the munitions. That was her exact word: "adore". She wasn't on the assembly line. She was superb at maths and she had to check various calculations. She loved it. She wanted to help win the war. I keep thinking about that – and about not loving childminding.' Joan added in a whisper, 'I feel guilty for seeing something war-related as an opportunity. And I'm dreading people thinking I'm not putting Max first.'

'It's not an easy choice for you.' Margaret released Joan's hand and slid an arm around her. 'Whatever decision you make, I'll stand by you. You adore that little godson of mine and you'd never do anything to his detriment.'

'Now it's my turn to say thank you.' Joan returned Margaret's hug. 'I've got a lot of thinking to do.' She released a brisk sigh, clearly wanting to move on from this topic, and glanced at Mabel's old bed. 'Do you mind sharing with Alison?'

The words gave Margaret a jolt. It was odd hearing from Joan's lips the very question she had asked herself numerous times. But being with Joan gave Margaret the chance to release some emotional tension. Joan knew about Margaret's miscarriage because she had been the first-aider who had helped her through it.

'No, I don't,' said Margaret, 'except that it has brought back memories that I would have much preferred never to be troubled by again.'

'It must feel strange,' Joan said sympathetically.

'It does,' Margaret admitted, 'but then I ask myself if I would have preferred Alison to stay in the old box room, to which the answer is a definite no. This room is much comfier and she's entitled to it. I've decided to look at it in a positive light. This is a chance for the two of us to get to know one another better. I do like her, you know.'

'Of course you do,' Joan agreed, 'and she likes you. She's never stopped admiring your leadership on the evening Max was born.'

'I'm glad we did that together,' said Margaret. 'It gives me something good to remember every time I think of . . . the other thing. Alison must never ever know about that.'

'Lord, no,' said Joan. 'She'd be devastated.'

'I wish it was possible for me to wipe my memory clean of it,' Margaret whispered.

Joan rubbed Margaret's back. 'I know. I'm always here if you need to talk. You know that, don't you?' She stood up. 'And now, Miss Thomas, it's time to go downstairs and show off your new frock to Mrs Cooper and Mrs Grayson. I know nothing can take away the bad memories, but a bit of admiration never hurt anyone.'

Margaret showed off her new dress to Alison, heaping praise on Joan's skills as she did so. 'No one would imagine this is a made-over dress, would they?'

'Joan is so clever,' Alison agreed. 'Tell you what: you should wear this when we go dancing. You'll be the belle of the ball.'

Margaret laughed. 'Not quite, but I'll feel special.'

She had Joan to thank for both of her good dresses, her other one being the one that Joan had originally made for her sister Letitia. Made from a lovely lilac, it had a collarless neck and a matching belt. Joan had lent it to Margaret to wear as her bridesmaid's dress at Joan's wedding, and on Margaret's next birthday she had given it to her outright. Joan was such a kind person.

Several of them were to go to the Ritz Ballroom the next evening. Margaret didn't mind being with Alison and Joel as long as they were part of a group. Persephone and Matt

32

were both due to have the evening free, but it depended on whether Matt's shift overran, which it often did because of all the delays on the railways these days. Persephone had said she would go even if Matt couldn't. Colette didn't go dancing, but Cordelia had given Emily permission to.

Margaret normally wore her lilac, which, after all, had been made for dancing, but now she looked forward to wearing her new dress. There was nothing like having all your worldly possessions blown to kingdom come to make you appreciate the nice things that came your way afterwards.

When they reached the Ritz, the doorman carefully closed the lobby door behind them before opening the door into the foyer. The girls queued up to hand in their jackets and hats in return for cloakroom tickets while Joel and Matt found a table that was big enough and sorted out drinks. The girls entered the ballroom, with its pillars, its art deco features and its balcony, just as the famous revolving stage began to turn. As the first band gradually disappeared from view, the other stage swung round with the second band playing exactly the same music. It was a sight and a sound Margaret never grew tired of. It felt special every single time – and it made her feel special too. Ballrooms, dance halls and cinemas enabled everyone to step into another existence, leaving the world of wartime behind for the time being.

Margaret danced a few times, twice with strangers, twice with men she'd danced with on previous occasions. When she returned to their table, Alison was there, sipping lemonade. She sat up straight as Margaret approached.

'There you are.' There was a warm glow in Alison's brown eyes. 'I thought you'd never come back. Joel and I have got someone we want you to meet.'

Alarm sent shivers through Margaret. 'A man?'

'Well, of course a man, silly.' Alison laughed. 'He's a doctor, which is how Joel knows him, and he's very handsome. Musical too. He comes from a family where they all play different instruments. Don't look so scared. I've met him and he's easy to talk to.'

'I really don't want to be fixed up with anyone,' Margaret began.

'But you're such a lovely girl,' Alison said persuasively. 'You deserve to have chap of your own. I've got Joel. Persephone has Matt. Mabel and Joan are both married. It's about time we got you sorted out. Why do you think I encouraged you to wear your new dress?'

Margaret made sure she kept her voice light and pleasant as she said, 'I don't want to be sorted out.'

'Oh, go on. It could be the last word in romance. Imagine if he turns out to be the man you've been waiting for all your life – and it's your friends who introduced you. Well, you never know,' Alison said breezily. 'It could happen like that. Persephone and Matt are seeing one another in spite of the social gap between them, and Joan and Bob met on a first-aid training day. You simply never know how you'll meet the man of your dreams. Come on, Margaret. You aren't shy, are you?'

In the end, Margaret felt forced to give in. Alison clearly wasn't going to, so Margaret just had to get it over with. She allowed herself to be introduced to Dr George Abernathy, who was indeed pleasant and easy to talk to. Under other circumstances, she wouldn't have minded him being a member of their group – but not with Alison watching her like a hawk, waiting for Cupid to take aim. She danced with George a few times, finding him light on his feet and an interesting conversationalist. But that was all. There was no spark there, just as she had known there wouldn't be.

'May I see you again?' George asked her. 'We could go to the pictures if you like.'

'Thanks, but I'm happier going out as one of a group,' said Margaret.

'Fair enough,' said George, looking disappointed.

A little later, Alison asked her, 'Didn't it work out?'

'I'm sure he's a perfectly decent chap and all the rest of it,' said Margaret, 'but I didn't like being put on the spot like that.'

'Maybe I shouldn't have told you,' said Alison. 'Maybe I should have just let him ask you to dance.'

Margaret felt like saying, 'Maybe you should leave me alone,' but what she said was, 'You're sweet to think of finding me someone, but I'd much rather you didn't. Honestly.'

'But you deserve to be happy,' said Alison. 'I'm not just saying that. I really mean it. I want you to be happy.'

Margaret made herself laugh. 'Organising an orderly queue of eligible bachelors outside the door of number one Wilton Close isn't the way to do it.'

'An orderly queue?' Alison's lips twitched into a wide smile. 'Now there's a thought.'

But Margaret realised she had made her point – or at least she hoped she had.

35

That night, she lay awake in the darkness, listening to the beat of her heart. Since getting over Joel all that time ago, she had never been attracted to another man. You heard about people playing the field, but she wasn't like that. She clearly remembered Mum telling her, 'Once I met your dad, I knew he was the one and only man for me.'

Had Joel been her own one and only chance? Was she destined never to meet anyone else?

Chapter Six

Bob had built Max a little box on wheels. At one end it had a lightweight piece of metal shaped like a giant croquet hoop. Max's great achievement was to grasp this handle in his chubby little fists and use the box to balance himself as he toddled along at a furious pace from one end of their sitting room to the other and back again, undeterred by bumping into their few pieces of furniture. Bob and Joan laughed as they watched, heaping praise and encouragement on their son. Then they looked at one another and exchanged rueful smiles.

'He's growing up so quickly,' said Joan. 'The days are flying by and I want to hang on to every new thing he does and every moment I have with him.'

'It won't be long before he's walking on his own,' said Bob. 'Then you'll have three toddlers to manage during the day. That'll keep you fit!'

It was too natural an opening to ignore. 'Actually, I'd like us to discuss that. You know that I'm not as happy child-minding as I might have been. I've been thinking seriously about going back to work at Victoria – and before you say it, I know that childminding is war work, but it doesn't feel like the right thing for me.'

'But it means you can stay at home with Max.'

Joan groaned. 'I know. And that's what makes this so hard. I adore Max and I know I just said that I want to hang on to every moment we have together – and that's true. I do. But I miss going out to work – and I'm aware that this is my last chance.'

'How so?'

'If we had another child, I don't think it would be possible.'

'Oh aye? If it was only the mothers of one who worked outside the home, the munitions factories would have hardly any employees.'

'I can't explain it in a rational way,' said Joan. 'It's a feeling I have. If proper arrangements could be made for Max, then I could cope with a job, I'm sure of that. But if we had another baby, I'd see it as necessary to stop at home.'

Bob shifted on the settee, putting a protective arm around her; she snuggled against him, feeling safe and happy.

'We do want more children, don't we?' he murmured.

'You know we do,' Joan answered. 'I'd never change my mind about that.'

'But before that happens, you want to have the chance of going back to railway work.'

'Call it my last hurrah.' Joan spoke lightly, but her heart swelled with gratitude for her husband's support.

'I'd rather call it you knowing your own mind. You love Max to bits, but this childminding lark isn't for you. I don't want you to be upset or frustrated at home. That wouldn't be good for the children and it wouldn't be good for you. Besides, this is wartime. In peacetime, you'd simply have been taking care of Max without the extra two to run around after and maybe you'd have felt differently about things. But in wartime, everyone has to do their duty. We thought yours was taking care of other people's children and it turns out we were mistaken.'

Joan slid her arm around Bob's waist and hugged him. 'Thank you for saying "we". That means so much.'

'Of course it's "we". My duty as a husband is to do the best I can to provide for my family and that means more than just putting food on the table. It means listening to my wife and taking her feelings into account. It also means looking to the future. I have enough relatives who lived through the last war to know that it's important to be proud of what you do in wartime. There is so much loss and unhappiness, and there will be so many difficulties afterwards, you have to take pride in what you did. I'll be proud to say that in my own small way I helped to keep the railways running. I want you to be proud too, Joan, and if being able to say "I worked on the railways" is going to make you prouder than saying "I looked after other people's children", then so be it.'

'Oh, Bob,' Joan murmured emotionally.

'Hey, cheer up. I know how proud I am of my mum having a job on the railways for the duration. When our son grows up and joins the railways too, he isn't just going to tell folk he followed in his father's footsteps. He's going to say that both his parents were railway workers. Won't that be something for us to be proud of?'

The single most important aspect of Joan's possible return to the railways was the difference it would make to Max's life. To this end, she was determined that she could only go back to work if she could find a job that didn't involve working shifts around the clock. There were many wives and mothers who had no option but to do this, but Joan promised Bob that she wouldn't. She promised it to herself too.

The top priority for her and Bob was making sure that Max would be properly cared for.

'Preferably by people he always knows and loves,' said Joan. 'It will be hard enough to leave him without having to contemplate leaving him with someone new. I know that Norman and Jeremy were left with someone new when they came to me, and I'm sure they didn't suffer because of it, but that's not the point.'

Only now was she truly beginning to understand how hard it must have been for those two mums whose youngsters she took care of. Until now, her thoughts of returning to railway work had centred almost entirely around her own frustration at staying at home. Now that it had started to become a real possibility, Max's welfare had very much taken centre stage, and rightly so. Part of her dreaded handing him over to be looked after by someone else, no matter how much she trusted them.

'Who exactly will take care of Max?' Bob asked.

'Gran could sometimes, though only sometimes,' said Joan. 'Certainly not on a regular basis. We couldn't ask a lady in her seventies to look after a little lad who has recently found his feet and wants to get about as much as he can.'

'Besides,' Bob added, 'we mustn't forget that we want her to enjoy being a great-grandmother.'

'I know,' Joan agreed at once. 'She never had the chance to be a grandmother because Letitia and I lost our parents when we were so tiny. Gran had to be the parent after that.

There's your mum and your sisters. They'd love it – shifts permitting.'

'But what if shifts don't permit?' asked Bob. 'On top of which, there'd be the matter of getting Max over to Stretford and back home again. It's one thing to go over there for Sunday tea, but it's not feasible on a daily basis.'

'Then that leaves a childminder and they're like gold dust,' said Joan, 'and we really don't want him to go to a stranger. I've been wondering about Mabel's nursery.' She smiled. 'I shouldn't call it that. I should use its proper name – the Lizzie Cooper Nursery. Dear Lizzie,' she added with a pang of sadness for her lost friend.

'Wouldn't the nursery be the same as sending him to a strange childminder?' Bob asked.

'Not quite,' said Joan. 'Some of the WVS ladies and the volunteers who work there are ladies we already know. Mrs Jenks and Mrs Broughton live up Torbay Road. Besides, I know how much Max loves being with Norman and Jeremy during the day when I'm looking after them. He adores their company and, being the youngest, he's always trying to do what they do. It's good for him to spend his days with other children and he'd certainly do that at the nursery.'

Bob grinned. 'And then there's the fact that our friend Mabel went to a lot of trouble to set it up. It would only be polite to send our lad there.'

'Idiot,' laughed Joan. 'Mabel went to endless lengths to make sure everything was exactly the way it ought to be. Well, she had to, because everything was done through the Corporation, so there's no question about the quality of the care.'

41

'Then the next step is to go there,' said Bob, 'and see if they have places left.'

'I'll let Norman and Jeremy's mums know – and we have to tell Gran what we're planning.' Joan's heart dipped at the prospect. It was a long time since she had been under Gran's thumb, but she still had moments of being wary of her. Gran could be uncompromising in her attitude.

'Yes, we should,' Bob agreed. 'Now that we've decided for sure, she's entitled to know.' He gave Joan a hug. 'And it'll get the scolding over and done with.'

Leaving Max snuggled up fast asleep, they went downstairs and sat with Gran in her parlour.

'We're telling you out of respect for you as Joan's gran and our landlady,' Bob made clear when they had explained what might happen.

And possibly out of respect for them, Gran opened her mouth – and then shut it again.

'Well, you know best, I suppose,' was all she allowed herself to say, 'but I find it a strange choice, especially when you're such devoted parents. No mother who has the option should go out to work. The best start for any child is in the home. The only exception to this is when the mother is inadequate, in which case a nursery is the desirable choice.'

'Times have changed,' Joan said. 'People are expected to do their bit – and I want to do mine on the railways.'

Gran's eyes glinted, but she simply stated, 'I know you'd never do anything against Max's best interests. When are you going to visit the nursery?'

'Tomorrow,' said Joan.

With three tots in her care, the easiest thing was to squeeze all of them into Max's pram.

At the nursery, Joan was met by Mrs Broughton.

'Have you any places available?' Joan asked.

'For three?'

'For one,' Joan said quickly. 'Just mine. Max.'

'Look at him. Isn't he growing?' Mrs Broughton said admiringly. 'Are you going back to work, then?'

Joan's gossip antenna started bleeping madly. 'Nothing has been decided yet, so I'd be grateful if you didn't say anything. Do you have any places?'

'We do,' Mrs Broughton told her, 'but only part-time ones. What sort of work hours are you contemplating?'

'As I said, nothing has been decided yet,' Joan said firmly.

Instead of heading for home with the boys, she took them round to Wilton Close.

In her old home, before she'd been bombed out, Mrs Cooper had provided Joan with a safe haven at a time when she had been deeply in need. Mrs Grayson had already been lodging there. Then Mrs Cooper's house had been destroyed and all three of them had moved together to Wilton Close, thanks to Cordelia's friendship with the Morgans. Not long after that, Mabel had moved in with them too. It was a part of her life that Joan held in great affection.

'Well, look who it is.' Mrs Grayson opened the front door as Joan heaved the pram through the wooden gate. Coming down the path, she peered into the pram, pretending not to see the boys. 'Goodness me, an empty pram! We'll have to fill it up with potatoes.'

'No!' and 'Yes!' the boys roared in delight.

'They really need a good run around,' said Joan, 'but I can't have them racing all over your vegetable garden.'

'I think that anyone who runs ten times around the dining table and then sits beautifully with their legs crossed can have a drink and a biscuit,' said Mrs Grayson. 'I'll help Max follow the other two.'

When this had been accomplished, Mrs Grayson dug about in the salvage box, producing some pieces of paper that she scrunched together to make little balls and presented to the boys, throwing them up and catching them again a few times first. The boys were thrilled with their new toys.

'You're very good with them,' said Joan, smiling.

'It's easy to be good with little ones when you don't have them all the time. Have you been out for a walk? Where did you take them?'

Joan decided to be open about it. If what she and Bob hoped for came about, then all their friends would know soon enough. She explained about wanting to return to work.

'But only if I can find the right daily care for Max. That goes without saying. I've just been along to the Lizzie Nursery to see if they have vacancies.'

'And do they?'

'Yes, but only part-time, so I still haven't solved the problem.'

Mrs Grayson looked thoughtful. 'You are just looking to see Max settled, aren't you? Not all three children?'

'No, it would be up to Norman and Jeremy's mothers to sort out their care.'

'Then – if it's just Max – why not let me do it?'

Joan stared. 'You? That's ever so kind, Mrs Grayson, but I couldn't impose.'

'You're not imposing. I'm offering. It would only be part-time, wouldn't it, so I'd still have ample time for my cooking and the jam- and pickle-making I do for the WVS. And part-time means I wouldn't find it too tiring. Think about it. I'm the sort of age to be Max's grandmother and there are plenty of grandmas who look after children.'

Joan thought about it. Mrs Grayson was right. Even so, the last thing Joan wanted was to take advantage.

'It's so sweet of you to offer, and I can't tell you how much it means to me, but you ought to have a good think first.'

'I don't need to.' Mrs Grayson drew back her shoulders, fixing Joan with a steady gaze. 'I know this is the right thing. There – there was my son, you see. My little boy who died. He was my only chance to be a mother and – well . . .' Her voice wobbled and she took a moment to compose herself. 'I love Max, you know I do. Nothing would give me greater pleasure than to help you to look after him. Think of all the fun he'll have in Wilton Close. It won't be just me all the time. He'll have Mrs Cooper and Alison and Margaret at different times.'

'And he already loves you all,' said Joan. It sounded perfect. Lots of other children to play with at the Lizzie Nursery and people Max had known all his young life here in Wilton Close. She hardly dared breathe lest the possibility wafted away.

'What do you think?' asked Mrs Grayson. 'Would you do me the honour of letting me take care of Max?'

Chapter Seven

Alison had spent all week looking forward to the weekend. She and Joel were both due to have Saturday and Sunday off and they planned to spend them together. Of course, this could change on the turn of a sixpence for Joel, depending upon what happened at Manchester Royal Infirmary. Alison understood that. She was proud to have a hard-working doctor as her boyfriend. People looked up to doctors and Alison enjoyed that. Best of all, though, was Joel's kindness, his optimistic nature and the way he made her feel she was the most important girl in the room. After Paul had trampled all over her heart, Joel had done wonders for her self-esteem – even to the extent that she hadn't been put off when he had shamefacedly admitted to her that he had got a previous girlfriend in the family way, something he himself had been unaware of until a considerable time later, long after the girl in question had suffered a miscarriage. It had been a shocking and difficult thing for Alison to hear, but her unswerving faith in Joel's love for her had helped her to accept it.

The way Alison saw it, it underlined the most important difference between her relationships with Joel and with Paul. As Paul's girlfriend, she had clung to the increasingly desperate fantasy of a romantic proposal followed by a lifetime of devoting herself to taking care of her husband. In complete contrast, her relationship with Joel was solidly based in real life. She hadn't given him the time of day to start with, but he had persevered – and the reason for his perseverance was that he knew he had met the love of his life.

Alison had known all along that he'd had girlfriends before her. She wouldn't have expected anything less from such an attractive man and she loved knowing that she was the one who had captured his heart. She wished, of course, that he had never got that other girl pregnant, but the fact that the baby had never been born and that Joel was not a father had enabled her to push the uncomfortable knowledge to the back of her mind.

On Saturday morning, Alison watched from the bay window in the front room. When Joel appeared, her heart bumped with delight and then gave an additional little lift as she saw the flowers he carried – carnations, if she wasn't mistaken. It was typical of Joel to be thoughtful. Generous, too. Fresh flowers cost an arm and a leg these days. She flew to open the door before he reached it. Removing his trilby as he walked into the house, he gave her a peck on the cheek, holding the flowers out of the way. Then, quickly scanning the hall and stairs, he dropped a kiss on her mouth, winking as he withdrew his head. Warmth flushed into Alison's cheeks.

Indicating the bouquet, Joel said, 'These are for the ladies,' and Alison realised it was not one bunch of carnations but two smaller ones. Joel presented her with a pretty corsage of a pink carnation with a froth of fern, bound together by a satin ribbon of pale pink.

'How lovely,' Alison exclaimed. 'Thank you.'

'And . . .' Joel removed a pin from his lapel. 'The most important bit.'

Alison fussed in front of the mirror on the hallstand, finding the right position on the lapel of her jacket and pinning the corsage in place, aware of Joel watching her, his expression full of love. She wanted to throw her arms around him, but settled for giving him a little push.

'Go in and deliver your flowers while I'll fetch my things.'

While Joel went into the front room, she put on her summery straw hat and checked the contents of her handbag, then stood quietly in the doorway, enjoying the sight of Mrs Grayson and Mrs Cooper cooing in delighted surprise over their carnations. What a kind man Joel was. He always thought about other people. Knowing him had made Alison consider others more than she used to.

Joel caught her looking.

'Time to go?' he asked.

'Alison, come and look at our flowers,' said Mrs Cooper. 'Aren't we lucky?'

'You shouldn't have, Joel,' said Mrs Grayson.

Alison gave her a nudge. 'Don't tell him he shouldn't or he might not do it again.'

'I was going to say, "but I'm glad you did". Such a treat.'

'You're very welcome, ladies,' said Joel, his manner warm but not fussy. He wasn't the sort to hog the glory. To Alison he said, 'We'd better get going.'

'Enjoy the day.' Mrs Cooper looked up from her yellow and white blooms to smile at the two of them.

'Thanks,' said Alison with a private sigh. A whole day in Joel's company was a huge treat. 'I'm sure we will, though I don't know what our plans are. Joel hasn't let on.'

'We'll make it up as we go along,' Joel teased.

First they went for a walk on the meadows, where Joel pointed out lady's mantle, its clusters of yellow flowers gracing the ends of the branched stems, and the purple flowers of wild thyme growing along the ground.

'It's good to see nature getting on with it,' he said, pausing to watch several bees crawling busily over a patch of white clover. Even Alison recognised white clover when she saw it. 'There's something reassuring about it.'

Alison squeezed his hand. Joel had been assigned to do intensive surgical training early on in the war in anticipation of the huge numbers of civilian injuries that had been expected. Although the air raids had tailed off now, he was still a surgeon and would be until the end of the war, after which he would go back to his original work, paediatrics, which was more than a job. It was a true vocation.

'Look at these over here.' Joel indicated a small cluster of pink flowers. 'Do you know what they are?'

'I haven't known any of the names so far,' laughed Alison, 'so I can't imagine why you think I might know these.'

'I think you might be able to make a wild guess.'

Shaking her head, Alison moved closer to take a look. 'Carnations!' She looked at Joel in astonishment. 'Did you do this?'

'I can't imagine what you mean.'

Stooping, Joel picked up the flowers, which were the same pink as Alison's corsage. To add to her surprise, he dangled them from his splayed fingers, showing off a loop of flowers.

'It should be big enough to go over the crown of your hat and sit on the brim.'

'You got the florist to make a daisy chain of carnations.'

'Nothing to do with me,' said Joel. 'The pixies must have done it.' He settled the flowers on her hat. 'Very fetching.'

'You're quite mad.'

'Madly in love, maybe,' but he said it with a twinkle that invited her to groan and administer a slap on his arm.

Hand in hand, they left the meadows and headed for the bus stop to catch the bus into town. Alison caught more than one girl looking at the flowers on her hat. She might be sitting in a bus that smelled of tobacco and old upholstery, but there was something magical about it.

When they alighted, Joel shot back his cuff and checked his wristwatch. 'We'll have a bite to eat at the Worker Bee and then . . .'

'And then?' asked Alison.

'We'll think of something.'

At the Worker Bee, when Alison would have walked over to a table by the window where a couple were just getting up to leave, Joel placed a gentle hand on her back and guided her to a table in the middle of the room that she would never have chosen because of the lack of privacy.

'Let's sit here, if you don't mind.'

'But it's got a *Reserved* sign.'

'It must be those pixies again.' Joel held her chair as she sat down. 'This was our table the very first time we went out together.'

'So it was,' Alison said with a smile. 'But you couldn't really call it going out. As I recall, I agreed to meet you here because . . .'

'It's all right. Don't be bashful. You can say it. Because I was handsome and charming and you were flattered and intrigued.'

'Well, it was flattering, I must admit. You went to all that trouble to track me down and I wasn't exactly gracious about it.'

'You were jolly hard work to start with,' said Joel. 'Every time I suggested meeting you, I never knew whether you'd turn up.'

'Ah, but I was worth the wait, wasn't I?' Alison teased.

Joel's expression turned serious. 'One hundred per cent.'

Alison's heart melted. Joel had never been shy of showing her how much she meant to him.

'We'll just have a sandwich now,' said Joel, 'and something more substantial later, if that's all right.'

The meat-paste sandwiches, made using the dreaded grey-looking National Loaf, were livened up by thin slices of tomato.

'Would you like to go and see *Blithe Spirit* at the Palace Theatre this afternoon?' Joel asked.

'I'd love to, but I imagine it'll be sold out.'

'We can but try.'

When they went to the theatre, Joel escorted Alison straight past the box office to the doors leading to the stalls. Alison opened her mouth to say something, then shut it again with a smile as, with the air of a conjuror, Joel produced a pair of tickets to show to the usherette.

'Dratted pixies,' he murmured. 'They get everywhere.'

Alison had a wonderful afternoon, not least because she nipped to the Ladies in the interval and had the chance to admire her flower-bedecked hat.

'Very pretty,' commented a matronly lady.

Another lady nudged the friend she was with. 'Such an extravagance,' she whispered with a note of disapproval.

'My boyfriend is very thoughtful,' Alison said, 'and,' she added with her nose in the air, 'stinking rich.'

She swept from the room, letting the door bang behind her. Back in the auditorium, Joel stood up politely as she approached. She reached up to kiss his cheek before she took her seat again.

'What was that for?' Joel asked. 'Not that I'm complaining.'

Relaxing after her moment of indignation, Alison explained.

Joel laughed. 'Then we'd better have something a bit more exotic than corned beef hash this evening. Shame. I was intending to take you back to the Worker Bee.'

But when they left, Joel escorted her to the Midland Hotel, a handsome building of Edwardian baroque. Crossing the foyer, they entered the dining room, where they were expected and were shown to their table at once. Alison looked around, admiring the wide arched windows and the air of pre-war elegance before she shook her head at Joel.

'Don't tell me. The pixies organised this too.'

'Dratted pixies,' said Joel.

The meal was superb. In keeping with wartime etiquette, they had just two courses. Alison chose the vegetable casserole while Joel opted for the mock duck and they both chose the rhubarb fool afterwards.

'That was delicious,' said Alison. 'You've spoiled me all day. Thank you – and thank you to the pixies.'

'The pixies wish you to know it was their great pleasure,' said Joel, 'but there is one last thing.'

'Another pixie idea?'

'No, this one is all mine and I hope you're going to like it.'

Alison started to say, 'Everything else has been perfect, so I'm sure I will,' but the words disintegrated after a couple of syllables as Joel rose from his seat at the table and sank down onto one knee. Alison's breath caught on a soft gasp. Joel produced a ring box from his pocket and opened it, presenting a beautiful emerald flanked on either side by a pair of smaller diamonds. Alison's heart delivered an almighty clunk and then seemed to stop. Her whole self hovered on the brink.

'Alison, I love you. You're the one and only girl for me and I want us to spend our lives together. Will you marry me?'

It took a moment for Alison's heart to commence beating again. 'I had no idea,' she whispered. Of all the stupid things to say! Her heart was singing her acceptance, but her silly tongue couldn't say the right thing.

Joel smiled, but a soft hitch in his breathing showed he was taking nothing for granted.

Emotion rose in Alison, tears filling her eyes and swelling inside her throat. Speech was impossible. She nodded, tears spilling down her cheeks before she managed to whisper, 'Yes.'

As Joel slid the ring onto her finger, there was applause from nearby tables. Alison smiled around blindly before her gaze settled on her ring. Her ring! She was engaged. She was going to marry Joel and be Mrs Joel Maitland. She lifted her swimming eyes to Joel's, sure that the glow of happiness in his face was mirrored in her own. She laughed with sheer elation, but there was a feeling of security and satisfaction and pure rightness too.

And to think she'd had no idea it was going to happen.

'We have to tell my parents first,' said Alison as she and Joel left the Midland. She couldn't wait to tell her friends and show off her ring, but Mum and Dad would be upset if they weren't the first to know. Besides, she wanted everything to be perfect and that meant doing things in the right order.

'No time like the present,' said Joel, flagging down a taxi and helping her in.

'We could have gone on the bus,' said Alison.

'No, we couldn't. This is quicker and we want to share our news.'

Alison angled herself towards Joel, giving him her hand to hold. He was doing all he could to make this day perfect for her. That made the tears well up again and she brushed them away.

When they got to Mum and Dad's, Lydia was there as well. Alison barely allowed time for the greetings before her good news came bursting out.

'Let's see the ring,' said Lydia, reaching for her hand, but Alison homed in on the looks on her parents' faces.

'You knew,' she realised.

'Joel was a complete gentleman,' said Mum. 'He came and asked for your father's permission.'

Alison turned to Joel. 'You thought of everything. Today has been wonderful.'

'Thank the pixies,' said Joel. 'I couldn't have done it without them.'

'Did you really not have any idea?' Lydia asked Alison.

'None,' said Alison.

She didn't intend to waste a single moment of today dwelling on times past, but she couldn't help but be aware of all the proposals she had expected from Paul and how confidently she had anticipated every single one of them, undaunted by previous disappointments. Yet this time, when it really happened, it had come completely out of the blue.

'You're so lucky that your husband will be in a reserved occupation,' said Lydia.

Alison focused on that delightful word 'husband' so intently that it took her a moment to realise what Lydia had said. She slipped her arm around her sister. 'I know how hard it was for you to marry Alec and then have to wave him off almost at once.'

'A weekend honeymoon coming up for two years ago,' said Lydia, 'and I haven't seen him since.'

'I know how fortunate I am.' Alison's heart filled. She had so much to be thankful for.

'When are you going to get wed?' Dad asked.

Alison laughed. 'Give us a chance. We've only just got engaged.' Then she added, 'It would be wonderful to be a summer bride.'

'Next summer it is, then,' said Dad.

'June,' said Mum. 'June is a lovely month for weddings.'

'Hadn't you better ask Joel if he thinks so too?' Lydia teased.

'I have two married sisters,' said Joel, 'so I'm fully aware that the bridegroom's job is to say yes to everything.'

Alison's pulse quickened. Plenty of couples were marrying very quickly these days – well, just look at Lydia and

Alec – but she wanted to spend months building up to her big day, planning every detail and making sure she had exactly the special day she wanted. Her wedding wasn't going to be just one day. It was going to be all the build-up too. Eleven blissful months of it. Mum would love it too. Everything for Lydia had been organised at top speed.

Before Joel took Alison home that evening, they crammed themselves into a telephone box so Joel could ring his parents. Alison's face broke out into fresh smiles as she heard the exclamations of pleasure at the other end of the line. When Joel hung up, he kissed Alison right there in the phone box. Maybe it was intended to be no more than a brief kiss, but it lengthened into something much deeper. They broke apart only when the person at the head of the queue for the box rapped on one of its small glass panes.

They returned to Wilton Close. Joel escorted Alison into the house, where they shared their news to cries of delight from Dot and Persephone, who had come round for the evening. Margaret gave Alison a hug.

'Congrats,' she said into Alison's ear. 'I'm delighted for you.' Turning to Joel, she said, 'You're a lucky man.'

'I know,' said Joel.

For half a moment, he and Margaret looked at one another. Alison guessed they were remembering their old relationship, which was only natural and she didn't mind.

Then Joel held out his arms to Mrs Cooper. 'Does the lucky man get a hug?'

'He does indeed,' said Mrs Cooper. 'I'm thrilled for you both. Another wedding. Now that's something to look forward to.'

'We'll organise a tea party to celebrate,' said Mrs Grayson.

Joel laughed. 'From what I know of all of you, the engagement won't be official until you've held a tea party.'

'I'll get everyone to tell me their shifts,' said Mrs Grayson, 'so we can choose the time when the most people can come.'

'When is the wedding to be?' asked Dot. 'Or is it too soon to say?'

'Next June,' said Alison.

'A June bride,' Mrs Grayson said emotionally.

In fact, 'A June bride,' said in happy and sentimental tones, often accompanied by a sigh, seemed to be the standard response when people were told. Alison lapped up every moment of being newly engaged. Because of the nature of her job, she had come across a lot of people in the course of her work –'And she won't rest until she's shown off her ring to every single one of them,' chuckled Persephone as the friends sat together in the buffet after Alison had shown her ring to Mrs Jessop.

'Well, I for one don't blame you, chick,' said Dot. 'You make the most of it.'

'Church or registry office?' asked Colette.

'Bridal gown or suit?' asked Margaret.

'Church and wedding dress,' Alison answered at once. 'Mind you, the dress could pose a bit of a problem. There are no new dresses to be had. At the start of the war, people were proud to have pared-back weddings because they were considered patriotic, but there's a feeling now that weddings should look as fancy and pre-war as possible.'

'Just to show the world that rationing and shortages aren't getting us down,' said Persephone, 'and we can still put on a good party.'

'And I do want a proper wedding dress,' said Alison. 'I wondered about borrowing Mabel's,' she added, a touch hesitantly.

'Oh, *yes*,' Margaret exclaimed. She had been one of Mabel's bridesmaids – Alison herself had been the other – and had admired the glorious silver-striped white taffeta first-hand. Margaret turned to the others. 'It has cap sleeves and a sweetheart neckline.' She moved her hands against herself, showing the neckline's shape. 'And it's longer at the back.'

'You said that Mabel left it with her mother for it to be lent to any of her father's factory girls who get married during the war,' said Cordelia. 'I think it would be perfect if you borrowed it, Alison.'

'Mabel would be thrilled,' Colette added. 'It would suit you,' she added warmly. She had been one of Mabel's two matrons of honour.

Alison hadn't really doubted that her friends would approve of the idea, but she felt relieved all the same. 'I'll write to Mrs Bradshaw and ask her.'

'Write to Mabel as well,' suggested Margaret. 'She'd love to know.'

'I'm glad you all like the idea,' said Alison.

'We don't just like it, chick,' Dot assured her. 'We love it.'

Alison leaned forward. 'There's something else I want to ask you. Joel and I are going round to see his sister Venetia. She had a go at splitting us up because she wanted him to get back with an old flame, so how do I behave towards her?'

'Tricky situation,' said Emily.

'Not necessarily,' said Persephone. 'How have you and she behaved towards one another since then?'

'Joel gave her a good talking-to and she's been charm itself ever since,' said Alison.

'Then presumably that will continue,' said Margaret.

'Presumably,' said Alison.

'Then what's the problem?' Cordelia asked. 'There must be a problem or you wouldn't have mentioned it.'

Alison thought about it. 'Getting engaged has reminded me of what she tried to do.'

'Sweetheart,' exclaimed Persephone. 'Don't let it spoil this happy time for you.'

'I know,' said Alison. 'I'm being silly.'

'It's not silly,' said Dot. 'Just tell yourself she tried but she failed.'

'In fact,' Cordelia added, 'she failed so spectacularly that you and Joel are getting married.'

But it was Emily, the youngest, who uttered the words that spoke most deeply and personally to Alison and made her feel stronger.

'If you feel iffy about seeing her, I bet she feels just as iffy every time she sees you. Her brother put her in her place when she tried to push you out. Whenever she sees you, she must remember how much you mean to him.'

A weight she'd been carrying since the spring of last year lifted from Alison, a weight she hadn't even known she was carrying.

'You're right,' she told Emily, gratitude lending warmth to her tone. 'I've always seen it from my side before, but you've made me see it through her eyes and that makes me feel a lot better.'

Sheer light-heartedness made her want to laugh, but that might sound as if she was glorying in Venetia's situation – though, if she was honest, that was no more than Venetia deserved.

Going to Venetia's house was a success. Venetia was as beautiful and poised as ever in a stylish linen dress with a boat neck that made her look cool and elegant. Her fair hair was caught up high on the back of her head from where it cascaded in masses of tiny curls. In her response to the engagement, she was everything that was gracious. She kissed Alison and made a fuss over her ring and was full of questions and congratulations. She even said 'A June bride' in the same happy voice as everyone else. Was it mean to wonder what she was thinking underneath all that?

All thoughts of Venetia were swept aside when Joel took Alison to the churchyard where his brother was buried. Nowadays, there were three young Maitlands – Joel, Venetia and Caroline – but until Joel was twelve years old, there had also been Jonathan. He had gone into hospital for a routine operation and died under the anaesthetic. The thought of it had the power to turn Alison cold all the way to her core. Imagine if Lydia . . .

She stood quietly with Joel beside his brother's headstone.

Joel shook his head. 'I've never got used to it, not deep down. I'm an adult. I'm a doctor. I'm used to death. Yet the thought of losing my brother so suddenly, so unexpectedly, still takes my breath away. He was only fourteen, for God's sake.'

Alison stood close to him, her fingers creeping into his. 'Life can be cruelly short.' She thought of Lizzie and Letitia, who had both died far too young, but now wasn't the moment to say it. This moment belonged to Jonathan.

'I wanted to bring you here,' said Joel, 'because I know how unspeakably precious life is. I know how easily it can be lost. We all know it these days because of the war, but I learned it when I was twelve and it was a hard lesson. If I operate on a patient and they don't pull through, I always think of Jonathan before I speak to the waiting family. I remind myself of the shock and the disbelief I felt over him before I give them the bad news. I hope that makes me do it in a better way, in so far as better is possible in those circumstances. I wish you could have known Jonathan. I wish he hadn't died.' Turning to Alison, he cupped her face in his hands. 'Life is precious,' he whispered, 'and you are my life.'

Chapter Eight

Several of the women and girls in the engine sheds had husbands, sons or sweethearts involved in the Italian campaign, so the capture of Palermo, which had been followed a couple of days later by the extraordinary news of Mussolini's fall from power, was still being discussed even though it was now Saturday, the first of August, and both events had taken place last week. Margaret noticed that Sally seemed rather distanced and wasn't joining in. Sometimes people didn't and you didn't always know why not.

After a long shift plus compulsory overtime, Margaret arrived home from work late on Saturday afternoon to find Dot in the kitchen, helping Mrs Grayson make baking-powder rolls and carrot scones for tomorrow's tea party for Joel and Alison.

'I didn't know you were coming round, Mrs Green.' Margaret was careful to use Dot's title. Using first names was something that convention dictated they should do only when outsiders weren't present. Or rather, convention dictated that they shouldn't use one another's first names at all, which was precisely why they did it only when nobody else was present.

'I just popped round with a knitting pattern,' said Dot, 'and then stayed to lend a hand.' She glanced at her wristwatch.

'Actually, I ought to be making tracks. Why don't you walk down to the terminus with me, Margaret? You can tell me how Anna and the children are getting on.'

'Give me a minute to get changed and have another go at washing my hands.'

Five minutes later, they left the house, but after leaving the little cul-de-sac, Dot steered Margaret across the road to the rec, which was now given over to allotments.

'Let's find a bench where we can have a chat, love.'

'What about?'

For reply, Dot gave her a sideways look. The warmth that rose in Margaret's cheeks owed nothing to the August sunshine.

'So that's why you came round to the house,' she said.

'Of course it is,' said Dot, as if this was the most obvious thing in the world. 'I wanted to make sure you're all right.'

'There was really no need,' Margaret started to say.

'Codswallop. There's every need – unless you've already poured your heart out to Joan.'

'I haven't seen her.'

Plonking herself down on a bench, Dot patted the wooden slats, inviting Margaret to join her.

'Now I know I'm a nosy old bag,' Dot began, 'but I care about you and I want to find out if Alison and Joel getting engaged has rattled you.'

Dot was the one other person who knew the truth about Joel and Margaret. Confiding in Dot had been a big decision for Margaret, because she had been desperate to keep the lid on her secret – but it had been the right decision. Dot's suggestion last year that instead of agonising over what, if anything, to tell Alison, Margaret should talk things over with Joel, had been exactly what was needed.

Margaret scooted along the bench to sit close and link arms. 'You're not a nosy old bag. You're a kind friend and I love you for it.'

'So, how are you feeling?' Dot asked.

Something made Margaret aim for a rather offhand tone. 'Well, let's face it, it was only a matter of time before it happened, wasn't it?'

'Is that you being evasive, Margaret Thomas?'

Margaret smiled. 'Partly,' she admitted, 'but it's true. We all more or less knew it was going to happen at some point, didn't we? Joel was so very sure from the start that Alison was the right girl for him.' She stopped, realising she had braced herself in case a powerful emotion floored her. It didn't happen. After a moment, she added ruefully, 'I can honestly say he never felt that way about me.'

'Does it hurt?' Dot asked softly.

'No, not now.' Margaret took her time answering. She owed it to Dot to find the right words. She owed it to herself too. 'I've accepted everything that happened. I've had to. Does it pain me that Alison and Joel have finally got engaged? No. I'm happy for them – genuinely. But . . .'

'But it brings back a lot of memories,' Dot finished for her.

Margaret nodded. 'Yes, it does.'

'And there's the tea party to face tomorrow,' Dot said softly.

A deep sadness made Margaret's chest ache, but then resolve took over and she looked directly at her friend. 'This situation isn't about me and my memories. It's about Alison and Joel being together and looking forward to their future.

I'm not going to think about myself. I'm going to concentrate on feeling happy for them.'

'You're a good lass,' said Dot. 'I knew you wouldn't be feeling sorry for yourself. I wanted you to know I haven't forgotten what you told me last year about you and Joel. I'm aware that Joan and I are the only ones in the know, and if you want to talk, you'd probably choose someone your own age, but don't forget I'm here too if you need me. Stiff upper lips are all very well, but there's summat to be said for not suffering in silence.'

'My suffering is over and done with,' said Margaret, 'but thank you for the support. Thank you for not judging me. Last year I was appalled when Joan said we should confide in you, but she was right. You took my sorry tale on the chin and knew exactly what I should do to resolve things.'

'Much as I love being admired,' said Dot, 'is this you evading the subject again?'

'No. Yes. A bit. Maybe.'

'That sounds like the cherry stones game. Did you play that when you were a nipper? This year, next year, sometime, never.'

'All right,' said Margaret. 'The truth. First and foremost, I am happy for Alison and Joel. And yes, of course the memories have come flooding back, but floods recede. Things feel a bit ropy at the moment, but that won't last. One thing I do know for certain is that getting used to this engagement will be a heck of a lot easier than what I had to face and get used to last year. That was hard.'

'It was, but you came through it.' Dot squeezed Margaret's arm. 'You're stronger than you think, chick.'

They walked to the terminus. Margaret waved Dot off, but instead of heading for home, she went for a walk, needing a bit of time to herself. How good Dot was, how kind and how utterly reliable. Her family were lucky to have her. There were times when Margaret missed her own darling mum terribly. Mum was the one who had held the family together. The Greens must view Dot in the same way – or maybe not. It wasn't until she was gone for good that it was obvious to Margaret's family how important Mum had been.

Margaret could have done with one of Mum's hugs right now. No matter how genuine her happiness was on behalf of Alison and Joel, the news of their engagement had been unsettling, not least thanks to the memories it had resurrected. Dot had been right about that.

But there was one memory Dot didn't know about. Only Joan knew.

The wedding dress.

Saints alive, how could she have been so unutterably stupid? But at the time it had seemed the natural thing to do. Aside from feeling daring, she hadn't questioned her actions. She had just fallen in love with a beautiful wedding dress and had secretly treated herself to it because the thought of leaving it in the shop until she officially needed it, thereby running the risk of losing it altogether, was simply not to be borne.

That's how much of a twit she had made of herself over Joel Maitland.

Alison hummed to herself as she got ready for the tea party, putting on a new-to-her white dress patterned with little red rosebuds from the WVS clothing exchange. Honestly, the things some women got rid of! This dress had been a real find and she loved it. Happiness swelled inside her. Today was her special day, hers and Joel's. Not all of their friends could come because of their shifts, which was a shame, but Mrs Cooper had invited Alison's family and that would be lovely. It had been rather a blow for Mum when Alison had moved to Wilton Close and she wanted Mum to see for herself that she had made a good choice.

Downstairs everything was ready. Persephone had cycled here early, her bicycle basket crammed with pastel-coloured sweet peas from Darley Court. Mrs Morgan's vases were too tall, but her rose bowl had come into play, as had the stash of jam jars that Mrs Grayson had received on Friday from the WVS for her next batch of jam-making. The pretty little flowers filled the house with their honey-sweet scent.

'You look thoughtful, chuck,' Mrs Cooper said to Alison.

'I was wondering about having sweet peas at our wedding reception.'

'Depends when in June you get married,' said Mrs Cooper. 'They don't really come into their own until a bit later in the summer.'

Alison didn't say anything, but she couldn't help wondering about the greenhouses at Darley Court. Would Miss Brown allow her to have one so that the sweet peas could be helped along? Miss Brown was the last word in good sense and sweet peas were hardly going to boost the war effort, but you never knew. The mistress of Darley Court might view a pretty wedding as being one in the eye for Hitler. It was worth bearing in mind.

Alison smiled to herself. This was why she wanted loads of time to build up to her wedding. She wanted to have as much fun as possible making choices and looking into all the possibilities. She thought of Lydia, who had got married on next to no notice. That had been exciting and romantic in its own way, but Alison fully intended to make the most of everything that preceded her own wedding. As for Mabel, her wedding had been organised miles away in her home town of Annerby by her mother, and apart from providing a guest list and dashing north for a dress fitting, all Mabel had had to do was turn up in time to get married. That wouldn't have suited Alison at all. She wanted to be deeply involved in every single moment of the preparations.

Joel arrived, smiling and handsome, his blue eyes bright with love when he saw her. Typical Joel, he immediately started helping, carrying the dining chairs through to the front room to provide the extra seating that would be needed. Mrs Cooper showed him where to place them.

Margaret and Persephone were busy in the kitchen with Mrs Grayson. Alison realised she ought to make herself useful too, instead of wafting about soaking up the atmosphere, but when she offered to help, the others shooed her away.

'Go and spend some time with your fiancé,' said Mrs Grayson.

Her fiancé! Happiness radiated throughout Alison's whole being. She felt as if she was glowing. How lucky she was. She was engaged to the most considerate, loving, hard-working man in the world and she was going to have a blissful time building up to the perfect wedding day. She couldn't ask for anything more.

Chapter Nine

Everyone was tired at the end of a long, physically taxing shift, but you'd never guess it from the level of chatter as the engine cleaners changed out of their dungarees and boiler suits and released their hair from their turbans. Most of them wore curlers under their turbans to keep their hair in shape, Margaret included, even though it was something her mum would have frowned upon. Or maybe, this far into the war, Mum would have got used to it, had she still been here.

Margaret fluffed up her hair, encouraging the shape back into it. She always styled her pageboy cut into full curls that waved away from her face and she had let her fringe grow long so that it too could be curled and sit in a froth at her temples. It was a pretty but uncomplicated style that was easy to look after and her friends said it suited her.

She was going to the pictures with Sally that evening, straight from work. After Sally had refused last time, Margaret had kept an eye on her, hoping her chum would get over her tiredness. When Margaret had again suggested the flicks, Sally had once more tried saying no, which had made Margaret feel all the more concerned.

'It's something more than simple weariness, isn't it? You're poorly.'

'No, honestly, I'm fine,' Sally protested.

'Well, if you're not poorly, you're run-down. Maybe a tonic would help.'

Sally gave her a smile. 'Actually, the best tonic would be an evening at the pictures. What do you fancy seeing?'

So this evening they were going to have a quick bite to eat in the buffet and then go to see the gorgeous Cary Grant in *Once Upon a Honeymoon*.

When she was ready, Margaret looked round and caught Sally's eye. Sally looked a bit washed out, but she answered Margaret's glance with a smile and Margaret's concern waned somewhat. An evening out with a friend could be just the tonic Sally needed – with Cary Grant thrown in for good measure.

But they never got as far as seeing the film. As they sat through the Pathé newsreel, Sally seemed to be sniffing a bit. Margaret assumed that the ubiquitous tobacco smoke must have got into her eyes, but when the screen brightened, Margaret got a better look and was shocked to see tears streaming down Sally's face. She wasted half a second trying to pinpoint which particular news item might be to blame, then she caught hold of Sally's hand.

'Come on. Let's get you out of here.'

Whispering 'I'm sorry. Excuse us,' Margaret led the way as they shuffled along the row to the aisle. She took Sally's elbow to escort her out. Seeing what was happening, an usherette lit their way for them by pointing her little torch at the floor.

When the door to the auditorium quietly swung shut behind them, Margaret put a comforting arm around Sally.

'Forget the tonic. You need to see a doctor.'

Sally mopped her face and breathed in hard a couple of times, mastering herself. 'I don't need to see anyone.'

'But—' Margaret began.

'I know exactly what's the matter with me,' said Sally. 'I'm . . .' She looked around to make sure they were alone. 'I'm pregnant.'

A sudden chill hit Margaret right in the centre of her being. It was the exact same feeling she'd had when she herself had realised she was in the family way.

'You're shocked,' said Sally in a dull voice.

'Obviously, yes, because I had no idea,' said Margaret, 'but I'm not going to turn my back on you, if that's what you're thinking.'

Sally covered her mouth with a trembling hand in obvious relief and Margaret's heart went out to her. She gave the girl a hug.

'You poor love. You must be worried sick. We need to go somewhere where we can talk.'

What with double summer time, it was still light outside. Margaret thought quickly. She needed to take Sally to a place where they could be alone.

'Whoever would have thought that a bomb site would have its uses?' she remarked lightly as they settled on what was left of a wall, behind which were heaps of bricks, plaster, timber and general rubble, all that remained of what had once been a pair of buildings. She stroked Sally's arm. 'It might help if you talked about it.' When Sally didn't answer, she added, 'Does anyone else know?'

'No,' said Sally, immediately followed by, 'Yes. That's the problem. My landlady twigged that there had been no

71

bloodstains on my knickers for some time. You know how it is. No matter how careful you are, and no matter how much you rinse your smalls, sometimes a little stain gets left behind. It turns out that when she does our laundry for us, Mrs Gilbey – well, she examines our underwear to make sure she can see signs we're still having our monthly visitor.'

'She does *what*?' Margaret asked. What an appalling intrusion.

Sally shrugged. 'She said she was entitled to make sure there was no immorality under her roof – and given my situation, I was hardly in a position to complain. She says I've got to get out or she'll report me to the billeting officer. She says she'll write to LMS as well and tell them what sort of girl they're employing.'

Margaret made a conscious effort not to respond to that. Forcing down her sense of outrage, she asked, 'What about the father?'

Sally tossed her head. 'What about him? Let's just say that when I told him, he turned out to be a bit more married than he'd led me to believe.'

'The swine.'

'That's one word for it, but most people would say it's my own fault. He had the proverbial silver tongue. He made me feel lovely and special and I was stupid enough to believe that as soon as I gave him my news, he'd immediately do the decent thing and marry me.'

'What about your family?' asked Margaret.

'I can't go home,' Sally said at once. 'My parents were bombed out and had to go and live with my auntie, so there's no room for me anyway. Not that I could ever tell them.

72

They'd be beside themselves with fury and shame.' Her voice fell on the final words.

'So you need somewhere to live,' said Margaret. 'How long have you got left at your current place?'

'To the end of next week at the absolute most. I truly have tried to find somewhere else, but you know how scarce accommodation is these days. Besides, any new landlady is going to chuck me out as soon as she realises. I know I'm going to end up in a mother and baby home, but what am I to do until then? Then, when we were in the flicks watching the Pathé News, my little problem seemed so sordid compared to what's going on in the world that it all got too much and I started blubbing. I'm sorry about that.'

'Nothing to be sorry for,' Margaret said. 'It's a good thing that you did because it made you tell me.'

'And that's a good thing?' Sally asked incredulously.

'Yes. A trouble shared is a trouble halved and all that.'

'Really? You aren't going to run a mile and never speak to me again?'

'Don't be daft. You need help and I'm not going to abandon you. I have an idea. I can't say anything now because that wouldn't be right, but let me see what I can do.'

Sally dissolved into tears.

Margaret got Mrs Cooper on her own while Mrs Grayson was making the bedtime drinks.

'Do you have any plans for Alison's old room, Mrs C?'

'Not at present, but I suppose I ought to offer it to the billeting officer, though I'd much rather find somebody for it myself. Once it's on the billeting officer's books, it'll be there for keeps and we won't have any choice as to who we're given. We're such a happy little home. I hate to sound mean, but I like the way things have worked out so far, with Lizzie's friends coming and going. It has felt natural.'

Margaret hid her dismay. 'Does that mean you don't want a stranger?'

Mrs Cooper looked directly at her. 'Does that mean you've got a stranger for me?'

'I have,' said Margaret, 'but you need to know right away that she's in a fix.'

'Oh aye? What sort of fix?'

Mrs Grayson chose that moment to walk in with the Ovaltine. She looked from one to the other.

Mrs Cooper spoke to her. 'Margaret has someone for the little bedroom, but apparently— No, Margaret, it's no use trying to stop me. Mrs Grayson is entitled to know whatever it is.'

Margaret swallowed hard, sure her ears had turned bright red, but this had to be done. Quietly, she explained Sally's predicament.

'The man pretended he wasn't married.'

'She still shouldn't have gone with him,' said Mrs Cooper.

'There's a lot of it about these days,' said Mrs Grayson. 'Not that I'm excusing it.'

'Her landlady is on the verge of throwing her out,' said Margaret, 'and she urgently needs somewhere to stay. I don't mean for her to have the baby here,' she added quickly. 'She just needs somewhere she can move into while she gets the next part sorted out.'

'The next part?' said Mrs Cooper.

'Somewhere to have the child,' said Mrs Grayson before Margaret could answer.

'I know it's a huge favour to ask,' said Margaret, 'but Sally made a mistake and now she's been left to pay the price. She's terrified of her family finding out. Things are going to be very hard for her for the next few months. I'm sorry to ask it of you, because I know you are both very respectable ladies, but I also know how kind you are and how beautifully you look after Alison and me, and Joan and Mabel before us – and not just us either, but all of our group of friends. You've made everybody welcome and you've hosted so many tea parties for us. Everyone loves coming to Wilton Close. You gave me something very special when I came to live here. I was in such a horrid dump before. Then you invited me to move in and I knew I was coming somewhere clean and comfortable, but this house is so much more than that. It's a place of warmth, kindness and friendship. I love living here and you two are the reason why I love it.'

'It's wonderful to hear all those compliments, dear,' said Mrs Cooper, 'but what you're asking is very serious indeed. I agree that the landlady who examines the lodgers' knickers is going beyond what's decent, but that doesn't alter the fact that she's within her rights to ask a girl in that condition to leave her house at once.'

'I hope you don't think badly of me for wanting to help her,' said Margaret, 'but you seem to be exactly what she needs for the time being. Even if you only let her stay for two or three weeks, it could make all the difference. I'd spend that time doing everything I could to find somewhere for her to move to.'

The two ladies looked at one another.

'I can't afford for this house to fall into disrepute because of a lodger who's no better than she should be,' said Mrs Cooper. 'But having said that, the poor girl must be desperate. Giving her a bed for a short time would be an easy thing for us to do, but to her it would, as Margaret says, make all the difference.'

'I know that as the housekeeper here, you shouldn't even contemplate taking her in,' said Mrs Grayson, 'but I've had my fair share of being judged by others. Plenty of people blamed me for the way my marriage ended, even though it was my husband who went off with someone else. It's always the wife who gets the blame. In this Sally's case, as with all girls who have fallen from grace, it's the girl who not just gets the blame but is left to cope with the very obvious consequences of a situation that was brought about by two people.'

Margaret held her breath. Were the ladies coming down on Sally's side?

'I'm not making any promises,' said Mrs Cooper. 'For a start, this isn't my house. It belongs to the Morgans and I couldn't do anything as serious as offering temporary refuge to a – a fallen girl without confiding in Mrs Masters as the Morgans' representative.'

'Oh,' said Margaret. 'I don't know about that.'

'Why not?' Mrs Cooper asked.

Margaret recalled how Cordelia had tactfully stayed away from Wilton Close last year while poor Mrs Cooper had been wrongly under suspicion for a spate of thefts from various houses where she cleaned. Normally, Cordelia checked the Wilton Close house for the Morgans once a month to make sure everything was just so, but she had written to them, pretending to be too busy. By staying away she'd been able to feign ignorance of the cloud hanging over Mrs Cooper – a cloud that, had they known about it, might well have resulted in the Morgans deciding to sack her and ask Cordelia to find them another housekeeper.

Nothing had ever been said to Mrs Cooper about Cordelia's absence from Wilton Close and she had never realised, but Margaret remembered it now. What on earth could she say to the proposition of informing Cordelia about the possibility of introducing, albeit temporarily, an unmarried lodger who was expecting a baby?

'That would put Mrs Masters in a difficult position' was the best she could manage.

'Says the girl who has already placed Mrs Cooper in a difficult position by making this request,' Mrs Grayson observed drily. 'Are you going to withdraw your request?'

Margaret took a breath. 'No. I promised to help Sally – and I want to help her. She deserves to be helped.'

'Plenty would say that that's a matter of opinion,' said Mrs Grayson.

'Well, I'm not one of them,' Margaret replied. 'She's working as hard as anyone for the war effort. It's just that in her personal life, she's made a mistake and fallen for a smooth-tongued rotter. She would never have – well, you know – if she'd known he was married.'

To Margaret's surprise, Mrs Cooper and Mrs Grayson exchanged smiles.

'If this Sally girl has you on her side, Margaret dear,' said Mrs Cooper, 'then she must be a good girl at heart. I agree she needs help, but you don't seem keen on telling Mrs Masters and I don't understand why not.'

'She'll be obliged to tell the Morgans,' said Margaret, 'and they'll probably say no.'

'In which case we would have to find another way to help her,' said Mrs Cooper.

That was the moment when Margaret knew everything was going to be all right. It was a silly thing to think, because how could she possibly know anything of the kind? But Mrs Cooper's simple statement of intent somehow made things slot into place.

'I wonder if Mrs Masters is going to come to the knitting circle this week?' said Mrs Cooper.

'She usually comes,' said Mrs Grayson.

'Margaret dear, perhaps you could catch her at work and ask her to pop in here on her way,' said Mrs Cooper. 'It'll add a few minutes to her walk, but I'm sure she won't mind.'

'She might have Emily with her,' said Margaret.

'Not to worry,' said Mrs Grayson. 'I'll ask Emily to walk with me to the church hall while Mrs Cooper has a quick word with her mother.'

'Or I could go with Emily,' suggested Margaret, anxious to play her part.

'No, you need to be here,' Mrs Cooper said decisively. 'Sally is your friend and you must speak up for her.'

Margaret gave both ladies a hug, careful not to spill their Ovaltine.

'You're so good. Thank you.'

'Actually, Margaret dear,' said Mrs Cooper, 'I think you are the good one. Sally is lucky to have a friend like you.'

Cordelia and Emily arrived, all smiles. Emily was looking brighter these days. It was some months on from the dreadful heartbreak of being dumped by her first love and the bleakness that had haunted her lovely blue eyes – cornflower blue, Cordelia called them – had gradually faded away. What a pretty girl she was, with her heart-shaped face and her naturally wavy hair. But then, with such good-looking parents – her distinguished father and her grey-eyed, ash-blonde mother – it was no surprise she was a looker.

No sooner had Cordelia and Emily set foot over the threshold than Mrs Grayson enlisted Emily's agreement to walk with her down to the church hall.

'The others can follow us when they're ready,' she added, 'but I'd like to get there. I've promised to teach Miss Travers to do fern lace stitch.'

'Will you teach me as well?' asked Emily.

When the front door closed behind them, Mrs Cooper got down to business with a speed that rather took Margaret's breath away.

'I need to ask you something, Mrs Masters. I hope you'll be sympathetic.'

'How intriguing,' said Cordelia. 'I'm sure I will if it's something that matters to you.'

'Margaret has a friend who needs our help,' said Mrs Cooper. She smiled encouragingly at Margaret. 'Perhaps you could explain.'

Aware of how important the next few minutes would be, Margaret launched into Sally's unhappy tale. She looked anxiously at Cordelia as she waited for her response.

'I see,' was all Cordelia said. She was always cool and grave, but she seemed even more so just now. Was that good or bad? 'And you are hoping to bring her here, Margaret?'

'I don't want to put words into Mrs Cooper's mouth, but she and Mrs Grayson have sort of agreed to it, but it's all down to you, really.'

'Actually, it's all down to the Morgans,' Cordelia pointed out. 'This is their house. Mr Morgan would be appalled if he knew what you were proposing.'

'I thought as much,' said Mrs Cooper. 'That's fine, Mrs Masters. We'll just have to find another way to support poor Sally.'

Cordelia smiled. Usually her smile didn't alter her composure, but there were times when it lit up her serious face. This was one of those times.

'Before the war, I'd have said, "How disgraceful. Absolutely not," but I've grown up a lot in recent years – oh, Margaret, your face! Do you imagine the over-thirties don't grow and change? I can assure you that isn't the case. One never stops learning – or rather, one shouldn't stop. I'd hate to be so set in my ways that I was incapable of . . .'

'Of growing and changing?' Margaret prompted, intrigued by the very idea.

'Of becoming a better person,' said Cordelia. She reached out and placed her slender hand on top of Mrs Cooper's work-worn one. 'Knowing you has made me a better person.'

'Oh my goodness,' Mrs Cooper murmured.

'So has knowing Mrs Green. If Sally's landlady intends to throw her out, then more fool her. She might be following society's rules, but she's losing the chance to be a better person. In wartime, we live with so many sorrows and one of the antidotes, I have come to believe, is to be kind whenever we can.'

'Does that mean Sally can move in?' breathed Margaret. 'I promise we won't take advantage and try to spin it out for longer than we should.'

'It still isn't up to me,' said Cordelia.

Something inside Margaret slumped. 'I know. It's up to the Morgans.'

'What I learned before the war, in my days on the local charity committees,' said Cordelia, 'is that there are different ways of achieving something. For example, were I to write to the Morgans and make this request, the response would be utter outrage and Mr Morgan would probably think I've gone off my rocker. On the other hand, were I to write privately to Mrs Morgan and briefly explain Sally's situation, followed by a few discreet words along the lines of "And you, of all people, will understand the poor girl's fears at this time," well, you never know what the response might be.'

'Why would Mrs Morgan understand?' asked Mrs Cooper. Then she caught her breath, her eyes widening. 'You surely don't mean that she . . .'

'Heavens, no, not Mrs Morgan. The very idea! No, it was their daughter who let's just say was interestingly plump when she walked down the aisle and then produced a so-called premature son.'

'And you don't think he was premature after all?' said Mrs Cooper.

'I think we can all recognise a bouncing ten-pounder when we see one,' Cordelia said wryly.

'Ten pounds?' murmured Mrs Cooper. 'The poor girl.'

'I suggest that I write the letter,' said Cordelia, 'and we'll see what happens. I rather imagine it will be good news for Sally.'

Chapter Ten

It came as no surprise to Alison to be sent for by Miss Emery. It was something that happened every so often. The thing that in recent months had come as something of a surprise was the way Miss Emery continued to behave precisely as she had always done. Last year, as a direct result of helping Alison and her friends, she had been dismissed from her post, whereupon the others had organised a successful campaign to have her reinstated. You'd think that after all that, she would have softened in her professional attitude towards them, but no. She conducted herself now just as she always had. At best you could call her professionally pleasant, even with Alison, who saw her on a regular basis.

When Alison presented herself at the large alcove that served as Miss Emery's office, Miss Emery immediately got up from her desk. As always, she was immaculately turned out. She could climb Mount Snowdon in gale force winds and would walk back down again uncrumpled.

'Good morning, Miss Lambert,' she said. 'I hear congratulations are in order.'

'Yes.' Alison held out her emerald ring.

'It's beautiful,' said Miss Emery.

'Thank you.' Alison never got tired of hearing how lovely her ring was.

'Have you set the date yet?'

'Not the actual date, but we've decided on next June.'

'June. I see. Would you come with me, please?'

That didn't come as a surprise either. Miss Emery's alcove was hardly suitable for private conversations and she routinely had to borrow a proper office to hold her meetings and interviews. Alison always felt indignant on her behalf, but Miss Emery, professional to the last, never betrayed a shred of displeasure with the arrangement.

On previous occasions when Alison had spoken privately to Miss Emery, it had been to learn which job she was being sent to next. Generally this was done in the alcove, but sometimes it had taken place in a real office and Alison had quite liked that. It made her feel important.

Miss Emery knocked on a door and seemed to start to walk inside, only to stop, her hand resting on the doorknob. Alison just managed not to cannon into her from behind. Beyond Miss Emery, there were two gentlemen in the office. Had she and Miss Emery turned up earlier than expected?

'Miss Lambert is here,' said Miss Emery. 'She is due to marry next June.' To Alison she said, 'You remember Mr Mortimer, don't you?'

Mr Mortimer rose to his feet. He was the official who had spoken to them all on their very first day here and had doled out their jobs. An old-fashioned watch chain hung in a loop from the little pocket in his waistcoat, which was a snug fit. Had his slicked-back hair been salt and pepper when Alison last saw him?

'Come in, Miss Lambert,' said Mr Mortimer. 'This is Mr Samuels.'

'Oh.' Alison's voice betrayed her recognition of the name.

Mr Samuels paused in the act of offering his hand for her to shake. 'Have we met before?'

'No, sir.' She knew the name because it had come up early on in the war when she and her friends had investigated a series of thefts from a secret store of food set aside lest the country be invaded. 'I just . . . know you're an important person in the company.'

Mr Samuels chuckled. 'I've been called worse things in my time. How do you do, Miss Lambert?'

'Please take a seat,' Mr Mortimer invited her.

That was the moment when Alison realised Miss Emery was no longer there. She had slipped out, closing the door silently behind her. What was this about?

'First of all,' said Mr Mortimer, smiling in a way that made his chubby cheeks bunch up beneath his eyes, 'please accept my hearty congratulations on your engagement. Is your fiancé a serviceman?'

'No, he's a doctor, a surgeon,' said Alison, 'but only for the duration. His true calling is to be a paediatrician. That's what he was doing before the war.'

'Very worthy,' said Mr Mortimer.

'And you have set the date for next June,' added Mr Samuels.

'Yes. Not the day, just the month.'

The two gentlemen looked at one another. Then Mr Samuels leaned on the arm of his chair in a way that looked casual, yet there was nothing casual in his tone or manner when he spoke.

'Miss Lambert, I must make it clear that whatever the outcome of this interview, you are not permitted to discuss it with anybody. Is that clear?'

'Including your fiancé,' Mr Mortimer added. His cheeks were no longer bunched up.

'Is that clear?' Mr Samuels repeated. It wasn't a bullying demand. His voice was quiet, all his attention focused on her.

Alison felt an internal flutter and wasn't sure if it was confusion or panic. 'Yes, sir.'

'Very well,' said Mr Samuels. 'You are required to change the date of your wedding. You may not get married next June. In fact, you may not get married next year.'

'What . . .?' She couldn't believe her ears.

'You may marry before the end of this year, if you wish,' said Mr Samuels, 'but no later.'

With a hundred questions jostling for position, all that emerged was: 'Why?'

Both gentlemen looked at her for some moments.

'Miss Lambert,' said Mr Mortimer, 'you have spent nearly two years working in various parts of the railways, have you not?'

'Yes. Being trained up.'

'For what purpose?' asked Mr Samuels.

'I – I don't know.' She felt foolish admitting it.

'Good. You aren't supposed to know, but your intended wedding date of next June has obliged us to tell you.'

There was a pause. Alison willed the men to get on with it.

'We could, of course, have simply given you instructions regarding your wedding arrangements without explaining,' said Mr Samuels. 'We could simply tell you that you're a sensible, patriotic girl and it is your duty to fall in with our wishes. Instead we have decided to tell you something that, under other circumstances, we wouldn't share with you yet.'

'Tell me what?' asked Alison.

'You are aware, of course, that the tide of the war has turned,' said Mr Samuels. 'One day the liberation of Europe will begin, Miss Lambert, and it cannot happen without the railways of Britain playing their part.'

Alison's skin tingled all over. 'And . . . is this going to happen next year?' The liberation of Europe. She was actually sitting here, having a conversation about the liberation of Europe.

'Who can say?' Mr Samuels replied.

'This is what your training has been for,' said Mr Mortimer. 'Many men and women on the railways will simply do their normal jobs but in different places and in secret. There will be others whose job will be to ensure that the onward journeys of troops and weapons take place without a hitch, and others whose role will be to maintain the day-to-day network of passenger trains and freight so that the general public has no idea that anything out of the ordinary is going on. This is why you have had the chance to learn about all areas of railway work – because you are going to be one of our onward-travel organisers. As far as your family, friends and most of your colleagues will be concerned, you will simply be continuing to work as you always have, but really you'll be doing something different, something secret. This is why you cannot get married next year, Miss Lambert. We cannot have you being distracted by your wedding plans.'

'Do you have any questions?' asked Mr Samuels.

Any questions? Yes. About a million of them. But her voice simply wouldn't work.

Joan felt fluttery with anticipation as she approached Miss Emery's office. Well, that might be its official name, but really it was a large alcove off a corridor that was otherwise lined with doors leading into real offices. At the open end of the alcove, Miss Emery had a desk on one side and a table with a typewriter on the other, with a swivel chair in between that she could angle to face either. At the back of the alcove were a tall cupboard, a coat stand and an extra chair.

Joan stood on the invisible line that marked the edge of Miss Emery's domain and tapped her knuckles on the wall to announce herself. Miss Emery was standing at the open cupboard and looked round. She wore a neat brown jacket and skirt with a cream blouse and her short string of graduated pearls.

'Mrs Hubble, how nice to see you. How are you?'

'Very well, thank you.'

Miss Emery shut the cupboard and turned the key. 'I was intrigued to receive your letter. I've arranged for us to have the use of an office so we can discuss the matter in private.'

'Thank you,' said Joan. Honestly, Miss Emery must spend half her time dashing about booking other people's offices.

Miss Emery escorted Joan further along the corridor, where she knocked on a door, opening it into a small outer office in which a middle-aged woman with salt-and-pepper hair sat at a typewriter, her desk at right angles to the inner office.

'Good morning, Mrs Cartwright,' said Miss Emery. 'This is Mrs Hubble. I believe you're expecting us.'

The secretary smiled briefly at Joan. 'Mr Ridley won't be back until gone eleven, so you've got plenty of time.'

Joan followed Miss Emery into Mr Ridley's office.

'Do sit down, Mrs Hubble. So, you wish to return to LMS.'

'Yes, please.' Joan put her handbag on the floor and folded her hands in her lap. 'I've been working as a childminder, which is important, of course, because it enables other mothers to go out to work, but I do miss being here. I loved my job as a station porter and I'd like to return to working on the railways. I want to do my bit for the war effort.'

'And childminding isn't your bit?' Miss Emery quirked an elegant eyebrow. 'There's no need to answer that. You have a very good work record at LMS, Mrs Hubble, and in principle we would be pleased to have you back. Do you see yourself returning to your old role as a station porter?'

Joan's fingers tightened together. 'Not as such. I know it's a lot to ask, but I really need a purely daytime job – because of Max and the arrangements I've made for his care.'

'I see. Yes, that is a lot to ask, especially in wartime when people don't ask, they get told.'

Joan felt worse. 'I'm sorry. I know it must sound like I'm trying to have my cake and eat it.'

'I do understand your situation,' said Miss Emery. 'I may not be married with a family of my own, but that doesn't mean I'm not sympathetic to the dilemmas and sacrifices that the country's mothers face every single day.' She paused. She still looked serious, but her features softened.

'It so happens that a new office-hours post has been created that I think might be suitable. In fact, I would urge you to apply for it.'

Joan's heart delivered a little bump of excitement. This sounded promising.

'As you are probably aware,' Miss Emery continued, 'each railway company employs a woman to act as the welfare supervisor for all the women and girls in the company's employment. In addition to this, LMS also employs an assistant welfare supervisor.' A faint smile indicated that she was speaking about herself. 'I'm pleased to say that I am now to be given an assistant whose role will be clerical, but who will also handle some of the less intricate cases. This new welfare clerk will be based in Hunts Bank and won't be required to travel around, which means that when I go away, as I often have to, there will still be a welfare person here.'

Joan leaned forward slightly. This sounded better than promising. It sounded perfect.

'As my assistant,' Miss Emery went on, with a glance that could only be described as encouraging, 'you – that is, the successful candidate would be trained to handle complaints, worries and concerns posed by the women and girls working for LMS. Both the welfare officer and I spend a large part of our time travelling around the region. Occasionally the new welfare clerk might be required to visit someone at another station, but it would be local and there would be no requirement to be away overnight.'

'It sounds very interesting,' breathed Joan.

'I am also pleased to tell you that my days in the alcove are numbered. I am to have a proper office. It might be that this is a large office that will become the women's welfare office, with space for both myself and my new colleague, or it could be that the new person might have a small office of her own. She will not,' said Miss Emery crisply, 'be expected to use the alcove.'

Joan was tempted to say how bad everyone had felt for Miss Emery while she had been forced to make the best of the alcove, but it wasn't her place to say such things.

'To start with,' Miss Emery continued, 'the successful applicant would work alongside me to learn the ropes and to see how various personal and professional matters are dealt with, according to whatever issues arise from the female employees. Sometimes the women need information, so it is essential to be familiar with all the rules and regs. On other occasions, they require support in a difficult situation, which might be connected with their family circumstances or could be work-related. Having worked as a station porter, and having a young child of your own, would give your application a solid basis.'

'I'd love to apply.' Joan's smile was so broad her face was in danger of cracking in two. 'The work you do is so important and worthwhile. I'd like the opportunity to be part of it.'

'Good. I'm glad to see your enthusiasm.' Miss Emery smiled. 'You have a very nice manner, Mrs Hubble. You're pleasant and polite and you listen. I would be very happy to see you in this post. It won't become available for a while. I believe it won't be advertised until September. I must stress,

Mrs Hubble, that there is a proper application process to go through.'

'Of course,' said Joan.

. . . important and worthwhile . . . opportunity . . . suitable background . . .

She was already writing the application in her head. She felt like running a victory lap all around Victoria Station. It was better than anything she could ever have hoped for.

Chapter Eleven

Joel was perfectly happy to bring their wedding forward to December. The sooner the better as far as he was concerned. They had decided to marry on Christmas Eve. Not just a winter wedding, but a Christmas wedding. What could be more romantic? Alison was grateful that Joel fitted in with her apparent change of mind so readily. It felt strange pretending it was because she simply couldn't bear to wait until next summer when all the while she was tinglingly aware of the real reason. She – she, Alison Lambert – had been picked to be one of the onward-travel planners for supporting and helping to make possible the eventual liberation of Europe.

She'd had to sign a paper to promise she wouldn't speak of it to anybody.

'This isn't the Z-list,' Mr Samuels had told her, 'but make no mistake, it is profoundly important.'

'What's the Z-list?' Alison had never heard of it.

'It's the same sort of thing as this. It is a declaration that you will keep details of your work secret, the difference being that if you fail to live up to your promise when you are on the Z-list, I believe they shoot you.'

Alison went about her normal daily routine in a state of shock for the first few days. The level of responsibility she was to be given took her breath away. Never for one moment had she imagined when she was being shunted from one post to another that it might lead to something like this. It was scary – but what an honour. Most of all, she felt a deep determination to do her very best for her country.

The first thing she had to do – for her country! – was rearrange her wedding.

'I thought you wanted months and months of planning and building up to it,' Persephone said when the friends met in the buffet.

'I did,' said Alison, 'and I still do. I just don't need as much of it as I thought. Next June is nearly a year away.'

'And you can't wait that long to be Mrs Joel Maitland,' said Emily.

'No, I can't,' said Alison. 'There's quite a while between now and Christmas. There'll be plenty of time to make everything perfect.'

'It'll be here before you know it,' said Dot.

'A Christmas Eve wedding,' said Cordelia. 'It might snow. It sounds beautiful.'

Alison laughed. 'I sincerely hope so. I don't want to walk up the church path ankle-deep in slush.'

'The path will be swept clear,' Dot proclaimed.

'There's just one problem,' said Alison. 'I wrote to tell Mabel's mum about the change of date and she sent a letter by return saying that the wedding dress won't be available, because it's already been promised to one of the factory girls.'

'No,' and 'What a shame,' said her friends.

'It's rather a blow,' Alison admitted, 'but worse things happen at sea, as the saying goes.'

'Good for you, taking it on the chin,' Dot said approvingly.

'I'm sure another lovely dress will come your way,' said Margaret. 'Things have a way of working out.'

'Fingers crossed,' said Emily.

'Shall you be getting married from your parents' house?' asked Persephone.

Alison nodded. 'Of course.' She hesitated, wondering whether to say what had popped into her mind, but if she couldn't say it to these dear friends, who could she say it to? 'Don't misunderstand this, but I have an odd little feeling that I'd have been just as happy to marry from Wilton Close. When I moved in, it was only meant to be a place of refuge, but it's come to be a true home to me.' She glanced around the table. 'I don't want to sound disloyal to my parents.'

'You don't, chick,' Dot assured her at once. 'You're paying a great compliment to Mrs Cooper and Mrs Grayson. Your mum and dad would never begrudge them that.'

Persephone turned to Margaret. 'I hope your friend Sally feels the same when she moves in. It's frightfully bad luck that her landlady's circumstances have changed.'

'The billeting officer wasn't best pleased when Sally's landlady said she wanted Sally's room for her daughter,' said Margaret, 'but you can't blame her.'

'It's fortunate that Mrs Cooper has a spare room again,' said Emily.

'When does Sally move in?' asked Colette.

'Saturday,' said Margaret. 'It's only temporary while she gets herself sorted out.'

Dot laughed. 'Temporary? In my experience, when girls move into Mrs Cooper's, they're there for keeps.'

That gave Alison something to think about. 'If she does stay longer than expected, I'll have to invite her to my wedding. It would be rather awful to invite everyone else and leave her out. I'm sorry,' she added. 'That sounded ungracious and it wasn't meant to.'

'You don't need to invite her to your wedding,' Margaret said at once. 'She won't be with us that long. Besides, nobody would expect you to invite her, especially not with wedding numbers being so strictly limited.'

Alison looked around at the others. 'As long as you're all able to come, that's what matters.'

Her friends had accepted her supposed change of heart over her wedding date without a qualm and so did her family. Mum went into a bit of a panic, but Alison could tell it was an enjoyable panic.

'We'll have to get a move on,' said Mum when Alison went round to her parents' house on Saturday.

Alison, Mum and Lydia were sitting at the table. Brilliant summer sunshine poured through the window, the lines of anti-blast tape creating zigzag patterns on the floor. Mum had a piece of paper in front of her. It was the back of a letter from Auntie Rosalind on which Mum had previously made some notes regarding the June wedding, some of which had now been crossed out. The sweet scent of Dad's pipe tobacco occasionally wafted through from the parlour, where Dad was tucked behind his newspaper, safe from wedding matters.

Alison glanced at what remained on Mum's list. 'I'm glad to see something has survived,' she joked. 'You've still got my list of attendants.'

Mum huffed a little sigh. 'Do you really need so many? There's a limit of forty on the number of people who can be there, you know,' she pointed out, as if Alison might have forgotten. 'That's only twenty for our side. Just look at all these names. Joan, Persephone, Emily, Margaret, Colette, Mrs Masters, Mrs Green, Mrs Cooper, Mrs Grayson. That's nine, Alison. Nine! Out of twenty.'

'Joel said we could have some of his allocation,' said Alison, 'because my friends from the railway are his friends too.'

'None of them can bring a husband or boyfriend,' Mum declared. 'It isn't fair on the family. And that's another thing. I know you've made a lot of friends through your work and moving into digs, but – so many bridesmaids?' She held up a hand to stop Alison from replying. 'This isn't a matter of money. Your father doesn't begrudge you anything, and I know your friends are important to you, but a wedding is a family thing. Think of the photographs in years to come. Lydia will always be your sister, but do you want your children asking who all the other bridesmaids are and you having to explain that they were girls you knew in the war and you haven't seen them since?'

Alison was startled. 'What makes you think I won't see them again? I'm sure we're going to be friends for ever.'

'You feel that way now,' said Mum, 'but things will go back to normal after the war. You won't be going to work then. You'll be looking after Joel's home and bringing up your children. Even if you do stay in touch with all these girls,' Mum went on, ploughing over what Alison attempted to say, 'it doesn't alter the fact that there are so many of them. Joan, Margaret, Emily, Persephone, Colette. You've even added

97

Mabel with a question mark. Then there's Lydia, of course – and what about Joel's sisters?'

'I wasn't intending to ask Joel's sisters.'

'You should, really. You should ask them before your friends. Have you already asked your friends?'

'Not yet,' said Alison. 'You and I agreed not to do anything until we had all the plans in place.'

'It makes me glad I got married at top speed when Alec had a seventy-two-hour pass,' said Lydia. 'No time at all for disagreements.'

If that was Lydia's attempt at introducing a light-hearted note, it didn't work. Alison and Mum both looked daggers at her.

Mum sighed again, this time in a sorrowful way. 'And then there's your friend Colette.'

'What about her?' asked Alison.

'She's separated from her husband.'

'Yes, and a jolly good thing too, from what Alison has told us,' said Lydia.

'It's a shocking thing to leave a marriage,' said Mum. 'I'm fully aware of the reasons why, and my heart goes out to the poor girl for everything she had to cope with, but the fact remains that leaving your husband is shocking and – well – not the kind of thing one looks for in a matron of honour. What sort of message does that send out to the congregation? "I'm getting married and by the way, one of my matrons of honour has left her husband." It doesn't create the right atmosphere.'

'No one will know about Colette's situation apart from her friends,' said Alison. She was starting to feel mutinous. 'She was a matron of honour for Mabel.'

'Yes, way up north, where nobody knew her,' said Mum. 'I'm sorry, Alison. I know you think I'm being harsh, but it's the way of the world. I'm just asking you to think about it, that's all. Now then, you and I will need to go to the Food Office to arrange the permits for the extra food . . .'

A bit later, when Mum had disappeared to make them all a cup of tea, Alison and Lydia looked at one another. For a moment there was silence, then they both giggled.

'It's a good job you've changed to Christmas,' Lydia whispered. 'Just think of all the organising she could do if she had until next summer.'

'I don't know why we're laughing,' said Alison.

'Personally, I'm laughing because I now realise that by getting married in such a rush, I got off lightly. You, on the other hand, aren't just getting the work Mum would always have put into your wedding, you're also getting the work she never had the chance to put into mine.'

'Thanks very much.' Alison pulled a face at her sister.

'You don't know how lucky you are,' said Lydia. 'You can take your time over your wedding and then you get to live with your husband. Some of us aren't so lucky. But I don't want you to think I'm not happy for you, because I am. You've been a wonderful sister to me and you deserve the very best. I – I never said anything at the time, but I know what a brick you were when I got married. It must have been pretty hellish for you, what with Paul having left you not long before. You could easily have spoiled things for me if you'd felt like it, but you didn't, and now I want only the best for you.' She grinned, looking for all the world like an impish eight-year-old. 'And if that means you need someone to gang up with you against Mum, just say the word.'

After spending Saturday afternoon with Lydia and Mum making plans for her wedding, Alison then spent Sunday afternoon with her friends in Wilton Close, doing the same thing.

'I might have suggested that you'll get tired of talking about your wedding, Alison,' Mrs Grayson gently teased her, 'but somehow I can't see that happening.'

Alison laughed good-naturedly. 'Definitely not.'

It was a drizzly afternoon. Alison glanced out of the window, unable to suppress thoughts of what weather might greet her on her wedding day.

'You're wondering about winter weather, aren't you, chuck?' asked Mrs Cooper.

Alison turned away from the window. 'You read my mind.'

'It rained solidly every day for a fortnight before my wedding,' Mrs Cooper told her. 'I was dreadfully upset about it to start with, but then, a couple of days before the wedding, I realised it didn't matter. Yes, sunshine would be wonderful, but actually, whatever the weather did, I knew I was going to be so happy and excited that I would barely notice.'

'You're right. It's no good agonising about the weather.'

'Everyone hopes for a fine day, of course they do, but you might find it more useful to spend your energy on the things you can control rather than the things you can't.'

'Did it rain on your wedding day?' Alison asked.

Mrs Cooper smiled. 'Until about eleven. We got wed at half past twelve and the sun shone all afternoon.'

It wasn't long before all their guests arrived. Persephone cycled across from Darley Court. Cordelia and Emily walked from their house on Edge Lane. Dot and Colette came by bus from Withington and Seymour Grove respectively, and Joan's grandmother had offered to take care of little Max so Joan could come too and not have to rush back.

Alison thanked them all for coming. 'I do appreciate it, especially as you were all here only a fortnight ago for my engagement tea party.'

'You can never have too much wedding talk,' said Dot.

'Let's start with the dresses,' said Alison. 'No, not mine, before you ask. Attendants' dresses. I'm going to ask you all to do the usual thing of wearing your best dress, the way you did for Joan's and Mabel's weddings.'

'I have an idea,' said Mrs Grayson, 'if you don't mind me butting in.'

'You aren't butting in,' said Alison. 'What is it?'

'Since it's a winter wedding, I wondered about crocheting some pretty shawls for the attendants.'

'That's a good idea,' said Cordelia. 'I imagine it might be fairly cool, shall we say, in the church in December.'

'Would you like everyone in the same colour, Alison,' asked Mrs Grayson, 'or in colours that tone in with their dresses?'

'Which is easier in terms of getting hold of the wool?' asked Joan.

'It's as broad as it is long,' said Mrs Grayson. 'Sufficient wool in a single colour would be tricky to find, but it might be difficult to find exactly the right toning colours.'

'Let's go for toning,' said Alison.

'And each girl can have the job of searching out her own wool,' said Cordelia. 'That takes the pressure off Mrs Grayson.'

'Where will you hold the reception?' asked Margaret.

'Mum has booked the church hall,' said Alison.

'I have an offer for you from Miss Brown,' said Persephone. 'She says would you like to borrow the decorations we had at Darley Court for the Christmas events last year?'

Everyone exclaimed in delight.

'Oh, *yes*!' said Margaret. 'All those garlands and streamers. Do you remember the tartan streamers?'

'And the strings of coloured beads,' Cordelia added.

'Those beautiful glass baubles,' Colette recalled, 'and the paper lanterns.'

'And those stockings,' said Dot. 'Red velvet with fur round the top.'

Joan laughed. 'I think we've all just said yes on your behalf, Alison.'

'It is what you want, isn't it?' Emily encouraged her.

It took Alison a moment to speak because she was overwhelmed by the generous offer.

'Thank you,' she said to Persephone. 'I'd love to have the use of all of that.'

Alison beamed at her friends. She felt like giving each and every one of them a hug and a kiss.

'Well, if you will get married on Christmas Eve,' Persephone said lightly, 'you've got to expect a bit of Christmas magic.'

Chapter Twelve

Joan had already warned her two mums that they would need to make alternative arrangements for their sons' care in the not too distant future when she returned to working for LMS. She knew them well enough to know that Norman's mother would start looking at once, but Jeremy's mother was more likely to ignore the problem until finally forced to do otherwise.

'Have you got a start date yet?' she had asked Joan.

'I haven't actually applied for the job yet,' Joan had told her.

Jeremy's mum looked relieved. 'Well then, there's plenty of time and you might not even get it.'

It had been on the tip of Joan's tongue to say she was sure of getting it, but she stopped herself. She didn't want to sound big-headed. Besides, she didn't want to risk Jeremy's mum not keeping the news to herself.

Joan found out when her friends were next due to meet up in the buffet and made arrangements with Mrs Grayson for her to take care of Max.

'Lovely! A trial run,' said Mrs Grayson.

Joan tried to see it as a trial run for herself too, but she knew that leaving Max for a trip to the buffet was a very different prospect to leaving him all day, every day throughout the working week. The trickiest part of the process, actually, was arranging for Norman and Jeremy to be looked after until their mums finished their shifts, but her sisters-in-law Glad and Petal both had a day off that day and were happy to help out.

Catching the bus into town to meet up with her friends felt like an adventure. Victoria Station was busy, as it always was at this time of day, the concourse crowded with passengers and their luggage, all in a fug of tobacco smoke. Some lucky travellers were able to take the weight off their feet by sitting on the benches, but most people had to stand, some chatting to acquaintances, others buried in their newspapers, some looking first at the station clock hanging from the gantry, then at their wristwatch and then back at the station clock, apparently unable to believe how slowly time was passing.

Joan eased her way through the crowds, smiling happily with a sense of homecoming as she made her way to the buffet. As soon as she walked in, she spotted her friends and waved, delighted by their looks of surprise. Persephone and Margaret came over and offered to stand in the queue for her so she could head straight to the table.

'That's kind of you,' said Joan, 'but I'd like to say hello to Mrs Jessop.'

Soon, with her cup of tea carefully balanced, she arrived at the table, where she was greeted warmly.

'What brings you here?' asked Dot. 'Not that I'm complaining. It's lovely to see you.'

'And to see you too, Dot,' said Joan, 'and the rest of you, of course. I've come to give you my news.'

'My goodness,' Alison exclaimed. 'Another baby.'

'No,' said Joan, taken aback. 'It's nothing like that.' She felt wrong-footed. If her friends thought the best possible news would be a little brother or sister for Max, what would they think of her real news? But she needn't have worried. As soon as she said, 'I'm coming back to the railways,' there was an eruption of pleasure followed by what felt like dozens of questions all at once.

She explained about Mrs Grayson and the Lizzie Nursery taking care of Max between them, and then told her friends about the job Miss Emery had described to her.

'Well, it's about time there was another girl working on behalf of all the female employees,' said Dot. 'It's mad that there's just the welfare supervisor and Miss Emery. Good for you, Joan. I'm pleased for you.'

'I haven't got the job yet,' said Joan. 'I have to apply for it.'

'These things have to be seen to be done properly,' said Persephone.

'But Miss Emery was very encouraging,' Joan added. 'She said that I've got the right sort of experience. I've worked on the railways and I'm also a wife and mother, so I understand about domestic pressures. She said I have the right sort of manner too.'

'If you think it would help,' said Cordelia, 'I might be able to arrange for you to sit in on some Citizens Advice interviews. It could give you a wider idea of the sorts of problems women face.'

'And it would be a good thing to put in your application letter,' Margaret added. 'Just think. When you're appointed, you'll be able to meet up with us in the buffet after work. Won't that be grand?'

'If you ask me,' said Dot, 'that's the real reason she wants the job in the first place.'

They all laughed. Joan felt warm inside. It was wonderful to be back in the buffet again – and it would be more wonderful still when she could come here with her friends regularly.

Before she left the buffet, Joan had intended to arrange to go round to Wilton Close to meet Sally, but as it was, Margaret made the suggestion first – not for Joan to visit Wilton Close, but for Margaret to bring Sally round to Torbay Road.

'That would be lovely,' said Joan. 'I'd like to meet her. When can you come? Bob's just started a run of two-till-ten shifts, though he'll be working until midnight, so my evenings are free once his lordship has settled for the night.'

Joan looked forward to their evening together. She made some ginger biscuits from a recipe Mrs Grayson had given her and gave the sitting room a quick once-over with Gran's home-made lemon polish so that it smelled fresh. When the doorbell rang, she ran downstairs to let her visitors in. Sally was a pretty blonde with light blue eyes and a quiet, rather shy manner.

'Come and say hello to my grandmother first,' said Joan, 'then we'll go upstairs.'

She and Bob had got into the habit of this. They and Gran lived mostly separate lives, which was how they all wanted it, but it was important to keep up a sense of family feeling too, so Joan and Bob almost always took their own visitors into Gran's parlour for a few minutes.

When they went upstairs, Joan put the kettle on, bringing a tray into the sitting room, where she found her guests fussing Brizo. Sally was kneeling on the rug in front of the fireplace, scratching his ears.

'He'll take any amount of that,' Joan told her, putting down the tray. When Sally sat on her heels, Joan added, 'Have one of the armchairs.'

'I'm fine on the rug,' said Sally. 'I'm delighted to meet the famous Brizo at last.'

'You've heard of him?' Joan asked, pleased.

'Everyone who works for LMS has heard of Brizo collecting money for charity on the station.'

Joan glowed. She was proud of Brizo. He visited Victoria Station regularly, wearing a little collecting box strapped to his back. It had been Persephone's idea. She'd been sure that passengers would be only too pleased to slip a few coppers into the box, happy both to support a good cause and to have a minute to fuss a friendly dog. Brizo certainly loved all the attention.

Sally gave Brizo a final hug and reached for her tea. 'You have a nice room.'

'Thanks. We might not have much, but we've got a lot more than many people.'

'My parents were bombed out,' said Sally. 'They lost everything.'

Joan glanced round, seeing her sitting room through Sally's eyes. It was a big room to contain no more than a couple of armchairs, a table with mismatched dining chairs, and a wooden cupboard with a drawer at the bottom, not forgetting the toy box and, of course, the rocking chair her friends had given her.

They drank tea and nibbled the biscuits as they chatted, but Joan sensed a certain air of restraint between the others and felt puzzled. She and Margaret were good friends. Was it Sally's shyness? Even as she thought it, Joan recognised that this wasn't quite the right word. Sally wasn't shy exactly, but something told Joan she wasn't comfortable.

At last, Margaret exchanged looks with Sally and then said, 'We're here under false pretences. That is, I wanted the two of you to meet, and I hope you'll be friends, but we have another reason for being here. It was what you said about your new job, Joan, that made me think of it.'

'My new job?' What on earth could this be about?

'Yes, it was when you said that Miss Emery thinks you've got the right sort of background.'

'I haven't started the job yet,' said Joan. 'I haven't even been appointed.'

'No, but you're going to be.'

Joan frowned. 'If you need some kind of help, Sally, you really ought to make an appointment with Miss Emery.'

Sally didn't say anything. After a moment, Margaret stepped in.

'I think Sally would be happier with you, because you're my friend and I've told her how kind you are. It'll only be anticipating your new job by a few weeks and Sally needs help now.'

'I'll gladly help,' said Joan.

Margaret and Sally exchanged another look.

'Miss Emery doesn't just want you because you've worked on the railways, Joan,' said Margaret. 'She wants you because of your personal background as well, because you're a wife

108

and mother. That was what gave me the idea of coming to see you – that, and also because I know how kind and trust-worthy you are. As a – as a mother, I think you might be able to give Sally some advice.'

Sally pressed her lips together. She opened her mouth to speak, then shut it again. Finally, she blurted out, 'I'm in the family way.'

Before Joan could say anything, Margaret said, 'The poor girl was led up the garden path by a man who turned out to be married. That's the real reason she had to leave her old billet.'

'Does Mrs . . .?' Realising she was whispering, Joan started again in a normal voice. 'Does Mrs Cooper know?'

'Yes,' said Margaret. 'So does Mrs Grayson and so does Cordelia, because she had to square it with the Morgans. I'd never have tried to move Sally into Wilton Close without telling Mrs Cooper the truth.'

Joan looked from one girl to the other. She was sure there was more to this than Margaret being a good friend. Had it brought back Margaret's memories of her own unwelcome pregnancy? She and Joan had been stuck in the cellar beneath Margaret's severely bomb-damaged house when Margaret had suffered a painful miscarriage and Joan, an inexperi-enced first-aider, had had to cope. It wasn't just Margaret who had memories of that time. *A flighty piece, a common little tart, who couldn't keep her knickers up.* That was what Gran had said. Not that Gran had any idea who the unfortunate girl had been. Joan had grown up a lot that night. Marga-ret's pregnancy had come as a shock because Joan, like all decent girls, had been brought up to believe that nice girls didn't sleep with their boyfriends. Joan had always assumed that girls who had more elastic in their morals than in their knickers would be easy to tell apart from decent girls, but the fact that she had known Margaret for some time and liked her had made her rethink all that.

Since then, of course, Margaret had confided the truth about her doomed relationship with Joel. For Joan, this had underlined the knowledge, already gained through learning about her own family's secret past, that life wasn't as black and white as she had been brought up to believe.

She said decisively, 'I want to help you, Sally.'

Sally's shoulders sagged and she buried her face in Brizo's gingery coat for a few moments. When she looked up, her eyes were bright with tears. 'Thank you. You can't imagine what this means to me. Margaret said you . . . but I didn't dare believe it. I'd be so grateful to discuss things with someone in authority.'

'Steady on,' said Joan. 'I'm not in the job yet.'

'Someone with information, then,' said Sally.

'Miss Emery could give you far more information than I can,' Joan said gently.

'She's also a spinster,' said Sally, 'and you've only got to look at her perfect hair and perfect clothes to know her life runs utterly smoothly. I can't go to her. I'd be too ashamed. You've no idea of the courage it took to come here.'

'Well, I do know about maternity food entitlements,' said Joan.

'Oh, I shan't be able to keep the baby,' Sally exclaimed.

'I don't mean later on. I mean while you're expecting. You need to get a letter from your doctor and take it to the

Food Office. It'll be embarrassing because it'll say Miss instead of Mrs, but that can't be helped. You're entitled to orange juice and vitamin tablets and an extra half-ration of meat. You get additional milk as well at a reduced price.' She smiled. 'One of the first people to know your condition is the milkman.'

Sally looked like she was about to object.

'If you're thinking of not bothering,' Joan cut in, 'that would be a big mistake. You'll need the extras because you're going to get tired and you've got to keep your strength up. The Food Office will issue you with a green ration book.'

'It sounds so public,' Sally whispered.

'I knew we were right to come to you, Joan,' said Margaret. 'Thanks for the information. I'll come with you to the Food Office if you like, Sally.'

'Thanks,' said Sally, though Joan wasn't sure if she was taking everything in.

Joan moved to sit on the rug, which Brizo seemed to think was for his benefit and he leaned warmly against her, inviting attention.

'Sally, I know about green ration books, but I don't know the first thing about what you're going to have to face.'

'Mother and baby homes,' said Sally dully. 'The adoption process.'

'But I know all about backache and being too uncomfortable to sleep. What I mean to say is, if you want to ask anything about what's happening to your body, I'm happy to talk about what it was like for me.'

The look Sally gave her was filled with gratitude. 'I wasn't sure about coming here when Margaret suggested it,' she

111

said, 'but I'm glad we did. You're going to be wonderful in your new job.'

Joan felt concerned about Sally and was glad to have helped her with some useful information, but there was more to it than that. It made her even more keen on the welfare post. Imagine being able to assist women every single day. How fulfilling – and interesting. She couldn't wait.

Just as Cordelia had promised when the friends had met up in the buffet, she had made arrangements for Joan to spend a morning in the Citizens Advice Bureau, sitting alongside a lady helping whoever came in with enquiries.

'I've explained about your proposed new role at work,' said Cordelia, 'and the head of the local bureau has agreed to let you have this experience. It's the sort of thing their own people do when they're training.'

'Thanks for arranging it for me,' Joan said sincerely.

She had her own arrangements to make before she could go. She had three little boys to be looked after by someone else. Mrs Grayson had offered to have Max again, but what was Joan to do with Jeremy and Norman? She was on the verge of asking whether she could pay for them to go to the Lizzie Nursery for the morning, and wondering what Bob would make of that, when Mrs Cooper stepped in.

'I'll change my cleaning rota so I can stop at home,' she offered. 'Then you can bring all three of them round.'

'Are you sure?' asked Joan. 'They have a nap in the afternoon, but I'm afraid they're on the go all morning.'

'It's in a good cause,' said Mrs Cooper. 'We'll have Brizo as well on the days he doesn't go to the station to raise money. Might as well make a full house of it.'

Joan kissed her cheek. 'What would I do without you?'

'Oh, you'd manage,' said Mrs Cooper. 'You're a capable girl, and kind with it. Sally told me how you'd helped with the green ration book and all the rest.'

'It wasn't exactly difficult for me,' said Joan.

'You made her feel better – well, after she'd got over the fright, anyway.'

'I never meant to scare her,' said Joan.

'Not that kind of fright. The kind where it's brought home to you that a situation really is happening.' Mrs Cooper sighed softly. 'I imagine there have been several such moments for Sally in recent weeks.'

'How long are you going to let her stay with you?' Joan asked.

'My instinct is to let her stay as long as possible, but I have to think about the Morgans. I can't have them coming home afterwards to hear the neighbours gossiping about what went on in their house during the war, so Sally has to leave before her condition becomes obvious. Mrs Grayson and I think she needs some coddling and as much rest as possible, so Mrs Grayson is going to feed her up. We want her to be fit and healthy when she . . . moves on.'

Joan shuddered. 'The very thought of having a baby and not being able to keep him is unbearable. I can't imagine my life without Max.'

'And I could never have imagined mine without Lizzie, and yet here I am trying to make the best of it without her,' said Mrs Cooper. 'That's why I want to help Sally, even though most people would have turned her away. I know how hard life can be. Just because something bad happens to you doesn't mean you're a bad person.'

Joan put her arms around her former landlady and held her close.

'You're the best person,' she whispered.

Joan sat to one side of the table behind which sat Mrs Humphreys from the Citizens Advice Bureau. She was a double-chinned lady with a fox fur around her ample shoulders. She greeted everyone with a smile that showed her dimples, but once she got down to business she was brisk and efficient. Each time a new person came forward with an enquiry, she gave Joan a brief introduction.

'This is Mrs Hubble, who is here to observe. If you object, she can withdraw, but I assure you she will keep your confidence.'

'That's all right. She can stay,' said the first lady, a timid-looking wisp of a woman.

'Thank you, Mrs Cutler,' said Mrs Humphreys, her dimples popping into action. To Joan she added, 'Mrs Cutler has been before – haven't you, Mrs Cutler?'

'Yes,' said Mrs Cutler. 'It's my house, you see,' she told Joan. 'We were bombed, not bombed out, you understand, just bombed, so we had to get repaired, but the repairs aren't much good.'

Joan smiled and nodded, but she was under strict instructions not to stick her oar in, so she couldn't say a word.

'The problem here,' said Mrs Humphreys, 'is that the Poor Man's Valuer wrote a report to say that the house wasn't built to a good standard in the first place. "Shoddy" was the word he used.'

'Now the damp is getting worse,' said Mrs Cutler, 'and the lodger is leaving.'

'I'm afraid the Poor Man's Valuer has done as much as he can.' Mrs Humphreys drew a form towards her and sat there with her pen poised. 'All I can do is refer the matter to the Poor Man's Lawyer to see if it is possible to take action against the builder who did the repairs.'

'Poor lady,' Joan whispered as Mrs Cutler went on her way.

'You see everything in this job,' said Mrs Humphreys.

The next person was Mrs Murphy, whose fifteen-year-old son was six foot one and still growing. Mrs Humphreys told her firmly that she had all the clothes coupons she was entitled to and suggested she join a sewing class. Another lady, who had taken in her late sister's children, also wanted clothing coupons.

'Will the children be living with you permanently?' asked Mrs Humphreys.

'Oh, yes, definitely. I wouldn't see our Audrey's kids going anywhere else.'

'Then you are entitled to extra coupons. Here's the form you need to fill in. Do you need help with it?'

When that lady had departed, Mrs Humphreys murmured, 'Lord, here we go again,' as an elderly woman came forward. Out loud she said, 'Good morning, Mrs Perkins. What can I do for you?'

'You can find me somewhere new to live, that's what you can do.'

'We've been over this before, Mrs Perkins.'

'For all the good it does,' Mrs Perkins said glumly. 'I can't stick living with my daughter-in-law much longer. I've got to get out of there.'

'You are on a list, Mrs Perkins,' said Mrs Humphreys. 'Everything possible is being done.'

When she had got rid of Mrs Perkins, who grumbled under her breath as she departed, Mrs Humphreys told Joan, 'In all probability, the daughter-in-law will be here tomorrow with the same complaint. We have each of them in here at least once a week.'

The next person was another elderly lady called Mrs Channing.

'I've been living with my daughter since I was bombed out and it's a bit of a squeeze, but it's all right. But I've got my furniture in store and the firm says I have to get it out of there by the end of next week because they're giving up the building.'

'I have a list of furniture storage companies,' said Mrs Humphreys. 'Let me see if I can find one that can take your belongings.'

All in all, it was an interesting morning, though Joan didn't think the problems were of much use or relevance to likely railway problems. Or did Miss Emery also help with issues in the women's home lives? Joan had always supposed that Miss Emery's work was based mostly around situations caused when there was inappropriate behaviour by men – or did she just imagine that because of Mr Clark, the horrid beast who had made her sit on his chair with him on her first day on the railways? On another occasion, he had commented on her legs in a quiet voice that no one else had heard – and then there had been the time when she'd made a mistake in her typing and he had threatened her with the sack.

'Or, if you prefer . . . I could smack your bottom for you.'

That was what he'd said and she had been too young and inexperienced to play merry ruddy heck. In fact, she'd been so young and inexperienced that she'd even questioned whether it was her own fault. If anybody came to her with a complaint about a man's conduct, she would be sure to deal with it promptly and efficiently. It would be satisfying to help a girl who found herself in a similar situation to the one that had made Joan so wretched.

Joan found herself feeling even more determined to make a good fist of this new job. She had enjoyed being a station porter, but she was going to love this new post in the same way that Letitia had loved her maths-based job at the munitions. It would be a way of honouring her much-loved sister's memory.

Chapter Thirteen

Margaret made sure she did her share in the garden at Wilton Close these days. They all had to pull their weight now. Tony, Colette's husband, used to do the garden for them. Looking back, that now felt creepy. Sometimes Dad came along and mucked in. He had always enjoyed a spot of gardening. After their house had been severely bomb damaged in one of the early air raids, he had moved into digs further along the road from where they lived opposite Alexandra Park, and when the park had been turned over to allotments, he had taken one on. He had subsequently moved out of the disagreeable Mrs McEvoy's house, but he had kept the allotment.

On the final Sunday in August, Margaret was busy sowing winter cabbage and lettuce, helped by Sally, who had settled in well.

Sally glanced around to make sure there was no one in next door's garden to overhear. 'It's high time I sorted out where to have the baby. Mrs Cooper and Mrs Grayson have been so kind, but I mustn't take advantage of their good nature.'

'Since coming here, you're looking better than you've looked for some time,' Margaret told her.

'I'm feeling better too – as long as I don't look too far into the future. My big worry is that because I feel stronger, my tummy will suddenly burst forth all over the place.'

Margaret laughed. 'That would be a sight to behold. Seriously, though, we do need to make arrangements for you. Are you still with your old doctor from where you lived before?'

Sally squared her chin. 'Yes. He wants to put me on a hospital list. The nearest maternity ward to Chorlton is at Withington Hospital, but obviously I want to go further afield than that. I need a mother and baby home where they'll . . .'

'Where they'll arrange an adoption,' Margaret finished gently.

Sally sucked in a breath. 'Yes. I don't know why it's so difficult to say it.'

Margaret didn't want to go down that road. 'Why does your doctor want to put you down for a local hospital?'

Sally looked away. When her gaze swung back, there was defiance in her eyes. 'He doesn't know about the adoption.'

'Does he think you're going to keep it?'

'He thinks I'm getting married. That's what I told him. I couldn't tell him the truth, could I? It was only because I was prepared to lie through my teeth that I was able to make an appointment at all. And I was right to hide the truth. The way he looked at me when he knew I was pregnant out of wedlock wasn't just disapproving. He was disgusted. Then I said I was getting married and he said, "I should jolly well hope so." I wanted to sink through the floor.'

'That was a disgraceful thing to say,' Margaret declared stoutly. 'He's a doctor. He's meant to look after his patients, not put them down.'

But she knew the doctor's attitude was perfectly normal. She remembered all too clearly how she herself had cringed with dread at the prospect of having to present herself at the surgery. She'd put it off and put it off . . . and then she'd lost the baby and ended up in hospital, where everybody knew she was a single girl. A single girl – a slut. All the neighbours back at Alexandra Park knew too. It had come close to destroying her relationship with her father. Margaret experienced a renewed determination that Sally's parents must never find out about their daughter's disgrace.

'I suppose I'll have to ask the doctor about a place with an adoption procedure,' said Sally.

'Yes,' Margaret said kindly. 'Either him or Miss Emery. I'm sure it wouldn't be the first time she's been asked.'

'I don't want to ask Miss Perfect.'

'As long as you aren't waiting for Joan.'

Sally sighed. 'I know, I know. She isn't in the job yet. It won't be advertised until September.'

'I don't want to make you feel pressured,' Margaret began.

'I know I'm being selfish. I've got to move on from Wilton Close. I'm just . . .' Sally's eyes filled ' . . . scared.'

If they hadn't been standing outside in the garden, Margaret would have taken her in her arms. 'I know. I'm here to help you and I don't just mean by bringing you to Wilton Close. I want to see you through . . . everything.'

Sally dashed away her tears. 'I can't believe how stupid I was. All those snatched liaisons that seemed so romantic – and really they were just plain tawdry. I'm so grateful to you for sticking by me. I was in despair before you brought me here.' Her smile was brittle as she added, 'I don't feel like a slut any more.'

'You never were one,' said Margaret. 'You were in love and you believed in the man you cared for. You had every reason to think he loved you just as much. You weren't to know you were . . .' Her voice trailed off.

'His bit on the side,' Sally finished for her. 'I never would have known if I hadn't fallen pregnant with his baby.' She shook her head. 'It does no good to dwell on it.'

'Something else we ought to think about,' said Margaret, treading carefully, 'is how long you can carry on in the engine sheds. I know you don't want to confide in Miss Emery, but she could arrange for you to move into a different job.'

'You're trying so hard to look after me. I do appreciate it, you know. As for the job, yes, it's hard graft, but it's elbow grease rather than physical strain.' Sally pressed her lips together for a thoughtful moment before saying, 'If cleaning every inch of the motion work or shifting clinker from the tubes was bad for the baby, then believe me, I'd have lost it weeks ago. I tried to,' she admitted. 'I worked like I've never worked before, hoping that – that it would solve my problem for me, but the greater the physical effort I put in, the harder the little blighter clung on.'

'Oh, Sally,' Margaret whispered.

'Plus I can wear dungarees in the engine sheds,' Sally added in an artificially bright voice. 'You can hide the proverbial multitude of sins inside a pair of dungarees.' She glanced down at herself. 'Joan's an angel. She let out the waist on my skirt and she's lent me a blouse that she made for herself when she was fuller-figured while she was pregnant. And I was able to swap my summer dress for a bigger one at the clothes exchange, but you're only allowed to go there once a month. I can get away with wearing a bigger size for a while, but I know there'll come a time when I won't be able to hide my condition. I have to have left here before that.' She breathed in, as if about to release a sigh, then didn't. 'I've stuck my head in the sand for too long. Please will you help me find a mother and baby place?'

Alison walked down the path with Joel. He stepped ahead to open the wooden gate for her as she called goodbye to Margaret and Sally, who were meant to be working in the garden but looked more like they were having a good old natter.

'Have a lovely afternoon,' Margaret called.

Frankly, Alison could think of a hundred ways she would rather spend a precious Sunday afternoon with Joel, but they were going to Venetia's.

'I don't know why she's invited us,' said Joel. 'She just said it's important.'

Venetia and her husband, Larry, had a handsome house with stone steps leading up to the front door, which stood in between a pair of wide bay windows. The front garden had been turned over to growing vegetables, but its smart layout was still there to be seen – a large square divided by paths into four smaller squares. The squares must have been sections of a no doubt immaculately manicured lawn before the war. In the centre stood an elegant fountain, its spray sparkling in the summer sun.

Larry was a doctor, who had joined up to do his patriotic duty in the navy. In civilian life, he had been a consultant – hence the gracious house. This was the kind of lifestyle Venetia had wanted for her brother, which was why last year she had preferred Rachel Chambers as his prospective wife. Rachel had poise and grace and would have made the perfect wife for an ambitious, up-and-coming doctor. But Joel had had his own ideas about the wife he wanted. He also had his own ideas about his career. Not for him the dizzy heights of professional fame and dignity that his father enjoyed and to which Larry presumably aspired; or if Larry didn't, then Venetia certainly did. No, Joel's vocation was to work with children, not by aiming for a consultancy and making his name through writing academic papers, but by working on the wards and devoting himself wholeheartedly to the families who needed him. It was an ambition that made Alison love and admire him all the more.

The door was answered by Venetia's maid, Grace, an older woman in a black skirt and blouse.

'Good afternoon, Grace,' said Joel. 'We've been summoned.'

They went into the front room, where they were met at the door by Honey, the yellow Labrador. Venetia put down her book and rose to greet them. She was as lovely as ever in a pretty dress with a pussycat bow instead of a collar. She managed to look casual and devastatingly elegant at the same time.

She kissed Joel's cheek and then Alison's. Honey's rear end wagged from side to side with pleasure as Joel and Alison bent to fuss her.

'I'm so glad you've come,' said Venetia. 'Thank you for sparing the time. Do sit down.'

Since the sofa belonged to Venetia and the dog, Alison and Joel sat in the wingback armchairs upholstered in caramel and beige tinged with pink. Honey, instead of returning to the sofa, plonked herself down next to Joel, leaning against him. Joel looped his arm around her and tickled her tummy.

'What's this about, Vee?' Joel asked. 'You made it sound special.'

'It is,' said Venetia, 'but not for you. You're nothing more than a means of getting in touch with Alison.' She smiled at Alison. 'Joel said you haven't found a wedding dress yet. Is that still the case?'

'No, I haven't.'

'And there's so little time,' said Venetia.

'There's weeks to go yet,' said Alison. 'It won't even be September until Wednesday.'

'No time at all,' said Venetia. 'That's why I asked you here. I wondered if you would like to borrow my wedding dress.'

Alison blinked. Her immediate, instinctive response was that she would sooner stick pins in her eyes. She drew a breath, inflating a smile.

'How kind of you to offer, but—'

'Come and try it on.' Venetia bounced to her feet. 'Then if another dress crops up, you'll have a choice.'

'Do I get to see Alison in it?' asked Joel.

'Foolish boy,' said his sister. 'Keep Honey company. That's all you're good for.'

Alison found herself being guided up the stairs and into a spacious bedroom at the front of the house. She managed not to let her eyes pop out at the sight of the bed. It wasn't a four-poster but a two-poster – a half-tester, if that was the right name – with embroidered curtains hanging from the frame, then looped back and tied with bows. The walls were duck-egg blue, the carpet a richer blue, and the furniture had been polished to a warm gleam – Grace's handiwork, presumably. A padded window seat stretched from one end of the bay window to the other and the scents of lemon and lavender mingled subtly in the air.

Alison gazed round, committing it all to memory so she could take every detail home with her to share.

Venetia opened a wardrobe that was practically the size of the back of a bus and took out a long gown covered in protective tissue paper. She carefully removed the fragile paper before holding up the dress for Alison to see.

'What do you think?' she asked.

It was a floor-length silk gown with a boatneck edged with pearls and leg-of-mutton sleeves that ended in points that would lie on the backs of the wearer's hands. Venetia lay the dress on the bed and produced a headdress of silk flowers with a floor-length veil.

Up until now, Alison hadn't felt gracious, but a spontaneous remark was surprised out of her.

'You must have been as slender as a reed when you wore this.'

'I can't claim the credit,' said Venetia. 'It was all thanks to the Women's League of Health and Beauty. All those daily exercises.'

'You're still slim,' said Alison. 'It's a beautiful dress.'

'Thank you. I felt like a princess.'

'I bet you did, but I'm not sure I could squeeze into it. Even if I did, I wouldn't be able to breathe.'

'Not to worry. Mummy had it made with generous seams in case I let myself go before the big day. I don't want to push you into borrowing it, but I'd be more than happy for you to do so. It's hard to get hold of a good wedding dress these days and most girls have to borrow. I wore this just over ten years ago – as you can tell from the style. Would you like to try it on?'

What girl wouldn't leap at the chance to put on a dress of this calibre?

Venetia helped her into it. 'You need to put this on first.' She held out a slinky ankle-length petticoat. 'This will make the dress sit smoothly on you. No – turn away from the mirror. You aren't allowed to see yourself yet.'

When the dress was on, Venetia fussed with it, spending ages fastening a long row of tiny pearl buttons up the back. Alison stood up straight and took shallow breaths.

'And last but not least: the headdress and veil.' Venetia positioned them and fluffed out the veil. 'There. Now you can look at yourself.'

Alison turned to the long mirror and her breath caught softly in her throat. She looked as if she had stepped out of a fairy tale.

'It's glamorous,' she breathed. 'I don't think I'm a glamorous person.'

'Every girl is glamorous on her wedding day,' said Venetia. 'Every girl should have the chance to look her very best.' She hesitated before adding in a less assured voice than Alison had previously heard from her, 'I know we didn't get off to the best possible start, but we're going to be sisters-in-law.'

'No thanks to you,' Alison said bluntly.

A flush rose in Venetia's smooth cheeks. 'I know and I apologise. I do love Joel most awfully and I want to be on the best of terms with his wife. I hope we can put that other business behind us – for the good of the family.'

Alison considered what to say. This would be her one and only chance to speak frankly on the subject and she decided to take it.

'The way you tried to come between Joel and me – or rather, the way you tried to thrust Rachel Chambers between us – isn't something I'll ever forget, but we're going to be family and that's important. I know how much you and Caroline mean to Joel.' Glad to have said her piece, and to have said it with dignity, Alison was able to add on a lighter note, 'And when you come to the party for our silver wedding, maybe you'll realise how wrong you were.'

Venetia smiled and tilted her head in gracious acknowledgement. Was she going to say anything else? But the moment passed and she returned her attention to the dress.

'The offer of the dress is made in good faith. It's not a peace offering – well, it is in a way, but mainly it's an offer from one future sister-in-law to another. It's a symbol of what I hope will become a genuine friendship between us ... even though I got us off to a rocky start.'

Alison gazed at her reflection, startled by her appearance. No two ways about it, the dress was utterly beautiful, but somehow she didn't look like herself any more. It hadn't occurred to her that she might adore a dress and yet know it wasn't the right one for her. Nor had it occurred to her that she would turn down Venetia's offer because the dress itself wasn't right. She had been so set on turning it down purely because it was Venetia's and for no other reason.

'You don't have to decide now, if you don't want to,' said Venetia. 'The offer's there if you want it. And for the record, I know you'll never forget what happened with Rachel. I'd hate me for that if I were you. But I'll tell you the memory of you that matters most to me. It was when you came here for the first time and you brought presents for my sons, whom you'd never even met. That was such a sweet thing to do. There is no more certain way of getting into my heart than by being good to my children.'

'Did you put Venetia up to that?' Alison asked Joel as they headed towards Chorlton on the bus after leaving his sister's house.

'Definitely not,' said Joel. 'Honest Injun. But I do remember what a smasher she looked on her wedding day.'

'Do you mind that I said "No, thank you," or would you have liked me to look a smasher too?'

'I don't mind what you wear as long as you say "I do", but I also want you to have the dress that makes you happy, because I know how important it is. That's all that matters, you being happy and having the Christmas wedding of your dreams.'

Alison looked out of the window as they passed the row of shops opposite Southern Cemetery. 'It's odd to picture a winter wedding on a sunny day like this.'

Joel smiled. 'The leaves will start falling before you know it and we'll have to get our winter woollies out.'

Alison looked at him. With his blazer and trilby, he wore flannels, a blue cotton shirt and a dark blue tie. His clothes were smart, but he wore them with a casual air that Alison found very attractive. She was sure other girls did too, and she enjoyed that. She had no reason to feel jealous or insecure. Joel loved her so much.

When they got off the bus at the terminus in Chorlton, Joel knelt to retie his shoelace.

'Drat,' he said. 'This lace is nearly worn through. I'll have to get more laces – if I can find any in the shops. I hope this one lasts out until I get home.'

'Mrs Cooper might have some string we can pinch,' said Alison.

They walked along Beech Road through the golden afternoon.

'I wonder if Margaret and Sally will have finished working in the garden,' remarked Joel.

'I should hope so. We've been gone a good while.'

'What's Sally like?' Joel asked. 'When she moved in, I was surprised because she's not part of your regular group.'

'She's Margaret's chum from the engine sheds. She lost her billet, so she's moved in with us temporarily while the billeting officer finds her somewhere new. Mrs Cooper and Mrs Grayson are making a bit of a fuss of her—'

Joel laughed. 'They make a fuss of all of you.'

'That's true,' Alison agreed with a smile. 'I don't know what made me notice it in particular with Sally.'

'It's probably their way of making her welcome.'

'Probably,' said Alison. 'It's not as though she needs to be coddled. She's not the fragile sort. If you think of the job she does, she must be as tough as old boots.'

'Talking of old boots, my lace has given up and snapped,' said Joel.

They slowed their pace so Joel could get along without walking out of his shoe, arriving at the house to find the garden empty and Colette emerging through the front door.

She spoke over her shoulder to Mrs Cooper, who was seeing her out. 'Here come the happy couple. Have you had a good afternoon?' she asked them.

'We went to see Joel's sister,' Alison told her.

'I hope you had a good time,' said Colette. 'I must go because of my bus. Nice to see you both.'

Mrs Cooper stood aside to let Alison in, asking Joel, 'Are you coming in for a while before you go home?'

Alison laughed. 'He has no choice. I've hobbled him so he can't get away. Broken shoelace,' she added by way of explanation.

'Can I beg some spare string off you?' asked Joel.

'If we have any,' Mrs Cooper said to Alison, 'it'll be in the middle drawer of the sideboard.'

While Mrs Cooper and Joel went into the front room, Alison went to the dining room. The handsome old sideboard had two large cupboards with three drawers above. She tried the middle drawer and found no string. Then she had a quick look in the left-hand drawer. None there either. She rifled through the right-hand drawer, disturbing the household's ration books as she did so and her mouth dropped open.

A green ration book. Everyone knew what that meant. Alison took it from the drawer. Who did it belong to?

Chapter Fourteen

Alison kept her mouth shut all evening. Sally was in the family way and there was no doubt at all that Mrs Cooper and Mrs Grayson knew, because Sally's green ration book was in the sideboard. Alison was appalled. She wasn't stupid. She knew perfectly well that plenty of girls were going all the way with their boyfriends these days. The wartime culture of living for today because who could say what might happen tomorrow had brought about a loosening of moral standards, a powerful desire to live for the moment and make the most of the present. Well, Alison wasn't that way inclined and she didn't care if that made her sound old-fashioned.

She remembered Mum having words with Lydia back at the start of the war when Alec had received his call-up papers.

Lydia had come creeping into Alison's bedroom one day to whisper about a problem one of her friends was having. Her boyfriend was due to go away soon and he was pressing his attentions on her, wanting her to 'give him something to remember her by,' as Lydia had delicately phrased it.

At that point, Mum had burst in, having clearly earwigged on every single word.

'You can tell your *friend*, Lydia, that if she gives her boyfriend something to remember her by, he might give *her* something to remember *him* by as well, and *her mother* won't be at all amused if she comes home with a bun in the oven.'

'Mum!' the girls had exclaimed in shock.

'It's all very well for a man to sow his wild oats,' declared Mum, 'but in the end he'll marry a decent girl. Make sure you tell your *friend* that, Lydia Lambert.'

In all the time Alison had spent waiting for Paul's proposal, the thought had sneaked into her head more than once that maybe she should tempt him into bed in the hope of getting pregnant, because that was bound to result in the wedding she'd so desperately wanted, but she had resisted the temptation. In the end, it was her need for a proper proposal, with Paul down on one knee and her feigning surprise, that had won the day.

Now, with all kinds of thoughts and feelings churning inside her after stumbling across the green ration book, Alison forced herself to bide her time. As much as she felt like striking a pose in the middle of the front room and announcing she had uncovered Sally's shameful secret, she knew the best way was to tackle Margaret. She was the one who had brought Sally here, so she must know.

Talking to Margaret meant waiting until bedtime.

While Margaret was in the bathroom, Alison got into bed, then immediately got out again. You couldn't hold a conversation like this from your bed. She sat on the covers and waited.

'Do you need the bathroom again?' Margaret asked, walking in. 'Sally's just gone in there.'

'No, I wanted a word,' said Alison, adding bluntly, 'I know about Sally. I found her green ration book.'

Margaret froze. Her cheeks stained pink.

'I wasn't snooping.' It felt important to say so. 'I was looking for something else and I just came across it.'

'So now you know,' said Margaret. 'We were hoping you wouldn't have to. It's nothing against you personally, but in these cases, the fewer people who know, the better.'

Alison lifted her eyebrows. 'Really? "In these cases"? I can't say I have any experience in such matters.' Discomfort made her skin prickle. 'I'm sorry. That was a horrid thing to say.'

'As long as you don't say anything of the sort to Sally.' Margaret's voice was cool, but then she added in a conciliatory tone, 'Look, I know this has come as a shock.'

'You can say that again. When is it due?'

'The end of January.'

'Is the – the father a serviceman? Did he – did they – did it happen when he was on leave?'

Margaret sank onto her bed. 'Nothing so straightforward, I'm afraid. The father – well, let's just say Sally has been badly let down.'

'So she wasn't in a proper relationship,' said Alison.

'I hope you aren't suggesting it's her own fault.'

'Well, you would defend her, of course. She's your friend.'

'It's not just because of that,' Margaret replied. 'People can get carried away in the emotion of the moment.'

'Look, I like Sally, I really do. I feel sorry for her and I wish her all the best, but I can feel that way and still feel critical of her at the same time.'

'So it seems.'

'I'm not heartless,' said Alison. 'I know what temptation feels like, but I believe in being pure before marriage.

Suppose I had given myself to Paul and then he'd left me. I'd hate Joel not to be my first.'

'That's all well and good, but it's different for Sally. She was taken in by a married man and now she's the one paying the price. I hope you aren't going to look down your nose at her. I told her this would be her safe haven until she finds somewhere else.'

Alison bridled. Truth be told, she had thought she might be cool towards Sally just so everyone would know she didn't approve, though she couldn't have said what made her want to do that. Being challenged on the point made her see that she didn't really want to make things hard for Sally – so why had she felt like being cool?

'She's come to the right place to be taken care of,' said Alison. 'How long will she be staying?'

'She has to leave before she starts showing,' said Margaret. 'She'll go into one of these mother and baby places where they organise adoptions.'

'She has a difficult time ahead.'

'Yes, she does,' said Margaret. 'You ought to tell Mrs C and Mrs G that you've found out. It'll make it easier in the house if the rest of us aren't having to keep it secret from you. Cordelia knows about it as well. She's made it right with the Morgans.'

Alison felt miffed. She might believe Sally's secret was grubby, but she didn't care for the idea that the others had kept it from her. She didn't feel she'd come out of this conversation very well, but then what had she expected? Had she thought Margaret would admit to being ashamed of her friend? All Alison knew was that she herself felt unsettled and was afraid she'd been bitchy. But what was bitchy about considering girls who gave themselves freely to their boyfriends were, to coin a phrase her mother liked to use, no better than they should be? That wasn't bitchy. It was what all decent people thought.

Except that it clearly wasn't. Mrs Cooper and Mrs Grayson evidently didn't think so and Alison had always held them in high regard. As for Cordelia making it right with the Morgans, how had *that* been achieved?

But no one explained and Alison could hardly ask. She was acutely aware of having stumbled across this secret by accident and that she wasn't really supposed to know about it.

She discussed the matter in the kitchen while Mrs Grayson showed her how to make sardine rolls. Mrs Grayson had given Mabel cookery lessons before she married Harry. Alison had learned to cook from Mum, but she still hoped that some of Mrs Grayson's magic would rub off on her now that her own wedding was coming up.

Alison set about wielding the tin opener.

'Sally was wrong to go to bed with her chap in the first place,' she said, determined to set out her stall of personal beliefs, 'and now it's even worse because he turns out to be married. But even if he hadn't been, I still think she shouldn't have done it.'

'She regrets it bitterly now,' said Mrs Grayson. 'Drain the oil carefully. For every tablespoon of oil, you need four tablespoons of flour. You have to remember that Sally thought she was in a loving relationship. She thought marriage was on the horizon.'

'She can't have done. Everyone knows that men don't marry the girls they sleep with. They want to marry decent girls.'

'Do you think Sally isn't a decent girl?'

'Well, she isn't.'

'Honestly, you make it sound as if girls should have "Decent" or "No Morals" tattooed on their foreheads.'

'No, I don't.'

Mrs Grayson added a pinch of salt. 'Have you got a tea-spoon? Three teaspoons of water for each tablespoon of oil. What about before you knew of Sally's condition? What did you think of her then?'

'That's not a fair question,' said Alison.

'Yes, it is. Don't overdo the water. What would your opinion be of Sally right now, right this minute, if you hadn't gone rummaging in the sideboard?'

Heat flooded Alison's cheeks. 'I didn't go rummaging.'

'This comes down to the green ration book. We all know you aren't a nosy parker, if that's what you're worried about. Now then, make a pastry from the mixture. But suppose Joel's shoelace hadn't broken and you'd never had cause to open that drawer, what would you think of Sally now? Be honest.'

'I don't know her all that well.'

'That's not an answer. You know her well enough to have formed an impression.'

'She seems nice enough. Pleasant, good-natured. She appreciates you and Mrs Cooper.' Yes, and now Alison knew why. 'Margaret likes her and I'm fond of Margaret and trust her judgement.'

'In other words, you've got no fault to find.'

'Maybe not, but—'

'But what?' asked Mrs Grayson. 'Count the sardines, then cut the pastry into pieces for the rolls.'

'It's important to have standards,' said Alison.

'I agree, but I also think standards should be applied with compassion. I've been on the receiving end of other people's standards in my time, so I know what I'm talking about. People had very definite opinions about me when my husband left me for another woman. Not that it affected me in the same way as it would have if I'd led a normal life and had gone out to the shops and to church and so forth. Even though I lived my life entirely inside the house because I was too frightened to set foot outside in those days, I was still well aware of the ill-feeling and, in some cases, the suspicion.'

'Suspicion?'

'Oh aye. People always blame the wife. Some neighbours who had previously helped me by doing my shopping stopped offering. I was lucky to have true friends who stood by me, especially Mrs Mitchell and also Mrs Warner, who was my next-door neighbour in those days. But Mrs Tomlinson, who was next door on the other side, would have nothing more to do with me in case I started finding little odd jobs that needed doing around the house. She was scared I'd ask her husband to do them and she wasn't having that. She wasn't about to risk losing her husband to the abandoned wife who needed a new man.'

'That's horrible,' said Alison.

'The point is that people saw me in a certain way, but that doesn't mean they were right about me.'

'But what happened to you, your husband leaving you, wasn't your fault,' said Alison.

'Some realised that, but others saw it as my fault, partly because of how I was in those days. They weren't going to blame my husband for getting fed up of the weird wife who couldn't even set foot across her own front doorstep. Others blamed me because people always think it must be the wife's fault. Ask Colette if you don't believe me.'

Alison fell silent, carefully placing each sardine on its piece of pastry and making a roll out of it. It gave her a bit of thinking time. The story behind Colette's marriage was well known. It had even been in the *Manchester Evening News*, so everyone must know what a cunning so-and-so Tony Naylor had been. Yet Colette occasionally made a remark that showed she was regarded with a certain wariness by folk in her neighbourhood.

'It's so unfair,' said Alison. 'Colette didn't do anything wrong, and nor did you.'

'No, we didn't, but we got judged all the same. Colette is still being judged and always will be as long as she keeps on living in that house. And the reason for it? Standards.'

'You're trying to make me say that my standards are wrong.'

'No, I'm not. I'm just saying that it's easy to have standards when you aren't the one at fault.'

'There you are, you see,' Alison retorted. 'There's no doubt Sally did something she shouldn't. That makes her situation different to yours and Colette's.'

'You seem determined to blame her,' said Mrs Grayson.

'I know what my mother would say if she knew.'

'You need to do that roll again,' said Mrs Grayson. 'The sardine's poking out.'

On their way to the pictures to see the matinée of the Flanagan and Allen comedy *Theatre Royal* when they both had an afternoon off, Alison confided in Joel about Sally being strung along by a married man. It was a glorious September day that seemed to suggest an Indian summer. Over her dress, Alison wore the lightweight wool bolero jacket she'd made for herself after all Joan's bridesmaids had worn boleros.

'So, Sally didn't have to leave her old billet because of the landlady's daughter coming home,' said Alison. 'She was chucked out for having got into trouble. Apparently, she's too scared to tell her family.'

'Poor girl,' said Joel. 'That's a lousy position to be in.'

'Yes, it is,' said Alison, 'but . . .'

'But?' asked Joel.

'It was her choice to do what she did with her boyfriend.' To do what she did? How prim she sounded!

'True,' said Joel.

Alison felt a twinge of irritation. She had been hoping for more of a response. 'Aren't you shocked at Mrs Cooper for taking her in?'

'You're always saying what a caring person she is. It's good of her to help.'

'Yes, it is. Margaret got Mrs Cooper and Mrs Grayson to agree to let Sally stay until she goes into a mother and baby home.'

'Margaret did?' Joel looked at her.

'Yes. Sally's going to have the baby adopted. Obviously.'

139

'Well, if the father's already married, I suppose there's no alternative. Poor Sally.'

Why was everyone's attitude 'poor Sally'? Why couldn't just one person say, 'She had no business sleeping with him' or 'She couldn't have known him all that well if she didn't even know he had a wife'? Why couldn't just one person say what Alison was thinking? She knew her mother would, but Mum would say a lot of other things too, such as, 'I'm not having you staying in that house any longer. It's time for you to come home. I'd thought better than that of Mrs Cooper.' And Alison couldn't have that. She loved living in Wilton Close and didn't want to jeopardise it.

The odd thing was that she didn't think worse of Mrs Cooper for taking Sally in. She admired her for her loving heart and her courage in the face of Sally's downfall. Alison felt the same way towards Mrs Grayson and Margaret. All three were good, kind people, big-hearted and broad-minded.

Was that the problem? In these modern times, was she herself narrow-minded? Was that why she seemed so fixed upon disapproving of Sally?

And just what did it say about her that she wanted Joel to disapprove too?

Chapter Fifteen

Max made a good start at the Lizzie Nursery. Joan and Bob had decided that the best thing for him was to begin going there before Joan went back to work.

'It'll get him settled in while you're still around to mop up any problems,' said Bob.

It made sense, of course it did, Joan could see that, so why did her eyes fill with tears as she left Max at the nursery for the first time? Did all mums feel this way?

Later, Joan told Mrs Cooper, 'To make it worse, I had Norman and Jeremy with me and I had to take them home while leaving my own little boy behind.'

But the worst moment came when she had to pick him up. Her heart gave a leap of pure delight when she saw him looking rosy and happy, having clearly had a wonderful time. Mrs Broughton assured her that he had settled in well. Then Max saw her and his face lit up. The next moment, Joan had him in her arms and was snuggling him close – only to find that his skin smelled of someone else's perfume. Joan felt a huge wave of – she wasn't sure what it was. Jealousy? Insecurity? Another woman had cuddled her little boy. Oh, she was being stupid. She loved it when her friends and family showed Max affection. She wanted him to be surrounded by adults who cherished him.

Drawing in a deep breath, she focused on what a good time Max had clearly had in the Lizzie Nursery. With the experienced staff and dear Mrs Grayson taking care of him, he would flourish.

And I'll flourish too, Joan thought. This would be the start of a new chapter for the Hubble family. She was going to take a leaf out of Letitia's book and contribute to the war effort by doing work she loved. She could be a doting mummy to Max at the same time as watching over the welfare of other women in the workplace.

A pang of loss smote her for the sister she had loved and looked up to. Losing Letitia made it doubly important that she make the most of her own life now.

The landing of Allied troops on the Italian mainland was followed a few days later by the announcement of Italy's surrender, strengthening Joan's resolution to return to work and do her bit. She had given Jeremy's and Norman's mothers ample notice of the date of her interview, which was due to take place on the Friday after Italy's surrender. Joan had received a letter about it and had told the two mums that same evening when they came to collect their little lads, which meant they had known about it even before Bob. Nevertheless, the day before the interview, Jeremy's mum tried it on.

'I haven't been able to make other arrangements,' she said with a winning smile. 'You couldn't ask your friend who's having Max to take Jeremy an' all, could you?'

'No,' Joan said firmly. 'I'm sorry, but that's not possible.'

The cheek of it! Jeremy was a little sweetheart, but his mother would try the patience of a saint. Joan wouldn't be sorry to see the back of her when she returned to her railway work.

Now it was the day of the interview, which was to be held that afternoon. Joan was excited, but scared too. She wished it was taking place this morning so she could get it over with. It was a long time since she'd felt nervous like this. Then she pictured meeting up with her friends in the buffet afterwards and the nerves gave way to a shiver of delight. This was really happening. She would be going back to work. Her friends were looking forward to it as much as she was.

Bob was working nights at the moment, but he got up earlier than normal so that they could have their midday meal together with Max before it was time for Joan to go. While Bob entertained their little boy, Joan got ready, then put on her dressing gown over her interview outfit to protect it from Max's messy eating habits. Alison had lent her a charcoal-grey jacket and skirt, which Joan wore with a simple white blouse. She wished she had a special necklace to wear for luck, but the locket Bob had given her and her much-loved silver filigree heart from Letitia had both been lost when Mrs Cooper's house was bombed.

Joan went into the sitting room, where Max was playing with his dad.

Bob looked at her and laughed. 'I was all set to tell you how lovely you look – and here you are, ready for bed.'

'Ready to feed your son, you mean.'

Leaving Bob and Max playing upstairs, Joan went down to the kitchen, where she put her apron over the dressing gown and made a tomato pie as well as cauliflower in white sauce. While they were cooking, she made sandwiches for

Bob to take to work later. When everything was ready, she carried the finished meals upstairs on a tray.

'I'm glad you're here to wish me luck,' she told Bob as they tucked in.

'You won't need luck,' said Bob. 'You're a natural for this post. You're kind and efficient and you love the railways. What more could they ask for?'

After dinner, Joan cleared away, then removed her dressing gown and got her things together. She had to take Max to Wilton Close first.

'I'll take him.' Bob grinned. 'It'll reduce the chances of turning up for your interview with smears of white sauce on your jacket. What d'you think, Max?' he asked, picking up his son. 'Should we send Mummy out with sauce on her jacket?'

Soon Joan was on her way. On the bus, she sat beside the window, supposedly gazing out, but she didn't see anything. Her mind was too occupied rehearsing answers to the questions she hoped to be asked, and her nerves were equally busy.

At Hunts Bank, she presented herself at the reception office window. One of the women put a tick next to her name on a list and pointed to the door opposite. Joan went in. She found another girl of a similar age to herself, her blonde hair draped across her cheek à la Veronica Lake, and two middle-aged ladies, one of whom looked up and smiled. Joan smiled back, not just at her but at the others as well.

'Good afternoon,' she said. She had planned this. Greeting the other candidates would make her look confident.

She took a seat, tucking her crossed ankles underneath, and prepared to wait. Presently the door opened again and a young woman walked in. A few years older than Joan, she looked to be around thirty. She exuded assurance, but in a quiet, self-possessed way; she didn't come across as cocky. She had intelligent hazel eyes in a fine-boned face and she wore her deep red hair in a victory roll. Her jacket and knee-length skirt were olive green and her hat boasted a jaunty feather. She smiled and nodded a general greeting before sitting down.

A few minutes later, a young woman looked into the room. 'Miss Brewer, please.'

The striking-looking redhead stood up and followed her out. Miss Brewer – Joan knew that name. It had been a Corporation lady called Miss Brewer who had been such a help to Mabel when she was setting up the Lizzie Nursery. Might this be the same person? Mabel had thought the world of Fay Brewer.

After twenty minutes by the wall clock, Miss Brewer returned and Miss Earnshaw, the girl with the Veronica Lake hairstyle, was taken from the room. Joan clasped her hands in her lap as she watched her go. As Mrs Hubble, would she be next?

It turned out that she was. The clerk led her upstairs to Mr Mortimer's office. Joan felt a little burst of confidence. Yes, she was nervous, but she'd also been looking forward to this and was determined to do her best and show her interviewers how perfect she was for the post.

Mr Mortimer, in the pinstripes and bow tie he always wore, sat behind his desk, flanked by another gentleman and Miss Emery. It was all Joan could do to rein in her smile at the sight of the assistant welfare officer. The two men rose to shake her hand. Mr Mortimer introduced Mr Prescott.

'And of course you know Miss Emery, don't you, Mrs Hubble?'

To Joan's surprise, just as she sat down, Miss Emery stood up.

'The welfare officer for women and girls isn't available to help us conduct these interviews today,' said Mr Mortimer, 'so we have Miss Emery with us, but since you and she are known to one another, it is only fair to the other candidates, none of whom has worked here before, that Miss Emery withdraws from your interview.'

Miss Emery gave Joan a small smile as she passed her. Joan wished she could have stayed.

The interview began with a recap of Joan's previous jobs at Victoria Station. She was glad to have the chance to use the sentences she had prepared about her work. Then the interview moved on to personal matters.

'You have a baby son, do you not, Mrs Hubble?' said Mr Mortimer.

'Yes. He was born in May of last year.'

'What arrangements have you made for his care?' asked Mr Prescott. He nodded his head while Joan explained. 'And should this Mrs Grayson be ill? What then?'

Joan explained about Gran and Mrs Cooper as well as Bob's family. 'Everyone loves Max and they'd be happy to help out by taking care of him in an emergency.'

'Is it your intention to increase your family?' Mr Mortimer asked her.

Warmth rose in Joan's cheeks. That was a highly personal question, but a prospective employer was entitled to ask it. 'Not at present.'

The two men shared a glance.

'Nevertheless, these things can happen . . .' Mr Prescott murmured.

Joan straightened her spine. 'All I can tell you is that me and my husband are happy for now with our family the way it is.'

'Mr Hubble is a railwayman, isn't he?' said Mr Mortimer.

'Yes. He has a signal box. He's pleased to think of me coming back to work here.'

'Let's talk about the job itself,' said Mr Mortimer. 'It is a new post and the successful candidate will support the work of the welfare officer and assistant welfare officer for women and girls.'

'I'd work very hard if you give me the post,' said Joan. 'I'm already familiar with the railways, and being a married lady, I understand what it's like to go out to work and then go home and complete all my domestic duties.'

'And no doubt you understand all about little marital tiffs,' Mr Prescott said with a chuckle.

'Bob and I get along very well, as a matter of fact.'

'You aren't very old, Mrs Hubble,' said Mr Mortimer.

'I finished school at fourteen, sir, and started work the next day.'

'What I mean is that because you are young, nearly every lady you have to assist will be older than you. Many will be old enough to be your mother. How would you cope with that?'

'I think it's to do with how you talk to people. They need to have confidence in you. Up-to-date knowledge of the rules and regulations is important, and obviously I would keep up with any changes, but it isn't just about having the correct information at your fingertips. It's to do with the way you treat people. It is important to be courteous and listen carefully to what they say and not make assumptions. As for differences in age,' Joan went on, taking a chance on speaking frankly, 'I don't think that matters as much as you make it sound.'

Mr Prescott raised his eyebrows. 'Indeed?'

'I think something we have all learned in wartime is that it's essential that everyone pulls their weight. That's nothing to do with how old you are. It's about working hard and doing your best and treating other people decently.' She went on to explain about sitting in on the interviews at the Citizens Advice. 'I know those problems weren't to do with working on the railways, but I saw for myself how important it is for people to have someone to turn to when they're in a fix.'

The two men exchanged glances.

'What made you arrange to observe at the Citizens Advice Bureau?' Mr Mortimer asked. 'You wouldn't have time to work for them as well as taking on this post, should you be offered it.'

'I don't intend to work for them,' Joan said quickly. 'I went along to one of their sessions because I thought it would give me some valuable experience that would contribute towards my application for this post.'

Mr Mortimer nodded. 'Very commendable.' He looked at Mr Prescott. 'Have you any further questions?'

Mr Prescott glanced down at a few notes he had made, then shook his head.

Mr Mortimer stood up, coming around the desk to shake hands and open the door for her. 'Thank you for attending,

Mrs Hubble. If you return to the room downstairs, we will make our decision after the final interview and inform the candidates of the result after that.'

Joan went back downstairs, feeling quietly confident. She had acquitted herself well, she knew she had, and she was even keener than before on the post. Thank heavens she had gone to see Miss Emery that day back in August. This job was perfect for her, not just because she felt she could do it well, but also because it would fit in with her home circumstances. Not having to work shifts would be a dream come true.

She smiled briefly at the other candidates as she entered the room and sat down. The red-headed Miss Brewer was writing in a notebook. Joan considered asking if she was indeed Mabel's Miss Brewer, but she didn't want to interrupt.

When the final candidate returned to the room, the atmosphere altered subtly. A few nervous smiles were exchanged. Joan realised that the flutters she felt weren't due to nerves so much as to anticipation. Miss Emery had invited her – more than invited her, warmly encouraged her – to apply for this post and Joan was sure she was right for it.

After some minutes, the door opened and Miss Emery preceded Mr Mortimer into the room.

'Miss Brewer, would you come with me, please?' asked Mr Mortimer.

Miss Brewer stuffed her notebook into her bag and stood up. Mr Mortimer moved aside so she could lead the way out. He shut the door behind them, leaving Miss Emery looking around at the remaining candidates. Joan's heart thudded.

'Thank you all for coming, ladies,' said Miss Emery. 'I'm sorry to tell you that on this occasion your applications have been unsuccessful.'

Joan felt as if she had frozen on the inside. She had been so sure she would be offered the job. Miss Emery herself had suggested she apply for it, had encouraged her to do so, and she'd worked hard on her letter of application. She'd even done that stint in the Citizens Advice Bureau to show how keen she was on helping people with their problems. And yet she'd been turned down. It was – well, frankly, it was humiliating. She'd been so *sure* and so had her friends. The frozen sensation changed, as if the ice was not melting but shattering. She seemed to be about to collapse in on herself.

Leaving Hunts Bank and heading for Victoria Station, she sniffed sharply and pulled her shoulders back. Reaching the other side of the road, she stopped. Some of her friends would be waiting for her in the buffet, ready to celebrate. How was she to face them? She felt swamped by a huge temptation to head straight for the bus stop and go home so she could lick her wounds, but that wasn't possible. The others were expecting her. If she failed to turn up, they would worry. Besides, seeing them now would get it over with.

She set off towards the station. How should she behave? Stiff upper lip or floods of tears? She would try with all her might not to succumb to the latter, though she wasn't sure she could manage it.

The concourse was packed. Loudspeaker announcements echoed around the vast area. Joan squeezed her way through the crowd and made it to the buffet. She was a little earlier than arranged, so maybe only a couple of her friends would be there and she could tell them, then slink away, leaving them to pass on her news to the rest.

No such luck. Joan was going to pause on the threshold to gather herself, but a group of lads behind her didn't stop and she almost stumbled inside. The first thing she saw when she righted herself was – not just one or two of her friends but all of them. They waved and smiled, their faces lighting up.

Joan went straight to them. She didn't want to sit down, but how could she not? It would be so rude.

'Surprise,' Margaret sang out. 'We let you think we couldn't all get here on time, but that was just a ruse.'

The others laughed, enjoying the moment, believing they had given her a lovely surprise. Joan almost burst into tears – not from disappointment or humiliation, but simply because these dear friends cared about her so much.

'How did it go?' asked Emily.

'I take it congratulations are in order,' Cordelia added.

'Well, actually – no,' said Joan in a hollow voice. 'I – I didn't get it. They offered the job to someone else.'

'Someone else?' Alison repeated. 'But I thought – I mean, we all thought—'

'We were all wrong.' Joan tried to smile. Her face felt brittle. 'I feel such a chump for thinking the job was mine for the asking.'

'Eh, chick,' said Dot. 'I thought Miss Emery made it sound as if you were just what they were after.'

'She encouraged me,' said Joan, 'but I evidently read too much into it. It's my own fault.'

151

'Don't say that,' said Cordelia. 'I seem to remember all of us being every bit as sure that you'd be selected.'

'I feel rotten now for encouraging you,' said Persephone.

'Well, we were hardly going to do anything less,' Dot pointed out.

'It's such a shame,' said Margaret. 'From everything you said about it, you'd have been perfect.'

'I think they might have offered it to the lady from the Corporation who was such a big help to Mabel when she was setting up the Lizzie Nursery,' said Joan, 'though I don't know that absolutely for certain.'

'If this Corporation lady was better than you,' said Dot, 'then all I can say is, she must be a blinking marvel.'

And then they were all at it, telling her how good she would have been in the job and how much she had deserved it and what a shame it was that she hadn't got it. It wasn't what Joan wanted to hear. She didn't actually know what she wanted to hear, but how good she would have been in the job wasn't it.

She felt emotionally exhausted when she left the buffet, surrounded by her friends. Now she had to go home and tell Bob and Gran. And after that Bob's family. And the ladies at Wilton Close. And Mabel in her next letter. Not to mention Norman's and Jeremy's mothers. They would try to hide it, but it would come as a relief to them. Come to think of it, Jeremy's mum probably wouldn't even bother to hide it.

How could she have been so certain? So sure of herself? So . . . stupid?

Chapter Sixteen

Sally had decided to go to the lady almoner at Withington Hospital. 'That's where the nearest maternity ward is, so their lady almoner must know all about other maternity services. She'll be the best source of information. I can't put it off. It's just that I hate the thought of being looked down on, but then, I suppose I deserve it.'

'No girl in your situation deserves to be treated in a snooty fashion,' said Margaret, 'but it's the way of the world and people who work in hospitals can be every bit as judgemental as the general public. You ought to prepare yourself for that.'

Sally shuddered. 'Why d'you think it's taken me this long to build up the courage?'

'You should go as soon as you can,' said Margaret. 'Don't wait for us to be on the same shifts again.'

She despised herself for saying that. Yes, it was important for Sally to get the information she needed as soon as possible, but Margaret was grateful to avoid going with her. Did that mean she wasn't as much of a friend as Sally thought she was?

But a sickness bug forced a drastic change around of the work rosters in the engine sheds and all of a sudden the two girls had a morning off together.

'You'll come with me, won't you?' asked Sally. 'Please.'

'Well . . .' Margaret struggled for a reply.

'You won't be able to come into the lady almoner's office with me,' said Sally, seeming not to notice the hesitation. 'When I rang up, the clerk said that only family are allowed in. Would you mind waiting for me outside? I know how feeble I sound, but I'd feel braver if I knew I had someone cheering me on close by.'

'Of course I'll come,' said Margaret, relief rushing through her now she knew she wouldn't have to see the lady almoner. She was probably making a mountain out of a molehill anyway. As if the lady almoner would remember her after all this time.

The girls' morning off took place in the week following Italy's surrender.

'Let's go to Joan's before we set off for Withington,' said Margaret. 'I haven't seen her since the day she didn't get the job.'

If she had questioned whether she was as good a friend as she should be to Sally, she felt something similar towards Joan and wanted to make amends.

When Margaret and Sally got to Torbay Road, they found Joan playing with Max and a toddler.

'I thought you minded two, not one,' said Margaret.

'I did,' said Joan, 'but I warned my mothers that I'd be returning to work and Norman's mum very efficiently made other arrangements for him. She decided to stick with them even though I didn't get the job. Jeremy's mum, on the other hand, was only too delighted to leave him here with me. It saved her the trouble.'

'I'm sorry you didn't get the post, Joan,' Margaret told her. 'I feel bad about the way I took it for granted.'

'If my friends took anything for granted,' said Joan, 'that was my fault. I was so pleased and excited that I let my feelings run away with me. Miss Emery did encourage me to apply, but she never promised me the post. In fact, she made sure I understood that I had to go through the application process. I took her encouragement to mean more than it really did, I'm afraid, and that's my own silly fault.' She turned to Sally. 'But I'm glad to have had the chance to help you. I just wish I could have ended up in a position to have helped lots of others too.'

'You were a big help to me,' Sally said at once.

They couldn't stay long at Joan's. When they were on the bus heading for the hospital, Sally lapsed into thought and Margaret didn't disturb her. It didn't take long to reach their destination. A clerk at the front desk gave them directions and they headed upstairs and along a corridor. Rounding a corner, they saw several wooden chairs lined up against the wall.

'This must be where we wait,' Sally whispered.

A woman who was sitting there looked up. 'The clerk's in there. You have to give your name.'

Sally secretly squeezed Margaret's hand, then she stepped forward and opened the door. Margaret didn't follow her in. After a moment, Sally emerged and sat down, Margaret taking the seat beside her.

'Is that the lady almoner's office?' Margaret asked.

'No, that's just a little office with a clerk doing the typing. There's another door, which must be to the office.'

155

Oh, good. Margaret nodded. She knew she was being daft, but having two doors between her and that woman felt far safer than having just one.

After a few minutes, the door opened and a middle-aged couple emerged, smiling at one another.

'That'll be a great help, won't it?' said the man and they went on their way.

Sally nudged Margaret. 'He seems pleased,' she murmured. 'Sounds like the lady almoner is a good egg.'

There was a pause, then the clerk opened the door and looked into the corridor.

'Mrs Carpenter, please,' she said.

An elderly lady in a long brown coat stood up, as did a younger woman. The clerk had already ducked back inside, leaving them to walk in and shut the door behind them. When they left some ten minutes later, it was Sally's turn to go in.

'Good luck,' Margaret whispered. She hoped the lady almoner wouldn't give Sally a rough time and make her feel like a harlot. Unfortunately, that might be the price Sally would have to pay in order to be given the information she needed.

When Sally emerged, she hurried straight past Margaret. 'I need the Ladies. Won't be a mo.'

Margaret stood up and smoothed her jacket, intending to walk along the corridor to meet Sally outside the Ladies. She glanced round automatically as the door behind her opened – and there stood the lady almoner herself.

The lady almoner's gaze landed on her, carried on towards someone else, then swung back.

'I remember you,' she said. 'Good grief, young woman. Don't tell me you're here because you've got yourself into trouble *again*.'

Margaret's heart delivered an almighty clout and all the blood in her body seemed to plunge towards the floor. All at once she was back in that hospital bed after her gruelling miscarriage, exhausted, in pain and shaken to her core because her father, shocked at learning that she'd been pregnant, had lost his rag and berated her in front of all the neighbours as she was carried away on a stretcher. The ambulancemen had strapped her to the stretcher and her arms had been under the straps, so she couldn't even cover her face.

She had been kept in hospital for a couple of days. Before she was discharged, the lady almoner came to see her. Her manner was brisk. She had sat down to speak to two other women in the ward as she discussed how their daughters would watch over their convalescence at home, but she hadn't sat next to Margaret. No, she'd stood beside the bed, looking down on her – figuratively as well as literally.

'Your home is too severely damaged to return to, Miss Darrell. The billeting officer has found places for you and your father along the road with a neighbour. Your father is already living there.'

'Thank you,' said Margaret.

The lady almoner turned away, then apparently thought better of it and turned back. 'Did you throw yourself down the stairs or take some other foolish action to bring about your miscarriage, Miss Darrell?'

'No,' whispered Margaret.

'Because if you did, it was unpatriotic to do it during an air raid, when we are most in need of our ambulances.'

With that, the lady almoner had turned on her heel and swept from the ward, leaving Margaret gawping after her, scarcely able to breathe. Then she'd realised that all eyes were upon her. If the other patients hadn't known before why she was here, they certainly knew now. Margaret had wanted to sob her heart out, but how would it look if she did? Then again, how would she appear if she didn't? Brazen? Shameless?

Those memories flooded her mind, her whole being, when the lady almoner recognised her now in the corridor and uttered those frightful words in front of the line of people waiting for assistance.

'Don't tell me you're here because you've got yourself into trouble again.'

Margaret was frozen to the spot, incapable of moving. Then Sally appeared at the corner of the corridor.

'Ready?' she called.

That was the one good thing about what had happened: Sally hadn't witnessed Margaret's moment of desperate shame. Her appearance galvanised Margaret into action. Darting down the corridor, she grasped Sally's arm and hurried her away under the pretext of catching the bus. It was an effort to listen to Sally's description of her meeting with the lady almoner. In fact, she had to ask her to repeat it.

'Just so I've got it clear in my head,' Margaret claimed, trying to force a path through her memories.

'I would have thought it was pretty self-explanatory,' said Sally. 'Yes, there are places hereabouts, but they're privately run and when she told me the fees, I knew I couldn't afford them. Still,' she added, 'at least we tried. Thanks for coming with me. The lady almoner might have been a good egg with that couple we saw, but she was distinctly unimpressed with me. She gave me the information, but in a way that suggested she would rather have fed me to the snakes.'

'I can imagine,' said Margaret.

'Believe me, you can't,' Sally answered. 'Nobody who hasn't experienced it could possibly put themselves in that position.'

Margaret released a silent sigh. 'You're right,' she said softly.

The little boys were having their afternoon nap, but there was no time for Joan to put her feet up. She put on her pinny and covered her hair with a scarf, tying it under her hair at the back of her neck. After cleaning the bathroom, she swept and dusted the landing and stairs. She would happily have done the hall as well, but Gran had made it clear that downstairs was her responsibility and she didn't expect Joan to act as her maid.

Just as she finished the bottom stair, the doorbell rang. Opening the door, she looked in surprise at Miss Emery.

'Good afternoon, Mrs Hubble. I'm sorry to trouble you at home. May I come in?'

'Of course.' Joan swiped the scarf from her head and practically ripped off her pinny, feeling caught out. 'We live upstairs. Do go up.'

She ushered her unexpected visitor into the front room, wishing the hearthrug wasn't littered with makeshift toys. Gran had brought her up to be house-proud, but it was impossible to keep the place tidy during the day – well, it was if she wanted to be a good childminder and do lots of playing on the floor with the children.

'Have a seat,' Joan offered. 'Would you like a cup of tea?'

'That's kind, but no, thank you.' Miss Emery took one of the armchairs. Sitting with her ankles together, she placed her dark brown leather handbag by her feet. Indicating the rubber toys made from worn-out hot-water bottles, she smiled. 'Where are the children? This looks like the *Mary Celeste*.'

'They're asleep,' said Joan.

'Then I'd better say this before they wake up.' Miss Emery's voice was quiet and serious. 'I owe you an apology, Mrs Hubble. I'm afraid you must have been very disappointed not to be offered the new welfare post and part of the responsibility for that disappointment lies with me, I'm afraid.'

'You mean you changed your mind about wanting me?'

'No, you misunderstand. I mean that I was the person who built up your hopes in the first place and I shouldn't have done that. It was unprofessional of me. But I was keen for you to apply, you see. I was sure you'd be good at it and I thought we'd work well together too. Hence the encouragement. I'm sorry.'

Joan uttered a shaky little laugh of relief. 'Thank you. That makes me feel better.'

'We didn't expect to attract an applicant of Miss Brewer's calibre,' Miss Emery explained. 'Her qualifications and experience outstripped everyone else's by a mile. It simply wasn't possible to offer the job to anybody else. But I'd like to assure you that you submitted a very good application.'

'Thank you,' Joan murmured.

Miss Emery stood up. 'I'd better leave you to it.'

Joan rose as well. 'Thank you for coming and for . . .' She hesitated, not sure how to express it.

'For coming clean?' Miss Emery raised an eyebrow.

Joan smiled. 'Yes.' Another hesitation. Should she say it? 'I want you to know that I won't tell anybody about this – apart from my husband. I tell him everything. But neither of us will pass it on. I – I wouldn't want anyone to think that maybe you'd . . .'

'Overstepped the mark? Thank you for that reassurance, Mrs Hubble.'

Their gazes met and Joan knew that she wasn't the only one remembering another occasion when Miss Emery had overstepped the mark. That had been when Colette's husband had refused to give Miss Emery permission to pass on Colette's address to her friends. Tony believed he had tied Miss Emery's hands, but she had cleverly untied them by giving the friends directions to Colette's house instead. It was a kindness that had cost her her job when Tony Naylor had made an official complaint about the breach of confidentiality. Colette's friends had gathered together to launch a campaign that eventually led to Miss Emery's reinstatement.

Joan saw her visitor out, pausing to lean against the front door after she closed it. She was grateful to Miss Emery for coming clean, as she'd put it, and Joan felt rather better about things. It didn't make up for the deep disappointment of not getting the position she had wanted so much, but it was . . . something.

Chapter Seventeen

Alison was as surprised as anyone that Joan hadn't been given the job she had seemed ideal for. She felt bad for her, but if this Miss Brewer was a better person for the post, then obviously she was the right choice. It was hard on Joan, though. She'd set her heart on working in women's welfare. She'd have been good at it too. Alison went round to Torbay Road to commiserate, but Joan wasn't keen to talk about it.

'It's my own silly fault,' she maintained. 'I got carried away. Miss Emery made it clear I had to go through the application process, and I should have thought more sensibly about there being other candidates who might be just as qualified as I was, if not more so. I just thought, when Miss Emery told me about the job and was so kind as to encourage me, that, well . . .'

'That it was being handed to you on a plate,' said Alison sympathetically.

Joan pulled a face. 'I hate to say it, but you aren't far wrong.' She smiled. 'That's enough of my woes. What about you? What work are you doing at the moment? You look surprised.'

'I thought you were going to ask about the wedding,' said Alison. 'That's what most folk want to know about.'

'Are you any closer to finding a dress?'

Now it was Alison's turn to pull a face, but she quickly smoothed her features. She didn't want to get lines. 'Not yet.'

The conversation moved down the familiar wedding route. Alison was always more than happy to discuss her wedding plans, but she felt a touch of relief, too, at having neatly dodged the question about her current role as a station announcer. The role she had once been very keen on having was now a useful job that enabled the powers that be to send her off elsewhere, supposedly to be an announcer, but really to give her special training to support her in her forthcoming role as an onward-travel organiser.

'We believe you will do a better job if you have a greater understanding of what is going on in the country,' Mr Samuels had told her when she'd been summoned back to Mr Mortimer's office last week.

Now she was due to be taken she knew not where for a purpose she wasn't sure of, other than that she was to learn something she had to keep utterly secret. Ought she to feel bad about telling her friends she was filling in for another announcer who was off sick? As much as her friends meant to her, she didn't feel uncomfortable letting the fibs roll off her tongue because she understood the importance of what she was involved in, and how essential it was to maintain absolute secrecy. But it was hard telling the same lies to Joel. There ought to be complete trust between them and here she was telling fibs.

At the start of the week following Joan's interview, Alison was taken to a small rural station. She wasn't told its name and of course there were no station signs with the information. It had rained earlier, but now the September sun was shining and the air was filled with the scent of damp grass. As far as Alison could see, this was nothing more than a once pretty but now tired-looking little station in the middle of no-where, next to a wood. Another girl and a middle-aged man were already there, apparently waiting for . . . whatever was going to happen.

Mr Samuels introduced the three of them, but conversation was discouraged.

'As you can see,' said Mr Samuels, 'this is a rural station with a small goods siding over there. Beyond the siding is a field where work is being carried out, and then we have the woods. The work in the field is to extend the siding. Just an ordinary piece of railway work, wouldn't you say? Anyone passing through on a train will see it and think nothing of it. In due course, they'll notice that extra wagons have been shunted in there – and they'll think nothing of it. What they can't see, what they won't have any idea of, is what you're about to see now.'

Another man led Alison and the other two down the slope at the end of the platform. They crossed the sidings, taking care with their footing, and walked around the edge of the field. Alison couldn't imagine what they were going to see in the woods. It turned out to be two lengths of railway track that ran parallel to one another between felled trees to a vast open space with yet more sidings and an array of buildings.

'And the passengers who travel through the station have no idea,' Alison marvelled.

When the trio returned, silent with awe, to Mr Samuels, he told them, 'This country has been working with the Americans for more than two years on the strategy for the invasion of Europe. What you have just seen is a small part of a huge national machine. I'm sure I have no need to remind you that you mustn't breathe a word about it, but I did want you to see it, so that you can start to understand what will be asked of you and what you'll be responsible for. You might work as onward-travel organisers for troops and munitions when the time comes, or you might organise onward-travel for passengers who have absolutely no idea what is going on all around them. I hope that because of what you've seen today, you will be all the more determined to do the best job you possibly can.'

'Yes, sir,' they all answered at once and Alison was sure the other two felt every bit as fired up with patriotism as she did.

For Alison, the feeling lasted all the way back to Manchester Victoria. When she disembarked from the train, she reminded herself that she mustn't give anything away. It wasn't just a matter of keeping the secret. It was to do with her manner in general. No one must be allowed to guess that there was anything different about her.

She was going out with Joel that evening. They had arranged to meet outside Manchester Royal Infirmary as his shift was due to coincide, more or less, with when she would be finishing her day's work. Alison loitered in the evening sunshine, happy to wait. She just hoped that Joel wouldn't be called upon at the last minute to do an extra shift. If it did happen, it wouldn't be the first time.

When he emerged, Alison ran to him and they embraced.

'I was worried you might get lumbered with another shift,' she told him.

'Quick,' Joel said with a grin. 'Let's escape before they realise I've slipped out.' As they walked along arm in arm, he asked, 'How was your day? You went off to be the announcer at another station, didn't you?'

'That's right. It was all fine, thanks.'

'Are you sure? You seem a bit – I don't know – a bit wound up.'

And no wonder after what she'd seen today. Oh, how she hated keeping the truth from Joel. But there was something else that had been on her mind that she wanted to discuss with him and his suggestion of her seeming wound up actually made a good introduction to it.

'There's something I've been thinking about a lot. It's Sally.'

'Oh yes?'

'I know how unsympathetic I must have sounded when I told you she'd got herself into trouble. I've been thinking about her situation – or rather, I've been thinking about my own reaction to it. I do think she was wrong to have that sort of relationship with that man, but – but I also think I may have been too quick to judge her.' Alison took a moment to find the right words to express precisely what she meant. It wasn't easy for her to talk about this, but she wanted Joel to understand. 'Don't get me wrong. I'd have frowned on any girl in Sally's situation. It's just that with Sally being Margaret's friend and moving into the house with us, it feels very close.'

'I can understand that.'

'It's . . . well, the truth is, it's made me think all over again about that old girlfriend of yours and how she got herself into

166

trouble. Hark at me! That's the point, isn't it? She didn't get *herself* into trouble. You were the one who did that. I'm sorry. That was a crude thing to say.'

Joel took in a breath. 'True, though. Girls don't end up pregnant on their own.'

Alison dashed away a tear. Joel stopped and turned her to him, putting his arms around her and holding her close, and never mind that they were out in public.

'We can't talk about this while we're walking along,' said Joel. 'Let's drop into the Claremont and find a quiet corner.'

Did he realise what he was suggesting? The Claremont was where he had told her what had happened to his old girlfriend. He and the girlfriend had been at a party where they'd both had too much to drink and had ended up in bed together. Immediately afterwards, the powers that be had spirited Joel off to Leeds. He'd admitted to Alison that it was a relief to get away as the girlfriend might now have had expectations and he didn't have marriage in mind. Ages later, he had bumped into her again and learned that as a result of their drunken encounter, she had fallen pregnant with his baby, which she had subsequently miscarried.

'The poor love had spent all that time thinking I'd set out to seduce her,' Joel had explained to Alison, 'and then, having had my wicked way, that I'd taken to my heels, but I swear to you it wasn't like that.'

Alison had been shocked by the story, but she hadn't entertained a moment's doubt that he was speaking the truth. The words that had followed only strengthened her belief in him.

'I don't want to have secrets from you,' Joel had assured her. 'You've had one boyfriend and it was a long-term relationship for you. Me, I've had a number of girlfriends, but that's all behind me now. You're the only girl I want.'

Now it was Alison's turn to be open and truthful with Joel – and with herself too. She had spent some time wrestling with her thoughts about Sally and it had taken a while for her to appreciate that the deep disquiet she felt wasn't necessarily because of Sally's position, even though that was what had opened it up.

They came to the Claremont and Joel escorted her up the steps. The top-hatted doorman admitted them. Under other circumstances, Alison would have loved to swan into the pillared foyer, with its polished woodwork, handsome furniture and elegant flower arrangements, but today she was churned up with nerves.

Joel glanced around and then guided her over to an alcove with two empty chairs and a table. A waiter appeared and Joel ordered drinks. By unspoken agreement, they waited for the drinks to arrive before resuming the conversation.

Joel lightly clasped Alison's hand in both of his, turning it over and stroking her palm as if he was about to read her fortune.

'I can't tell you how much I wish it hadn't happened,' he said. 'I had no idea that I had made her pregnant. The first I knew of it was a long time later when she told me that there'd been a baby, but she'd lost it. I felt wretched for her, not just because of having to go through the pain and distress of the miscarriage, but because of what she'd suffered before that: the fear and the worry of what she was going to do. She hadn't got a mother to turn to.'

'I understand why that would make you sympathetic to Sally's situation,' said Alison, 'but it's also the reason why I've been so dead set against her.' She inhaled to steady herself. 'If you didn't have a – a pregnancy in your background, I would have looked down on Sally, but only in the way that it's normal to do so. I think I'd probably have been more accepting of her for Margaret's sake and for Mrs Cooper's. But – but you do have an unwanted pregnancy in your past, and I know I said at the time that it didn't matter, that all I cared about was how you felt towards me, but it turns out that it *does* matter. The reason I've been so down on poor Sally is that it hurts and upsets me that you and another girl . . . well, that there was going to be a baby. That's more than just sleeping with someone. And I know you didn't know about the baby, and I know she lost it anyway, but . . . but this business with Sally has brought it all bubbling up to the surface.'

'Alison, my love, I'm so sorry.'

'I know you are. I know that before you met me, you had a string of girlfriends. I also know that since you met me, you haven't looked at anyone else. You told me early on that I was the only girl for you and I know that's true. I've believed it all along. It even made me accept the baby and the miscarriage – or I thought it did, but I've realised now how very much all that hurt me. Even though it happened ages before we met. Even though it's really none of my business.'

Joel leaned closer, speaking in a low voice. 'I had no idea you felt this way.'

'Neither had I. At the time, I was very grown-up and modern about it and felt I was facing up to the truth, but I know now I didn't face up to it. I tucked it away in the back of my mind. I decided it didn't matter. And it *doesn't*. That's the silliest thing. I know you love me. I know we are perfect for one another. And it doesn't matter that you've had other girlfriends, it honestly doesn't. But knowing about Sally has made me see that – well, that maybe I'm not as modern and grown-up as I thought I was. Knowing about that baby – your old girlfriend's, not Sally's—' Alison broke off abruptly. 'You see? I call it your old girlfriend's baby, not *your* baby. I can't bear the thought of you having a baby with somebody else. The whole business has rattled me deep down in a way that I didn't realise when you first told me.'

'But you realise it now. I can only repeat what I said to you before. I never knew about the baby. When my old girlfriend was pregnant, it wasn't because we slept with one another on a regular basis. It happened once, just once, because the alcohol was flowing and we both had one too many. I'm sorry that she fell pregnant. I'm sorry because of what she then had to go through, and I'm sorry because it's hurt you too.'

Alison gave him a shaky smile. She felt wobbly inside, but warm as well. 'I'll tell you something else I know. I know that I trust you completely. And I know I'm being silly to feel upset about something that happened in your life way before I met you.'

'That isn't silly,' Joel reassured her. 'I can understand why what's happened to Sally has brought it all back. I'm sorry if I expected you to accept it without a murmur. I thought at the time what a brick you were and how lucky I was. I told you the truth because I didn't want there to be any secrets between us. I was enormously relieved and grateful that you took it so well.'

'I took it well because it was in the past and we all know the importance these days of living for the moment and making the most of all the good things that come our way. And *you're* a very good thing. You're the best thing that's ever happened to me . . . in case you were wondering,' she added, looking into his eyes.

'That's handy,' said Joel, 'because you're my best thing.' Lifting her hand, he kissed it, sending little darts of delight skittering through her. 'I don't know what to say. I can't make the past unhappen.'

'I don't mean to make you suffer for it, but I needed you to know what I feel. I don't want you to think I was cold and uncaring about Sally,' said Alison. 'I feel better for having talked about it.'

'Do you? It hasn't made you have doubts?'

Alison shook her head. 'Not even for a moment.' She looked at her emerald ring. Being engaged to Joel was what she wanted and nothing could shake that certainty. 'In fact, I'd like us to help Sally as a way of making up to her for all the horrid things I've thought about her. I don't know whether she's found a place to have her baby yet, but if she hasn't, could you ask your colleagues for a recommendation?'

Chapter Eighteen

'I'm sorry, Sally, but you really will have to leave soon,' said Mrs Cooper as she, Margaret, Sally and Mrs Grayson sat together nursing cups of tea while they waited for the nine o'clock news on the wireless. Alison was with Joel, but Margaret wasn't getting out much these days. Sally was saving every penny and Margaret stayed at home to keep her company.

Mrs Cooper's words made Margaret's heart sink into her shoes. She felt guilty for not having already helped Sally to move on. 'We have tried to find somewhere,' she told Mrs Cooper before Sally could say anything, 'but it's difficult.'

'How so?' asked Mrs Cooper. 'I'm sympathetic, Sally dear, you know I am, but I have the reputation of Mr Morgan's house to think of and you've gained weight recently. You're five months along.'

'The last thing I want to do is take advantage of your hospitality,' said Sally. 'I don't want you thinking I've got my feet under the table and have no intention of moving out.'

'We don't think that at all, do we, Mrs Grayson?' said Mrs Cooper. 'But we do need to know when you'll be leaving.'

'You said it's proving difficult to find somewhere,' Mrs Grayson prompted Margaret. 'Do you mean all the maternity homes are full?'

'We have to find one that handles adoptions,' said Margaret. 'That will be much more straightforward for Sally than if she has to get the welfare people involved.'

'I can see that,' said Mrs Cooper, giving Sally a smile of encouragement. 'It's going to be hard for you whatever happens, so it makes sense to go down the least upsetting road.'

'I went to see the lady almoner at Withington Hospital last week,' said Sally. 'Margaret came with me – not into the lady almoner's office. She had to wait outside, but just knowing she was there gave me the courage to face the interview.'

'Was the lady almoner of any help?' asked Mrs Grayson.

'She told me about two maternity homes in Manchester, but when she explained what the fees were, I couldn't afford them. I've got a bit put by, plus a little something my grandma left me, but it's not enough.'

'What about the father?' Mrs Grayson replied at once. 'He should put his hand in his pocket. It isn't right that you're left to deal with this on your own – and don't give me any nonsense about never wanting to see him again. You're in a fix, young lady, and a financial contribution from the man who landed you in it would make life a lot easier.'

Sally's mouth twisted. 'For the record, I don't ever want to see him again, but even if I did want to, I couldn't, because I don't know where he lives.' Her expression crumpled, but only for a moment. 'I've been a first-class idiot. I'll never trust a man again.'

'I know you can't afford either of the homes,' said Mrs Cooper, 'but what were they like?'

'We didn't go and see,' said Margaret. 'There didn't seem to be any point.'

'I have heard of another place where they arrange adoptions,' said Sally, 'and apparently they go to a lot of trouble to find good adoptive parents, but it's quite a distance away. I'd have to stay overnight if I visited and I can't afford to do that, not with the fees to pay. I might have to take it on trust.'

'I don't like the idea of you going to live in a place you haven't had the chance to look at first,' said Mrs Cooper, 'but it sounds like you'll have no choice.'

'Don't worry,' said Sally. 'I promise I'll leave here soon.'

Getting up, she gathered the cups and saucers and took the tray to the kitchen. Margaret was about to follow to help wash up, but Mrs Grayson put out a restraining hand.

'Let her go. She could probably do with a few minutes on her own.'

Margaret nodded and sat down. 'You've both been so good about this. I'll never forget it and nor will Sally.'

'She's jolly lucky to have a friend like you, chuck,' said Mrs Cooper. 'I don't imagine it was easy for a respectable lass like you to accompany her to the lady almoner's.'

If only she knew!

'It's not as though I went in with her,' said Margaret. 'I waited outside in the corridor. The clerk said that only family are allowed in.'

And thank goodness for that. Even now, a week later, the memory of seeing the lady almoner again still had the power to bring Margaret to the verge of tears. She turned her face away, picking up the *Radio Times* and pretending to scan the lists of wireless programmes so that Mrs Cooper and Mrs Grayson wouldn't realise. Sally returned from the kitchen, her eyes betraying that she had indulged in a little weep.

Margaret's heart reached out to her. Whatever distress she had suffered, it was nothing compared to what Sally was facing.

Margaret could see that the two ladies had noticed Sally's slightly swollen eyes, but neither of them said anything.

'Switch on the wireless, would you, Margaret?' said Mrs Grayson. 'It's nearly time for the news.'

Being on the early shift tomorrow gave Margaret a good excuse to head off to bed. Not that she expected to get much sleep. She read for a while and then tried to settle down, though it was hard to steer her thoughts in any direction other than that of the lady almoner. Honestly, she had thought that she'd left that chapter of her life well and truly behind her. Mind you, she'd thought that once before, only for Alison to meet Joel and start going out with him. Was she going to be haunted by her mistake for ever?

She didn't want that to happen to Sally. She wanted Sally to get through this dire experience with the least possible upset. It would be hard having to give up her baby, but that would draw a line underneath everything. Margaret wished a line could be drawn under her own situation.

She had to stop thinking about herself and concentrate on her friend. There had been no one for her to turn to when she'd been in the family way and she was determined to give Sally the staunch support she herself had lacked. She hadn't told Sally about her own experience. It would have felt self-indulgent somehow, as if she was trying to divert attention away from Sally's situation. What had happened to Margaret had happened in the past and she didn't want it to hog the limelight now.

Besides, she felt it was important that Sally receive help from a girl she thought of as decent. It meant a great deal to Margaret that Joan hadn't spurned her after the miscarriage. Joan had in fact made a point of befriending her when their paths had later crossed. It was because of Joan that Margaret was now surrounded by such dear friends and lived in Wilton Close. Joan had done all that for her even though Margaret was a fallen girl.

Margaret wanted Sally to feel she was receiving the same kind of support. The way Margaret's father and her old neighbours had viewed her after her miscarriage had added to her feeling of being unclean. The neighbours had given her narrow-eyed glances as they exchanged remarks in low voices. As for Dad, he had practically hunched over in shame. When she had been most in need of his love and support, he had barely been able to look at her. Joan's friendship had gone a long way towards helping her feel better about herself – and she wanted her own friendship to give Sally's morale a boost in the same way.

Thinking about Sally made Margaret feel less troubled on her own account and she began to relax, the tension sliding away from her limbs. The bedroom door opened softly.

'Are you awake?' Alison whispered.

Margaret turned over. 'Is something the matter?'

'It's nothing bad, but I've got something to say and I need to say it to all of you. The others are still downstairs. Do you mind getting up for a few minutes?'

Intrigued, Margaret swung her feet to the floor. Alison passed over her dressing gown and they padded downstairs.

Margaret sat beside Sally on the sofa, wondering what was going on.

'I want to apologise,' said Alison, 'to all of you, but especially to you, Sally.'

'To me?' said Sally. 'Why?'

'Because I've been hateful about you behind your back, because of you being in the club. You're a decent girl and you don't deserve this. I wish you well with all my heart and I'm sorry for being beastly about you. It was mean of me. I can see that now. And I'm sorry if I've made the atmosphere in the house unpleasant. I won't do it again. I wanted to say this to all of you, because you all deserve the apology. I especially wanted to tell Sally I'm sorry in front of the rest of you. It's the least I owe you, Sally.'

'Thank you.' Sally nodded and there was a sheen of tears in her blue eyes. 'I didn't know you were being nasty behind my back, though you have been rather cool to my face.'

'I'm sorry,' Alison started to say again, but Sally waved her words away.

'I didn't say that to wring another apology out of you. I said it because I want you to know how much it means to me that you have seen through the shame and the stigma to the real me underneath.' Sally pressed a hand against her heart. 'I've had so much support since I came here.'

'And now you'll have my support too,' Alison told her, making Margaret fill with pride and gratitude.

'Thank you, Alison dear,' said Mrs Cooper. 'That's very generous of you. Let's leave it there, shall we? We don't want Sally getting too emotional.'

When Margaret returned to bed, Alison followed her up and sat on her own bed.

'I couldn't say it to the others,' she began, 'but I can tell you. The real reason I was so out of sorts about Sally was because of – ' she drew in a breath ' – how Joel's old girlfriend was going to have his baby, only she lost it. When you and I talked about it last year, I said I could accept the past and not let it spoil the present – and I meant every word at the time. But it turns out that maybe I didn't mean it deep down. Sally's pregnancy out of wedlock bothered me so much because it dug up all that upset. I thought I was down on her because she'd been free with herself and got into trouble, but I know now that I've been churned up at the thought of Joel and this other girl, even though it happened a long time ago. But I've got it out of my system now. Joel and I had a long talk this evening and I feel I can let go of the bad feelings that have been spoiling things for me recently.' She smiled at Margaret. 'I just wanted you to know.' She stood up. 'Mrs Grayson is making bedtime drinks. I'll leave you to get some shut-eye.'

Alison left the room and Margaret lay there, eyes wide open and her heart hammering.

Chapter Nineteen

Since failing to be appointed to the new welfare post, Joan had found herself in the position of dropping off her own little boy at the nursery or Wilton Close and then taking Jeremy home with her. It seemed a bizarre state of affairs and Jeremy's mother's delight at her continuing to be a childminder didn't help.

'As long as you understand that I'm still looking,' Joan told her.

'As long as looking is all you do' was the cheery answer and Joan could have crowned her.

'You could walk into a job at the munitions,' said Petal, Bob's middle sister, a lovely green-eyed blonde. She was a real beauty, as was the oldest sister, Maureen, with her plentiful chestnut-brown hair, brown eyes and fine cheekbones, and her tall, slender figure.

'But I don't want to have to work nights,' said Joan. 'I know how wrong it is to be picky in wartime, but I have to put Max first.'

'At least you've still got the childminding while you wait for the right job to come along,' said Petal.

Later, when Joan repeated Petal's comment to Gran over a cup of tea, Gran snorted.

'Is that what you intend to do? *Wait*?' Gran invested deep scorn into the word in the way that only she could. 'I didn't bring you up to be a milksop. I didn't bring you up to *wait* for things to happen.'

'No,' Joan said drily, 'you brought me up to do what you wanted.'

'You didn't always do it, though, did you?' Gran shot back at her.

Was Gran referring to Steven? A chill swept through Joan at the memory of how, in the depths of her grief for Letitia, she had lost her way emotionally and had ended up two-timing Bob. Surely Gran wasn't dragging that up?

'Look at how you joined the railway without asking for my permission,' said Gran. 'That was because you were determined. You need to show a bit of that determination now. You'll have plenty of time to be at home with Max when peace comes – and believe me, you'll definitely be at home then. I've lived through one of these wars before, remember. The government needed women to step into men's jobs, so all of a sudden we were being told that it was all right to work outside the home, that it wouldn't damage family life or be detrimental to the children. Then the war ended and women weren't needed any longer, so then we were told that our families needed us at home. Now it's happening all over again. Women are necessary to keep the country running, so once again it's the done thing to go out to work at the same time as keep house. But mark my words. The minute the war is over, the women will all get "Thank you and goodbye" letters and be sent back to the kitchen sink.'

'I thought you'd prefer women to be at home, looking after their families.'

'Everyone has their duty and a woman's is to look after her home and her family. Speaking as a grandmother who was called upon to act as parent to two little granddaughters, I know that better than anyone. But in wartime, there are two lots of duty, the domestic and the contribution to the war effort.'

'Are you saying,' asked Joan, 'that if I love the railways, I should find another job and go back?'

'What I'm saying,' answered Gran, 'is that it is the government's job to win the war, which requires women to undertake all manner of war work. You and I both know that you could make more of a contribution to the war effort than by childminding. So stop walking around with a face like a wet weekend and do something about it.'

The last day of September brought good news. That evening in Wilton Close, Alison gave Sally the name of a mother and baby home in Sale which arranged adoptions privately.

Margaret perked up, pleased. 'Sale? That's not far as the crow flies, though the journey will be a bit fiddly. The main thing is we'll be able to visit and take a look.'

'What about the fees?' Sally asked.

'Eight guineas a week,' said Alison, adding quickly when Sally flinched, 'but Joel was told that the home has a bursary system to assist unmarried mothers, so you can apply for that. You have to be interviewed.'

'We need to make arrangements as soon as possible,' said Mrs Cooper. 'I'll come with you, Sally dear, if Margaret can't.'

'Would you really do that?' Sally asked.

'Of course,' said Mrs Cooper. 'I wouldn't say it if I didn't mean it. I feel responsible for you – and not just responsible. You've lived here for a while and I've become fond of you.'

'Thank you,' said Sally, her voice warm with sincerity. 'You've been so good to me – both of you,' she added, looking at Mrs Grayson.

Margaret's eyes filled with tears of gratitude towards her landlady and Mrs Grayson. She felt proud of them too, for setting aside their natural reservations about unmarried mothers and taking Sally to their hearts. She was grateful to Alison as well for overcoming her own feelings to the point where she had ended up wanting to help. Joel's access to information looked like it had made all the difference.

Did this mean the end was in sight? Margaret shut her eyes for a moment, relief making her realise the strain she'd been under. Not that she begrudged a single moment of it. She was glad to have helped Sally, both in practical ways and with moral support. She'd tried to make her feel better about herself, remembering all too well what it was like to feel grubby and terrified.

She was also glad and grateful that Alison seemed to have found peace in the matter of Joel's former relationship. It honestly scared Margaret to know that the anguish and shame of her miscarriage still lived on in other ways and she hated to think that she carried some of the responsibility for Alison having been unhappy deep down. Margaret hoped with all her heart that Alison and Joel's discussion had finally laid the matter to rest.

The atmosphere in the house became one of relief mixed with optimism now that it seemed a suitable maternity home had been found. Margaret shared those feelings, but she felt unsettled too, her mind teeming with what-ifs. What if she hadn't lost her own baby? What if she'd had to find somewhere to give birth? What if – what if she'd had to give up her child? Really and truly, there was no what-if about that one. She had known all too clearly at the time that it was her only option, though she hadn't permitted herself to dwell on it. She'd been too busy being frightened and overwhelmed, too busy battling feelings of dread.

But she thought about it now, about having her baby and giving it up, never seeing it again. She pictured Joan and how much she loved Max. Margaret was his godmother and she adored him too. When she was pregnant, she hadn't thought of giving up her baby in terms of it being a huge emotional wrench, but she thought of it that way now.

Oh, she was being foolish. She'd lost her baby and that's all there was to it. Why was she allowing all these what-ifs to creep into her mind?

It was the first of October, a new month and, if Joan had anything to do with it, a new start. Imagine Gran of all people making her feel better about herself and her future. Gran! Wonders would never cease. Today was Jeremy's birthday and his mum had got the day off work, which added to Joan's sense of well-being. She had changed Max's childcare arrangements so that they could have a precious day together, just the two of them, then Mrs Grayson was going to have him later, allowing Joan to go to Victoria Station to meet up with her friends in the buffet. Joan couldn't wait.

Late in the afternoon, she caught the bus into town, feeling uplifted after a day spent with her son and no Jeremy. Was that rotten of her? Walking from the bus stop to Victoria Station, she paid special attention to the buildings she passed. Some stood empty, damaged beyond repair. It added to her resolve to return to 'proper' war work.

Entering Victoria, she paused beside the handsome memorial to the men of the old Lancashire and Yorkshire Railway who had perished in the Great War. Beneath a vast mosaic-tiled map depicting the lines of the network, a series of seven bronze panels recorded the men's names, more than fourteen hundred of them. Here was another reason for Joan to make a meaningful contribution to the war effort. All those men who never came home, all those bereaved families, all those young Great War widows who were now middle-aged women, forced to live through another war, many of them with sons who were fighting. Thank goodness Bob was in a reserved occupation – and Joel, and Persephone's Matt.

Filled with a potent mixture of pride and sorrow, Joan wended her way through the busy station to the buffet. As she walked in, Mrs Jessop gave her a wave from behind the counter. When she'd bought her cup of tea, her friends made room for her at their crowded table.

'Where's Max?' Dot asked.

'With Mrs Grayson,' said Joan, settling in for a good natter. 'The little lad I look after is with his mum today, so I've had a lovely time with Max.'

'And now you've come to have a lovely time with us,' Margaret added, making the others laugh.

'Don't let me interrupt,' said Joan. 'What were you talking about?'

'Fay Brewer, as a matter of fact,' said Cordelia. 'The word is that she did an outstanding interview.'

'So you mustn't feel bad about not getting that job,' said Dot. 'It sounds as if you were up against stiff competition.'

The others agreed. Miss Emery's apology had meant a lot to Joan, but knowing that Fay Brewer had been not just the best candidate for the post but far superior to the other candidates was of no consolation. No – she wasn't going to think that way. Fay Brewer had got the job fair and square and Joan had put all that behind her.

Just when she thought the conversation was going to move on, Alison said to Cordelia, 'Tell Joan about meeting her and what you found out.'

'Dot and I happened to bump into Miss Emery when she was showing Miss Brewer round,' said Cordelia. 'She introduced us. We had a little chat and it turned out that Miss Brewer is indeed the Miss Brewer from the Corporation who was such a support to Mabel when she was busy setting up the Lizzie Nursery. Fancy that!'

'We did wonder about her when we heard the name,' Emily reminded Joan – as if she needed reminding.

'Fancy that,' Joan murmured.

After that the conversation did move on, but the gloss had gone off the occasion for Joan. Was she a meanie to feel a bit huffy about Fay Brewer? She hadn't enjoyed hearing the friends who'd had such sympathy for her when she didn't get the job now heaping praise on Miss Brewer. Now that really was childish, she admonished herself.

Back at home that evening, she curled up with Bob on the sofa when Max was in bed.

'Did you have a good time in the buffet?' Bob asked.

'So-so.' Joan wanted to be honest with Bob. 'They were singing the praises of Miss Brewer – you know, the lady who got the job.'

'Ouch,' said Bob.

Joan smiled. 'Yes, it was a bit ouch. She came to the railways from the Corporation and she was the one who helped Mabel with the Lizzie Nursery.'

'That makes her a good egg in my book.'

'In mine too,' said Joan. 'Mabel said at the time that Miss Brewer made everything a whole lot easier for her. But . . .'

'But what?' asked Bob.

'Oh, nothing. It's just me being daft. I'm all right, honestly.'

'It must have brought it back,' said Bob, 'you not getting that job you wanted so much, I mean.'

'Yes, it did.' Joan snuggled closer. Bob always understood her so well.

'Well then, you know what you need to do, don't you? You need to put that well and truly behind you and set your sights on a different job. It's time to show 'em what you're made of, Mrs Hubble.'

Chapter Twenty

Because of Sally's work roster, Margaret and Mrs Cooper went to see Rookery House on her behalf. On the way, they speculated as to what it might be like.

'At least it already existed as a mother and baby home before the war,' said Mrs Cooper. 'I take heart from that. So many women now have to go into wartime maternity places that used to be orphanages or even former Poor Law institutions.'

She gave a little shudder that Margaret felt because their arms were touching.

When they got there, they found that the home had obviously been built years ago as a posh house. They exchanged glances before they approached the front door and rang the bell. They were shown to the superintendent's office, where a middle-aged, well-groomed lady rose to greet them. She introduced herself as Mrs Walters and offered them a seat before resuming her own behind a large desk. She looked at Margaret and enquired, 'Miss Bennett?'

'No,' Margaret said quickly. 'I'm her friend, Margaret Thomas – Miss Thomas. Miss Bennett couldn't come today.'

Mrs Cooper said, 'And I'm Mrs Cooper, Miss Bennett's landlady. I'm here in place of her mother.'

'Who presumably also can't come today,' said Mrs Walters.

'She doesn't know about the baby,' said Mrs Cooper. 'Sally – Miss Bennett – is in quite a fix, as you can see.'

'Then she is fortunate to have friends like the two of you to support her,' said Mrs Walters, 'especially you, Mrs Cooper. You seem respectable. Or are you helping Miss Bennett simply to move her on from your house?'

Mrs Cooper bridled, but then nodded. 'I took Miss Bennett in, knowing what her condition was, so, yes, I've been a friend to her, but I'm also helping her to move on. You said I seem respectable. Well, I'll tell you this. I'm thoroughly respectable and so is the house I take care of. I can't and won't have any scandal attached to it. Its owners will come home after the war and they'll expect to find it in the same condition as when they left it, not just clean and tidy, but with its reputation unblemished an' all.'

It was the turn of Mrs Walters to nod. 'Miss Bennett is fortunate to have such staunch support. Many girls in her position find themselves abandoned. There is one important question I must put to you.' Mrs Walters shook her head. 'It is most unfortunate that Miss Bennett isn't here to answer it herself, because her being accepted here depends upon it.'

'What is it?' breathed Margaret, feeling oddly chilly.

'Here at Rookery House, we only accept unmarried girls for whom this is their first slip,' said Mrs Walters.

'Slip?' said Margaret.

'Their first pregnancy,' Mrs Walters clarified. 'It is essential that we are able to assure the adoptive parents that the mother is a girl of good character, who has never fallen from grace in this manner before. The baby of a loose girl who has had more than one child out of wedlock might well inherit its mother's morals, or lack of them, and the adoptive parents could expect to face problems with the child as it grows. No adoptive parents want that.'

Mrs Cooper looked at Margaret.

'Of course it's never happened to Sally before,' Margaret exclaimed.

'I'm pleased to hear it,' said Mrs Walters, 'though naturally I shall require a written assurance from Miss Bennett herself.' She glanced at a piece of paper on her desk. 'I require her full name for our records. Is Sally short for Sarah?'

'No,' said Mrs Cooper. 'I thought you might need to know, so I asked her. She is Sally Annabel Lucy. Annabel with one L, not double L E.'

'Thank you.' Mrs Walters made a note. 'I believe Miss Bennett is interested in the bursary we offer to some girls in her position. If she applies and is successful, the bursary would pay half of Miss Bennett's fees.'

Margaret and Mrs Cooper exchanged looks of relief.

'But if she decided to keep the baby, she would be required to return all the bursary funds,' Mrs Walters added.

'Give back the money if she keeps the baby?' Margaret exclaimed. 'That's bribery. Of course she couldn't repay the money.'

'Bribery?' Mrs Walters lifted her eyebrows. 'On the contrary, it is a perfectly reasonable condition. It is most generous of the benefactor to take pity on unmarried mothers. It is not just generous but highly unusual. We don't want anyone taking advantage of it.'

'You mean, accept the bursary and then keep the baby?' said Mrs Cooper.

'Precisely so. It isn't bribery and it isn't payment for the child. It is simply a means of assisting an unmarried mother who sees adoption as the solution to her problem.'

The solution to her problem! Margaret flinched inwardly. How heartless it all seemed. But who was she to climb on her high horse? Hadn't she regarded her own pregnancy in exactly that way?

'We'd like to apply for your bursary on Miss Bennett's behalf.' Mrs Cooper fished in her handbag. 'Here is the letter she has written.'

Mrs Walters held out her hand and took the letter, producing a pair of spectacles to enable her to read it. 'I will put it before the board, but I can't see any reason why Miss Bennett would be turned down. Shall we make a provisional date for her to move in? When is she due?'

'The end of January,' said Mrs Cooper. 'I know your married ladies probably come here for only two or three weeks, but Miss Bennett needs to be here longer than that if she is to hide her condition from the world. I imagine it's the same for other unmarried girls.'

'Those that can afford it,' said Mrs Walters in a dry voice.

Mrs Cooper turned to Margaret. 'You do realise that Miss Emery will have to be informed, don't you? I'm sorry. I know it isn't what Sally wants, but she can't have all that time off work without explaining why. I don't suppose she's the first, but from what I've heard about her, I'm sure Miss Emery will keep her confidence.'

Margaret nodded. In the engine shed, they would have to come up with a fictitious sick granny who needed looking after, or something of the kind, to explain Sally's absence. It was unusual for anybody to be granted extended leave from their war work, but emergencies happened and if Sally and Margaret played their cards right, their colleagues would be sympathetic.

They talked on for a while, Mrs Walters giving them the information they would need to pass on to Sally.

'One final thing,' she said as they were about to get up to leave. 'When Miss Bennett arrives to stay here, please could you ask her to come to the back door.'

'Is that where you sign in the new patients?' Margaret asked.

'It is where we ask the *un*married patients to present themselves,' said Mrs Walters. 'Our married ladies naturally use the front door.'

On a chilly October day, Alison and Joel stood in front of the semi-detached house at the end of the road, next to a field. It had a large, semicircular bay window on the ground floor, with a second one above it, each boasting no fewer than seven panes of glass, each of them criss-crossed with plenty of anti-blast tape. Two steps led up to the front door, which was sheltered by a wide porch. To one side was an integral garage. Alison didn't know which was more impressive – having a garage or the garage being integral. She laughed at herself. It wasn't as though Joel had a motor. But one day . . .

Joel squeezed her hand. 'Here it is. What d'you think?'

'It looks fine from the outside,' said Alison, feeling all quivery with excitement. Was this really going to be their first married home? 'Can we go in?'

Joel laughed. 'Of course we can. They're expecting us.'

The house was currently occupied by Dr Solomon 'Grundy' Phipps and his wife, Clara. Grundy and Joel had worked alongside one another during the air raids and Joel had asked him to be his best man. In a few weeks, Grundy and Clara were going to move to the West Country, where he would be taking up a new post. Grundy had had a word with the rent man about letting Joel and Alison have the house and the landlord had agreed. According to Joel, he was glad to have another doctor lined up.

Joel knocked and the door was opened almost immediately, which made Alison feel welcome. Joel performed the introductions.

Clara, a fair-skinned, light blonde lady in her thirties, laughed as she said to Alison, 'I'm sure you're far more interested in seeing the house than in meeting us. Let me show you round.'

Alison went with her willingly, looking into the various rooms, downstairs and up. Several items of furniture – a couple of simple armchairs and a side table, even the bed in the master bedroom – had tubular steel frames. Clara noticed her looking and Alison hoped she had concealed her dislike.

'Most of the furniture comes with the house, but the modern stuff is our own,' said Clara. 'The bathroom is over here.'

Alison peered inside, noting the cork floor and the chrome taps, which, unlike Mum's brass ones, wouldn't need polishing, as well as the oil-baize curtains that went well in bathrooms because of being waterproof.

Back downstairs, she gazed lovingly at Joel. How clever of him to find this house for them.

'Will it do?' he asked in a teasing voice.

'It's perfect,' said Alison. 'I never imagined us getting so much space of our own.'

'There's going to be a short gap between us moving out and you getting married and moving in,' said Grundy, 'but as long as you're happy to pay the rent on the unoccupied house, the landlord is happy for you to have the place.'

'We've been happy here, haven't we, darling?' said Clara. 'I'm sure you shall be too.'

'Oh, we shall,' breathed Alison.

Alison went across the road to Hunts Bank. Miss Emery had sent for her. Up until now, this generally meant she was about to be given yet another new role within the railway, but this time Miss Emery informed her that Mr Samuels was in the building and wished to speak to her.

Alison had to wait a while for him to become available, then the door opened and a man emerged, closing the door behind him. Presently, the door opened again and Alison was invited inside.

'Good morning, Miss Lambert. My apologies for keeping you waiting,' said Mr Samuels. 'Please sit down. This won't take long.'

And it didn't. It took a lot less time than she had been kept waiting.

'You shall be going away for the last week of October,' Mr Samuels informed her. 'The official reason will be so that you can train up new station announcers, but really . . . well, you will understand that I can't tell you why in advance.'

And that was all the information she was given. Alison returned to her duties feeling excited and a bit scared, though what she had to be scared of, she didn't know. Well, that was just it, wasn't it? The not knowing. But there was one thing she did know and she used the thought of it to stiffen her spine. This was something to do with the special role she was to play next year. The fear dropped away and she felt proud. If only she could tell someone!

That evening was a buffet meeting and although Alison joined in the conversation, part of her boggled at the way she was behaving as normal while the awareness of her forthcoming special job was swirling around inside her.

The conversation turned to Christmas.

'Just think,' said Alison, 'this will be the fourth Christmas of the war.'

'Fifth,' said Emily.

'Surely not.' Alison counted on her fingers, starting with '39. 'Crikey. You're right. Five.'

'Let's hope it's the last wartime Christmas,' said Persephone. 'What do you think the chances are?'

'Even if it isn't the last one,' said Cordelia, 'at least we can now confidently look ahead to the end of the war.'

'The war against those U-boats is being won at long last,' said Dot.

'Shall I tell you what I managed to buy the other day?' said Colette, smiling. 'Small coloured candles for the Christmas cake.'

'No' and 'You didn't' were the responses.

'Yes, I did,' said Colette. 'Ninepence a dozen. They had those little flower-shaped candleholders as well, but I didn't know whether to get them. They were four shillings a dozen.'

'Four bob,' Persephone exclaimed. 'That's daylight robbery.'

'I know,' Colette agreed, 'but I thought about it and I knew that if I didn't get them, I'd wish I had.'

'So you got them,' said Dot.

'They'll look lovely on Mrs Grayson's Christmas cake,' said Colette.

'Are you spending Christmas Day in Wilton Close?' asked Emily and Colette nodded.

'You'll be an old married lady by then,' Dot said to Alison with a smile. 'Married for a whole week.'

'Have you found somewhere to live yet?' asked Persephone.

'Yes,' Alison reported happily. 'We looked at it yesterday.' She spent a few minutes describing the house and answering questions.

'That must be a weight off your mind,' said Colette. 'I'm pleased for you.'

'Just wait,' said Persephone. 'We'll all be coming round to yours for tea.'

'You'll be very welcome,' said Alison. She was looking forward to being the lady of the house.

'We've got to get her married off first,' said Dot with a chuckle. 'Have you got any more wedding plans to share with us?'

'I have, actually,' said Alison, thriving on all the attention. 'We've just been talking about Christmas and I want to incorporate some Christmassy details into the wedding. For starters, the choir is going to sing carols as the guests arrive and also while we sign the register. And we've been given permission to decorate the church with holly – if we can get hold of enough of it.'

'I'm sure Darley Court can help with that,' said Persephone.

'I know it isn't anything to do with Christmas,' said Alison, 'but we're going to start the ceremony with prayers for absent friends.'

'Very appropriate,' Dot said approvingly.

'And I need your help, all of you,' said Alison, which made the others sit up straighter. 'Christmas is a time for presents for children, which is hard these days with so few toys in the shops, so we want to get as many toys made as we can. Mrs Grayson has already offered to knit and crochet some. She's still got a pattern for a crocheted horse called Dobbin that was in *Woman's Weekly* back in 1940, so I'm expecting a whole herd of little Dobbins.' She smiled at her friends. 'If nothing else, we're all experts at making toys after supplying that great quantity to Mabel's nursery.'

'I've still got the patterns that the handicrafts lady gave me when she did the activity day at the orphanage,' said Emily.

'If you could all help,' said Alison, 'that would be wonderful. It would be especially right for our wedding, because when I first knew Joel, he tackled a war profiteer in a toy shop who was trying to get his hands on as much of the stock as he could.'

'The rotter,' said Persephone.

'What did Joel do?' asked Emily.

'He outwitted him and made him leave,' Alison told her. 'And there was another time when Joel and his sister were involved in providing toys for children who were facing prolonged stays in hospital.'

Colette nodded. 'So it would be fitting for you and Joel to celebrate your wedding by providing toys.'

'Yes, it would,' Alison sighed happily. 'And with your help, we'll be able to.'

Chapter Twenty-One

On Sunday afternoon, Alison sat with Mum and Lydia, telling them all about the house she and Joel were going to have.

'Can we go and see it before you move in?' asked Lydia.

'I'm sure the current tenants won't mind at all,' said Alison, picturing how friendly Clara had been.

'Is the house furnished?' asked Mum. 'You'll have to put your names down quickly if you need to buy Utility furniture.'

'Nearly all the furniture is included,' said Alison. 'The Phippses have added some pieces of their own, hideous stuff with tubular frames, which they'll be taking with them.'

'That was all the rage a few years ago,' said Mum. 'Now folk are grateful for anything they can get.'

'You've really fallen on your feet,' said Lydia.

Mum sighed. 'I had hoped you'd live over on this side of town, nearer to us.'

Alison pressed Mum's hand. 'We're lucky to get a house at all. We're lucky to get *anything*. It's only because Joel and Grundy are colleagues that we had the chance of this.'

After that, they moved on to wedding talk.

'Flowers,' said Mum.

'Joel says his parents want to contribute to the wedding,' said Alison, 'and they've offered to pay for the flowers.'

'That's good of them,' said Lydia, adding bluntly, 'Isn't his father some sort of high-up consultant? I expect they're rolling in it.'

'Lydia!' said Mum. 'Don't be vulgar.'

'Joel did say not to stint ourselves,' Alison said lightly.

'Good-oh.' Lydia laughed. 'We'll fill the church with exotic orchids.'

'We'll do no such thing,' Mum replied primly. 'I refuse to spend money just for the sake of it. Really, Lydia, I don't know where this attitude of yours has come from.'

'I was joking,' Lydia pointed out.

'I don't want something that costs a fortune,' said Alison. 'I want something lovely, of course, but not something that involves hothouses.'

'I've already spoken to Mrs Hanberger and Miss Grain at the florist's,' said Mum, 'and they've been very helpful. Mrs Hanberger has suggested eucalyptus for the greenery, which I think is a very good idea.'

'Oh yes,' Alison agreed readily. 'I like eucalyptus.'

'You might not be so keen on this,' Mum went on, 'but Miss Grain said that rather than setting your heart on flowers they might not be able to get hold of, if you will trust them to give you the best of what they can get, they'll make sure you have a beautiful bouquet.'

'I never thought I'd hear myself say this,' Alison replied, 'but that sounds perfect.'

'Really?' said Lydia, not troubling to hide her surprise. 'I thought you'd be determined to have exactly what you wanted and nothing less would do.'

'I think the ladies at the florist's will produce something wonderful,' said Alison. 'People do when it's for a wedding. When Joan got married, the church hall flooded, so we simply moved the reception to the station buffet and had a splendid time, probably better than if we'd been in the church hall because everyone mucked in and made the best of things. I quite like the idea of not knowing what flowers I'm going to have.'

What she meant was that she liked the thought of one day telling the story to her children, but she didn't say so.

'I'm having trouble finding a photographer,' said Mum.

'They can't all have been called up,' said Alison.

'It isn't the photographers that are the problem,' said Lydia. 'It's the scarcity of photographic materials. One of the girls at work had her wedding pictures taken by a friend. Would you mind that?' she asked Alison.

Mum jumped in before Alison could respond. 'Taken by a friend? No, I'll find a proper professional photographer if it's the last thing I do. You don't want amateur snaps, Alison.'

'I'd rather have snaps than an empty wedding album,' said Alison. 'At least the wedding cake is taken care of,' she added to divert Mum's attention before she could get a bee in her bonnet to add to all the other bees already swarming around in there.

Mum visibly relaxed. 'Yes,' she said with satisfaction. 'I do want you to have a cake, whatever the difficulties, because I wasn't able to have one in 1918.'

'Three cheers for your Mrs Grayson,' said Lydia with a smile.

Alison smiled back. 'She says her secret is that she makes her own caster sugar by putting ordinary sugar through the mangle.'

'Through the mangle!' Mum looked horrified.

Alison laughed. 'She does put it inside a calico bag first.'

'We need to make the final decisions about the food for the reception,' said Mum. 'Everything has to be made to stretch as far as it can.'

'I know it doesn't sound glamorous,' said Lydia, 'but scrambled dried egg makes a good sandwich filling. Oh, that's something I meant to ask you.' She looked at Alison. 'Is Mrs Grayson using real eggs or dried for the cake?'

'If she uses dried, no one will be able to tell,' Alison declared loyally. 'She'll make sure it's every bit as delicious.'

'I don't mean that,' said Lydia. 'I mean if you're going to have two tiers and keep the top one for the christening. The lady over the road from me kept her top layer, but when she cut into it a year later, it crumbled practically to dust because of the dried egg.'

Alison was distracted by the thought of a christening. Both she and Joel wanted children, but not right away. Alison had once glimpsed a saucy postcard that a male colleague had brought back from a trip to the seaside and which all the men had chuckled over. It showed a bosomy lady in a frothy nightie lying on a bed, wearing her gas mask and saying to the man beside her something along the lines of, 'My mum told me to take precautions.'

Alison had no intention of entering into a baby conversation with Mum. Back when she was going out with Paul, she and Mum had often indulged in baby talk, because having a child as soon as nature allowed had been very much part of Alison's plans – but not any longer. Yes, she wanted to have a family with Joel, but they wanted time together on their own first, something that seemed far too modern an approach to marriage to discuss with her mother. Besides, Alison hadn't forgotten that Lydia had hoped to fall for a honeymoon baby, but it hadn't happened – and she hadn't seen her husband since. The last thing Alison wanted was to rub her sister's nose in it.

'What other food are we going to have?' she asked, changing the subject.

'I've been given a beautiful black and white rabbit,' said Mum.

'I don't think I want to hear this,' said Lydia.

'Don't be silly, darling,' said Mum. 'It's what domestic rabbits are for. You know that. Dad has got the old hutch out of the shed. It's a good job I never let him chop it up for firewood. I'm feeding up the rabbit at the moment.'

'No,' breathed Alison.

Mum gave her a look. 'Are you going to turn vegetarian on me? No? Good. That means you'll be enjoying chicken in aspic jelly at your reception.'

'You mean mock chicken,' said Lydia.

'Everyone knows mock chicken is really rabbit,' said Mum. 'I want to raise the tone. We'll call it chicken because everyone says that's what rabbit tastes like, and no one will know the difference once I've flavoured it with herbs. Don't look at me like that, girls. We've always kept rabbits to eat. That's why you were never allowed to give them names.'

'I'll type the invitations at work this coming week in my dinner breaks.' Lydia scrunched up her shoulders and grinned. 'It's only a couple of months away.'

'I know. It's eleven weeks from the day before yesterday. Not that I'm counting,' Alison added with a laugh.

'Do you want me to give you back all the things you gave me from your old bottom drawer?' Lydia asked. 'Sorry to mention it, but I've been wondering.'

'Keep it. Keep everything,' Alison said at once, shaking her head at the memory – at herself for ever having been so obsessed with getting married to Paul. She had stored all kinds of household and kitchen items and linen in her 'bottom drawer', ready for the day she finally became Mrs Paul Dunaway. Some of her hoard had been pretty and decorative, such as the cushion covers and the photograph frame. Other items had been pretty but practical – the milk jug and matching sugar bowl, the vases, the pillowcases she'd embroidered. Good grief, she'd even bought a sturdy cloth bag for when she went to the grocer's to buy potatoes. She'd ended up giving the lot to Lydia – and she categorically didn't want any of it back.

Lydia squeezed her hand. 'Sorry,' she whispered.

'It's all right,' Alison replied. She understood why Lydia had felt she ought to make the offer.

'We need to get you sorted out with a wedding dress,' said Mum.

'I've had an idea about that,' Lydia piped up. 'What about your friend Joan's dress?'

'The dress you wore for your wedding?' Mum looked at Lydia.

Lydia nodded. 'I'd understand if you didn't fancy it,' she told Alison, 'but I think it would be rather special, the two of us getting married in the same dress. Think about it.'

'I will,' said Alison.

'Well, don't take too long,' said Mum. 'The wedding will be here before you know it. And if Lydia's doing the invitations, I want to talk about your friend Colette. I asked you to reconsider having her as one of your attendants.'

'She's a dear friend,' Alison said in a steady voice. 'I'm not going to leave her out.'

'You don't have to. She can come to the wedding.'

'As long as she doesn't follow me up the aisle,' said Alison.

'It's plain wrong, Alison. She's separated.'

'Mum, the last thing I want is to hurt you, but you're wrong. Colette's been a good friend to me and I couldn't possibly ask her to be an ordinary guest when my other friends are being my attendants. It wouldn't be right.'

'You just need to take her to one side and explain. I'm sure she'll understand,' said Mum. 'If you find it hard, I'll come over to Victoria Station and do it myself. It's all about having standards. It's about the way we behave and how we appear to other people. It's very important.'

Alison spoke quietly. 'Colette's husband was very keen on how things appeared to other people. For several years, Colette lived in fear of him and nobody had any idea, because outwardly everything looked just the way it should. We were all taken in by his performance. But in terms of social standards, they looked like the perfect couple.'

'I'm not saying she hasn't suffered—'

'Mum, you're right,' Alison went on. 'It is about standards.'

'Oh, good,' breathed Mum. 'I knew you'd see sense.'

'What I see, Mum, is another standard: that decent people stick by their friends through thick and thin. I'm sorry if it upsets you, I truly am, but I hope you can see this matter from the standard of being a loyal friend rather than the standard of what the neighbours will say. Colette is my friend and I want her to be one of my matrons of honour. And don't forget,' Alison added with a smile, 'I learned my standards from you and Dad.'

Joan sat on the bus, heading once again for Hunts Bank. She felt both hopeful and determined. She had put the disappointment of not being appointed to the new welfare position well and truly behind her and now wanted to put her best foot forward. After Bob had advised her to 'show 'em what you're made of' the Friday before last, she'd written to Miss Emery requesting an appointment and now, at the start of this new week, she was on her way. She knew Miss Emery thought well of her. That had been plain both when they'd discussed the new post and also when Miss Emery had come to Torbay Road to offer her apology. Now Joan needed Miss Emery to know that she was definitely still looking for a way to return to working on the railways.

At Hunts Bank, Joan presented herself at the little window that gave on to the reception office to announce her arrival. The receptionist checked the diary.

'Miss Emery is expecting you, Mrs Hubble. I'll have you taken upstairs.'

'No need.' Joan smiled. 'I know my way. I used to work here,' she couldn't help adding.

She was still smiling as she ran lightly up the stairs and made her way to Miss Emery's alcove-office, where she found Miss Emery seated at her desk, reading something and making notes in pencil at the side.

Miss Emery looked up. 'Good morning, Mrs Hubble. I'm pleased to see you. Would you like to hang up your coat and take a seat? I'll be with you in one minute.'

It felt welcoming to be invited to hang up her own coat, as if she belonged here. That was a promising start. Joan sat in the other chair and waited. After a few moments, Miss Emery looked round.

'Thank you for waiting. I'll lock this report away and then we can pop along to an office I've arranged to borrow so we can talk privately.'

She took Joan to an office further down the corridor and around the corner.

When they were settled, Miss Emery said, 'I've been given the office for the rest of the morning, but I do need to keep an eye on the time as I'm expecting someone else. I was pleased to receive your letter. It's good to know that you weren't put off by your unsuccessful application.'

'I would have loved that job, obviously,' said Joan, 'but my main aim is to work on the railways. I was very happy here and I'd like to come back.'

'Good.' Miss Emery smiled in that restrained, professional way she had. Joan had never seen her let rip with a huge grin. 'Not all vacancies have to be applied for. The welfare post did because it was new and it required particular skills. Also, to be frank, it was important to establish it as a real job, for want of a better word. In other railway companies, they have only one woman acting as welfare officer and those ladies must be rushed off their feet. LMS has always been unusual in having an assistant welfare officer as well. When the decision was made to bring in a third person, there was some . . .'

'Resistance?' Joan suggested.

'Let's say that questions were asked in high places. Hence the thorough selection process. The good news is that your previous application letter and interview can be used towards a suitable post.'

'You mean I wouldn't have to apply again?' That would be a relief.

'No, you wouldn't. With existing jobs, it's standard practice simply to transfer people. As long as we can find a position for you quite quickly, I can justify using your welfare application and interview, plus your previous experience here, to appoint you.'

'Thank you,' said Joan.

The door opened and in walked Fay Brewer.

'I'm so sorry,' she said. 'I thought you'd have finished, Miss Emery. My mistake. I do apologise.'

Joan looked at her. She had only seen her with her hat on before and now she was able to see her hair properly. Frankly, it was gorgeous, thick and glossy and a really unusual dark red. Did Miss Brewer recognise her from the interview waiting room? Joan hoped not.

'I'll come back later,' Miss Brewer said to Miss Emery.

'No, please come in,' Miss Emery replied. 'This is Mrs Joan Hubble, who used to work on Victoria Station before she left when she became a mother.'

'Congratulations,' said Miss Brewer.

'Max is well over a year old now,' said Joan, 'and it's high time I came back. And – congratulations to you too on becoming the new welfare clerk.' *It's time to show 'em what you're made of, Mrs Hubble.* 'I – I tried for the post myself, but the word on the station is that you romped home.'

'Thanks,' said Miss Brewer. 'I recognise you from the day of the interview.'

Thank heaven she had offered her congratulations.

'Just one thing,' Miss Brewer added. 'I'm not the welfare clerk.'

For one wild moment, Joan imagined that Miss Brewer had somehow ended up in a different post, leaving the way free for Joan to work in welfare—

'With Miss Brewer's knowledge and experience,' said Miss Emery, 'it didn't seem appropriate for her to be just a clerk. Therefore she is our new welfare support officer.'

'Oh.' Joan swallowed. 'Well – congratulations again.'

Miss Brewer nodded her acknowledgement.

'Miss Brewer,' said Miss Emery, 'Mrs Hubble is anxious to return to work on the railways. If I furnish you with her work record, please could you find her a suitable position?'

A couple of evenings later, Joan hosted a toymaking session upstairs in Torbay Road. It was the middle of October now and although the days were often fine, the evenings and nights were distinctly chilly. Bob was out at work and Joan was looking forward to having her friends round. When all of them got together, it was normally either in the buffet or at Wilton Close, so having them at her house felt like a treat.

'Where's young Mr Maxwell?' asked Persephone.

'Fast asleep,' said Joan.

'Just as well,' chuckled Dot. 'He's old enough to be more than a bit interested in what we're up to.'

Joan had made a couple of jam jars of flour-and-water paste. Emily produced a pot of Gloy to loud cheers.

'The real thing,' said Colette. 'I don't remember the last time I used proper glue.'

They started off by making crackers, following instructions in a copy of *Vera's Voice* that Dot had brought with her.

'I had a go at home,' said Dot. 'They're a bit fiddly to start with, but you'll soon get the hang of doing them. You roll up a strip of card, cover it in crepe paper and twist the ends tightly. There won't be a "crack" inside, of course.'

'That won't matter,' said Cordelia. 'The children will love shouting "bang!" They'll probably enjoy that more than if they had proper crackers.'

'And Jimmy and his mates came up with some jokes to pop inside them,' said Dot.

'Proper cracker jokes, I hope,' said Alison. 'The sort that make you groan.'

'Knock-knock jokes mainly,' said Dot.

'When we've made the crackers,' said Alison, 'I've got a bag of beads that my auntie Stella found on the market, so we can make some bracelets and necklaces as well.'

They chatted as they worked.

'Holly,' Persephone said to Alison. 'You were hoping to decorate the church with holly and I said Darley Court might be able to help. Well, we can indeed. There are two types on the estate – dark green with berries and green-and-yellow variegated. You're welcome to lots of both.'

'That's wonderful,' breathed Alison. 'What with this and the promise of the Christmas decorations for the church hall, I feel quite overwhelmed. Miss Brown is so generous.'

'What would we do without Darley Court?' said Colette. 'Or rather, what would we do without Miss Brown?'

'Look how she let us have the children's Christmas party there last year,' Margaret said appreciatively.

'Not to mention not one but two Christmas dances,' Cordelia added.

'And all three events were held on the same day too,' Joan remembered. 'It took a lot of organising.'

'We've got Cordelia to thank for that,' said Dot, which made Emily look proudly at her mother.

'I couldn't have done it without all my friends,' said Cordelia.

'And I wouldn't be able to have the wedding I want without the help of my friends,' said Alison.

Dot laughed. 'Don't let your mum hear you say that.'

'It's true,' said Alison. 'Look at all of us here now. You're all joining in so that Joel and I can have our wish of providing presents for local children and children in hospital at Christmas.'

'It's our pleasure,' Cordelia assured her. 'It's lovely to know that you both want to share the happiness of your wedding with the children.'

'At Christmas too,' Emily added. 'That makes it more special.'

'It's all part of us being friends,' said Joan. 'It's nice to think of all those children benefiting from our friendship.'

'Just like they did on the orphanage activity day back in the spring,' said Emily.

'It makes you realise,' Margaret mused. 'Our friendship isn't just for us. It makes a difference to other people too.'

'We all owe a debt of gratitude to Miss Emery,' said Alison.

'True,' said Dot. 'She brought us all together in the first place, but we owe our gratitude to someone else an' all.'

'Who?' asked Colette.

Dot smiled. 'Mrs Jessop, of course. It was all very well Miss Emery telling us to be pally, but how easy would it have been without Mrs Jessop saying we could keep our notebook under the buffet counter so we could arrange our meetings? Cordelia said, "What would we do without Darley Court?" and she's right. But I also reckon, what would we do without Mrs Jessop?'

'Hear, hear,' said Persephone.

'Very true,' said Colette.

'I think we should do something special for Mrs Jessop,' said Alison. 'I know I shouldn't really ask it of you when you're all working on making things to give to children to celebrate my wedding, but do you think we could do something for Mrs Jessop as well?'

'It would be perfect,' said Emily.

'Yes, it would,' said Margaret.

'What, though?' asked Cordelia.

Alison smiled and her eyes shone. 'Let's decorate the buffet for Christmas.'

'Yes, let's,' said Persephone.

'It's a lovely idea,' said Dot. 'What with?' Trust Dot to be practical.

'Paper chains,' said Emily. 'If we start collecting paper now, we'll be able to make plenty.'

Cordelia nodded. 'Simple but effective.'

'That's a good idea, Emily,' said Colette, smiling at the younger girl.

Joan smiled too. It sounded perfect. Dot was right. They owed so much to dear Mrs Jessop and this would be more than a way of thanking her. It would be something to bring a spot of Christmas cheer to her many customers.

Chapter Twenty-Two

After Lydia had made the suggestion about Alison borrowing Joan's wedding dress, Alison gave herself plenty of time to think it over. She felt very drawn to the idea, but didn't want to be hasty. Her wedding dress had to be perfect. In the week that followed, the war news was good. Italy had declared war on Germany and Alison felt her own small part in the eventual invasion of Europe coming a step closer. Another piece of good news was that twenty-eight million tons of oranges had arrived in the UK from South Africa and all children under sixteen were going to be allocated up to two pounds, depending on how old they were. Joan was thrilled.

'The things that make us happy in wartime,' she said. 'We all took oranges for granted before the war.'

When Mr Mortimer sent for Alison, she knew at once it must be in connection with the trip Mr Samuels had organised, supposedly to train up new station announcers. She was going to be away from home for the whole of the final week of October.

'Your week away will be of great importance to you, Miss Lambert,' Mr Mortimer told her. 'I hope that what you learn will be of benefit and support to you in the future. After you come back, you will be moved out of your position as a station announcer and will start working in onward travel.

When the call comes for the railways to begin the process that will, God willing, end with the liberation of Europe, I want Victoria Station's response to be second to none.'

Which might not have told Alison anything helpful, but definitely underlined the seriousness. She didn't even know where she was going. Her friends naturally assumed that she would be within LMS territory, but Alison was aware she couldn't take that for granted.

She was instructed by Miss Emery to report to Mr Gordon in the ticket office.

'Don't go to a ticket-office window,' said Miss Emery. 'If you walk round the side of the office, you'll find a door. Knock and ask for Mr Gordon.'

His name rang a bell and Alison recalled Colette mentioning him a while ago when Persephone had told their group about a problem with fare-dodgers. She had never noticed the side door before. All she had been aware of was the impressive front of the long ticket office, with its wood panelling gleaming with polish and the line of small windows, each with a shelf beneath onto which the clerks pushed the tickets for passengers to pick up.

Alison found the door she needed without any trouble. She knocked politely and turned the knob, but it was locked. She waited and after a few moments the door opened and a clerk looked out enquiringly.

'I'm here to see Mr Gordon,' said Alison.

The clerk stood aside to let her in, then took her to a small office in one corner of the long room. The door was open and Alison could see in. There was already a lady clerk in there, talking to the man behind the desk, who must be Mr Gordon, a good-looking man in his forties or possibly older, with a high forehead and thinning golden-brown hair. When the lady clerk left the office and Mr Gordon looked her way, Alison saw the intelligence in his eyes. He looked shrewd, but not in an unkind way.

He gave her the tickets and she signed for them. At long last she knew where she was going. London, to start with, and then to various destinations in the south of England.

As well as thinking about her forthcoming trip, Alison had the chance during the week to try on the wedding dresses of a couple of girls at work. Lovely as their gowns were, the more she thought about it, the more she liked the idea of wearing Joan's dress. After all, one reason why she had hoped to borrow Mabel's was precisely because it was Mabel's. She had imagined herself one day showing her wedding pictures to her children and explaining to them about wartime brides borrowing one another's dresses and how her own dress had belonged to her chum Mabel, one of the girls she'd shared digs with.

Now she rearranged those details in her mind to fit in with the new story.

'My wedding dress was previously worn by Auntie Lydia and before that by my friend Joan, who was the very first railway girl I ever met. We had to sit tests in English, maths and geography and Joan and I arrived for the test session at the same time. And before the dress was Joan's, it was in the keeping of another friend called Margaret. She was given it by a friend of hers who joined up, though Margaret never wore it as a wedding dress. She just took care of it. Margaret and I were in the same digs and we shared a bedroom for a while. Knowing this wedding dress was connected to Auntie Lydia, Joan and Margaret made it all the more special to me.'

That in itself was something of a revelation. The Alison who had dreamed of marrying Paul Dunaway would never have settled for anything less than a brand-new gown, but this more mature Alison was charmed by the thought of a shared dress with its own tale to tell. Perhaps she wouldn't be the last girl to wear it and its story would continue.

Making up her mind, Alison gleefully added her intention to a letter she was writing to Mabel before she popped it in the pillar box.

Talk about bad luck. Unfortunately, because of her shifts, she wasn't free to get round to Torbay Road until after work on Friday. She would only have a few minutes there because of needing to get home to Wilton Close, but she wanted to ask Joan about the dress since her commitments meant this was her last chance to do so before she went away first thing on Monday.

When she rang Joan's doorbell, Alison was ready to burst with excitement. Joan would be thrilled, she knew.

'It's lovely to see you,' said Joan, leading the way upstairs. 'What brings you here? Not that you need a reason.'

'I haven't got long,' said Alison. 'After this I need to dash home and grab a bite to eat, then get changed—'

Joan laughed. 'Don't tell me. Get changed and rush to meet Joel when he comes off shift.'

Alison laughed too. 'You know me so well. I've got something to ask you, something important. Please may I borrow your beautiful wedding dress?'

Joan's lips parted, but instead of exclaiming in joy, she looked – well, dazed was the only word. It definitely wasn't the reaction Alison had anticipated. She tried to laugh it off.

'You don't seem exactly thrilled at the prospect. I thought you'd be pleased.'

'It's not that,' said Joan. 'I think . . . maybe it wouldn't suit you.'

'I don't see why not. It looked lovely on you and Lydia. Why not on me as well?'

'I know you're finding it hard to get a dress. I just don't want you to borrow it out of desperation because you can't find anything better.'

Alison couldn't quite believe what she was hearing. 'If Letitia had lived, wouldn't you have been happy if you and she had worn the same wedding gown? Honestly, to hear you, anyone would think you didn't want me to wear your dress.'

Joan caught hold of Alison's hands. 'Oh, Alison, don't be like that. Of course I can understand why you're drawn to the idea of wearing the same dress as Lydia. I'm just not sure it's the right one for you.'

'There's no time to try it on now,' said Alison, 'and I'm away next week, training up station announcers. Just make sure you've got the dress out of mothballs by the time I get back.'

Margaret arrived home, hungry as a hunter, in the middle of the evening to find Joan sitting with Mrs Cooper and Mrs Grayson. Margaret was pleased to see her.

Mrs Grayson stood up. 'I'll go and get you something to eat, Margaret,' she said.

'Joan has come round to see you,' Mrs Cooper told Margaret. 'Why don't the two of you pop upstairs while Mrs Grayson is in the kitchen?'

'Is everything all right?' Margaret asked Joan.

'I just need to ask you something.'

They went upstairs. Joan shut the bedroom door behind them and took Margaret by surprise by taking both her hands.

'Alison wants to borrow the wedding dress.'

A nasty chilly sensation rippled all down Margaret's spine. She hadn't known what to expect, but she would never have thought of this. Joan tugged her towards the bed and they sat down.

'It was Lydia's idea,' Joan told her. 'You know, two sisters wearing the same dress.'

'And that's what Alison wants,' said Margaret.

'She seems to have set her heart on it,' said Joan. 'She came round to our house earlier to ask. Thank goodness there wasn't time for her to try it on. What are we going to do?'

For a single mad moment, Margaret imagined letting Alison wear the dress, then cringed inwardly at the very idea. It would be the most appalling betrayal of their friendship.

'She can't wear it,' Margaret whispered. 'We can't let her. Oh my godfathers.'

'How are we to talk her out of it?' asked Joan. 'I tried to and she got annoyed. She said it was as if I didn't want her to wear it – which of course I don't, but I couldn't have her realising that.'

'There must be another dress we can get our hands on that she'd like,' said Margaret.

'I wouldn't count on it. She loves the idea of this one. She even said I'd have loved Letitia and me to wear the same dress, so why not her and Lydia?'

Margaret clenched her fists. Her palms were clammy. 'She's not going to be talked out of this, is she?'

Joan shook her head. Her eyes were huge.

'I don't want to tell her the truth,' Margaret said softly.

'I know.'

'Joel and I had the chance to do that last year and we didn't. We thought it was best not to. We just wanted to put it all behind us and never think of it again.' Margaret laughed, a harsh sound. 'That's worked out well, hasn't it?' She shook her head. 'We can't let her wear the dress.' Her muscles tightened as if in readiness. 'I don't want to tell her the truth, but there's nothing for it. We'll have to.'

Margaret had spent the morning avoiding Alison at home. Alison had gone to work during the afternoon and wouldn't return until the early hours, at which point Margaret could pretend to be asleep. That she would be wide awake she did not doubt. She had stayed awake all last night and felt as though she would never shut her eyes again until this painful matter had been . . . had been what? Finished with? Sorted out? How could it possibly be sorted out? Alison was going to be devastated, and rightly so.

Margaret waited now at the hospital for Joel. She had sent him a note saying she needed to see him urgently, though whether he had received it she had no way of knowing.

Perhaps Matron or someone had decided not to trouble him with it, reckoning that his concentration mustn't be disturbed. Margaret heaved a sigh – or tried to, but it was nothing more than a shallow, shaky thread of breath. Alison – the wedding dress—

On the other side of the reception area, one of a pair of double doors swung open and Joel came striding through. Even though his face showed the long hours he had put in that day, his eyes were alert. Margaret came to her feet as he headed straight towards her.

'I was given your note an hour ago, but I couldn't come until now,' Joel said, not giving her a chance to speak. 'What's happened? Is it Alison?'

'She's fine,' Margaret reassured him at once. 'You and I need to talk. It's urgent, Joel, or I wouldn't be here. Are you seeing Alison tomorrow?'

'Just briefly. We're snatching an hour together, then she's away all next week. What's this about?' Joel didn't even pause before he added, 'I can only imagine it's about one thing.'

Margaret nodded.

'*Damn.*'

The word was softly spoken but loaded with the same worry and anguish that Margaret had been battling ever since her conversation with Joan yesterday evening. Joel rubbed the back of his neck, then blew out a couple of short, sharp breaths as if gathering himself.

'Come with me,' he said. 'I've got half an hour, then I have to get back.'

He took her – just like last time – to a small consulting room. Last time it had been a ground-floor room with frosted windows brightened by the spring sunshine. This time it was a room on the first floor and the blackout was in force, but there was still a desk with one chair behind it and two in front, and in the corner a narrow examination bed with a curtain on a ceiling track.

Almost before they had sat down in the two chairs in front of the desk, Joel said, 'Tell me.'

'It's about Alison's wedding dress. She wants to borrow Joan's. Joan wore it when she got married in the June of 1941, and then that September she lent the dress to Lydia, Alison's sister.'

'I know who Lydia is,' Joel said with a trace of impatience.

'Of course you do. I'm sorry. I'm just trying to explain this as fully as I can.' Yes – as fully as she could while missing out the most important detail. 'The problem is that before the dress belonged to Joan, it was mine.'

'Yours?' Joel's surprise was obvious.

Margaret kept her voice steady. 'Yes. I told everyone that it was given to me by a friend who was about to join up. I said she couldn't take it with her and she wanted it to go to a good home. She knew I'd take care of it. And when Joan needed a wedding dress, I gave it to her. That's what I told everyone.'

'I see,' Joel answered slowly. He frowned. 'But that wasn't the truth?'

Margaret wanted to take a deep breath, but stopped herself. Looking as if she needed to prepare herself to speak might make Joel twig that there was more to this than she was about to reveal.

'I bought the dress for myself.'

221

Joel closed his eyes for a moment as he shook his head. 'Now I'm really confused. I didn't know you'd been engaged.'

'I haven't.' Margaret injected brightness into her voice as she said, 'Oh, it was a silly thing, really. A lot of girls did it. Everyone knew the war was going to bring terrible shortages. We weren't supposed to buy extra and hoard it, but people did. You know, a couple of extra tins of peaches or tuna in with the weekly shopping, to be tucked away in the back of the cupboard.'

'Are you telling me that girls hoarded wedding dresses?' Joel was clearly amazed – as well he might be, as Margaret and Joan had conjured this up between them.

'I've already admitted that it was silly, but it happened. The only other person who knows about this is Joan. What matters now is that Alison wants to borrow the dress that I purchased.' Determined that Joel should set aside his bafflement at the notion of hoarding wedding dresses and fix his mind on what mattered, Margaret said in a stronger voice that bore no traces of her deep anxiety, 'Your fiancée wants to wear the dress that was bought by the girl you got into trouble.'

Joel sucked in a breath and scrubbed his face with his palms. When his hands fell from his face, he stared at Margaret, looking drained and dazed.

Margaret's heart clenched. She shook her head and blinked back the tears that welled up. 'We can't let her wear that dress,' she whispered. 'We just can't. It would be a betrayal of her trust.'

'There must be another dress,' Joel insisted.

'She tried on a couple more during the week,' Margaret told him, 'but neither of them was right for her. She's set her heart on wearing the same dress as Lydia. We can't let her do that, not when – not when it used to belong to me.'

'You're right,' said Joel. 'It's one thing to keep the extent of our old relationship a secret. We did that with the best of intentions. But this . . . If Alison had found out the truth about us, I could have explained why we didn't tell her and I could have held my head up while I did it. But if we were to let her wear your wedding dress and *then* the truth somehow came out, I couldn't give her a good, honest reason for letting her wear your dress. You're correct to call it a betrayal of trust.'

He spent a few moments thinking. Margaret watched him, knowing he had to cram into his head everything that she'd been struggling with ever since Joan had dropped her bomb-shell yesterday evening. Well – everything except one crucial detail.

Joel raised her eyes and looked into Margaret's. 'There's nothing for it. I have to tell her, but it'll have to wait until she gets back from this work trip. I can't let her go away with this hanging over her. Besides, I'll only be seeing her for a short while tomorrow, nowhere near long enough to discuss it properly.'

Unease shivered inside Margaret. There would be just over a week to get through before Alison was told – a week of anxiety and regrets. But anything that Margaret felt during that time would be nothing compared to what awaited Alison upon her return.

The only consolation was that she had been able to with-hold the one vital detail.

Chapter Twenty-Three

Alison was deeply put out that Joan hadn't fallen with cries of delight upon her wish to borrow Joan's wedding dress. She was even more put out because she wouldn't be at home to get to the root of the problem. It made her feel disquieted and fidgety not to have her dress situation sorted out. Then she thought back to being told that she wasn't allowed to have her wedding in June so as not to be distracted next spring and summer – and now here she was feeling frustrated and distracted as her winter wedding approached.

She vowed to set aside her wedding worries and concentrate on whatever the week away brought. She anticipated having a lot to learn and intended to do her very best.

Her journey to London on Monday seemed to go on for ever. Several times the train halted for long periods for no obvious reason, which made Alison recall being at that unnamed rural station with Mr Samuels and being shown the extra sidings and buildings tucked away in the woods.

The train was packed solid, but at least she was one of the lucky ones who had a seat all the way to London. It was a different story during the next part of her journey. She had to stand all the way. As the day wore on, she was exhausted and aching all over and felt like sinking to the floor, except that the press of bodies all around her was so great that even if her legs had given way, she would have remained upright.

Her week away involved making various journeys that ranged from the tiresome to the arduous, sleeping fitfully in strange beds and agonising over getting off at the right station.

But that all paled into insignificance as she glimpsed the wartime work of the railways. One night, she was taken to the south coast to see the extraordinary sight of a colossal piece of artillery mounted on a flatbed wagon behind a loco. The gun fired shells across the Channel from one end of a long tunnel, then the loco hauled it to the tunnel's far end so it could fire from there before being returned to the near end to start again.

'It makes Jerry think we have more guns than we've really got,' Alison was told.

She also met some of the railway engineers who had spent the war dealing with emergencies – damage to bridges, tracks and locos – often under aerial bombardment. One of them told her, 'Jerry makes the holes and we fill 'em in again.'

The chap who was her designated guide for the following day took delight in baffling her by announcing they were going to Woolworth's. He took her to somewhere in Hampshire, where 'Woolworth's' turned out to be a vast depot, so called because it could supply nearly everything.

'Spare parts for machine guns and tanks, any kind of medical equipment you care to mention, anything at all that our boys overseas need, it's all right here in these huts. We get requests scribbled on bits of paper from the front line, from back-up positions, from field hospitals. Everything is parcelled up immediately and sent by train to Southampton. Our trains get priority over everything else on the line.'

Alison was amazed, humbled and profoundly impressed. More than anything, she felt patriotic. This was the war work of the railways and she was part of the railways. This made the sacrifice of her June wedding more than worthwhile.

Alison arrived home late on Sunday night. The next day was the first of November.

'Now I can officially say I'm getting married next month,' she announced happily at the breakfast table to Mrs Cooper and Mrs Grayson. Margaret and Sally were on earlies this week and had left ages ago.

'How exciting,' said Mrs Grayson. 'I hope your plans are coming along nicely.'

'Between her WVS work and my wedding, I don't think my mother ever sleeps.'

Mrs Cooper poured Alison another cup of tea. 'Maybe she will have had some luck in finding you a wedding dress while you were away.'

Alison's pleasure dipped, but she kept her smile in place. 'Lydia wondered about Joan's wedding dress.'

'Isn't that the dress Lydia wore?' asked Mrs Grayson.

'How lovely if you both wear the same,' said Mrs Cooper.

'It's not definite,' said Alison, feeling uncomfortable at the memory of Joan's inexplicable lack of enthusiasm. 'I need to check with Joan. I did ask her, but I think it took her by surprise.'

'She'll say yes,' said Mrs Cooper. 'She's bound to.'

'She was happy to lend the dress to Lydia,' Mrs Grayson added.

'I'll get an answer from her in the next day or two.' After all, what problem could there possibly be? Joan was probably kicking herself for not having said yes right away. Alison glanced at the clock. 'I'd better got a move on.'

'Don't forget Joel is meeting you after work,' said Mrs Cooper.

'As if she'd forget that,' said Mrs Grayson.

Happiness bubbled up inside Alison, lending a sensation of lightness to her limbs. Yesterday's journey had dragged on interminably, but every time she'd felt exhaustion begin to swamp her, the thought of seeing Joel again soon had left her rejuvenated.

Now, she spent her day looking forward to the coming evening with her handsome, loving, considerate fiancé.

Joel met her on the crowded concourse after work. Alison had to restrain herself from running into his arms, as she was in uniform and so had to conduct herself with decorum. After they had greeted one another, she nipped into the Ladies to change into her cherry-coloured jumper and wool skirt. Now she really could hurry into Joel's arms.

'Guess what,' she said.

Joel smiled, his eyes warm. 'What?'

'I'm getting married next month.'

'What a coincidence. So am I.'

Alison slid her arm through the crook of his elbow. 'What are we doing this evening?'

'I'd like you to come to my rooms so we can talk,' said Joel.

Alison had never been to his rooms. Joel had been to both her homes, Wilton Close and her parents' house, but she hadn't visited his home because he lived in a bachelor apartment and it wouldn't be respectable for her to go there.

'We can talk anywhere,' she said.

'It's private and I don't want us to be interrupted.'

'Is it to do with the wedding?' Alison asked. 'There's nothing wrong, is there?'

'It isn't about the wedding,' said Joel, steering her towards the taxi rank and giving the driver his address.

'Give me a clue,' said Alison once they were on their way. She said it in a jokey manner.

Joel took her hand. 'Can you hang on until we get there? I don't want to start talking about it now.'

'Should I be worried?'

'Alison, please. I know how unusual this is, but I'm asking you to bear with me.'

She subsided. In spite of the mystery, it was exciting to think of seeing where Joel lived. Exciting – and a bit daring. She felt ultra-aware of being engaged, of being the future Mrs Joel Maitland.

Joel's rooms were in a pair of large Victorian villas that had been knocked together. The accommodation was purely for bachelors, which was why it couldn't be their matrimonial home. Each floor in the building had a landlady, which in this case was short for 'landing-lady'. The apartments were service flats and each landlady did the cooking and cleaning for the rooms on her own landing.

Inside Joel's front door was a hallway with a coat stand and extra pegs on the wall. Joel hung up their coats, then opened one of four doors leading off the hall and Alison entered his sitting room. She looked around with interest, noting the smart furniture, the bookcase, the gramophone and the sideboard with decanters on top.

'Is the furniture yours?' she asked.

'It's a furnished flat,' Joel told her.

'Shame. The sideboard would have looked good in our new home.'

Joel smiled. 'We can't have the sideboard, but we can have what's on top.'

'The decanters and glasses.'

'They were a house-warming present from Venetia and Larry,' said Joel. 'I'd offer you a drink, but the booze ran out long ago and I haven't been able to buy more – not through legal means, anyhow.'

'Never mind.'

'Have a seat.'

Alison sat on the settee, surprised when, instead of sitting next to her, Joel chose the armchair. Maybe he was maintaining a respectable distance.

'What have you brought me here to discuss?' Alison asked him. Her pulse was starting to speed.

Joel hesitated, swallowing hard and pressing his lips together.

'Whatever it is, you don't seem eager to talk about it,' said Alison.

Joel sat forward. His blue eyes, which were so often bright with laughter, were sombre.

'Alison, I'm sorry. I have something serious to tell you. First of all, let me say that I love you with all my heart and I hope you'll understand and forgive me.'

Alison's heart thudded inside her chest. 'What is it? Tell me.'

'There's no easy way to say this, so I'll just have to come right out with it. You know that Margaret and I went out together a few times early on in the war.'

'Yes,' said Alison. 'She told me that last year after I came home from Leeds.'

'And you also know that I once got a girl in the family way,' said Joel.

'Yes,' Alison said again. Was Joel about to bring up that conversation where she'd admitted to having been ratty about Sally? It was the only thing Alison could think of.

'What I never told you,' said Joel, 'is that the girl it happened to . . . was Margaret.'

Alison felt disoriented. 'No,' she said, rejecting the idea. She must have misheard. It sounded as if Joel had said—

'I'm sorry, but it's true,' Joel said quietly. 'Margaret was the girl who had the miscarriage.'

'*No.*' The word burst from Alison's lips. 'No,' she repeated, followed incredulously by, 'Margaret? My Margaret? My *friend* Margaret?'

'She wasn't your friend when it happened,' said Joel. 'It was long before you met her – and before you met me.'

'Oh, well, that's all right then,' Alison flared bitterly.

'I know this is a shock.'

'Why didn't you tell me before?' Alison demanded. 'You could have told me last year. Last *year* – and you're only telling me now.'

'I don't want there to be secrets between us,' said Joel.

'Really?' Alison was scathing. 'You're finally telling me so that there aren't any secrets. It's funny, but I seem to recall you saying precisely that when you owned up to having got a girl pregnant. Correct me if I'm wrong,' she taunted him, 'but on that occasion didn't you fail to mention that the girl in question was my friend? So much for not keeping secrets.'

'I know how bad this looks, Alison. Believe me, I do understand. Last year, when we decided not to tell you—'

'Whoa!' Alison exclaimed. 'Hang on a minute. You said, "when *we* decided". Do you mean to tell me that you and Margaret got together and decided what you would and wouldn't say to me?'

'Yes,' Joel admitted, 'though you make it sound callous and it certainly wasn't that.'

'So why didn't you tell me?'

'Partly it was to protect Margaret's privacy,' said Joel. 'She was entitled to that.'

Alison knew Joel was right, but she still felt as if cold water had been dashed over her. 'What about me? Wasn't I entitled to anything?'

Joel looked her straight in the eye. 'You were entitled to be protected. We knew how much it would hurt and upset you and we both wanted to avoid that.'

'And it conveniently fitted in with protecting Margaret's privacy.'

What a catty thing to say. But it was so hard to take this in. It was unbelievable. And to think that at the time, she'd been grateful – *grateful* – that the pregnant former girlfriend hadn't been Rachel Chambers, the girl Venetia had tried to ease back into Joel's affections. All along it was Margaret. *Margaret*.

Joel's face had stiffened at Alison's words, but now he nodded. 'It seemed the best outcome for both of you.'

'And presumably for you too,' said Alison. 'It saved you from having to face an awkward conversation with me.'

'I did have the awkward conversation, as you call it,' Joel said firmly. 'I told you all about the pregnant girl and the miscarriage, and how I hadn't known anything about the pregnancy or the miscarriage because I was away in Leeds. The only detail I missed out was Margaret's identity. That was the choice Margaret and I made, to protect her reputation and your feelings. Whether we were right or wrong is a matter of opinion, but you can't blame Margaret for wanting to keep her identity quiet.'

Alison was silent. She was still struggling to comprehend all the ramifications. Much as she might resist the thought that Joel and Margaret had been in any measure at all in the right, she had to admit to herself that she understood why Margaret had been anxious to maintain her anonymity. Any girl would want that.

Joel said, 'Margaret and I – what I mean to say is, it happened just the once.'

'I don't want to hear this. I listened to you last year, and then again when we talked at the Claremont, but that was different. That was before I knew that – that—'

'Please,' said Joel. 'It's important that you keep in mind that it happened once and only once, when we'd both had one too many. It wasn't – it wasn't a love affair.' He came to kneel in front of her, but didn't try to touch her. 'You're the girl I love. You're the only one I've ever wanted to spend my life with. I've never wanted to marry anybody else. You know that, don't you?'

Alison swept away some tears. She had to be strong to negotiate her way through this conversation.

'Why tell me now?' she asked. 'If you kept it from me before so as to preserve my feelings, why hurt me now?'

'Because things have changed.'

'What has?' Alison asked sharply.

'Joan's wedding dress.'

Alison's thoughts seemed to freeze, then all at once they raced in a dozen different directions.

'It used to belong to Margaret,' said Joel.

Alison delved into her memory. 'Yes. It was given to her by a girl who joined up – *oh*.' Alison went cold as realisation sank in. The dress Lydia had worn, the dress Alison had wanted to wear specifically because Lydia had worn it, had, before it belonged to Joan, belonged to Margaret – the girl Joel had got in the family way.

'Actually, the dress wasn't given to Margaret by a friend. She bought it for herself.'

'What? I didn't know she was ever engaged.'

'She wasn't. She bought the dress as a sort of investment. Apparently other girls did the same thing. You know, hoarding in case of need.'

'Well! It's the first I've heard of such a thing.' The chill that washed through Alison was evident in her voice. 'But, yes, I can see how tasteless it would be to let me wear that dress.'

'Joan and Margaret were beside themselves when you asked to borrow it,' Joel told her. 'For you to wear a wedding dress that had once been Margaret's property, when Margaret was the girl who—'

'You don't have to spell it out,' Alison snapped. 'Oh, my stars.'

'They felt it would be a kind of betrayal to let you wear a dress that had once belonged to Margaret before she passed it along to Joan.'

Alison fought with this new idea. Then her thoughts zinged into sharp focus.

'Joan knows about you and Margaret? *Joan* does?'

Joel nodded. 'Yes. Margaret confided in her last year.'

'So it's not just you and Margaret. It's Joan as well.'

'Margaret needed support,' said Joel. 'She had to face that pregnancy all alone back in 1940. She didn't know what had made me leave Manchester so suddenly after she and I had spent the night together. At the beginning of last year, when she saw you and me together, she thought I was a cad who'd seduced her and gone on my merry way. She was appalled to think I was your new boyfriend. She wanted to warn you against getting involved with me, but at the same time she dreaded telling you about her and me. Then you were sent away to Leeds and it gave her a chance to decide what to do. It was a difficult time for her. As I said, she needed support.'

'And she turned to Joan.'

Alison tried to make sense of it. Had her friends been lying to her all this time – or had they been protecting her? No, she didn't need to ask. They'd had her best interests at heart and she knew it, but that didn't stop her feeling sore. She couldn't decide if they'd been right to withhold the truth from her, but she knew they had done it for the right reasons.

'So it was time for you to come clean,' Alison said to Joel. How hard her voice sounded. Well, she felt hard. This had tilted her whole world sideways. 'You're only telling me this now because Joan and Margaret made you. If I hadn't asked to wear Joan's dress, this would never have happened.'

A flush stained Joel's countenance. 'That's true – except for the part about me being made to do it. You make it sound as if they backed me into a corner and held a gun to my head.'

'Didn't they?' Anger was starting to bubble up. 'Last year, you told me about your conveniently nameless girlfriend. You drip-fed me as much of the truth as it suited you to provide. You'd never have admitted that the girl was Margaret if this business with the dress hadn't happened – would you?'

'No, I wouldn't,' Joel said quietly.

'You thought you were going to get away with it.'

'It wasn't a question of getting away with it,' said Joel. 'I wanted to be honest with you—'

'Up to a point,' Alison chimed in.

'—and I also wanted to spare you the hurt of knowing that the girl later went on to become your friend. I also wanted to spare Margaret from having another person who knew what happened to her. I make no apology for that. It was the least I could do for her.'

'How very gallant,' Alison said sarcastically.

'Margaret and I acted for the best when we decided not to name her. But now, with you wanting to wear that wedding dress – well, she and Joan couldn't let you do that.'

'So while I've been away from home, doing my duty—' She stopped, then remembered to say, 'While I've been training up new station announcers, this was going on behind my back.' Thoughts rattled around inside Alison's head. 'Margaret came to see you last week, did she?'

Joel drew in a breath. 'Actually, it was before you went away.'

'*What*?'

'Only just before. She sat in a hospital waiting room for hours on the Saturday until I was available. You went away on the Monday.'

'So we could have had this conversation before I went.'

'There wasn't enough time. We only had an hour together on the Sunday before you left. I decided to leave it until you came back. I didn't want you to be upset while you were away from home.'

'How considerate of you,' Alison said crisply. 'I can hardly believe what I've heard. You and Margaret. What am I meant to make of that? You and Margaret,' she said again, but it didn't matter how many times she said it. It didn't make it any more credible. Joel and Margaret. *Margaret*.

'I know you're shocked,' said Joel.

'Flabbergasted, more like. Stunned. Aghast.'

She stood up. She had no idea she was going to do it. She just found herself on her feet. Joel stood as well. When he attempted to reach for her, Alison moved away.

'I want to go home. I need to think about this.'

Joel asked, 'Are we . . .?'

'I don't know,' said Alison. 'I honestly don't know.'

Chapter Twenty-Four

Joel got a taxi for Alison and insisted on giving her the money for her fare and a tip. Alison travelled home feeling fluttery and disoriented. She didn't know what to think. Sally's pregnancy had brought her old feelings to the surface and made her appreciate that the accidental pregnancy in Joel's past had upset her far more than she'd let herself be aware of, which was why she had come down so hard on Sally. Once she'd accepted the truth behind her angry reaction, it had not only softened her towards Sally, but had also enabled her to set aside the hurt and disappointment linked to Joel and his old flame.

But now – now – Joel's past had returned with a vengeance and this time it was much worse. Last year, Joel and Margaret had owned up – eventually – to having gone out together for a short spell ages ago, but that was all they'd said and Alison had accepted it at face value. More fool her. And they would have let matters rest like that, except for her wanting to wear the same wedding dress as Lydia, the dress they all thought of as belonging to Joan, though actually she had received it from Margaret. And now it turned out that Margaret had bought the dress for herself in case she should ever need it.

A bitter taste invaded Alison's mouth. How was she supposed to cope with this? She didn't know what she wanted to do. Pain swept through her at the thought of her precious wedding possibly being in jeopardy.

At least she wouldn't have to face Mrs Cooper and Mrs Grayson when she arrived home. They would have already gone out to their knitting circle. Maybe she should keep the taxi waiting while she stormed in and packed her belongings. She could get the driver to take her to her parents' house. That would teach Margaret a lesson. Let her explain *that* to the ladies when they came home. But arriving unannounced on Mum and Dad's doorstep would trigger a hundred questions, not one of which Alison could bear to answer. No, she was well and truly stuck in Wilton Close.

She paid the driver and stood on the pavement. In the cold November evening, the house was a large shape of deeper darkness in the blackout, but Alison's mind filled with how they had all congregated in the front garden in June for Mabel's pre-wedding photos. Mabel had worn Joan's dress on that happy occasion. Wearing it had been a piece of fun, but underneath the fun it had been deeply meaningful, because it meant that those friends who couldn't attend her wedding were able to see her in a wedding gown. It also provided Mabel with very special additional pictures for her album.

They had all mucked in so as to make Mabel's wartime wedding as memorable as they could, but now Alison's was blighted by what had happened in the past between her fiancé and her friend.

Throwing open the gate, Alison marched up the path, banging the gate shut behind her. The front door opened before she got there. Margaret stood in the doorway, her face pale and anxious against the unlit hallway behind her. She stood aside and Alison swept past her, muscles tense and her pulse speeding.

As Alison turned to confront her, Margaret said hastily, 'I know you must be angry, but please keep your voice down. Sally's in the front room. She's dozed off.'

Without a word, Alison entered the dining room. Once again, she turned to face Margaret.

'How could you lie to me all this time?' she demanded.

'I didn't actually tell lies—'

'Don't give me that! You lied – you both did. Not saying something can be just as much of a lie as telling a rotten great whopper, and you know it.'

'I'm sorry.' Margaret's voice was quiet. 'Joel and I agreed not to tell you about the baby because—'

Alison waved a dismissive hand. 'I've heard it all from him. You didn't want to hurt me, blah blah blah. Oh yes, and let's not forget your reputation. We can't have that sullied, can we? No wonder you took Sally's side so determinedly. You see yourself in her.'

'Shh . . . please,' Margaret begged. 'Not so loud.'

'Is that all you care about? Me keeping my voice down? Let me tell you what I care about. I care about discovering that my fiancé and my friend got sloshed one night and ended up making a baby.'

'Don't!' Margaret exclaimed. 'You make it sound sordid and it wasn't. It was a mistake. We got carried away.'

'*Yes*,' said Alison, making a meal out of the word. 'I re-member a conversation you and I had just after Joel told me about the mystery girl he'd got in the family way. You said then that people could get carried away. Little did I know you were speaking from experience. I was trying to get to grips with what Joel had told me and you helped me.' A laugh escaped her, even though laughing was the last thing she felt like doing. 'No wonder you helped. It was in your interests, wasn't it?'

'I remember that conversation,' Margaret said in a tight voice. 'I was scared at first in case Joel had told you it was me. He'd said he wouldn't, but . . .' She shook her head. 'Then I realised you didn't know.'

'What a relief that must have been,' Alison said with false sweetness.

'You're right. It was a relief. But it was also a chance for me to be a good friend to you. That was what I wanted, what I tried to be. It was what you deserved.'

'Just so long as you avoided the truth, eh?'

'Stop it – please.' Although she sounded anguished, Margaret's voice remained quiet. 'You've every right to be upset. But *I* was upset when I realised you were Joel's new girlfriend. I agonised over whether to tell you. At that point I thought Joel had abandoned me on purpose. I thought he was – well, I thought he was as bad as we all think Sally's boyfriend is now. I thought you should be warned against him – but I held back because I was ashamed of what had happened to me. I wanted to keep it private.'

For the second time that evening, and still against her will, Alison had to concede – though not out loud – that she understood Margaret's need for privacy.

Then Margaret spoiled it by saying, 'If you'd been in my position—'

That was too much. 'I'd never be in your position,' Alison flared, 'because I don't get drunk and sleep around.'

Margaret's lips parted on a gasp and her hazel eyes widened. 'How *could* you say that? I've never . . . I made one mistake. *One!* And I paid the highest possible price. I found out I was having a baby. I believed I'd been abandoned. I was terrified. I had no one to turn to. My mother had died some years before and my sister had been evacuated. Can you imagine what that was like?'

It was on the tip of Alison's tongue to repeat the remark that she didn't need to because it would never happen to her, but no matter how angry and betrayed she felt, she couldn't be so harsh in the face of Margaret's evident distress.

'And then – and then I miscarried. Our house was badly damaged in an air raid. I was trapped in the cellar and – and—' The words were choked off as Margaret fought with her emotions. Her voice dropped to a whisper. 'I don't know what I'd have done if Joan hadn't been there.'

'Joan was there?' said Alison. 'That's how she found out about you and Joel.'

'Not Joel specifically. I never told her about him until – until I'd seen him with you and I was trying to decide what to do for the best.'

'Clearly, Joan's advice didn't involve telling me the truth.'

'We didn't know what to do,' said Margaret. 'Remember, this was when I still believed Joel had cleared off and left me. We wanted to warn you – but I couldn't bear to share my secret. In the end, Joan thought of asking Dot.'

'*Dot*! She knows too?' cried Alison. 'Dear heaven, am I the only person who *didn't* know?'

Margaret huffed out a long breath. 'Nobody else knows. Believe me, I never wanted Joan or Dot to know. I never wanted *any*one to know. But circumstances were such that I had to confide in them.'

'Presumably, Dot also said to keep the truth from me.' Alison's sense of betrayal was growing by the minute.

'Actually, no. Joan and I were fixated on whether to tell you, but Dot said I should talk to Joel, and she was right. It was the first time we'd spoken since the night we got drunk. That was when I found out he hadn't left me in the lurch.' With sudden vigour, Margaret went on. 'If you feel shocked now, Alison, believe me, I know exactly how that feels. I'd spent two years thinking the worst of Joel when really it hadn't happened that way at all. He hadn't run for the hills to get away from me. He'd been spirited off by the army to do special training in severe burns and serious injuries likely to be sustained in air raids. He was in Leeds after that. He did try later to get in touch with me, but the mail train was hit in a raid. He even came back to Manchester to our house, but it was an abandoned wreck. Someone sent him up the road to where Dad and I had been billeted, but I'd long gone. The lady of the house hated having me there because of me being a scarlet woman.' Margaret uttered a bitter laugh. 'Did I say Joan and Dot are the only ones who know my secret? They're the only ones who know about Joel, but all my old neighbours know about the miscarriage. Mrs McEvoy couldn't stand having me under her roof, so I left.'

Was that when she had moved into the grotty bedsit? Alison had never seen it, but Joan had spoken of it as if Margaret had needed rescuing. Margaret had always said how happy and grateful she was to move into Wilton Close, taking Joan's place after she left to marry Bob.

'There you are,' said Margaret. 'That's everything.'

'It's a bit late to tell me now,' said Alison. 'You should have told me last year. I had a right to know.'

'And I had a right to my privacy,' Margaret shot back.

Heat flushed through Alison. Margaret should be grovelling, not sticking up for herself.

'You'd never have told me if Lydia hadn't suggested Joan's dress,' said Alison. 'Or *your* dress, should I say? Honestly!' She could almost feel the scorn seeping out through her skin. 'Fancy buying a wedding dress just in case. I've never heard anything so ridiculous in my entire life.'

Margaret went very still. 'It didn't happen like that. That was something Joan and I made up because we had to be certain Joel would see how impossible it was for you to wear the dress. It having passed briefly through my hands might not have seemed like a compelling reason.'

Alison's breath caught in her chest. This whole evening was becoming stranger by the minute. She felt trapped.

Margaret continued, her voice steady. 'I didn't buy it before the war. I didn't hoard it on the off chance of getting married.' The tip of her tongue ran across her upper lip. 'I bought it during the phoney war. I saw it and fell in love with it and bought it. I knew it was a mad thing to do, but that didn't stop me, because supposing I'd left it in the shop and another girl had come along and bought it. I couldn't take that risk. I – I thought I was going to get married, you see.'

Now Alison was even more confused. 'So you *did* have a reason to buy it.' A chap in the forces? A man who'd copped it at Dunkirk?

'You don't have to have a ring on your finger to believe you're on the way to getting married. I was so sure . . .' Were those tears in Margaret's eyes? A chill trickled through Alison. Did Margaret mean . . .? Could she possibly mean . . .?

'I worshipped Joel,' Margaret told her. 'And I really and truly believed I would end up married to him. That's why it felt right to buy the dress – and that's the real reason why you had to be prevented from wearing it.'

Margaret was exhausted. She had known that talking to Alison would be challenging, but she hadn't appreciated she would end up feeling like a wrung-out dishcloth.

Afterwards, Alison had gone for a walk, clearly not caring about the dark or the cold.

'I need to be alone' was all she'd said, darting an angry look in Margaret's direction.

Margaret had taken that as her cue to go to bed early so she could pretend to be asleep when Alison returned. It was a beastly nuisance that they had to share a room. How were they going to cope with that?

Before she went upstairs, Margaret looked into the front room. Sally wasn't there. She must have gone to bed while Alison and Margaret were talking. Talking? Locked in conflict, more like. Sally had been getting tired recently. Margaret silently opened Sally's bedroom door and peered in, hearing

244

Sally's steady breathing. She dearly hoped that things would work out as well as possible for her.

Sally was to move into Rookery House tomorrow. Mrs Cooper was going to take her. Until now, Margaret had wished she could be the one to accompany Sally, but now it was a relief not to. It was bound to be emotional and Margaret wasn't sure she would have been up to it. She would miss having Sally here in Wilton Close.

She got ready for bed and lay awake, waiting for the sheets to warm up. She'd forgotten to prepare a hot-water bottle, but she didn't like to creep downstairs and make one in case Alison returned. She couldn't face her again so soon. Thank goodness they were on different shifts tomorrow. Margaret would be getting up early, leaving Alison in bed, no doubt feigning sleep.

Emotion swelled inside Margaret and tears rose behind her eyes, but she refused to shed them. However distressing this was for her, it was a hundred times worse for Alison.

She tried to put herself in Alison's position. It wasn't just the shock of knowing the truth. It was the thought that the man she loved and her friend had kept a secret from her. And not just one of her friends, but three. They had all decided that Margaret's privacy trumped telling Alison the truth. That was how it must seem to Alison.

Margaret shuddered. Could their friendship survive this? Could Alison and Joel survive this?

Chapter Twenty-Five

Joan tapped a curled knuckle against her mouth. Margaret had told her that Joel was going to admit the truth to Alison about the baby on Monday evening, and that she would stay at home so as to be there when Alison came back. Now it was Tuesday evening and Joan had spent all day fretting over what might have happened.

When the doorbell rang, she flew to answer it. Fortunately, it was second nature to check the hall light was switched off before pulling back the floor-length curtain that covered the door. Otherwise she would have broken the blackout in her hurry. Margaret slid inside and Joan reinstated the precautions.

'How did it go?' she asked at once.

'Who is it?' Gran called.

'It's for me,' Joan called back.

Usually, when one of her friends came round, Joan would take her into Gran's parlour for a few minutes, but this time she took Margaret straight upstairs. Max was in bed and Bob was at work. They sat on the hearthrug in the sitting room, close to the fire. There wasn't much coal. This had once been the master bedroom, which was why it had a fireplace.

Joan gazed at Margaret, who looked like she might cry. Joan's heart melted. She cared deeply for Margaret, partly because of the tough hand life had dealt her. She cared for

Alison, too, and hated to imagine the wall that might now exist between them.

'Was it horrid?' Joan asked. 'Of course it was. Stupid question.'

'I don't know if I've made things worse.'

'How so?'

'Alison obviously intended to wipe the floor with me. I think I was supposed to stand there and take it.'

'But you didn't?' Joan prompted gently.

'I was trying to explain everything to her, but I think it came out less as me explaining and more as me fighting back.'

Joan nodded slowly, unsure what to say.

Closing her eyes, Margaret breathed in deeply, then tipped her head back to release the breath. 'Joan, it was beastly. Poor Alison was in a real state. Do you think Joel and I should have told her the whole truth last year?' She didn't wait for an answer. 'But we had good reasons not to, or we thought we did.'

'You must stop thinking like that,' said Joan. 'You acted for the best for Alison and also for you.'

'That's the trouble,' said Margaret. 'As far as Alison can see, I'm the one who benefited because my secret was preserved.'

'Couldn't she see that you and Joel wanted to protect her from being hurt?'

Margaret shrugged heavily. 'I don't think she cares about that. She said she had the right to be told. She made me feel so guilty for not telling her before.'

'You couldn't tell her then,' Joan replied staunchly. 'Having a pregnancy out of wedlock simply isn't something you tell. I just wish you hadn't had to share it with Alison now.'

'Oh, that blasted dress,' Margaret exclaimed. 'I wish I'd never clapped eyes on it.'

'How did you leave things with her?' Joan asked.

'I told her the whole story, including why I'd bought the dress. She was . . . stunned. She went out. I don't think she could bear to be with me a moment longer. I'm going to keep out of her way as much as I can. I just hope that Mrs Cooper doesn't twig that something's up. You know what a love she is. She'd be certain to try to help.'

'Well, if you need a bolt-hole . . .'

Margaret smiled and for the first time since she'd arrived, Joan saw her eyes soften.

'Thanks,' said Margaret. 'I knew yesterday was going to be bad, but I had no idea how bad.'

Joan gave her a hug. 'All we can do is wait and hope Alison can come to terms with it.'

The following morning, Joan put on the smart grey jacket and skirt Alison had lent her. Today she was due to see Miss Brewer to find out about the job she was to be assigned to. She took Max to Wilton Close to be taken care of by Mrs Grayson.

'I'm delighted you're going to have a job at last,' said Mrs Grayson. 'I was concerned you might change your mind after you weren't given that post you'd set your heart on – and then I wouldn't have the chance to look after this handsome young man.'

'I hope he won't wear you out,' said Joan.

'We'll be fine,' said Mrs Grayson. 'It's not as though I'll be having him full-time. We'll have a grand time together, won't we, Max?'

Joan dropped a kiss on top of her son's head. She felt like scooping him up for an enormous hug, but didn't want to make a big thing of leaving him.

She caught the bus from the terminus. On the way, she gazed out of the window at the wartime landscape of public shelters, which had played such an essential role when air raids had taken place night after night, and the rows of houses in the middle of which sat demolished buildings that had taken direct hits. Everybody was so accustomed to being surrounded by evidence of destruction that nobody batted an eyelid. An urgent need swept through Joan that her Max wouldn't grow up thinking this was normal.

As she walked to Hunts Bank, she felt edgy, which was silly. There was nothing to be nervous about. She looked through the hatch into the reception office to say good morning and give her name.

'I'm here to see Miss Brewer.'

The lady in the office reached for the internal telephone. 'I'll let her know you're here. If you'll kindly take a seat over there.' She nodded to a couple of wooden chairs standing against the wall in the corridor, then dialled and began to speak.

'That's all right,' said Joan. 'I know my way.'

Something inside her baulked at waiting meekly for Miss Fay Brewer in the corridor by the front door. Joan wasn't new here. She had worked for LMS from not long after the start of the war. It was Fay Brewer who was the newcomer. Normally Joan was the politest person in the world, but today she felt a strong urge to assert herself and show Fay Brewer that she wasn't a meek little girl.

She felt good about herself as she ran upstairs and made her way to Miss Emery's alcove. To her consternation, it was empty. Dismay poured through her. What a twit. Miss Emery had talked about having a new office, a proper one. There was still time to redeem the situation. All Joan had to do was hurry back down to the reception office and ask for directions.

On her way down, she met Fay Brewer coming up.

'There you are,' said Miss Brewer. 'Mrs Burroughs in reception said you'd bolted, so I assume you went to the old alcove. It looks a bit different now, doesn't it?'

Heat flooded Joan's cheeks. Drat. 'Yes. I should have realised you wouldn't still be there.'

'I'll show you to our new billet. I think you'll find it's a big improvement.'

It was indeed. Mind you, the simple fact that it boasted a fourth wall with a door ensured that. There were two desks, one that faced into the room as normal and the other pushed up against the wall. Miss Brewer went to this one, turning the chair so that when Joan sat in the visitor's seat, she and Miss Brewer faced one another without a desk in between. Joan wasn't sure she liked it. It felt informal.

'Thanks for coming in,' said Miss Brewer. 'I see you've worked as a clerk before, so that's the sort of work I've found for you.'

'Oh.' The word was out before Joan could stop herself.

'Is there a problem?'

'Well . . . I was hoping for something on the station itself, if possible.'

'I see,' said Miss Brewer. 'As you know, Miss Emery asked me to find you a suitable post, not just in terms of your abilities, but also one that won't involve shift work. You can't work on the station without committing to shifts.'

Joan felt two inches tall. Not because of Miss Brewer's words or her attitude, both of which were perfectly polite, but because of her own idiocy. She must seem like a spoilt brat who wanted everything her own way. But the truth was that clerking was the very last thing she wanted. There were clerks in all professions and walks of life. Joan had the same dream now that she'd had back in 1940 when she'd first applied to become a railway girl. She wanted a job that was specific to the railways. That was why she'd loved being a station porter so much – because it was a railway job and only a railway job.

'I realise that,' she said quietly. 'I simply wish to work for LMS and do my bit.'

'Good show,' said Miss Brewer. 'There is a vacancy in one of the wages departments. It's a new office, actually, that's been set up to handle the PAYE tax. Have you heard of that? It stands for pay as you earn. How's your maths?' she asked with a smile.

Crikey. Letitia had been the maths wizard. 'I didn't get a distinction or anything.'

'That isn't a requirement,' Miss Brewer told her. 'On the subject of wages, you'll be on Class Five and you'll be paid fortnightly on Thursdays. If you prove yourself, there may be the chance of a promotion that would put you up to Class Four, which brings in an extra three and sixpence a week.'

Joan nodded, but she didn't hold out much hope. She was a plodder when it came to maths.

251

'It would be very pleasing if you did get on.' Miss Brewer sighed. 'You probably remember that Class Five is referred to as the women's grade. I'd like to see more girls doing well. Women aren't even considered for the highest female rate of pay until they're twenty-eight.'

'I've a few years to go before that,' Joan said.

'When can you start?' asked Miss Brewer.

'I've got my childminding arrangements in place already,' Joan said with a touch of pride.

'Good-oh,' said Miss Brewer. 'I take it that means you can start next Monday.'

Alison, Lydia and Mum were meant to have a wedding meeting this coming weekend, but Alison couldn't face it. On Wednesday afternoon, she sneaked a telephone call to Lydia at the shipping office where she worked and cried off.

'I'm really sorry,' and there was a genuine wobble in her voice. 'I've got overtime.'

'Not to worry,' Lydia said. 'When can you come instead?'

Alison's mind froze over. She tried to dodge the question. 'I haven't thought that far ahead.'

'Come off it. It's the first thing Mum will ask.'

'Say I'll let you know.'

'Well, don't leave it too long. Mum has found a photographer. She wants to plan the group photos.'

Alison quickly ended the call and sat back, heart thumping. She couldn't possibly spend any time with Mum and Lydia. It wasn't just that she wanted to avoid planning the wedding. It was also because she knew they would see straight through her. The one thing holding her together at the moment was the fact that the bombshell that had dropped on her life was a closely guarded secret. That was what enabled her to carry on as normal at work. She had started her new job in onward travel now and it was essential that she concentrate and do her best.

At home, Margaret was evidently keeping out of her way. And so she jolly well should, Alison thought angrily. But she was careful not to display that anger in front of Mrs Cooper and Mrs Grayson.

Cursing herself for that happy letter announcing her intention of borrowing Joan's dress, Alison wrote a few lines to Mabel to say the dress wasn't right for her. She dithered over the wording, refusing to say it didn't suit her, because that would make it sound as if she'd tried it on. The way things were now, she would set fire to it sooner than put it on. *It's not right for me* felt closer to the truth. Not that Mabel would have any idea what she meant.

She ended the letter *Yours in haste,* as if she had a million things to do. It saved her having to pen a proper letter with lots of news. Signing her name, Alison felt ill. Short as it was, never had a letter been so painful to write.

Chapter Twenty-Six

Joan hid her disappointment at being put into a clerical position by making a joke out of how she wasn't exactly a genius at maths. The joke also covered her nerves at the thought of the responsibility of dealing not just with wages, which was scary enough, but also with tax.

She was severely taken aback when Alison came to see her on the Saturday before she was due to start work. Was she in for an earbashing? But Alison had come to do her a favour.

'You can hang on to my grey jacket and skirt for the time being, if you like. I wear a uniform for work.'

'Thanks.' Joan didn't know whether to smile. She felt fluttery. 'That's a big help. It saves me having to rely on the clothes exchange.'

They looked at one another and Joan's heart beat faster.

'You might have told me,' said Alison.

'I couldn't,' said Joan. 'That was the whole point. We wanted to keep Margaret's secret. She agonised over the right thing to do, she honestly did.'

'And you took her side.'

'It wasn't a question of sides.' Joan wanted nothing more than to go to Alison and put her arms around her, but she was sure there would be nothing that Alison wanted less. 'Poor Margaret was beside herself. She wanted to warn you against getting involved with Joel, because at that point she believed he'd heartlessly deserted her, but she also wanted to keep her horrible secret locked away. You can't blame her for that, surely?'

'I suppose not,' Alison answered in a brittle voice that made it clear this was a big concession on her part.

That riled Joan. 'You *suppose* not?'

'Yes, all right, I can understand that no girl would shout that particular secret from the rooftops.'

Joan's heart went out to her. 'You sound so grudging,' she whispered, her tone one of kindness, not criticism.

'Frankly, I feel grudging.' Alison's voice was breezy, but Joan wasn't deceived. 'When I have to listen to you coming down so heavily on Margaret's side, it makes me feel grudging.'

'Oh, Alison, sweetheart, I've already said it isn't a matter of sides. It's just that I was the one Margaret turned to because I was the one who was with her when she miscarried.'

'So you're bound to see it from her point of view,' said Alison crisply. 'What about trying to see it from mine? How would you feel if Bob kept a secret from you and it turned out some of your friends knew about it too? Just look at your face. I know what you're thinking. "That would never happen with me and Bob." Well, guess what. Up until the start of this week, I'd never have imagined it happening to Joel and me, but now it has and I'm . . .' Her voice tightened and she gulped. 'I'm *struggling*.'

Now Joan did go to her and put her arms around her, not deterred by the stiffness of Alison's body.

'Alison, you're my friend and I care about you. You were the very first one of our group I met and I knew right from the start that I wanted to be friends with you. Do you remember us leaving the building with Colette and Lizzie after sitting the railway tests? We asked who was going home on which bus. I hoped I'd be able to travel with you, but instead . . .' Joan heard her own voice tighten as a painful constriction filled her throat. 'Heaven help me, I was a bit disappointed because I was on the same bus as Lizzie.'

Alison drew back slightly and looked at her. For possibly the first time since she'd arrived in Torbay Road, she wasn't thinking about herself. Her brown eyes were filled with compassion.

'*No*,' she whispered.

'Yes,' said Joan. 'It's a funny thing to remember, such a tiny incident – hardly an incident at all, really, just a fleeting feeling, but I've never forgotten it. When I think of what happened to Lizzie a few months later . . .' She shook her head. 'Poor girl. The thought of her in that house when it took a direct hit—'

Alison moved to take Joan in her arms and they hugged. Alison was the one to break the embrace, but she kept hold of Joan's hands.

'It can be hard being friends,' said Alison. 'I'll never forget Lizzie.'

'None of us will.'

'Losing a friend is such a painful thing to happen. I felt so bad for you when you lost Letitia. She was your friend as well as your sister. It was a double blow. You said I'm your friend and you care about me. I feel the same about you.'

'I care about Margaret too,' Joan said softly. 'She needed me and I helped her, but all the time I was supporting her, I was thinking of you too. We were both thinking of you.'

Alison nodded slowly. Joan tried to read her expression, but couldn't.

'It hurts me that you and Dot – oh yes, I know all about Dot as well,' said Alison. 'It hurts me that you've both known all along and you never saw fit to tell me.'

'It wasn't our secret to share.'

Alison ploughed on as if Joan hadn't spoken. 'Joel and Margaret made a pact to keep me in the dark – and please don't trot out the line about Margaret being entitled to her privacy. I'm sick to death of hearing that. They decided not to tell me and if it hadn't been for Lydia, I still wouldn't know. I'd have gone through my whole life not knowing that my husband and my friend—' Her mouth twisted. 'You get the picture. How am I meant to feel about that? If it was you, Joan, how would *you* feel?'

Joan slept fitfully the night before starting her new job. Her conversation with Alison weighed heavily on her mind and she also felt concerned about her darling Max. Even though he was used to being with Mrs Grayson and at the Lizzie Nursery, it would still be a wrench to leave him in the morning. This was going to be the real thing.

She was also aware of how she would have to think ahead regarding Bob's shifts. On days when he set off while she was out at work, she would have to leave his snap tin ready for him to pick up, but whenever he arrived home from work during the day, Gran had agreed to provide him with a meal.

'Men have it easy, chick,' Dot had said with a chuckle when Joan explained her plans. 'They don't know they're born.'

Joan had long admired Dot for the way she ran her home and took care of her family while working full-time and coping with the compulsory overtime. Now Joan was about to get a taste of the same way of life herself and she had a suspicion it wasn't going to be as straightforward as Dot made it look. Not that Joan was going to whine. It might take some getting used to, but she was determined to make a success of it.

It was essential that her first day should go smoothly, not just the job itself, but getting Max ready and dropping him off. He was due to be in Wilton Close this morning and Mrs Grayson would take him to the nursery for the afternoon.

Up until now Max had always been perfectly happy to be left with Mrs Grayson – but not today. Maybe he had picked up on his mummy's nerves. Whatever the reason, when Joan attempted to hand him over, he clung to her and howled his head off.

Mrs Cooper unpeeled him from Joan. 'Off you trot. He'll be fine.'

Mrs Grayson steered her towards the door. 'Good luck. I hope it all goes well.'

Goes well? With her little boy desperate for her to stay with him? Feeling like the worst mother in the world, Joan forced herself to go on her way.

Joan was met at Hunts Bank by a lady who introduced herself as Mrs Marjorie Clements. She was wearing the red lipstick

Hitler was said to hate and was perhaps fifteen years Joan's senior, with light brown hair worn in a victory roll and grey eyes that made Joan feel she was being thoroughly assessed.

'I'm the acting deputy in our section,' Mrs Clements said as she shook hands. 'Leave your coat on,' she added as Joan automatically started unfastening her buttons, expecting to be shown upstairs. 'You'll need it.'

To Joan's surprise, Mrs Clements led her back outside into the cold and down the road. Before Joan could ask, Mrs Clements answered her question.

'There's no room for us in Hunts Bank. We've been put in a building beside the permanent way. It's just a few minutes' walk.'

Just? Those extra minutes might well force Joan onto an earlier bus in the mornings. Mrs Clements set a brisk pace and Joan soon realised that bringing Brizo to Victoria Station and dropping him off would be impossible.

After some minutes, she and Mrs Clements walked down a slope, heading for a brick building that was indeed beside the tracks. There were sidings here, with lines of wagons waiting. Above the scene, two vast barrage balloons glittered in the winter sunshine, their strong cables whining as they shifted in the breeze.

'We call them Flossie and Blossom,' said Mrs Clements.

Joan smiled, thinking of *The Adventures of John Balloon*, a children's book about a runaway barrage balloon that she was looking forward to reading to Max when he was older, while at the same time very much hoping she would never need to because the war would be over and the barrage balloons would have vanished from the landscape.

Mrs Clements led the way up some steps and opened the door on to a lobby-cum-cloakroom.

'Coats and hats over there,' she said, indicating coat pegs on the wall. 'Handbags under the desks.'

Joan quickly hung up her things, then followed Mrs Clements into a large office filled with tall stools in front of high, lidded desks. A fire burned in the grate. Mrs Clements introduced Joan and she was greeted with smiles and words of welcome.

'Mrs Hubble has worked on the railways before,' said Mrs Clements.

A pretty clerk called Miss Palmer said, smiling, 'So there's no point in sending her to ask for the key to the tunnel.'

Joan smiled back, starting to feel at ease. 'Long stands, glass hammers. I've heard all of 'em before.'

Mrs Clements took her to an inner office, where she introduced her to Mr Darwin, a cheery-looking young man who looked as though he should be in the forces until he stood up and came round his desk – an ordinary, flat desk, not a sloping one like everyone else had – to shake hands. He walked with, not exactly a limp, more of a lurch. Joan knew she shouldn't look, but couldn't help it. Her gaze was drawn to his feet. His right shoe had a built-up sole several inches thick to compensate for . . . what? Polio? A birth defect? Mr Darwin could have simply stood up and shaken hands across the desk. Had he walked around it to let her see and get it over with? Joan wished she hadn't looked. The last thing she wanted was to shame him. She also took a moment to bless all the stars that had given her a healthy child.

'Mr Darwin is the acting head of our section,' Mrs Clements told her.

'Pleased to meet you, Mrs Hubble,' said Mr Darwin. 'Mrs Clements here will show you the ropes. Good with figures, are you?'

'Well . . .' Joan hesitated.

'You're allowed to do your working out on paper while you get the hang of it,' said Mr Darwin. 'Soon you'll be doing mental calculations, the same as everyone else. We check the books regularly and they have to balance.'

He gave a nod of polite dismissal and Mrs Clements bore Joan away.

'This will be your desk over here, Mrs Hubble. Stow your bag underneath, then you can stand beside Miss Palmer and she'll talk you through what she's doing. Don't worry. We shan't let you loose until you're up to it.'

'We don't want to make mistakes,' said Miss Palmer, 'not just because it's bad practice, but because there'd be uproar.'

'Pay-as-you-earn tax has caused no end of vexation and suspicion in the workforce,' said Mrs Clements, 'but it's here to stay.'

Joan spent the morning alongside Miss Palmer. It was uncomfortable standing for so long, but she didn't like to ask if she could bring her stool across. A horrid thought smote her. Was she supposed to pick up the work really quickly and have no need to sit down? Did standing there all morning mark her out as a dunce? She had adored her clever sister and Letitia had never once made her feel inferior, but by crikey, Gran had.

Miss Palmer angled a smile at her. 'Going cross-eyed yet? Let's leave it for a few minutes. It's my turn to fetch the water for dinnertime drinks. I'll show you.'

She fetched her coat and hat and Joan did likewise. Miss Palmer had brought the kettle with her.

Once they were outside, Miss Palmer explained, 'We have to cross the line to get water from the water column, then we heat the kettle over the fire. We're given a coal ration. If you're sent to ask for more, always ask for Derby coal if they have it. It's really good for fireplaces.'

The November sky, which had been bright earlier, had now clouded over and there was a sharp nip in the air. Over on the far side of the permanent way stood a water column. It looked like a thick lamp post with an arm sticking out from its top. A wide rubber hose dangled from the end of the arm. It was from here that the water tanks on locomotives were filled. Beside the column was the water tower, a brick-built structure with a metal tank on top where the water was stored. The tank was higher than the column to ensure the water pressure was strong enough. A small building stood behind the tower.

Joan gazed at the sizeable hose hanging from the water column.

'We've got to get water out of that?' she asked.

'Yes,' said Miss Palmer. 'There's a bit of a knack to it, but you'll soon get the hang of it.' She held out the kettle. 'The best way is just to have a go.' She gave it a moment, then said, 'Your face! Of course we aren't going to get water out of the column. We'd both get soaked from head to foot.'

Joan grinned. 'I admit it. You had me fooled.'

'Sorry. Couldn't resist. Actually, we call it fetching water from the column even though this is where we really go . . .' She led Joan to the building on the other side of the tower. 'This is a workshop-cum-storage place. Best of all, it has running water.'

'I'd much rather turn on a tap than take my chances with the water column,' said Joan.

'You're a good sport,' said Miss Palmer. 'I had to get you on something after you already knew about the key to the tunnel. Is your husband in the forces?' she asked as they retraced their steps across the permanent way.

'He's a railwayman,' Joan told her proudly. 'He has a signal box.'

'Good-oh,' said Miss Palmer. 'Keeping it in the family.'

Back indoors, Miss Palmer hung the kettle on a metal arm and swung it over the fire.

Mrs Clements appeared. 'I see you're learning the important things,' she said to Joan. 'Miss Palmer will have her dinner break in a few minutes because she started at half past eight. You're on a nine o'clock start this week, so you'll have your break at half twelve. I'll give you some filing to do for now.'

Miss Palmer disappeared in the direction of the cramped staffroom and Mrs Clements led Joan to a filing cabinet.

'Mr Baxendale is very particular about keeping the filing up to date,' she said.

'Mr Baxendale?' Joan asked.

'He's the head of our section.'

'I thought Mr Darwin was the head.'

'He's the acting head,' said Mrs Clements, 'and I'm the acting deputy. Mr Baxendale will be off work for some weeks thanks to a broken leg, so Mr Darwin and I are both acting up.' Her eyes took on a flinty gleam. 'Have you heard of DOP?'

'No.'

'It means Difference of Pay. While Mr Darwin takes on Mr Baxendale's role, he gets the extra money to give him the equivalent of Mr Baxendale's salary.'

'That's a good idea,' said Joan, 'giving people the extra money while they take on the extra responsibility.'

'It's a very good idea,' said Mrs Clements, 'if you're a man. I'm the acting deputy, but d'you think I get DOP? No, I don't, and for no better reason than that I'm a woman. I'm no trade unionist, but, honestly, I can see why the workers at Rolls-Royce went on strike. The women wanted equal pay for equal work – and they got it too.'

'Good for them,' said Joan.

'The men walked out alongside them,' said Mrs Clements. 'That probably helped their cause. No one ever gave women more money just because it was the right thing to do and they deserved it.'

'It must be galling not getting DOP,' said Joan.

'It makes my blood boil, it really does.' Mrs Clements gave a one-sided shrug. 'But it doesn't stop me working my hardest. We all have to do our bit, Mrs Hubble, and do it to the best of our ability.'

Chapter Twenty-Seven

Margaret went to see Sally on her day off. Not only did she want to go, but also she was glad to escape from Wilton Close, because it was Alison's day off too. Just over a week had dragged by since Joel had told Alison the truth and there had been an atmosphere in Wilton Close ever since.

'Pre-wedding jitters,' Mrs Cooper said knowingly.

'I do hope Alison isn't regretting changing from a summer wedding to a winter one,' said Mrs Grayson.

Alison was being polite but cool towards Margaret, who compensated by being extra friendly towards Mrs Cooper and Mrs Grayson. Would that make Alison's coolness more obvious? But Margaret couldn't help herself. She had found refuge in Joan's home last week, but she was reluctant to continue doing that. Joan had started work this week and needed to get used to her new routine.

Margaret wrapped up warmly for her journey to Sale, choosing the russet-brown jumper with a single cream stripe about four inches above the waist that Anna had knitted for her. With it, she wore her 'W' necklace. She was wearing the jumper and necklace a lot at the moment, as if the two together made a lucky charm.

Mrs Grayson gave her some home-made ginger biscuits to take, wrapped in greaseproof paper.

'Sally might have made some friends she can share them with,' Mrs Grayson said.

'I hope so,' said Margaret.

She remembered her own short-lived pregnancy as the loneliest time of her whole life. She dearly wanted Sally not to have to endure anything like that.

When she arrived at Rookery House, Margaret walked to the back door. Although she understood why the front door was reserved for the married ladies and their visitors, she still felt a spurt of resentment at what it said about the girls who had got pregnant out of wedlock.

She told the woman who answered the door that she'd come to see Sally Bennett.

'Oh.' The woman raised her eyebrows. 'Well. I suppose it's all right for you to come in. The greenies don't normally get visitors.'

'Greenies?' Margaret asked.

'Wait here, will you?' said the woman and left her.

Presently, Sally appeared. She wore a voluminous dark green wrap-around pinny, with her blonde hair tucked inside a snood. Her cheeks were flushed as if from exertion.

Margaret would have been pleased to see her anyway, but after the strain of recent days in Wilton Close, gladness surged up inside her and she reached out to take Sally's hands. To her surprise, they were damp.

Sally withdrew them, looking self-conscious, and wiped them on her pinny.

'Sorry,' she said. 'I've been washing the window sills.'

'You've been *what*?'

Sally glanced around, then frowned at Margaret. 'Come to my room. I've got permission to take you.'

'Isn't there a visitors' room?' Margaret asked as she followed Sally up a staircase with bare treads.

'Us unmarried girls have a common room, but that's being cleaned at the moment.'

Sally led the way up two flights to a dark corridor with rooms on both sides and no natural light. She opened a door and Margaret entered, compliments at the ready. The room was small but spotless, with a bed and bedside cupboard, a narrow hanging cupboard with a drawer at the bottom, a washstand and a wooden chair with arms. Margaret was stumped for something to say. So much for admiring the room and lifting Sally's spirits.

'I know,' said Sally. 'It's . . . basic. Sit down. I'll have the chair, if you don't mind. It supports my back. It won't be long before I need to use the arms to push myself to my feet.'

Margaret sat on the bed. She took the biscuits from her bag.

'From Mrs Grayson. She thought you might have chums to share them with.'

Sally smiled and her light blue eyes softened. 'How kind she is. They feed us pretty well here, actually, but it'll be nice to have a treat.'

Margaret couldn't hold in the question a moment longer. 'Have they got you doing housework?'

Sally plucked at the green pinafore and held it away from her swollen belly. 'Behold the greenie. We all wear them, all us unmarrieds, I mean, and yes, we do the cleaning.'

'But you're paying to be here.'

'So what? It's normal practice, apparently, for the unmarried girls to do the housework in these places. It's not so bad. One girl knows someone who was sent to a convent to have her baby. You'd think nuns would be kind, wouldn't you? These weren't. They had the girls slaving eight or more hours a day in the laundry, heaving sopping sheets around and putting them through a giant mangle. At least all we have to do here is ordinary housework.'

'It's not what I expected,' said Margaret.

'Me neither,' said Sally, 'but let's face it, after cleaning locos in the engine shed, a spot of housework is a doddle.'

'Have you settled in all right?' Margaret asked.

'Well enough. I've got pally with one or two others. It's a relief not to have to pretend any longer.'

'That's something,' said Margaret.

'We compare notes about how we got in the family way. What happened to me turns out to be depressingly common. But not everyone is like that. There's a girl called Betty who celebrated getting engaged by going all the way with her chap. Now he's back on the front line and she's here, having his baby. Goodness knows when he'll get leave again so he can make an honest woman of her. Poor Betty is a greenie like the rest of us, even though she's not really a fallen girl and she'll be keeping her baby.' Sally broke off and bit her lip.

Margaret hesitated before asking, 'Do you know how the adoption process works?'

'There's nothing to know. You hand over your baby and that's that.'

There had to be more to it than that. 'Don't you get told about the new parents?'

268

'No. Mind you, that's probably for the best, because what difference would it make?' Sally sounded flippant, but Margaret wasn't fooled.

'I'm sorry,' she said. 'That was a bit near the knuckle.'

'There's something I'd like to ask you,' said Sally. 'Maybe I shouldn't, but I've been thinking about it ever since I found out.'

'Found out what?'

Sally pressed her lips together for a moment. 'The night before I left Wilton Close to come here, I overheard a conversation between you and Alison.'

Margaret's lips parted, but she didn't speak. She couldn't.

'I know I shouldn't have,' Sally said quickly. 'I was dozing and half woke up when Alison arrived home. The two of you went into the other room, presumably so as not to disturb me, so I got up to come and tell you that I'd go and lie down so you could have the front room, but when I reached the dining-room door, I heard my name. I thought Alison might have changed her mind again and gone back to thinking of me as a slut, so I stayed where I was and listened. It turned out the conversation wasn't about me. It was about you.'

'How much did you hear?' Margaret asked.

'Pretty much all of it. You and Alison's fiancé. The baby you lost. The wedding dress. Ever since then, I've been wondering why you never told me.'

'It's not exactly something you proudly share.'

'Not that I'm in a position to criticise,' said Sally. 'I know all about keeping secrets. To start with, I was angry with you for not telling, for letting me think you were whiter than white, for letting me think you were better than I was.'

'I never thought of myself that way.'

'I know you didn't. That was just me being silly. But I couldn't understand why you didn't say anything. It didn't seem fair. You knew everything about my situation. I thought the least you could do was let me in on yours. But it's really none of my business. I know that.'

'I'll tell you why I kept it from you,' said Margaret.

'There's no need, honestly. I wish I'd never brought it up.'

'I'm glad you did. Since you know what happened to me, I'd rather you knew why I stayed quiet.' Margaret took a moment to pull her thoughts together. 'There were various reasons, actually. I didn't want to seem obsessed with what happened to me all that time ago, when I ought to be concentrating on you in the here and now. And – and I did want you to think of me as whiter than white, as you put it – oh, not for my sake, not for my reputation, but because it meant the world to me when Joan was prepared to be my friend even though she knew about the baby. Knowing that a decent girl didn't look down on me helped me a lot and I hoped you would feel that way too.'

Sally looked thoughtful, then she nodded.

'There was another reason too,' Margaret added. 'I'm very aware that you're facing something I never had to face. What happened to me was bad enough, but I didn't want to seem to compare my experience with yours. What's going to happen to you is so much worse than what I had to contend with.'

'It isn't a competition,' Sally said. 'And if it were, believe me, it isn't one I'd want to win.'

Chapter Twenty-Eight

Alison sat in the darkened cinema, not even trying to concentrate on *The Adventures of Tartu*, even though she was a huge fan of Robert Donat and had loved him in *The 39 Steps* and *Goodbye, Mr Chips*. Joel sat beside her. Was he, too, going through the motions? Seeing the film had been Alison's choice. She still felt raw and injured and this was a way to avoid conversation, but maybe it had been a mistake.

At the end of the film, everyone stood for the national anthem before shuffling along between the seats to the aisles and making slow but steady progress towards the doors out of the theatre – and theatre was the right word. The cinema screen stood on the stage where once actors and music hall performers had trodden the boards. Velvet curtains from the old days were pulled open with a grand swish at the start of the evening and drawn again at the end.

Alison and Joel made their way out along with everybody else. Normally Joel would have held Alison's elbow or her hand to ensure they stayed together, but this evening he didn't touch her. That was her own fault, she knew. She hadn't permitted any intimacy since the revelation – revelation? Bombshell, more like – since the bombshell about Joel and Margaret and the baby. The *baby*.

Last year, when Joel had quietly admitted to having got a girl in the family way, Alison had instantly assumed that the baby had been born and she was appalled to think he already had a child. Horrid as it made her sound, she'd been overwhelmed with relief when he told her there had been a miscarriage. If Joel had been a father, there would always have been a part of him that would never belong to her. As it was, the baby had been lost and Joel hadn't even known about it until a long time afterwards, which meant he was all hers. That was how she had seen it last year. Was that wrong of her? Selfish? Heartless?

Heartless was the last thing she was. There could be no doubt about that. She felt as if she was nothing but heart at the moment – feelings, turmoil, questions, confusion, pain.

They walked out of the cinema into the total darkness of the blackout. Alison had a mad idea that she would like to walk deep into it and never come back. People were always getting lost in the dark. It didn't matter how well you knew the vicinity. The blackout disoriented everyone, even four years into the war when you might suppose everybody had got used to it.

Here and there were tiny glows from tissue-muffled torchlight. A motor car went by, its headlights fitted with metal grilles to dim the light and reduce its spread. The various instances of muted light merely emphasised the depth of the blackout.

Above, clouds wafted across the heavens like the tobacco smoke that had drifted inside the cinema, but where there were no clouds, the stars showed as brilliant pinpricks of sparkling light, utterly beautiful in the wide skies.

Looking up at the stars, Alison was aware of her engagement ring inside her glove. Her lovely emerald. After Joel had first placed it on her finger, she had often gazed at it, drinking in the sight and significance of it, feeling she was the luckiest girl in the world. Now when she looked at it, she boggled at how everything could have gone so wrong.

Joel's voice broke into her thoughts. 'What did you think of the film?'

'It was . . . To tell you the truth, my mind was elsewhere.'

'Same here. We need to talk about this, Alison.'

'What else is there to say? I'm shocked that you and Margaret . . . you know. What makes it worse is that you could have told me more than a year ago, but you chose not to. That *hurts*. Shh,' she added, which was daft when she was the one who was speaking, but she didn't want him to answer because they were approaching a bus stop with a queue of people and she couldn't bear anyone to overhear.

Behind them, a bus came trundling along and pulled up. A few people got off, then the queue moved forward and passengers climbed onto the platform at the rear and either stepped up onto the lower deck or else mounted the narrow curved staircase to the top deck. The conductor dinged the bell and the bus moved off, leaving the pavement empty.

Joel guided Alison towards the bench for waiting passengers.

'Can we sit and talk?' he asked. 'Please?'

They sat. Previously, they would have sat close together, bodies touching, especially on a cold night like this, but now their bodies didn't touch. It felt right that way but also horribly wrong.

273

'I don't know how to put this right,' said Joel.

'Everything used to be perfect.'

'I know how deeply upset you are.'

'Not just upset,' said Alison. 'My perfect world has turned out to be fragile. I'm more than upset. I'm scared and angry. This is like when Paul left me. When that happened, I got this idea in my head that it served me right. I'd been so sure that the two of us were a permanent couple, so confident that we'd spend the rest of our lives together. I felt sorry for girls whose relationships didn't last, and it wasn't a nice kind of sorry. It was a condescending sort of sorry, because I knew that such a thing could never happen to me and Paul. And then it did.'

'He left you for another girl,' said Joel. 'Margaret and I – it feels strange even saying "Margaret and I" because we didn't know one another all that long.'

'Long enough to make a baby.'

Joel was silent for a moment. 'I've explained that. We both had too much to drink.'

Alison pressed her lips together so hard it seemed they might never come unstuck. She knew Joel was being reasonable. The trouble was that she didn't feel reasonable. Something inside her wanted to stamp and scream, but that would put her in the wrong.

'What I mean,' said Joel, 'is that I don't think you can really compare you and Paul with Margaret and me. The two relationships were entirely different.'

'I'm not comparing the two. I'm telling you how I felt after Paul ditched me. It was like being punished for daring to believe in our relationship. It was as if the world wanted

274

me to know that what I'd thought was me being confident was actually me being cocky and superior to other girls. As if I needed to be brought down a few pegs.'

'This situation with Margaret is nothing to do with teaching you a lesson,' said Joel.

'I *know* that.'

'The most important thing is that what happened with Margaret happened at the beginning of the war – during the phoney war. I understand why you're hurt, but I also think you're blaming Margaret and me for something that happened way before either of us ever met you. To be honest, Alison, that isn't fair.'

'I resent that,' Alison said at once. 'When Venetia did her utmost to get rid of me and get you and Rachel Chambers back together, and I walked in to find you holding Rachel's hand in both of yours—'

'I was comforting her, that's all,' Joel interrupted. 'I'd told her I had no intention of resuming our old relationship and she was upset.'

'I could have caused all sorts of trouble at that point,' said Alison. 'I could have been a dozen different kinds of difficult. I could have refused to speak to you ever again, but I didn't. I was sensible and reasonable. I heard you out and hey presto, the Rachel situation was dealt with and I knew how strong we were as a couple. And now I'm supposed to do that all over again, but this time it's Margaret and the baby – and I'm perfectly well aware that it happened before I knew you, which apparently means I'm not supposed to have an opinion on the subject—'

'I never said that—'

'—but it wasn't just the miscarriage, it's the fact that you kept it secret from me. You *all* kept it secret from me – you, Margaret, Joan, Dot. All of you, all this time, and you've only owned up now because Lydia suggested borrowing Joan's wedding dress. I *know* you didn't all choose Margaret over me, but it *feels* as if you did. And once again, I find myself being expected to be sensible and reasonable. Well, I'm not sure I'm capable of it this time.'

Chapter Twenty-Nine

It was the middle of November and Joan was now in her second week at work. It ought to be a happy time. Tiring, yes, but satisfying. Only it wasn't and she felt ashamed of herself. On top of coping with the new job and the new routine, she had had to make fresh arrangements for Brizo. Instead of dropping him off at Victoria herself, which she had confidently expected to do but she simply didn't have enough time, the old system had had to be reinstated whereby he was collected from Torbay Road by Alison or Margaret. Not being able to handle a simple task like taking her dog to the station in the morning made Joan feel a complete twit. She tried to tell herself not to be idiotic about it. She had wanted a job outside the home and she'd got one. She ought to be grateful, not fed up.

She pinned on her best smile as she entered the buffet – and walked straight into Fay Brewer, who evidently thought the smile must be for her.

'Mrs Hubble,' she said in a friendly voice. 'How are you? How are you getting along with the PAYE?'

'So-so,' said Joan. 'I'm getting the hang of it.'

'Jolly good,' said Miss Brewer. She was about to continue on her way when another voice chimed in.

'Miss Brewer, what are you doing here?' It was Dot, friendly as always. 'Hark at me. What a daft question. Are you on your way in or out?'

'Out,' said Miss Brewer.

'That's a shame,' said Cordelia, who had arrived with Dot. 'You could have joined us.'

'You still can,' said Dot, 'if you've a few minutes to spare. Come and sit with us and meet our friends.'

'I don't want to intrude,' said Miss Brewer.

'Nonsense,' said Dot. 'You were a big help to our Mabel and any friend of hers is a friend of ours.'

'Strictly speaking, I wasn't her friend,' said Miss Brewer. 'I was just doing my job.'

'Ah, but there are ways and ways of doing a job,' said Cordelia, smiling. 'We are aware, Miss Brewer, that at the time Mabel needed help, there was another lady at the Corporation who definitely didn't conduct her work affairs in a friendly and helpful manner.'

'But you did,' said Dot, 'which means you helped set up the Lizzie Nursery and that means the world to all of us.'

'Do join us,' Cordelia urged her, 'just for a minute or two.'

'Yes, do,' Dot added.

Joan felt obliged to say, 'Yes.'

Miss Brewer laughed. 'Very well – and thank you.'

She stayed in the queue with them while they lined up for their cups of tea, then she accompanied them to where the others had bagged two tables to push together. Joan found herself sitting beside her. Everyone was here except Alison. Cordelia performed the introductions.

'Not that you'll remember all the names straight off,' said Dot, 'but we won't hold it against you if you forget any.'

'What made you move from the Corporation to here?' asked Persephone.

'I have an interest in welfare, especially women's welfare. My mother once endured a hunger strike in prison.'

'Your mother was a suffragette?' asked Colette.

'A suffra*gist*, wanting to get the vote through legitimate means, rather than a suffra*gette*, advocating achieving it by any means, however violent. And my father is a doctor who, apart from when he worked in field hospitals during the last war, has always worked in the community, providing health care for the poor alongside his regular paid work.'

'No wonder you got the job,' said Margaret, 'with a pedigree like that.'

Joan watched the others taking to Fay Brewer – and quite right too that they should. She was friendly and capable and Joan was as grateful as any of them for the support she'd given Mabel. So why did Joan feel miffed that Miss Brewer was receiving this warm welcome? Was she still vexed at not getting the welfare post? Was she really that petty?

'You were a bit quiet in the buffet, chick,' said Dot as they were all getting up and gathering their things together, ready to go home.

Joan could have kicked herself. 'I'm fine. I was just listening.'

'Aye, not everyone wants to yack all the time – like me.'

'You don't talk all the time. You're the best listener I've ever met,' Joan said warmly.

'That's handy, because I think you could maybe do with someone to listen,' said Dot. 'Am I right? Look, love, I don't need to rush home tonight. My Reg is on the evening shift, so he won't be there, and the kids are with their mams, so if you need to talk, I'm here to listen.'

'Honestly, Dot, I have to get home.'

'I'll come with you.'

'We can't talk on the bus.' Joan glanced around. She and all the others except for Dot went on the same bus, unless anyone peeled off and went to the pictures.

'I'll come on your bus.' Dot raised her voice and spoke to the group in general. 'I need to drop in on Mrs Cooper and now is as good a time as any.'

'Lovely.' Persephone linked her arm through Dot's. 'You can sit next to me and tell me how Jimmy and Jenny are getting on.'

They all headed for the stop and managed to pile onto the same bus. Colette got off first, at Seymour Grove. Cordelia and Emily got off at the stop before the terminus. This was also the closest stop to Torbay Road, but Joan had to collect Max from Wilton Close, so she stayed on with the others. After the bus turned in a tight hairpin into the terminus and they all got off, Persephone plunged into the darkness, calling goodbye as she headed off to Darley Court, leaving Joan, Margaret and Dot to head down Beech Road.

Happiness grew inside Joan as they walked. She always felt like this when she was going to collect Max.

'Someone can't wait to get to Mrs Cooper's,' chuckled Dot.

'I can't think why,' Margaret teased.

At the house, Joan gave Max a big cuddle and felt complete once more. He and Bob were the centre of her world.

'I'll drop round and see you when I finish here,' Dot said softly as Joan prepared to leave.

Joan nodded. Dot was such a dear friend, always keeping an eye on all of them. Would her own long-dead mother have been like this? Always wanting the best for her? Caring about all the small details of her life?

When she reached home, she gave Max his bath and a bedtime story. Bob's mum said he wasn't old enough for stories yet, but Joan loved sharing them, convinced that Max enjoyed hearing her voice. He definitely liked snuggling up at story time and she couldn't think of anything better than being snuggled up to by her darling little boy.

Not long after she put Max down, Dot arrived. Joan took her to peep at him.

'Eh, he's a handsome little lad,' said Dot.

'Like his daddy,' said Joan.

Leaving Max, they went into the sitting room.

'Now then, what's going on in your head?' asked Dot. 'Are you regretting going back to work? No one would blame you. It's obvious that you adore young Max.'

'I don't regret it as such,' said Joan, wanting to be honest. 'I just wish I wasn't in an office job.'

'That was bound to happen, though, wasn't it?' Dot asked. 'They're the only jobs without night shifts.'

'I know,' said Joan. 'I'm being silly, that's all. I just need to knuckle down and get used to it. The thing is, I'm very aware that it's something Letitia would have been brilliant at, whereas it doesn't come naturally to me.'

'You'll get to grips with it,' Dot said confidently. 'I expect part of it is that you're worried about this business with Alison and Margaret. Poor lasses.'

'Alison is so upset that you and I knew about Margaret's baby and she didn't. She's not just upset. I think she's furious. She's . . .' Joan searched for the right word. 'She's in turmoil.'

'You can see why.'

'Dot, would you talk to her?'

'Me?' said Dot in surprise.

'You're so good at that kind of thing.'

'Not on your nelly. Can you imagine it? I'm one of the people she's vexed at. If I turned up on her doorstep offering to talk things over, I'd look a right nosy old so-and-so.'

'I'm sure you wouldn't,' said Joan.

'Listen, chick. Ask any member of my family and they'll tell you that I'm always one to stick my oar in. Now that's not how I see it. I see it as helping when there's a problem that needs sorting. To me, that's being a good neighbour, a good friend. But Alison isn't going to see it that way at present. If she were to turn up on *my* doorstep, that'd be different.'

Joan sighed. 'I can't see that happening,' she said sorrowfully.

Alison had made her excuses for not meeting up with the others in the buffet a couple of evenings ago. She wasn't exactly keen to go now, but she was gasping for a cuppa before heading for home and she didn't want to use the staffroom because – well, she wanted a bit of time to herself. The girls she worked with were excited about her wedding, which was lovely of them, of course, and until recently

Alison had been only too happy to share all the details, but not any longer.

Sometimes her heart felt just too heavy to keep up the public pretence that all was well. Once or twice she had even wished Joel had never told her the truth, but she didn't really mean that. It was important that she knew because . . . because she feared that not knowing had made a fool of her. Moreover, she didn't want there to be any secrets between her and Joel, especially one as big as this. Knowing was painful, but the idea of not knowing was worse.

She hesitated outside the buffet door, then had to step aside to let a bunch of soldiers get past. She took another step so as not to get bumped by their kitbags. Before the door closed behind her, she saw them being passed straight to the head of the queue by those who were waiting. Quite right too. You heard of buffets where servicemen weren't required to pay or where, when stocks ran low, food was set aside purely for the country's brave boys and everyone else went without.

She was about to open the door and go in when behind her a familiar voice said, 'Evening, chick.'

Alison turned round. 'Dot – Mrs Green,' she added quickly, in case anyone had heard her slip of the tongue.

'I have to say you don't look keen to go in,' Dot said cheerfully.

'I was just letting the soldiers in first.'

'It was more than that, chick. I'm not as green as I am cabbage-looking. Tell me if I'm wrong, but I reckon you're feeling iffy about going into the buffet. Afraid you might bump into someone?'

Alison shrugged. 'I'm fine – honestly.' Then, before she knew it, the truth came tumbling out. 'Actually, I'm not fine at all, as you very well know. Can we go somewhere and talk?'

'Course we can, love. I know just the place, nice and quiet.'

Before Alison could have second thoughts, Dot linked arms and bore her away. Dot was wearing her navy blue coat, a loose-fitting garment with wide lapels and big patch pockets. It used to belong to Cordelia, but she'd had more than one and had given it to Dot after Dot had chucked her one and only coat onto an incendiary, then jumped up and down on it to smother the flames.

That was one of the things Alison liked about Dot. She didn't have misplaced pride. Some women would refuse to accept a cast-off garment, even from a friend, or else they would take it but keep quiet about its origins. Not Dot. When her navy coat was admired, she would say straight out, 'My friend gave it to me when she'd finished with it. Feel that for quality. It's the best coat I've ever had.'

They made their way through the crowds of passengers until they left the concourse behind, disappearing into the part of the station that the public never got to see. Alison recognised it as the way she had come with Margaret on the night of the air raid when Max was born.

'There's a bench round that corner,' said Dot. 'Some porters might see us as they go by, but they won't pay us any mind.'

They sat down together. Alison drew her green wool coat more closely around herself, but there was nothing she could do about the chill whipping at her ankles. She expected Dot, warm, motherly Dot, to say something, but she didn't.

Alison's mind was full to bursting and she didn't know where to start. A question from Dot would have provided something to focus on, but Dot simply waited.

Finally, Alison said, 'I don't know what to do. I can't stop thinking about it.'

Dot nodded. 'When you say you don't know what to do, do you mean whether to go through with the wedding?'

Alison was shocked. 'Good heavens, no.' It had never occurred to her not to marry Joel.

'Well, that's good,' said Dot. 'I'm glad we've got that out of the way.'

'In some ways, it would have been easier if I'd been able to explode and throw him out of my life. At least that would have brought this to an end.'

The corners of Dot's mouth turned downwards in a thoughtful way. 'True, but would that have been the ending you wanted?'

'Of course not. Even at the outset, when I was at my most shocked and hurt, I never thought of breaking off the engagement.' Alison faked a laugh. 'I don't think Mum would let me.'

'Then let me remind you that this wedding is – how many weeks away?' asked Dot.

'Five weeks on Friday.'

'You need to get to grips with this way before then.'

Alison frowned. 'You make it sound like I'm wallowing in it.'

'Nay, I don't think that at all. I think being told that your Joel made a baby with another girl must have come as a horrible shock. I bet you were relieved when he said she'd lost the baby.'

285

Alison looked at her. 'Yes,' she whispered. 'I feel as if I ought to be ashamed of that, but I just can't be. I've never felt colder in my life than I did during those few moments when I thought Joel was the father of an illegitimate child, when I thought he already had a child in his life. A child who was nothing to do with me.'

'It's a complicated business,' Dot said quietly.

'That bit didn't feel complicated at all. I was glad when he told me the girl had miscarried – and relieved, and grateful.'

'It meant you weren't sharing him.'

Alison nodded. 'It meant he didn't have a past. Well, he did, but not one that still existed.' She thought about it for a moment. 'I was so grateful for it that I didn't realise how hurt I was about this other girl and the pregnancy.'

'But it did hurt you,' said Dot.

'Yes, but I buried it. It wasn't until all this blew up that I truly realised how much it had affected me.'

'And it's added to the turmoil,' said Dot.

That drew a smile from Alison. 'That's not the sort of word I'd think of you using. "Turmoil" doesn't seem a Dot sort of word.'

'I can't take credit for it, chick. I pinched it off Joan. And before you ask, yes, her and me have talked about you. Not being nosy parkers, just being—'

'My friends,' Alison put in. 'I know that.'

'We're concerned about Margaret an' all,' said Dot.

'I know that too.' Something inside Alison hardened. She drew in a slow breath and forced the hard feeling to soften, imagining it as a piece of putty that needed to be manipulated by warm fingers to make it malleable.

'She's a good girl, you know, is our Margaret.'

'Please don't praise her,' said Alison. 'Not in front of me.'

'Why not? Doesn't she deserve it?'

'The girl who got squiffy and lost her respectability? Well, go on,' said Alison when Dot didn't answer. 'Aren't you going to say anything?'

'I was waiting for you to finish the sentence, love.'

'What?'

'I thought you were going to say "lost her respectability with the man I ended up engaged to". The man who, by my reckoning, you didn't meet for another – how long? Eighteen months? Summat like that, anyroad.'

Whatever it was inside Alison hardened again. Why had she ever imagined it might help her to talk to Dot? 'Are you saying it's before my time and none of my business?'

'It has very unfortunately become your business,' said Dot.

'Yes, it has,' Alison agreed crisply. 'Which brings us right back to where we started.'

'Not quite,' said Dot. 'You told me not to praise Margaret.'

'Damn right I did.'

'I don't need to praise her,' Dot said mildly. 'The road I remember it, she's had enough praise off you to last her a lifetime.'

Vexed as she was, Alison couldn't suppress her curiosity. 'What?'

Dot waved a hand to indicate their surroundings. 'Doesn't being here jog your memory? That evening when Joan was having Max in the first-class restaurant, you and Margaret came here and used a ladder to find your way up onto the station canopy and set about extinguishing all them Jerry incendiaries. By, that took some guts. I say "you and Margaret", but actually it was more like "Margaret and you", wasn't it? That's how you told it afterwards. You couldn't stop talking about how she was the one with all the courage and the initiative and you just tagged along, following her lead and doing as you were told. It warmed my heart to see how much you admired her, it really did.'

Alison was silent. It was more than not speaking. It was a stillness deep inside.

'Eh, we were all bursting with pride for our Margaret after that.' Dot slid her arm through Alison's and hoicked her closer. 'And you, my lovely lass, you were the proudest of us all.'

Chapter Thirty

With the wedding now only four and a half weeks away, Margaret hoped that Alison could come to terms with the past. She, too, needed to come to terms with her own past. She'd visited Sally on her day off and, on her way home, her mind was crammed full with thoughts of her own lost baby. Was that wrong of her? Ridiculous? There was certainly nothing to be gained by it, but she couldn't stop herself. Until she had started helping Sally and involving herself so deeply in Sally's troubles, she had pushed her ill-fated pregnancy right to the back of her mind and done her best never to dwell on it again.

But now she couldn't help wondering, and all the what-ifs were playing out in her mind. The mother and baby home. The shame. The being kept apart from the respectable married mothers-to-be. The waiting. Having to part with her child. The never knowing what had become of him or her afterwards.

The him or her question loomed large. What would she have had? Sally said it was a question that all the unmarried girls were interested in, even though all but a couple of them knew they would have to give up their babies. Would Margaret have joined in with those conversations and the speculation if she'd ended up in that position? Presumably. Certainly.

Would she – would she have been jealous of Anna, jealous of her own sister, for being married and able to bring up her twins? The thought of little Tommy and Anne-Marie made Margaret's stomach clench. What if – what if that ill-fated pregnancy represented her one and only chance to be a mother?

When she arrived home, Alison opened the front door as she walked up the path. Margaret's heart dipped in dismay.

'Can we talk later?' Alison asked softly as Margaret entered the hall.

Margaret pushed her thoughts aside and nodded. Her emotions were currently fixed on Sally and her own lost child, but now she would have to channel them in Alison's direction, although her thoughts of her own baby were a part of Alison's situation, so maybe the wrench wouldn't be so great. But Alison's attitude towards Margaret's pregnancy was anything but sympathetic and Margaret would have to gird herself for the encounter.

Mrs Cooper and Mrs Grayson were keen to hear how Sally was getting on.

'She's blooming,' Margaret told them. To be honest, she'd been taken aback by how Sally's girth had increased, but it wouldn't be ladylike to say so. 'She's uncomfortable and wants it to be over.'

Mrs Cooper sighed. 'When a married lady can't wait for it to be over, she'll have a baby in her arms at the end of it, but Sally and those other unmarried girls . . . Poor things.'

Margaret pictured herself as one of the 'poor things', then shook her head as if to dislodge the idea. She was being stupid. This was Sally's situation, Sally's problem, not hers. Why were her thoughts constantly dragging her down memory lane while adding what-if embellishments?

Later, Mrs Cooper and Mrs Grayson went out to play cards with the neighbours.

Wanting to get it over with, Margaret said, 'Should we have that talk?'

They sat in the front room. Over to one side of the fireplace was a box of toys for Max, building bricks that Joan had found at the market, a dog knitted by Mrs Grayson, a spinning top Persephone had found in the attics at Darley Court.

Having braced herself for an attack, Margaret was taken aback when Alison said, 'I'm glad Sally is doing well. She deserves to have something go her way.'

'Yes, she does,' Margaret agreed. 'She paid a heavy price for trusting her rat of a boyfriend.'

'You paid a heavy price too,' said Alison, 'although Joel wasn't a rat, even if you thought he was at the time.'

Margaret waited. What was Alison building up to? She needed to remain strong in case Alison let fly.

'I'm going to be honest with you. It might hurt you to hear this, but I wasn't sorry that Joel's baby had died,' said Alison, and Margaret caught her breath. 'I wouldn't have wanted him to have a child already. But of course, if he'd known about the baby, he would immediately have married the mother. You.'

Margaret swallowed. 'And that would have been a mistake. I would presumably have lost the baby anyway and he would have found himself married to the wrong girl. If the child – if my baby had lived, Joel would have made a good husband and father, obviously, but he wouldn't have been truly happy with me, and in the end I would have seen that. He never felt about me the way he feels about you. I'm not just saying that. It's true.'

'Do you still have feelings for him?' Alison asked.

'No – and that's the truth too.'

'Is it?' Alison asked at once. 'You loved him so much you bought a wedding dress.'

Margaret shut her eyes for a moment. 'Don't remind me. It was a mad thing to do.'

'It shows how deep your feelings were.'

As much as Margaret longed to move on from this, she recognised Alison's need for certainty. Leaning forward, she spoke earnestly. 'I swear I haven't cared for Joel for a long time. Even so, it came as a shock to see how much you meant to him. It made me realise he'd never felt like that towards me. You're his one true love, Alison. He liked me at the time, but I was just another girlfriend. He cared about me, but it was never going to last, not on his side. I promise you, I was happy for the two of you when you got engaged. You and Joel are right together.' Margaret spoke honestly, generously and without regret.

'Did you feel bad keeping the secret from me?'

'No,' Margaret said frankly. 'I honestly believed it was the right thing to do. Once I knew that you didn't need to be warned off Joel, there was nothing to be gained by telling you, but there was still a lot to lose – still a lot for me to lose. When you've had a pregnancy out of wedlock, it's a secret you carry with you for the rest of your life and it isn't something you share willingly.'

'Then I went and spoiled it for you by finding out. I'm sorry,' Alison added unexpectedly. 'That was catty.'

Margaret shrugged lightly. 'I've been honest. Now it's your turn. Weren't you happier before you knew?'

'Ignorance is bliss, you mean?' Alison sounded sharp, but then she admitted, 'Actually, it was bliss.'

'I'm truly sorry for my part in spoiling things for you,' Margaret said simply.

'Can I ask you about the pregnancy and the miscarriage? I – I'd like to understand.'

Was this some sort of trap? Would Alison use this information against her at a later date? But recognising this as a moment for trust, Margaret slowly started to talk about the fear that had streamed through her when she'd finally admitted to herself that she really was pregnant and then the horror and agony of the miscarriage.

'I don't know what I'd have done without Joan. I don't want her to take any of the blame for what's happened. I don't want Dot to either. If you want to blame someone, blame me. They don't deserve to be hated when all they wanted to do was help me.'

'I don't hate them,' said Alison. 'I was shocked and angry – furious – when I first knew what they'd done. It felt as if they'd chosen you over me, but I know now it wasn't like that. Of course they wanted to help you.' She hesitated before adding, 'I'm glad you had support when you needed it.'

Surprise left Margaret almost breathless. 'I never expected to hear you say that.'

'You aren't the only one Dot helped, as it happens. I had a long talk with her last week and she reminded me of how much I admired you for your bravery the evening Max was born. It's true. You were amazing. Your courage was outstanding. Dot made me see that there's more to you than being Joel's old girlfriend. I gave myself some days to think about it – and she's right, of course. I'm not saying I want us to collapse into one another's arms and swear undying friendship, but I know now that I can cope with what happened. Dot helped me put it into a different perspective.'

'Thank you,' Margaret whispered.

'I've decided to move back home until the wedding,' said Alison. 'When I came to Wilton Close, I was escaping from home. Paul had got together with Katie, and then there was Lydia's wedding. It was pure torture having to be her bridesmaid, but I had to do it for the sake of appearances. Coming to live here was the right thing to do. Going back to Mum and Dad's might sound as if I'm escaping again, but it doesn't feel that way. It's a way of creating a distance between me and what's happened recently. Also, it would mean the world to Mum to have me there before the wedding. It feels right to me too. I want you to know I'm not storming off in a huff.'

'One thing we never discussed,' Margaret ventured, 'was whether I should step aside and not be a bridesmaid.'

'I've given that a lot of thought these past few days,' said Alison. 'What girl wants her husband-to-be's old flame at her wedding, let alone following her up the aisle?'

Margaret held her tongue. What was coming next? Clearly, she wasn't going to be at Alison's wedding.

'But then, you see,' said Alison, 'there's Colette.'

'Colette?' Margaret asked, puzzled.

'My mum was dead against her being a matron of honour, because of being separated. But Colette is my friend and I care about her. I want her at my wedding, not just as a guest, but walking up the aisle with me. So I put my foot down and insisted on her being a matron of honour.'

'Good for you,' said Margaret, 'but I don't see what that has to do with my situation.'

'Neither do I entirely,' said Alison. 'All I can tell you is that the two feel connected. It was important to stand by Colette. I admire and respect her and she didn't deserve the bad things that happened to her, but every now and again she mentions being snubbed by a neighbour. Even after everything Tony did, some people look down on her for being separated.'

'It's horribly unfair,' said Margaret.

'It would also be unfair if people were to look down on you – and by "people", I mean me,' said Alison. 'Colette isn't the only person I admire and respect. I have finally allowed myself to see how hard it must have been for you when you thought Joel was a cad and you wanted to warn me against him. Everything that's happened . . .' She made a vague movement with her hand. 'I was swept along with it – swept aside by it. What I want now is to feel in charge of what happens next, and that includes having the bridesmaids I want.'

'Are you saying you want me to be one of them?' Margaret asked.

'I'm saying I want the brave girl who extinguished all those incendiaries to follow me up the aisle.'

'Oh, Alison,' breathed Margaret.

'There is another thing,' said Alison. 'Lizzie. The last time I saw her, I didn't know it was the last time. I think about that sometimes. I imagine having the chance to say goodbye – but that's stupid, because I wouldn't have said goodbye. I'd have dragged her out of that building so she didn't get killed and she'd still be here now. But she isn't here and you are. Regardless of anything that happened in the past, you're my friend and I care about you and I need you to know that – because I never said it to Lizzie.'

Chapter Thirty-One

Alison dressed carefully in the midnight-blue gown Lydia had given her in exchange for her old apricot dress. She smoothed her hands over the fitted bodice and moved a little so that the skirt's soft flare swung gently. She felt hopeful. She admired her reflection, appreciating not just the dress but also her complexion. Her skin looked brighter, as did her eyes, now that the weight of sorrow had lifted from her. It hadn't been just sorrow either. There had been anger – and jealousy. Yes, jealousy. She was able to face it now. She had been bitterly jealous of Margaret for making a baby with Joel. That was what it all came down to for her.

Thank heaven she'd found a way to make peace with it. After floundering around in fury and betrayal, she had taken charge of her thoughts and feelings, refusing to be bogged down in unhappiness any longer. It was time to move on. If she let the bad feelings continue, it would affect her relationship with Joel, placing a barrier between them, and that was the last thing she wanted.

Feeling confident, she went downstairs. Mrs Cooper and Mrs Grayson admired her appearance. Soon it was time for her to leave. She had rung earlier from the public telephone box to book a taxi to take her to Joel's building, where he stood ready on the pavement. He climbed in beside her and she sighed with pleasure. He was so handsome. But Alison didn't miss the anxiety in his eyes. She felt a sense of calm. She held this situation in her hands.

The taxi took them to the Midland Hotel, the scene of Joel's proposal.

'Before we go into the dining room,' said Alison, 'can we sit and talk? I want you to understand what it's been like for me these past weeks.'

They sat down. Alison had planned what she wanted to say. Speaking quietly, she described her anger and frustration.

'The worst part was that you and the other three didn't come seeking my forgiveness, because you all thought you hadn't done anything wrong. It might sound childish, but if you'd all said, "We're so sorry. We made a terrible mistake," I'd have felt better. I wanted you all to be sorry. That's the truth. But you weren't sorry because you all believed you'd done the right thing. It was as if I was supposed to see it through your eyes and just accept it, which I found galling, to say the least.'

'Darling, I know you were badly hurt,' said Joel, 'but Margaret was too and it really was important to respect her privacy.'

'And if this had happened to anybody other than you and me, I'd have agreed,' said Alison. 'But it didn't happen to someone else. It happened to us and it's not so easy to be high-minded when you're on the receiving end. I felt betrayed.'

'You can't imagine how many times I've wished I'd never met Margaret.'

'I can, actually,' said Alison, 'because you're an honourable man and I know this has torn you apart.'

'I love you so much,' said Joel.

'I never doubted that for a single moment. I love you too. That's why I want to put it all behind us.'

'You do?' There was a sudden light in Joel's eyes. 'You're my one and only. I've known that ever since I met you.'

'That's very important to me,' said Alison. 'Being Dr Joel Maitland's one and only is the best thing that ever happened to me.'

Joel reached to take her hand. 'Actually, I do need your forgiveness.'

'You don't need to say that now.'

'Yes, I do. I want you to forgive me for the way I told you last year about having got an old girlfriend in the family way. I shouldn't have done it the way I did. It happened straight after Venetia had tried to foist Rachel back onto me – the same day, the same afternoon. You already had the Rachel shock to cope with – and then I piled the pregnant girlfriend and the miscarriage on top. I shouldn't have done that. I should have told you on a separate occasion. Above all, I should have given you the chance to be upset. Instead, I told you so as to get it out in the open. That was selfish of me and I'm sorry. We never talked about it again and so I thought it was all right.'

'Thank you.' Alison thought she might sag with relief, but instead she sat up straight. 'Thank you for understanding why I've been so fraught. I've been jealous of you and Margaret, even though I knew there was nothing to be jealous of. And I couldn't bear to think of that baby. I know the child was never born, but I kept thinking that if it had been, then you'd already be a father. That was such a hard thing for me to contemplate, especially when you and I have agreed not to have a family right away.'

Joel nodded. 'Yes, I can see that. It's a strange thing to picture, isn't it? But it didn't happen. I know it's impossible not to imagine it – but it didn't happen and I hope the thought will fade away in time.'

Now that they were speaking with such openness, there was something else Alison had to bring up. 'If you'd known Margaret was expecting, you'd have married her.'

'Yes, I would. It would have been the right thing to do. But let's have one thing perfectly clear.' Joel leaned closer and looked deep into her eyes, holding her gaze. 'That would have been my one and only reason for marrying her.'

'To make an honest woman of her,' Alison murmured. She thought of the wedding dress Margaret had purchased. She could slide it into the conversation quite naturally – but she kept quiet. Margaret didn't deserve that kind of humiliation. It turned out that the others weren't the only ones who thought it important to protect Margaret's privacy and her reputation.

'It might sound harsh,' said Joel, 'but yes. Margaret's a lovely girl, but she's not the girl for me – not the wife for me. There's only one girl who has ever been the wife for me and I'm looking at her right now and hoping with all my heart that she can forgive me. Do you forgive me, Alison?'

Alison experienced a momentary giddiness as long-held tensions slid away. Then her heart filled with warmth that spilled over and cascaded all through her.

'Of course,' she told Joel. 'But let's make a promise that in future we'll always talk things over properly.'

'I promise,' said Joel. 'And I'm grateful for your understanding.'

'I don't want your gratitude.'

Joel smiled. 'Then how about my deep and undying devotion? Will that do?'

'For starters.'

Alison reached into her handbag.

'I've got something for you. It isn't new, but I hope you like it.'

Joel opened the box and took out a wristwatch with a dark green leather strap.

'I managed to get the strap changed,' said Alison. 'You can't imagine how hard it was to find a green watch strap, but I specially wanted a green one so that it matches my engagement ring.'

Joel smiled at her, his eyes full of love. 'An engagement watch. I love it.'

'It's to represent all the time we'll have together,' said Alison, sighing happily as the pieces of her world slotted back together again.

Chapter Thirty-Two

Now she was in her third week in her new job, Joan was slowly getting to grips with the new routine. There had been no problems with the arrangements she'd made for Max. Brizo's care was pretty straightforward. On the days when he wasn't taken to Victoria Station, he was looked after by the Wilton Close ladies or by Gran. Joan was aware of having to cram everything in – shopping, cooking, housework, taking Brizo for walks and, of course, spending all the time she could with Max. She had to do all the things she used to do, but in a fraction of the time.

Getting to work punctually posed a challenge, but she managed well enough when she had a nine o'clock start. Just when she thought she'd got to grips with that, she'd been put on the other shift, which required her to be at her desk for eight thirty, which ought to have been a simple matter of getting out of bed half an hour earlier but somehow wasn't. A strong part of her wanted to keep silent. She hated the thought of looking like she couldn't cope. But she also understood how important her friends' support was.

'How's the new job?' Alison asked her in the buffet.

'I'm learning a lot.'

Dot chimed in. 'Just as important, how are you finding all the rushing around that us working wives have to do?'

Joan plumped for honesty. 'I'm finding it hard, since you ask. It seems there's never enough time.'

'Welcome to the club, chick,' said Dot understandingly. 'Don't fret. You'll get used to it. It's extra hard for you because of having a baby to look after an' all.'

Some of Joan's burden lifted. 'Thanks, Dot. The hardest part is seeing others seeming to manage so well and feeling I'm not cut out for it.'

The others all spoke at once, surprised and concerned by her lack of confidence.

'It takes some getting used to,' said Dot, 'but you're doing fine.'

'Give it a while and let yourself adjust,' Cordelia advised. 'Taking on a full-time job on top of being responsible for a home and family is a considerable undertaking, especially when there's a baby.'

Joan smiled at her friends. 'Thank you. I've been feeling wobbly about everything.'

'Not to mention jolly tired, I imagine,' said Colette.

'You've all made me feel better,' said Joan. 'I've got to give myself time to get used to it.'

'Set your mind to it,' said Alison, 'and you'll be fine.'

Her friends' reassurance shored up Joan's confidence and made her feel she didn't have to keep her struggles a secret. Previously she had worried about appearing inadequate, but now she realised that a bit of cheerful honesty brought forth understanding from others. Even Gran, who was nothing if not judgemental, said 'Nobody said it would be easy' in a good-humoured voice and not the tone of criticism for which Joan had braced herself.

Feeling better in herself, Joan decided to go with Margaret to see Sally on Saturday morning. Bob's mum and dad had taken Max home with them yesterday evening and were keeping him until teatime today.

'Strictly speaking,' Joan told Margaret as they set off together, 'I ought to spend this morning doing housework and shopping, but you know what they say. All work and no play. I haven't seen Sally since she left Wilton Close. I wouldn't want her to think I've forgotten her.'

Any feelings of guilt Joan had about abandoning her duties were soon dispelled as she and Margaret chatted on their journey. Margaret described how she and Alison had made peace.

'I'm pleased to hear it,' said Joan. 'When Mrs Grayson told me Alison was moving back home until the wedding, I was scared everything had gone horribly wrong.'

Margaret smiled wryly. 'Even more horribly wrong than before? It's difficult to see how that could have been possible.'

'She's moving back to her parents' later today, isn't she? It'll be strange for you, being the only girl in the house.'

'That's how you started, isn't it?' Margaret reminded her. 'As the only one.'

'Then along came Mabel. I used to have the single room that Mrs Cooper now has and she had the double. When Mabel moved in, Mrs Cooper swapped things round. I wonder who you'll end up sharing with.'

'It's not as though we have any more friends in need of a billet,' said Margaret.

'Maybe the billeting officer will get wind of it and allocate someone. That's what happened to my gran at one point.'

After two bus rides and a short walk, they arrived at Rook-ery House. Margaret had already explained about having to go round the back. Joan had thought she was ready for it, but it made her feel that Sally and the other unmarried girls were having their noses rubbed in it.

Margaret led the way upstairs. Sally was in a plain little room, sitting on a wooden armchair, wearing a coat that didn't meet across her front.

After greetings had been exchanged, Sally said, 'I can't quite believe this is happening. It's another step along the way. From today, I'm going to be a respectable married lady. They've even given me a ring to wear – look. I had to pay a deposit to make sure I give it back.'

Her voice was neutral and it was impossible to be certain what Sally was feeling. Bitter? Angry? Ground down? There was one thing Joan was sure of.

She crouched beside Sally and took her hand. 'It's scary, isn't it? It's impossible not to feel scared of the birth.'

Sally gulped. 'Walking through that front door into the home will make it feel much closer. All the girls talk about how they can't wait for it to be over – and I want that too – but there's the small matter of the birth to get through first.' She left a silence before adding, 'Without the thought of a baby in my arms afterwards.'

Anxiety fluttered across Margaret's face. 'You aren't thinking of keeping it?'

'No, of course not,' Sally said at once. She looked at them with bleakness in her eyes. 'But what if I suddenly want to? What if I can't help it? The girls talk about this huge rush of love you're supposed to feel. Imagine feeling that – and then the baby gets taken away from you.'

Margaret looked stricken, which was understandable. She had become close to Sally in recent months. Joan knew it was up to her to say the right thing – whatever that was. She prayed she wouldn't make a hash of it.

'Sally, I can't begin to imagine the distress you're facing. My little boy means the world to me and I'm so sorry that you're in this position. You have to be strong. I know that's easy for me to say, but it's all the advice I can offer. A girl in your situation doesn't have choices. All you can do is be strong and get through it.'

Sally nodded tearfully. 'I wish I'd never set eyes on Alan. I wish I'd never listened to his lies.'

Joan rose as Sally pushed herself to her feet and made a show of glancing left and right as if she didn't know where her case was, so she had a moment to swipe away her tears. With a final sniff, she hauled a smile into place.

'Let's go,' she said. 'I'm about to become a respectable married lady.'

Margaret picked up the suitcase and they headed downstairs and outside, walking around the side of the old house to escort Sally through the front door.

Alison cycled over to Darley Court, wondering why Persephone had invited her and in particular why she'd been so insistent. She had nabbed her for five minutes at work yesterday to make the arrangement.

'But I'm moving back to my parents' house tomorrow,' Alison had protested.

'Come to Darley Court first,' Persephone urged her. 'Please. It'll be worth it.'

'Why?'

Persephone had glanced around. They were in the canteen and Alison was sitting at a table with some other girls who, no matter how politely they continued talking to one another, wouldn't be able to help overhearing what was said.

'Just come to Darley Court in the morning,' Persephone had encouraged her with a smile.

So here Alison was now, parking her bicycle under the sticking-out porch that was big enough for an old-fashioned carriage to go underneath so that its travellers could get out in the dry. The big front door opened before Alison reached the top of the steps and there was Persephone, ready to draw her inside, her violet eyes bright with excitement.

'I'm so glad you've come. Did you have a chilly ride? Never mind. I think what I'm about to show you might warm you up.'

Alison smiled, intrigued. 'What's this about?'

'You'll see. First of all, I've got some visitors for you. This way.'

Knowing she hadn't a hope of receiving an explanation, Alison didn't bother asking questions as Persephone took her to a small sitting room that felt cosy on a nippy winter's day like this, thanks to the deep red velvet curtains and pelmet and the crackling fire surrounded by a marble chimney piece. Miss Brown looked round as Alison walked in, but before Alison could utter a word, Mum and Lydia rose from the sofa to hug her.

'What are you doing here?' Alison asked them. She turned to Persephone, saying with mock severity, 'This time you really do have to tell me what's happening.'

'What's happening, my love,' said Persephone, 'is that we're going to play at trying on wedding dresses – or at least you are and the rest of us will ooh and aah and tell you how beautiful you look.'

'But first,' said Miss Brown, 'sit down and have a cup of tea to warm you up.'

Alison sank onto a seat. She must have looked as astonished as she felt because the others laughed.

Persephone explained.

'After you wrote to Mabel to say that Joan's dress didn't suit, Mabel wrote to me to suggest my coming-out dress, which was white, of course. Mabel's coming-out dress was sent to Barbara Cartland to add to her stash of wedding dresses for girls in the forces to borrow. So I was all set to write to Nanny Trehearn-Hobbs and ask her to parcel mine up, and then I thought what we really need is a selection, so I sent my sister a telegram.'

'A telegram!' Alison and Lydia exclaimed in unison.

'That's what one does in an emergency,' Persephone replied. 'SEND WEDDING DRESS STOP URGENT STOP. Iphigenia immediately telephoned here, demanding to know if the dress was for me. I explained about your big day looming and you still needing a dress and Iphigenia said, and I quote, "Tell her not to worry. Auntie Iphigenia will save the day." I hope she has. Even if she hasn't, you'll have a wizard morning trying on these gowns.'

'Gowns, plural?' asked Alison.

'Iphigenia never does anything by halves,' said Persephone with an airy wave of her hand. 'Have you finished your tea? Shall we all go upstairs?'

Alison seemed to float through the following hour. She kept having to tell herself that this was really happening. Laid out across Persephone's bed was an array of gowns that took her breath away. She laughed in amazement and delight at the thought of trying them on, and she shed tears of gratitude at the thoughtfulness and generosity of the Trehearn-Hobbs sisters.

'You might like to try this one first,' said Persephone. 'It's Iphigenia's wedding dress.'

She held up an ivory gown with sleeves that flared from the elbow. It had a knee-length skirt over the ankle-length underskirt, both superbly cut with a floaty flare. Trying it on, Alison couldn't tear her gaze away from her reflection.

'Don't forget the veil,' said Persephone. 'There's Iphigenia's, and she's also sent a couple of others that she borrowed off her chums.'

'I want to wear hers,' Alison said at once.

'You haven't seen it yet,' said Persephone.

'Or the others,' Mum added.

'I want to wear Iphigenia's,' Alison declared firmly. 'She's been so kind. I want to wear her veil.' She turned to her mother. 'You understand, don't you?'

Mum nodded. 'Of course. I'm overwhelmed by her kindness. Imagine doing all this for your sister's friend.'

'Everyone mucks in in wartime,' said Persephone.

She carefully undid a tissue-wrapped bundle. Out came a tiara of tiny wax and silk flowers with a dream of a veil of silk tulle. Persephone held it up to be admired.

'It's floor-length at the back, but the part you wear over your face just falls as far as the bust.'

'It's lovely,' breathed Lydia.

'My wedding veil,' Alison whispered.

Persephone was about to put it on Alison's head, then she stood back and offered it to Mum.

'Would you like to, Mrs Lambert?'

Mum fixed the tiara in position, looking critically at it before she moved her hands away. Alison turned back to the cheval mirror and her breath hitched in pure delight.

'You'll knock Joel's socks off,' Persephone said quietly.

'Now you've just got to choose the dress,' said Lydia. 'Try this one next.'

Alison laughed. 'Back to the dressing-up box.'

'Let me take the headdress off first,' said Mum.

Alison tried on Persephone's coming-out dress, which was of white taffeta with a fitted bodice, wide shoulder straps and a floor-length flared skirt. After that there was a creamy-white dress that fell to mid-calf and a winter-white gown with a short matching jacket. Then there was a dove-grey silk evening gown belonging to Iphigenia with a round neck and sleek long sleeves, the skirt spreading into a rippling train behind.

The moment Alison saw herself in it, she knew this was the one.

She turned to her mother. 'This one.'

'I'm surprised at you going for dove grey,' said Mum.

'So am I,' said Alison, feeling happy tears welling up. 'I thought I wanted white or cream, but this is perfect. It's so elegant, and I love the train.'

'Try it on with the veil,' urged Lydia.

Mum stepped forward again and placed the tiara on Alison's head. There were tears in Mum's eyes. She looked at Persephone. 'Will you give me your sister's address? I want to write and thank her.'

'We'll all write and thank her,' said Lydia.

Alison went to Persephone. 'Thank you as well. You're the one who made this happen.' She looked down at herself, hardly able to believe she would have such a glorious dress to wear.

'It's a pleasure,' said Persephone, giving her a gentle push in the direction of the mirror.

Alison let admiration wash over her for a while. When Mum said softly, 'Let's get you changed back into your own clothes,' Alison agreed with reluctance. She couldn't bear to take off her wedding dress.

'Before you do that,' Persephone said, 'there's one more thing Iphigenia thought you might care for.'

'Something else?' Lydia exclaimed in wonderment. 'What is it? *Oh*,' she breathed as Persephone produced a long fur cloak lined with a cream fabric whose faint glimmer pronounced it to be silk.

'It's rather gorgeous, isn't it?' said Persephone. 'If it's cold on your big day, you don't want to freeze.'

'You could wear it to travel to and from the church,' said Mum.

'Try it on,' Lydia urged. 'Let me lift the veil out of the way.'

Alison stood there in state of blissful disbelief as the long fur was draped around her shoulders. She had her wedding dress and veil and a wonderful winter cloak. If any remnants of yearning to be a June bride still lingered, they evaporated in that moment. She was going to be a winter bride – better yet, a Christmas bride. Her wedding was going to be everything she could have wished for.

'Walk over to the door,' said Persephone, 'then turn round and walk towards the mirror.'

Instead, Alison walked over to her friend and hugged her.

Chapter Thirty-Three

Alison was in her old bedroom, unpacking, when Lydia walked in.

'Some things don't change,' Alison remarked. 'You were always barging in, as I recall.'

'Who, me?' Lydia put on an innocent expression.

'Yes, you. You used to help yourself to my clothes.'

'That was your fault for having nice things.' Lydia sat on the bed. 'Seriously, does it feel like a step backwards to come here after living away from home?'

'I'm glad to be back,' said Alison. 'It feels right to be at home before the wedding.' Should she confide? Yes. After the emotion that morning of finding her beautiful wedding dress, she felt close to her sister. 'I left here in a state of such wretchedness, but the next time I leave it will be in a state of pure happiness. That's the way I want to leave Mum and Dad's house.'

Lydia nodded in understanding. 'You're lucky. All your tough times are behind you now. When you get married, you and Joel will live together. For most war brides, our tough times begin after the wedding with a long separation.'

'I do know how lucky I am,' Alison assured her. Lydia was fond of reminding her how fortunate she was to have Joel here. 'How is Alec? Any word?'

'Not recently. It's like that. No letters at all and then half a dozen all at once.'

'Does he write good letters?'

'Not bad, and at least they're letters. One of the girls at work, her husband sends those postcards where you cross out what doesn't apply. Next to him, Alec looks like William Shakespeare.'

Apparently not wanting to continue with the subject, Lydia got up and opened the hanging cupboard. She didn't remove the wedding dress but lifted the fabric, fingering it gently.

'It's heavenly,' she said. 'You're lucky to have friends in high places.'

Alison laughed. 'I won't want to give it back. I can tell you that for nothing.'

Mum walked in. 'Leave that gown alone, Lydia. It has to be kept perfect.'

'Honestly, Mum,' Lydia protested. 'I'm not a child.'

'You're tucked away in here just like when you were children playing at schools with your teddies and your dolls. Come downstairs. We need to talk about the wedding.' Mum turned and left the room.

'And we can't possibly talk about the wedding in here,' Lydia whispered.

'Heaven forbid,' Alison whispered back. 'It has to be done at the table.'

'Like all the most important events of the war.'

They went downstairs to go through all the arrangements. As Alison joined in, she felt aglow with happiness. Her troubles were behind her and she had acquired the most wonderful wedding dress imaginable, together with a fairy-tale veil.

When it was time for Lydia to head back to her flat, Alison walked there with her.

'Don't look now,' Lydia whispered urgently, 'but Paul and that Katie are over there.'

Alison was dismayed. They were the very last people she wanted to see.

'They're pretending not to have noticed us,' said Lydia. 'Look at them gazing into that shop window. As if there's anything on display these days! Come on.'

She hauled Alison across the road. Alison tried to pull away, but Lydia wasn't having it. She dragged Alison over to her old boyfriend and the girl he'd left her for.

'Hello, you two!' Lydia gushed. 'How lovely to see you. How *are* you?'

'Oh. We didn't see you,' said Paul, looking uncomfortable. 'How are you?' he asked Alison.

'She's *fine*, thanks for asking,' said Lydia before Alison could open her mouth. 'She just moved back home for the build-up to the wedding. It's all so *exciting*. My goodness, you should see the dress. A friend had it sent up from London. Well, we mustn't keep you. We're on an important wedding mission.'

They went on their way.

Once they were at a safe distance, Alison said, 'Lydia, you're dreadful.'

'No, I'm not. They deserved to squirm with embarrassment after what they did to you. "We didn't see you," my foot.'

Lydia's flat was the downstairs of a house near the cricket pitch. Dad had done up the kitchen with new cupboard doors, a big luxury these days, and he'd installed a new Belfast sink. Lydia had done her best with the sitting room, thanks to second-hand curtains and cushion covers, and it looked pretty in a faded way. Everywhere was tidy and clean, but then it was bound to be. There was only Lydia living here. Alison hadn't forgotten Lydia's sorrow about not having a honeymoon baby. If Lydia had actually had a baby, he or she would have been not much different in age to Joan's Max.

Lydia had borrowed a copy of the Utility furniture catalogue from a neighbour.

'Joel and I are lucky to be moving into an almost fully furnished house,' said Alison. 'I don't suppose we'd be entitled to anything.'

'There's no harm in looking,' said Lydia, flicking through the pages. 'It's the closest we get to shopping for furniture these days. Besides, you'll be newly-weds and that's who Utility is for – newly-weds and the bombed-out.'

'They aren't making sofas,' Alison noted.

'Too much wood and upholstery,' said Lydia, 'but these armchairs aren't bad and this fireside chair has an adjustable back. Two pounds, ten and six.'

'Just think,' said Alison. 'After the war, for years to come, heaps of families will be living with Utility furniture. It's a sobering thought.'

'No, it isn't,' said Lydia, eyeing up the choice of bedroom furniture. 'It's a patriotic thought. Utility is a way of sharing out what's available. It's about doing the best for the population in wartime. That's something to be proud of.'

When Alison went home, she smiled as she remembered Lydia's way of dealing with Paul and Katie. At least she needn't worry now about possibly bumping into them again. Lydia had effectively removed any reason for her to feel awkward. Mind you, after Lydia's performance, Paul and Katie would probably run a mile if they saw Alison coming.

Lydia was the best sister ever. Alison was delighted that she had managed to purchase a cake of Lux soap for her for Christmas. Lux was advertised by Judy Garland, who was Lydia's favourite film star.

Alison let herself into the house. It felt good to be back at home. Best of all, with her troubles well and truly behind her, she could concentrate on looking forward to the wedding on Christmas Eve. Joel was coming to pick her up that evening to take her out. There was something rather exciting about that. It had always been Paul who'd collected her from here and this was a way of wiping out that memory.

But when Joel arrived, he looked serious.

'I'm so sorry, Alison,' he told her. 'It's the house. We can't have it. It's been declared uninhabitable.'

'But we've seen it,' Alison protested. 'There's nothing wrong with it.'

'Grundy and Clara are moving out as we speak,' said Joel.

'What happened?' asked Dad.

'The house is at the end of the road,' Joel explained. 'Next to it is a field. Evidently, there was an underground cavern in this field which was created by a bomb that penetrated deep into the ground before it exploded. Because this took place underground, nobody realised and the bomb went unrecorded – until now. The ground on top of the cavern

317

collapsed in on itself yesterday, creating a whopping great crater. Unfortunately, all this happened near enough to the house to compromise the structure. It's undermined the foundations and there's a crack up the outside wall big enough to put your fist inside.'

Dad shook his head. 'That's serious.'

As the situation gradually sank in, Alison felt cold and wobbly. What a way to end the day that had started so gloriously with Iphigenia's wedding dress.

Where were they going to live now?

Chapter Thirty-Four

Monday saw Joan returning to a nine o'clock start. Phew. But it was important not to relax and feel she had lots of time. That would end in disaster. She left Brizo with Gran; he was having the day at home. Then she dropped off Max at the Lizzie Nursery and walked briskly to the bus stop. It was a grey day with a chilly breeze and she was glad of her warm gloves, though she'd forgotten her scarf because she'd been too busy ensuring Max was wrapped up warmly. He was more important than she was.

Arriving in town, she alighted and hurried to work. How much easier life would be if she was based in one of the offices inside Hunts Bank. It would save precious minutes. She still yearned for a job on the station. That was what had brought her back into the workforce. But in wartime, you didn't do what you wanted. You did as you were told. Drat Fay Brewer and her 'I see you've worked as a clerk before.'

Joan experienced the usual twinge of annoyance at the thought of Miss Brewer, and never mind that she was being unreasonable. She simply couldn't help it. If she was honest, she didn't want to help it. Being vexed with Fay Brewer was like putting petrol in a motor car. You needed fuel to make the engine run. Well, disliking Fay Brewer seemed to give Joan the fuel she needed to cram in all her responsibilities at top speed, which was how her life felt these days.

The cold wind caught her as she stepped out into the open beside the permanent way to head for the PAYE building. She had to snatch at her hat so as not to lose it. The barrage balloon wires thrummed in the stiff breeze, the giant oval-shaped balloons moving solemnly overhead.

Her face stinging with cold, Joan was glad to get indoors. It was the tail end of November now. December would start on Wednesday. As she pulled the door to behind her, it was almost yanked out of her hand. For a second she blamed a gust of wind, then Miss Palmer came hurrying in, bringing a waft of chill with her.

'It's proper parky out there,' said Miss Palmer. 'Look at you without a scarf. You're made of sterner stuff than I am.'

Joan hung up her coat and tidied her hair before going to her sit-up-and-beg desk. She felt she was doing better with the work now, though she worried all the time about making mistakes. Sometimes she lifted her head to glance around the room. Everybody else always seemed to be working steadily and without problems. She couldn't rid herself of the feeling that she shouldn't really be here, as if she had cheated her way into a grammar school class and it was only a matter of time before she was found out.

Halfway through the morning, the office door swung open, accompanied by the sound of laughter and followed by the outer door shutting. Fay Brewer appeared.

'Sorry about that, everyone. The wind's getting up and it blew open the office door as I came into the lobby.'

'Good morning, Miss Brewer.' Mrs Clements went over to her, glancing around the office at the same time, which had the effect of making everyone return their attention to their work. 'Would you care for a cup of tea? I believe we need more water. Whose turn is it?'

'Mine.' Joan capped her fountain pen.

Mrs Clements told Miss Brewer about having to cross the line to fetch water.

Miss Brewer gave Joan a polite nod. 'Good morning, Mrs Hubble.' To Mrs Clements she said, 'Thanks for the offer, but there's no need on my account.'

Joan slid from her high stool to the floor. 'We need the water anyway.'

'Then I'll come with.' Fay Brewer smiled at her. 'It'll give us the chance to have a chat.'

In the lobby, they donned their outdoor things, then went outside into the cold wind. The balloon cables sang with a long drawn-out whine. Fay Brewer said something, but her words were lost beneath a loud creaking sound from one of the cables.

'Sorry,' said Joan. 'I didn't catch that.'

'I asked how you're getting on.'

'Fine, thank you. I've learned a lot.'

'It's a big responsibility, handling tax. Is that what we're heading for?' Miss Brewer indicated the water column and water tower across the tracks.

'Yes, though we actually get the water in that small building over to the side. Hang on.' Joan looked up at the signals. 'There's a train on its way.'

'There's no sign of it yet.'

'You can't be too careful,' said Joan.

There was a loud scraping noise, followed by a sharp whipping sound. They both turned to look. One of the barrage balloons had broken loose.

'Quick!' Miss Brewer exclaimed. 'We have to secure it.'

They sprinted towards the dangling cables. The wind changed direction, snatching Joan's breath and slapping her face. Much worse, it sent the barrage balloon on a different course, this time heading across the railway tracks. The two of them launched themselves at the nearest cable, fighting with all their strength to tether the balloon to a signal pole. Having succeeded, they staggered backwards. Joan's hands felt red-raw inside her gloves. She was breathing hard, but she laughed in relief and triumph when she caught Fay Brewer's eye.

Miss Brewer started to say something, but then there was a new noise, a grinding followed by a crack, that happened slowly, then ended in a rush as the signal pole was torn from the ground. The barrage balloon moved on once more, dragging cables behind it. Fay Brewer and Joan leaped out of the way, but Miss Brewer caught a glancing blow that sent her sprawling. Joan went to help her to her feet, but Miss Brewer was already scrambling after the trailing cables.

'Come on!' she shouted. 'We have to fasten that wire.'

A familiar sound penetrated Joan's mind.

'The train's coming.'

There was a prolonged screech of brakes as the driver saw the danger ahead.

The two women threw themselves at the cable and hung on. Joan's shoulders all but tore from their sockets, but she didn't let go. Her only thought was for the safety of the train.

'The wagons!' Joan called.

Together they dragged the cable towards the line of goods wagons in the sidings – but how on earth were they to wrap it around a wagon?

'The couplings,' said Joan.

'The what?'

Joan didn't answer. Heaving with all her might, she hauled the cable towards the sturdy metal parts that linked two of the wagons near the centre of the line. Miss Brewer followed her lead, seeming to grasp what Joan intended. Together they heaved the cable across the coupling. Now they would have to bring it back underneath and up again, wrapping it around as many times as possible so it couldn't work loose. The couplings shifted and clanked.

Then all at once they weren't on their own. The other workers from the office came running and stumbling across the sidings to help them. More hands reached for the cable, more arms tugged hard and the stout wire was secured, the effort sending several women toppling over backwards.

'That's done it,' Mrs Clements declared breathlessly. 'It's going to hold.'

'We've saved the train,' gasped Miss Palmer.

'Not us,' said Mrs Clements. 'Mrs Hubble and Miss Brewer. We just came along at the end.'

'The cables wouldn't have knocked the train over – would they?' asked Miss Brewer.

'No,' said Mr Darwin, 'but they'd have bashed in some windows as they went on their way. Just imagine the injuries. You were splendid, ladies.'

'It wasn't me so much as Mrs Hubble,' said Miss Brewer. 'She was the one who realised we could make use of the wagons.' She smiled warmly at Joan. 'Well done. Good show.'

To Joan's surprise, Fay Brewer hugged her. Even more to Joan's surprise, she hugged her back.

In high spirits, the PAYE clerks saw the train on its way with much waving. The passengers waved back.

'What a tale they'll have to tell when they get home,' said Miss Palmer.

'That's nothing compared to the story our two heroines will have to tell,' said Mrs Clements.

It was quite some time before work resumed in the office. There was far too much adrenaline flowing for that. As they all poured indoors, the cry went up, 'Put the kettle on, someone!' and then there was a burst of laughter because water still had to be fetched from the column.

A wag said to Joan, 'Shirking your water duty, Mrs Hubble?'

'Some folk will do anything to get out of fetching the water,' said someone else.

Mr Darwin put a telephone call through to Hunts Bank and soon a squad of engineers arrived to take charge of the barrage balloon and check the wagon couplings for damage.

Joan felt all fired up. Only now that it was over did it really start to sink in what she and Fay – yes, Fay, no longer Miss Brewer – had achieved. They might have sustained nasty injuries if those cables had clipped them hard. Fay was lucky to have got off as lightly as she had. Joan was grateful she would be going home in one piece.

'You must be bursting with pride for saving the train,' said one of her colleagues.

'Actually, I'm more surprised than anything else,' said Joan. 'And I couldn't have done it on my own.'

She looked across at Fay, who was nursing a mug of tea in both hands. Fay gave her a nod but didn't come over.

Mr Darwin emerged from his office. 'Miss Brewer, Mrs Hubble, you shall both be required to go to Hunts Bank to write reports about what happened this morning.'

Fay put down her mug. 'I'm heading back there now, so I'll get mine done. Mrs Hubble can do hers when it's convenient.'

Joan made up her mind. 'Should I go now with Miss Brewer?' she asked her boss. 'That would be the most efficient way.'

'Very well,' Mr Darwin agreed, 'but come straight back. Everyone back to your desks, please. That's enough excitement for one morning.'

Joan and Fay donned their outdoor garb once more and set off. It wasn't a long walk and Joan didn't intend to waste a minute of it.

'I owe you an apology,' she said frankly.

Fay looked at her in surprise. 'What for?'

'Because I've been ungracious. I'd set my heart on the job you got and it was one heck of a blow when they gave it to you instead.'

'Miss Emery did mention what a good candidate you were – except that I came along.'

'It sounds big-headed now,' said Joan, 'but at the time I really thought I was going to be appointed.'

'It must have been a big disappointment,' said Fay.

'Then you were given the task of finding me a suitable position.'

'Thus adding insult to injury,' Fay suggested.

The glow in Joan's cheeks owed nothing to the chilly air or her lack of a scarf. 'I know nobody intended it to be that way, but you're right. That was how it felt at the time. I know how childish that makes me sound. And then you gave me a clerical post, which was the last thing in the world I wanted.'

'But you were a clerk once before,' said Fay. 'It says on your work record that you were good at it.'

'I was hoping for a job on the station.'

'I was told to get you something with office hours. That doesn't fit in with station work.'

'I know,' said Joan. 'It was just me being unreasonable.'

'I wouldn't have put you down as the unreasonable type.'

Joan was relieved that Fay recognised that. 'I'm not – well, not as a rule. I'm sorry I've been such a twerp.'

'No harm done,' said Fay.

'There's something more.' Now that she'd started, Joan wanted to get it all off her chest. 'My friends, the ones I meet up with in the buffet, they like you because of how you helped Mabel with the Lizzie Cooper Nursery.'

'That's nice to know.'

'They like you for yourself, too, and I – well, I was jealous, I suppose, but I'm not any more.'

'I'm sorry you didn't get a job you wanted, but it can't be changed now,' said Fay. 'It wouldn't be right to do that sort of favour for a friend.'

The beginnings of a smile tugged at Joan's lips. 'We're friends, then?'

'If we were enemies, I'd pack you off to the coalyard,' said Fay.

'Well then,' said Joan, smiling broadly now, 'we'd better be friends, hadn't we?'

Chapter Thirty-Five

That Monday was to be a buffet evening. Joan had an extra reason for wanting to see her friends. She'd asked Fay if she would care to join them and Fay had accepted. The thought of being on good terms with Fay Brewer put Joan in high spirits for the rest of the day. She hadn't known Fay very long, but now that she'd stopped being an idiot, she thought well of her – and, of course, Fay came with Mabel's highest recommendation!

When Joan joined her friends in the buffet, it wasn't too busy, so for once, instead of crowding around a single table, they could push two tables together and spread out a bit. Joan was nearly the last to arrive. Dot was already there, as were Cordelia, Emily, Persephone, Colette and Margaret. They just needed Alison – and Fay.

Joan put down her cup and saucer, peeling off her gloves as she sat down next to Persephone.

'Here she is,' Dot said warmly. 'Our heroine. There's no call to look surprised, chick. We've all heard what you did. You're the talk of the station.'

Joan's thoughts were so full of welcoming Fay into their group that it honestly came as a surprise to hear the barrage balloon incident being referred to.

'Tell us everything,' Margaret urged.

Joan laughed. 'It sounds like you already know.'

'We want to hear it from you,' said Persephone. 'Every single detail. I might make an article out of it, if you don't mind.'

Joan told her story, flattered and mildly embarrassed at the way the others hung on every word.

'You really are a heroine,' Emily said when she'd finished.

'I expect you can't wait to get home and tell Bob,' said Cordelia. 'Mrs Foster will be proud too.'

'Not to mention Mrs Cooper and Mrs Grayson,' Colette added.

'It'll make a wonderful bedtime story for Max when he's older,' said Margaret.

'It wasn't just me,' said Joan. 'The whole office mucked in.'

'But not until the end,' said Persephone.

'Fay Brewer was with me all along,' Joan pointed out. 'I couldn't possibly have done it without her. Actually, I've invited her along to the buffet. I hope that's all right.'

'Of course it is, chick,' Dot said at once. 'We already know her a little and we all like her – don't we, girls?'

'Yes' and 'Absolutely' were the answers and Joan smiled at her friends.

Persephone got up. 'Sorry, all. Got to dash. The rest of you might be going home after an honest day's toil, but I'm due to start work soon.' She wore her caramel-coloured wool coat over her uniform. Fastening the belt buckle, she pulled on her gauntlet-style gloves. 'See you all next time.'

After that, the talk turned to Christmas.

'They reckon that only one family in ten will be able to get a turkey or a goose this year,' said Cordelia.

'Mrs Grayson says we're due for a double ration of dried eggs in December,' said Margaret, 'so at least that's something.'

Dot chuckled: 'I hope you aren't suggesting scrambled eggs for Christmas dinner.'

'There's also said to be a scarcity of ready-made Christmas puds,' said Emily.

'That won't cause a problem in Wilton Close,' said Margaret. 'Not with Mrs Grayson and her magic mixing bowl.'

'I have to say,' Dot remarked, 'I'm tired of all the advertisements that at first glance make you think the item is available and then you see the bit saying "which we hope will soon reappear". Some hope.'

'It's to keep their products in your mind,' said Cordelia.

'What is everyone doing for presents this year?' asked Margaret. 'I've been using odd bits of wool to make egg cosies and ration-book cases.'

'Very useful,' Dot said approvingly. 'It's the useful presents that are the most welcome these days. I sacrificed an old towel to make face flannels hemmed in blanket stitch for Sheila, Pammy and Jenny. What bright ideas have you had, Cordelia?' Then Dot's gaze fell on Emily and she laughed. 'Sorry. Mum's the word.'

'In more ways than one,' Colette added.

'Daphne – she's one of the porters – has got her mum a tin of custard powder for Christmas,' said Emily. 'I know how important useful gifts are, but I wish beauty gifts were easier to find.'

'Bath salts cost twice as much as before the war,' said Margaret, 'if not more.'

Joan had managed to buy a bottle of bath salts, which she had divided into small amounts and put into pretty bags she'd made from bits of muslin, but she kept this to herself because her friends around the table would be receiving some of them, as would Bob's sisters and his mum, as well as the ladies at Wilton Close.

Alison arrived, frowning and looking tired. She dropped onto the chair vacated by Persephone.

'You look fed up, love,' said Dot. 'What's wrong?'

'Persephone told us you've got a wedding dress,' said Cordelia. 'I thought that meant all was now well.'

'It was – until our house fell through,' said Alison. To exclamations of 'Oh no,' she described what had happened.

'Where will you live instead?' asked Emily.

'That's the problem,' Alison said gloomily. 'Mum says we can stay with her, but I don't fancy it.'

'Why not?' Dot asked. 'Plenty of young couples live with one set of parents. It's normal.'

'I know,' said Alison, 'and I also know how ungrateful I sound, but it just doesn't feel right. My mum pointed out that if I'd married Paul, I would happily have moved in with him and his mother – but that was back then when all I could think about was getting married and being a wife. I'm a different person now. I've lived away from home. I've done essential war work. No matter how much I love them, moving back in with my parents would feel like a step backwards.' She glanced around the table. 'Like I say, I know how ungrateful I sound.'

'The chance of Joel's colleague's house has spoiled you for anything else,' said Colette. She sounded understanding, not critical.

'What about Joel's sister?' asked Margaret.

'She already has lodgers,' said Alison. 'Lydia offered us her flat, with her moving back in with Mum and Dad, until we find somewhere else.'

'How generous,' said Joan.

'Problem sorted,' said Cordelia.

Alison shook her head. 'If we did that, Joel and I would never be considered for anywhere else because we'd already be fixed up, and Lydia would be stuck at home for the duration.'

'The duration and beyond,' said Dot. 'The housing problem won't miraculously end when peace is declared.'

'Sharing homes is normal nowadays,' Joan said kindly, 'and not everyone gets to choose who they live with. It was really hard when me and Bob were looking for somewhere.'

'Daphne lives with her mum,' added Emily, 'and ever since the Christmas Blitz, they've had two aunties and an uncle squeezed in with them.'

Joan nodded, remembering. 'When we got married, we were meant to live with Auntie Florrie, but she was bombed out and she had to move in with Auntie Marie.'

Alison held up her hands in surrender. 'I know, I know. I'm being unreasonable.'

'It isn't unreasonable to dream of spending your early married life alone together,' Cordelia said, 'but unfortunately a dream is exactly what it is.'

'You're right, of course,' said Alison. 'I need to pull myself together and concentrate on how lucky I am that my husband won't be away overseas for months if not years on end.'

Under the table, Joan squeezed Alison's hand. Not all that long ago, she would never have believed it possible for her to live under the same roof as Gran, but it was surprising how things turned out sometimes.

'Here comes Fay Brewer,' said Emily.

The others looked round to welcome Fay.

'Park yourself, love,' said Dot. 'We've been hearing what you and our Joan did this morning.'

'Congratulations,' said Cordelia. 'You were very brave.'

'We just did what needed doing,' said Fay, smiling at Joan. 'Anyone would have done the same.'

'Aye,' said Dot, 'but it was you two that were on the spot, so take a bit of praise when it's given.'

Fay laughed. 'Thank you.'

'That's better,' said Dot.

'You work with Miss Emery, don't you?' said Alison.

'One of the best pieces of advice I've ever had came from her,' said Cordelia. 'It was something she said to all of us, actually, on our first day working for the railways.'

'Sounds intriguing,' said Fay. 'What was it?'

'She told us to be friends,' said Dot. 'She said it didn't matter who'd gone to which school or who came from which background. She said we'd need one another – and she was right.' Smiling at Fay, she waved a hand to encompass everyone seated round the table. 'Meet the best friends I've ever had.'

'Oh, Dot,' said Joan.

'Well, it's true,' said Dot.

'Yes,' Joan agreed, 'it is.'

Chapter Thirty-Six

The first of December. Alison was going to get married three weeks on Friday – Christmas Eve. Her heart leaped at the prospect. All that was needed to make it perfect was a home of their own – but she had to stop thinking like that. There must be thousands of young couples all over the country who dreamed of somewhere of their own, not to mention all the long-established families who had lost everything in a raid. As deep as her disappointment was, Alison made an effort to cheer up and count her blessings. After all, what was the need of a home to themselves compared to the anguish she had fought her way through?

'Someone dropped in to see you,' one of her colleagues told her when she came back from her dinner break. 'She left a message. "Please can you and Joel go round to Colette's house one evening?" She said she'll be in this evening, tomorrow evening and the evening after.'

'Thanks,' said Alison.

Colette hadn't invited them before. Did she get lonely living on her own? She never gave any indication of it, but then she wasn't the sort to moan and complain – which made Alison all the more determined not to grouse about her own forthcoming living arrangements. She and Joel were going to live with Mum and Dad and that was all there was to it.

Part of her wished now that she had accepted Lydia's offer of her flat, but that really wouldn't have been fair on Lydia. It meant a lot to Alison that her sister had made that generous offer. Not everyone had a sister who was willing to give up her home for them.

Mum had arranged to borrow a double bed from Auntie Stella, but it would be too big for Alison's room, so Mum's plan, suggested by Auntie Stella, was to give her and Joel the downstairs front room. There was something embarrassing about their sleeping arrangements being the subject of family discussions.

Thanks to their respective work schedules, Alison wasn't due to see Joel again until Friday, so that was when they went to Seymour Grove to see Colette.

'This brings back memories of us girls cycling over there after she came home from London,' Alison told Joel as they walked along Colette's road in the blackout. 'We were so excited to see her again. We had no idea Tony didn't want us there.'

'She's lucky to have such staunch friends,' said Joel.

'I'm glad she trusted us with the truth in the end,' said Alison, 'though it wasn't until Tony beat her so badly that she did. If he hadn't done that . . .'

If he hadn't, would Colette still be leading that horrible double life of public normality and private fear? It didn't bear thinking about. What mattered was that she had been rescued from that appalling situation and Tony was now gone, and good riddance to bad rubbish. Alison's blood heated up every time she thought of him and what her lovely friend had endured at his evil hands.

All the houses in the road looked blank and unwelcoming with the blackout curtains keeping every sliver of light inside. Guided by tissue-dimmed torches, Joel and Alison arrived at Colette's front door. When Colette opened it, they slipped inside so she could close it quickly. Not that the hall light was on, but everyone automatically nipped in and out of doorways during the blackout, so used were they to the strict rules.

Colette took them into her sitting room.

'Sit down and I'll put the kettle on.'

She returned shortly with a tray of tea and biscuits.

'They're honey biscuits,' she said. 'Mrs Grayson—'

'—gave you the recipe,' Alison finished, smiling. 'What would we all do without her?'

'I'm so pleased you finally found a wedding dress,' said Colette.

'I didn't find it, exactly,' said Alison. 'Persephone sorted it out for me. She sent her sister a telegram, if you please.'

'What was I saying about staunch friends?' Joel murmured.

'I'll tell you all about the dress when we're alone,' Alison promised.

'I'm not allowed to know anything,' said Joel.

'Quite right too,' said Colette. 'I'm sorry you lost the house you were supposed to move into. You must have been looking forward to that.'

Alison smothered a sigh. 'I can't tell you how much.'

'But Alison's parents have offered to have us,' said Joel, 'which is jolly splendid of them.'

'I'm sure it is,' Colette agreed. There was a twinkle in her blue eyes as she said, 'So you might not be interested in my suggestion, then.'

'Your suggestion?' Alison asked. 'As to where we live, you mean?'

'I shouldn't tease,' said Colette. 'Simple question: would you like to live here?'

'Here?' Joel asked. 'In your house?'

Colette nodded. 'I'm sure it would be very comfortable with Alison's parents, but if you'd prefer to have a place of your own, you're welcome to this house.'

It took a moment to sink in.

Had Colette just offered to let them have her house? Astonishment poured through Alison. 'Do you – do you mean . . .? Have I got this right?' No, she must have misunderstood. Colette couldn't possibly have made such an offer. It wasn't possible. She corrected herself. 'It's so kind of you to open your home to us. It would be much less of a squeeze to share with you than with Mum and Dad.'

'I'm offering you the house,' Colette said gently. 'I won't be here. If you move in, I'll go and live with Mrs Cooper. It's all arranged – but it's up to you. I'm sure your mum would love to have you living with her.'

Alison and Joel looked at one another.

'Are you offering to move out so we can move in?' Joel asked Colette.

She nodded, smiling. 'It makes sense, if you think about it. I'm rattling around here all on my own. I know I should have gone to the billeting officer to offer a room ages ago, but I could never bring myself to do it. It was such a relief to be here on my own without Tony. I needed to learn to feel safe here.' She sat up straighter. 'But now you need the house and I really don't want to be here. It's too full of memories.

I wanted to live here on my own to begin with, just to show the neighbours I could do so with my head held high. I wanted them to see I have nothing to be ashamed of – even though some of them definitely don't agree with me on that point. I also – I also wanted to live here and be seen around the neighbourhood so that any local married lady who lives a secret life of fear because her husband is being hateful to her could see that it's an experience you can survive. You can emerge from the other side of it.'

'You're so brave,' Alison whispered.

Colette shrugged that off. 'Why don't you go and have a look round and have a chat about what you want to do.'

As if there was a question about what they wanted! Alison and Joel got to their feet and started to go round the house. Joel had never been here before. Alison had, but only downstairs. It might be nothing like as big as Grundy's house, and certainly not as modern, but who cared about that? It could be theirs.

'I can't believe we have the chance of this,' Joel said when they were upstairs. 'When we lost the other place, I thought that was it until some unspecified point after the war.'

Alison took his hand. 'It's like you said. Staunch friends.'

They went back downstairs. Colette smiled as they entered the sitting room.

'What do you think?' she asked.

'I think,' said Alison, going to her, 'that you are the dearest friend anyone ever had. We can never thank you enough. I promise you that we'll make this into a happy home.'

'Thank you,' said Colette. 'I like the sound of that. The house deserves it. It never had a chance of it with Tony and me.'

'Not Tony and you,' Alison corrected her. 'It was Tony that made this an unhappy home. It was nothing to do with you.'

Alison and Joel sat down. Alison felt fluttery and eager. She sniffed away a tear or two and laughed at herself.

'Let me tell you how things will be arranged,' said Colette. 'The house is in Tony's name and I can't change what's on the rent book, but I have given the rent man due notice that I'm expecting to take in lodgers. I've let him believe you've been billeted on me. He doesn't know I'm going to move out. That's none of his business, but if he ever asks after me, say I've gone to look after a sick friend or something. As long as you pay the rent and it gets marked off on Tony's book, that's all there is to it.'

'Are you sure about handing over the house to us?' asked Joel. 'There's room for the three of us.'

'Tony left matters in such a way that I had to stay here – or so he thought,' said Colette. 'I know you think I'm doing something generous by offering you this house, but I'm going to benefit from it too. It's time for me to move on and I can't think of anything that would suit me better or make me happier than living in Wilton Close. Think of it this way, Alison. You and I will be swapping bedrooms. Doesn't that make it sound simple?'

'Thank you, Colette,' said Joel, 'from the bottom of my heart.'

'I'm glad to know you'll be with Mrs Cooper and Mrs Grayson in Wilton Close,' said Alison. 'I was very happy there and you shall be too.'

'I know,' said Colette.

Alison didn't think she'd ever seen her friend look so serene.

Chapter Thirty-Seven

In common with everyone else, Margaret was delighted at the news that Alison and Joel were going to move into Colette's house.

'It solves their problem as well as giving them a house the rest of us already know,' Margaret said to Mrs Cooper. 'It's wonderful that Colette's coming here too.'

'She's a dear girl,' said Mrs Cooper.

'I know how close the two of you are,' Margaret said fondly. 'I'd been wondering who I might end up sharing with. Come to think of it, Colette might prefer the box room so she can be on her own. Or I don't mind moving into the box room if you want to offer her the big room.'

'Bless you, how sweet, but let's just wait and see, shall we? I certainly won't move you out of your room.'

Even though she had been in the double room ever since Joan had moved out, Margaret couldn't help feeling that Colette had the greater claim to it. Later, she said so to Joan.

'I know it sounds daft, but I've realised that it's because Colette has been married.'

'What difference does that make?' Joan asked.

'There's a pecking order in life, isn't there? And married ladies take precedence over single girls.'

'I was about to say, "You're being daft," but actually, you're right,' said Joan. 'Married ladies do have more clout than spinsters.'

They looked at one another.

'And respectable girls are heaps better than unmarried mothers,' said Joan. 'Poor Sally. But the important thing is that she'll come out of the mother and baby home with her reputation intact.'

'Like me, you mean,' said Margaret, 'though of course I didn't get as far as the maternity-home stage.'

Joan placed her hand on Margaret's arm. 'You're living proof that a girl can leave such a thing behind and go on to make a success of her life. I hope Sally manages as well as you have.'

'So do I,' Margaret agreed. 'I couldn't have done it without my friends and a good home.'

Joan frowned. 'What difference did that make? I was the only friend who knew and then we told Dot.'

Margaret tried to explain. 'It's not a question of how many people knew. It's about being accepted by people I liked and admired. It's living in Wilton Close and feeling comfortable and wanted. You can't imagine what a boost it gave me after I'd felt so small and ashamed for such a long time. Scared as well, because I was all alone until you came along and drew me into the group and introduced me to Mrs Cooper. You made a big difference to my life, Joan Hubble. I can never pay you back.'

A pretty rosiness glowed in Joan's cheeks. 'You've paid it back by helping Sally. It sounds as if she must have felt every bit as alone and frightened as you did. If I made a difference to your life, I think you've made a bigger one to Sally's. You've stood by her through a horrid ordeal. Most folk would have called her a slut and turned their backs on her.'

'It wasn't just me,' said Margaret. 'I couldn't have done it without Mrs Cooper and Mrs Grayson – and Cordelia. And you, dear old you.'

'It's going to be a strange Christmas for Sally in Rookery House. I hope it won't put her off Christmas for ever.'

'I hope not.' Wanting to cheer up the conversation, Margaret asked, 'What are your plans?'

'We're going to pool our resources with Bob's family. They're all coming over to us. Gran will be in charge of the cooking. I can't wait. Max is of an age to take an interest this year.'

'What presents is he going to get?'

'His aunties have made clothes for him,' said Joan, 'and I found some gingery-brown velvet in the rummage box on the market that I've made into a Brizo dog for him.'

'How clever. He'll love it,' said Margaret. 'I found a couple of toy yachts, second-hand – if not third- or fourth-hand, judging by their condition. One's for Max. I know he's too young, but he can grow into it. It was too good a toy to miss out on.'

'Thank you. That's so thoughtful,' said Joan. 'What have you sent Anna for the twins? Is the other yacht for Tommy?'

'Yes, and I made a fabric dolly for Anne-Marie.'

'They're going to love them.'

'I hope so,' said Margaret. 'Christmas shopping has made me feel very aware of not having them near here so that I can watch them grow up.'

She and Joan looked at one another. Neither of them needed to say a word. Margaret knew the exact same thought had appeared in Joan's head as had appeared in her own.

Sally.

Because of work and overtime commitments and Alison's wedding, today would be the last time Margaret and Sally would see one another before Christmas. Margaret had moved heaven and earth to find a nice little Christmas present for her. Beauty gifts were hard to find, just as Emily had remarked upon in the buffet recently, but Margaret had managed to find a small jar of cold cream, which would double up as hand cream, the perfect gift for a girl whose war work was manual and grimy.

There was thick fog, so Margaret set off early. The fog was dense, the sort in which you couldn't see further than the end of your arm. Smelly, too, a bit like rotten eggs. Wrapped up inside her overcoat and hat, complete with scarf and gloves knitted by Mrs Grayson, Margaret settled herself on the first of the two buses that would convey her to Sale and prepared for a long journey along roads on which vehicles were moving at a crawl.

It gave her plenty of thinking time. She acknowledged once again her relief and gratitude that Alison had felt able to accept what had passed between her and Joel. It would have been understandable if Alison had chosen never to speak to her again. Margaret also felt admiration for the way she had elected to be in charge of how to cope with the situation. Alison had shown real strength of character in a sticky situation.

Then Margaret thought of Sally, who had no option but to be strong, on the outside at least, but how was she really feeling on the inside?

At long last it was time to get off the bus. She had to wait ages for the second one. When she finally climbed aboard, she was in serious danger of missing the visiting hours. The fog was less murky now and this bus travelled a little faster than the first one had, but Margaret still almost missed her stop because of the severely limited visibility.

She made her way to Rookery House only to be informed that she was too late for afternoon visiting.

'Come back this evening,' said the receptionist who answered the door.

'Couldn't I have just a few minutes? Please?' Margaret gave her most winning smile. 'It's taken me for ever to get here and I can't come back later. In fact, this will be my last visit before Christmas.'

'Who have you come to see?'

'Mrs Bennett.'

The receptionist flicked her a glance that said she knew full well that *Mrs* Bennett was no such thing.

'Step inside and let me close the door.' The receptionist shivered. 'It's a rotten old day. Wait here, please.'

She went into the office and Margaret saw her pick up the house telephone, though she couldn't hear what was said. When the receptionist returned, something in her manner had changed.

'We don't normally allow visitors for twenty-four hours following a birth—'

Margaret stiffened. 'You mean – she's had it?'

'—or, as in this case, for forty-eight hours if there have been complications—'

'Complications?' Margaret pressed, frightened.

'—but Mrs Walters says she will make an exception in this instance.'

'Thank you.' Margaret was poised to dash to Sally's side. 'Where can I find her?'

She was forced to wait while the receptionist summoned a greenie who was mopping the floor down the passage and gave her instructions. Margaret followed the girl up the stairs and then up more stairs. The greenie left her at the doors to a ward, where the sister wasn't best pleased at having a visitor foisted on her out of hours and made Margaret wait while she telephoned Mrs Walters, though judging from the length of time she took, she apparently did a couple of other jobs as well.

At last, Margaret was allowed in. Sally wasn't in the ward but in a small room of her own, lying up against her pillows, arms neatly by her sides on top of the covers. Her face was ghostly pale.

Margaret hurried to take her hand. 'How are you? The receptionist says you've had the baby.'

Sally's jaw tightened as if she was going to refuse to speak. Then she said, 'Yesterday evening.'

'But—'

'Yes, it was early.' Sally's voice was hard. 'I'm aware of that, thank you.'

'Are you – are you all right?' Margaret hardly dared ask with Sally in this mood.

'Never better.'

'Sally, please don't . . .' Margaret's voice trailed away.

'Don't what? Don't be like this? Sorry if I don't fall in with your expectations. I'm not exactly the proud mother, glowing with joy.'

'Of course you aren't,' Margaret said softly.

Sally sighed so deeply her body shook. 'I'm sorry to be so horrible. You of all people don't deserve it. It was pretty grim, if you must know. The midwife had to send for the doctor. Apparently, I have a weak cervix. He made it sound as if a weak cervix goes with having weak morals, but the nurse told me later that it can happen even if you're married.'

'I've never heard of a cervix,' said Margaret. She knew she wasn't supposed to be having this conversation. Single girls weren't meant to know anything about giving birth.

'It's something to do with the womb,' Sally told her. 'Mine wasn't strong enough to hold the baby in for as long as it was supposed to. As well as that, I had to have stitches afterwards and they hurt like billy-o. The doctor said maybe that would serve as a reminder to me not to be a naughty girl next time.'

Margaret tensed with anger. She made sure to keep her voice gentle. 'You poor love. He had no right to say that.'

Sally's reply was a shrug and she looked away.

'What did you have?' asked Margaret.

Sally looked at her. 'A little boy. Daniel.'

'You were allowed to give him a name?' Margaret asked, surprised. She didn't like to say so, but surely that was the prerogative of the adoptive parents.

'I didn't mean to,' said Sally. 'It just happened – like when someone blurts out something they really ought not to have said and they say, "Sorry, it just slipped out." The midwife showed him to me and all of a sudden, there it was inside my head. Daniel. It just slipped in there. I've been trying to unthink it, but . . .' Another shrug. Another hardening of her delicate jawline.

'Oh, Sally,' Margaret whispered. 'I don't know what to say.'

'You could try telling me I'm lucky to have got it over with so much earlier than I was expecting. That's what the others in the ward said when my waters broke.' Margaret's ignorance must have shown because Sally added, 'That's the way you know it's started.' She seized Margaret's hand. 'I wasn't *ready*. I thought I had weeks to go. I thought I had until the end of January and I hated the thought of having to wait that long. I was desperate for it to be over – but when it started, I wasn't ready.'

Margaret was stumped for what to say. The best she could come up with was 'It must have come as quite a shock.'

'You can say that again. I never imagined anything could hurt so much.' Sally swallowed. 'When the door opened and you walked in, I thought it was Mrs Walters again. She came to see me earlier. Apparently, you get a week of bed rest after a birth.' She laughed, a hollow sound. 'She wanted to know if I have somewhere to go after that— Oh,' and suddenly there was the old Sally, the real Sally. 'I didn't mean to sound as if I was angling to go back to Mrs Cooper's. Please don't think that.'

Margaret wanted nothing more than to scoop Sally into her arms and invite her home, but it wasn't her place to do any such thing.

'Mrs Walters says there's a hostel she sometimes sends girls to. She said I can stay there if I need to. I'm still trying to come to terms with what happened yesterday, never mind think about next week.'

Margaret hesitated, but she had to ask. 'Is ...?' She wanted, and at the same time didn't want, to say Daniel's name. It wouldn't be good for Sally – would it? – to let the name sink even deeper into her consciousness, into her heart. 'Is the baby all right? With him being so early, I mean.'

'You can use his name, you know,' Sally replied, 'and yes, he's fine. The nurse said that when babies arrive this early, they sometimes have problems with their breathing, but he's all right, apparently.'

'Apparently?' Margaret frowned.

'I said I didn't want to see him again. Don't look at me like that.'

'I'm not looking at you like anything.'

'Yes, you are. You're shocked that I've refused to see him. Don't you understand? I've never wanted anything so much in my entire life – and that's why I can't do it. I mustn't. If I want him this much now, how much more would I want him if they let me have him for a few days? Dear God, Margaret, how am I to face giving him up? It's so *final*.'

'It has to be,' Margaret whispered.

'Easy for you to say.'

'No, it isn't easy for me.' Something made Margaret fight back, though she kept her voice gentle. 'I'm trying hard to say the right thing, even though there can't possibly be a right thing that I can say in this situation.'

349

'Do you know what's going to happen when my baby is adopted?' Sally's voice was businesslike. 'When the adoption is confirmed, his new parents will be given a new, shorter version of his birth certificate, one that conveniently misses my name off it. That means he can go through his entire life not knowing he's adopted if his new parents choose not to tell him.'

'Oh, Sally,' Margaret whispered.

'And Mrs Walters says that if they do tell him, the advice she gives in wartime is to say that the father was a soldier who died on the battlefield and the mother . . .' The words choked in Sally's throat. She tried again. 'The mother was killed in an air raid. All very respectable.'

Margaret floundered for something positive to say. 'I suppose this is what's best for the child.'

'Oh yes, for the child – yes.' Sally sucked in a huge breath. 'And that's absolutely right and proper and just the way it should be.' Her hand shot out and grabbed Margaret's. 'But what about the real mother? What about me? I simply won't exist any more.'

Chapter Thirty-Eight

Alison and Joel's friends had all taken to Mrs Cooper's house the toys they'd made to be given away as part of the wedding celebration. Alison and Joel went to fetch them, lingering with delight over the various stuffed animals, peg dollies, woolly pom-poms, finger puppets made from the fingers of gloves, and 'binoculars' made from rolled-up card.

Margaret's father had made pretend cigarettes from little bits of wood, complete with a dab of paint on the tip to make them look as if they were alight.

'They'll make some lucky children feel very grown-up,' said Joel.

'Have you seen what Dad has made?' asked Mum.

Good old Dad. Using bits and pieces of wood, he had made some trains and motor cars, not to mention half a dozen forts. Forts!

They chatted with Mrs Cooper and Mrs Grayson about the wedding, which was now just days away, Christmas Eve being next week. Then Alison drew Margaret aside to ask after Sally. Margaret took her upstairs. They sat opposite one another on the beds.

'How is she?' Alison asked. 'Joan told me she'd had a boy.'

'I haven't seen her since the day after she had him,' said Margaret. 'As to how she is – or was – it's difficult to say.

She was upset when I saw her, shocked the baby had come so early. I gather she had a rough time. They had to have the doctor to her.'

'Then it must have been bad,' said Alison, 'but at least it's all over with.'

'I think the worst part was the emotional impact,' said Margaret. 'She decided not to see him again because it's going to be so hard to give him up.'

Alison felt unsettled in a way she hadn't anticipated. 'I'd never thought of it that way. I just thought . . .'

'That she'd be glad to get rid?'

'Don't say it like that,' Alison protested, 'as if I'm being heartless. That was the plan all along.'

Margaret let out a sigh. 'Sorry. I shouldn't snap at you, but seeing Sally all washed out and upset left me feeling raw around the edges. She didn't deserve any of this. She honestly expected the boyfriend to make an honest woman of her once she told him about the baby.'

Alison was silent, thinking of Mum's highly critical and unsympathetic attitude towards fallen girls. She had thought the same way too until all this had happened. If there was one thing she had learned in recent weeks, it was that life wasn't that simple. Was it this new sensitivity that gave her an insight into what Margaret must be feeling?

'You aren't just upset on Sally's behalf, are you?' Alison asked. 'You've been thinking all along about what happened to you.'

Margaret gave her a direct look. 'Do you really want to go down that road? Because I'll tell you if you want me to.'

Alison bit her lip, then nodded. 'I'd like to understand something of what you went through. The way I used to see things, it would have been so easy to put the blame on you for getting drunk.'

'And Joel,' said Margaret. 'He got drunk too. No one ever blames the man.'

Alison accepted the correction. 'And Joel. Both of you. You're right, of course,' she added drily. 'It's always the girl who gets talked about, always the girl who suffers. It's all too easy to make assumptions. I haven't said a word about any of this to my mother, but I keep hearing her voice in my head, making pointed remarks about "nice girls". That's how I was brought up.'

'So was I,' said Margaret with a touch of sharpness. 'I hope you don't imagine otherwise.'

'Of course not.' Alison had a stab at sounding indignant, but actually she'd needed telling and she knew it. 'I'm not saying Mum is wrong or that my personal standards have slipped, but I think I'm not as judgemental as I used to be. I think my morals have budged up a bit and made room for a spot of kindness. It's easy to believe in rules about how good people should behave – until you find a good person you like and care about who has fallen foul of those rules. So if you want to tell me about Sally's situation bringing your own back to you, I'll listen and do my best to understand.'

Margaret didn't say anything for a few beats. 'You're right. It has brought it all back. Or rather, it's made me think about all the things that never happened to me, that I never had to go through. I lost my baby relatively early on. Nobody

353

knew I was in the family way. I was scared silly of admitting it to my dad, but I didn't have anybody else to tell. I didn't know what to do. And then I miscarried.'

'Was it a relief?' Alison asked.

'You'd think so, but actually I never really had a chance to think of it that way, because things then became bad in other ways. My father knew; the neighbours knew. We'd lost our house and our new landlady knew. She was vile to me and in the end I left. I left my old job too because I was so frightened of customers who knew me coming into the shop and then complaining to the management about the quality of their staff.'

'I hadn't appreciated how hard it was for you,' said Alison. She thought but did not say that if she had realised previously, she would very likely have felt that Margaret had deserved it.

'But all of that isn't what Sally's pregnancy has made me think about,' Margaret continued. 'It's made me think about all the things that didn't happen. If your head has been full of your mum's voice going on about nice girls, mine has been stuffed full of what-ifs. What if I hadn't miscarried my baby? What if I'd had to find a mother and baby home that would take me? What if I'd had to face up to an adoption? What if I'd loved my baby and not wanted to give him or her up?'

Alison didn't know what to say. Margaret's words, though quiet, carried an intensity and she was shocked by their power.

'I have to keep reminding myself,' Margaret added softly, 'that all this isn't about me. It's about Sally.'

Alison reached for her hand. 'You're mistaken. It is about you. It's about everything you've lived with and kept hidden inside all this time.'

Margaret glanced away. Was she hiding tears? But when she spoke, her voice was breezy. 'Maybe. But mainly this is about Sally.' She swung her face back and looked Alison straight in the eyes. 'There's something I need to know. I'm terrified to ask, but . . . does Joel know the real reason why I bought the wedding dress? Did you tell him?'

Alison leaned towards her. 'No, I didn't – and I never will, I promise. There's no need for him to know.'

Margaret shivered, actually shivered, her whole body quivering as she again turned her face away.

'I would never tell Joel that,' Alison assured her softly. 'You can forget it ever happened.'

'Thank you,' Margaret whispered.

Wanting to bring the conversation into calmer waters, Alison asked, 'What will happen to Sally next?'

Margaret lifted her chin, composing her emotions. 'The Rookery House people offered to get her a place in a hostel while she recovers.'

Alison uttered a small 'Oh' of distress. 'It sounds pretty brutal. I don't mean the hostel sounds like a bad place. I mean,' she shrugged, 'it seems to be happening so quickly, like she's on a conveyor belt.'

'Mrs Cooper said she must come here, of course,' Margaret told her.

'Of course,' Alison repeated. Dear Mrs Cooper, always so generous.

'But Miss Emery stepped in,' said Margaret. 'Sally had given Mrs Walters at the home permission to inform Miss Emery when the baby was born. Because it came early and Sally had a difficult time and is going to need more recuperation than normal, Miss Emery has arranged for her to go into a convalescent home for a month. She'll still need somewhere when she leaves, but she's sorted out for the time being.'

'How do you know if you haven't seen her since last week?'

'She gave Miss Emery permission to tell me,' said Margaret.

'It's good to know things have been sorted out.'

'Yes.' Margaret smiled, her eyes thoughtful. 'It's the start of a fresh chapter for Sally.' Then her smile widened. 'Speaking of fresh chapters, you've got your own starting on Christmas Eve.'

Joy drummed inside Alison's chest. 'Yes. I can hardly wait.'

They stood up. Impulsively, Alison gave Margaret a hug, telling her, 'I'm glad you'll be at my wedding.'

'So am I,' Margaret whispered.

Chapter Thirty-Nine

Alison gave a wriggle of excitement when she woke up on Monday. Today she could say she was getting married this week – and she did say it. Out loud. More than once. Then she laughed at herself, throwing back the covers and emerging into the bedroom's chilly air.

She practically sang the special words as she gave Mum a hug before sitting down at the breakfast table.

Mum hugged her back. 'I just want to say how delighted I am for you. It broke my heart to see how desolate you were after things ended between you and Paul – and now look at you, all happy and excited because you're going to marry Joel.'

'I'm very happy,' Alison confirmed. 'For the record, I put Paul well and truly behind me long ago. I know I met Joel a relatively short time after Paul left me, but I wasn't on the rebound and he isn't second best.'

'I never thought for one moment—'

'Maybe not,' Alison put in, 'but if Auntie Rosalind or Auntie June drops a hint at the wedding, you can set them straight. I don't want anyone to have the slightest doubt about us.'

'As long as you have no doubts, that's all that matters,' said Mum.

'Not a single one.'

After breakfast, she headed to work with a light heart, not caring that the wind was bitter. As the bus made its way into town, Alison thought about her plans for the day. She intended to dash to the shops in her dinner break. She had a list from Mum, who had taken to calling her shopping list a wish list because the shortages were biting so deep. She also wanted to get one or two things for herself, in particular a length of petersham to give her going-away hat a new trimming. A new hat was out of the question. Hats weren't part of the coupon system and prices had gone up and up.

Lydia had found the instructions for fashioning a large rosette to decorate the side of a hat and Alison had set her heart on it. She and Joel weren't exactly going away because they both had to return to work on Boxing Day afternoon, so they were going to stay for two nights at the elegant Midland Hotel where Joel had proposed to her on that wonderful day in the summer. Alison wanted to look her very best as she entered through the Midland's doors as a married lady. To this end, she also hoped to find a new blouse and she had the last four coupons from her annual allocation to enable her to buy it.

Her dinner break was officially only half an hour, but Alison was able to be away from her post for longer because of her wedding. The others were happy to cover for her when they knew about her going-away hat and blouse. Everyone was interested in her big day and more than happy to help out.

Alison hurried along Market Street towards Ingleby's. Hearing voices singing 'O Come, All Ye Faithful' complete with soaring descants, she crossed the road to listen to a group of carol singers, wishing she could stay longer as she dropped a silver sixpence into their collecting box. She almost ran into Ingleby's, the long-established store that sold – or used to, before the war – everything the dressmaker could possibly wish for, as well as accessories such as gloves and scarves to brighten any outfit and a range of millinery. They still sold ready-made clothes for ladies, but their dressmaking department for customers who could pay for tailor-made garments had, shortly before the outbreak of war, started making blackout curtains and then moved on to dungarees for land girls. Joan had once worked as a sewing machinist for Ingleby's.

A helpful assistant showed Alison petersham in a couple of widths and she chose the wider one, which would make a showier rosette. Then she went in search of a blouse. Collars were smaller than they used to be and buttons were a little wider apart, according to clothes regulations, but you could always rely on Ingleby's for quality. There was one blouse that caught Alison's eye, a simple ivory-coloured one that seemed more sophisticated than plain white.

Close by, Alison noticed a soldier standing at one of the glass-topped counters, being shown ladies' hankies, each of them embroidered with an initial.

'My little girl would love one of those,' he said to the assistant. 'I have to leave tomorrow, so I won't be here on Christmas Day. I'd love to leave her a special present just from me.'

The middle-aged assistant smiled. 'What's her name?'

'Katharine with a K.'

The assistant ran her hand over the display and picked out a handkerchief. 'Here you are, sir. That'll be two shillings and one coupon.'

The soldier's face fell a mile. 'I don't possess any coupons.'

'I'm very sorry, sir,' said the assistant, looking upset. 'I can't let you have it without a coupon.'

The soldier lowered his head. 'Oh. Well, I'll have to leave it, then.'

'No – wait,' said Alison. Without another thought, she turned her back on the ivory blouse. 'You can have one of mine.'

'I couldn't—' the soldier started to say.

'Please do.' Alison smiled at him. 'You're so brave, fighting for your country, for all of us at home. It would be a shame if your daughter didn't get her special present.'

'Thank you,' said the soldier. 'You've no idea how much this means.'

'It's a pleasure,' Alison assured him, handing over one of her precious coupons.

'Happy Christmas, miss.'

'Happy Christmas to you too – and to Katharine.'

The plan was to decorate the buffet on Wednesday evening because that was the time the biggest number of them were available. Since it had been Alison's idea in the first place, her friends had insisted that she must be the one to tell Mrs Jessop what they wanted to do – and why. Alison had said Dot must be there too, since she was the one who had thought of thanking Mrs Jessop, and also Emily, who had had the idea of the paper chains.

'Bless your hearts, there's no call for you to do that,' Mrs Jessop had started to say.

'There's every need,' Dot had replied at once. 'It's made a huge difference to us, having your buffet as a meeting place.'

'And your kindness in letting us keep our notebook under the counter has made it even better,' Alison added, 'so please let us do this for you.'

So they gathered on Wednesday after their shifts. Alison, Dot and Colette arrived first. Persephone and Emily had yet to appear. Fay was there too. Alison had invited her to attend the wedding, though not the reception.

'I'm sorry about that,' Alison had said. 'It's because of the restrictions on numbers.'

'Don't apologise,' Fay had answered. 'I'm flattered to be asked to the ceremony and I'd love to attend.'

It couldn't be the easiest thing to join a group of such well-established friends at any time, but all the more so in the run-up to Christmas. Fay had initially held back when the others had made arrangements for putting up the paper chains in the buffet.

When asked, she had explained, 'I'm such a newcomer. It's not as though I've benefited from Mrs Jessop's hospitality for ages like the rest of you.'

Alison had liked her for that. There was something appealing about seeing someone with such professional and personal confidence displaying a touch of shyness and humility.

Colette's smile had warmed her blue eyes. 'You're one of us now, silly. Join in and be glad of it. There was a time when I couldn't join in the way I wanted and oh, how I longed to. Make the most of it, is my advice to you.'

That Wednesday evening, the buffet hummed with conversation. Heads turned as an older porter carrying a stepladder followed Emily in and she held the door for him.

'Shall I stay and help?' asked the porter.

'You're sweet to offer, Mr Buckley,' Emily said with her pretty smile, 'but it's important we do this ourselves.'

As Mr Buckley opened the door to leave, he stood back, holding the door for Persephone to enter pushing a sack trolley with two fat sacks.

'Are the Christmas elves all set to spring into action?' she asked, delight dancing in her violet eyes.

Emily opened the first sack and carefully began to draw out a long paper chain. It was all mixed up with the others and a whole clump emerged together. Alison and Colette gently disentangled the whole lot while Fay and Dot carried the stepladder into a corner, Dot calling out, '*Scusi, scusi,*' as they made their way between the tables. Some customers stood up to make way.

Mrs Jessop came over to Alison and Colette.

'It's going to be a bit disruptive,' said Alison. 'I'm sorry.'

'But it'll be worth it in the end,' Colette added.

'I'm sure it will,' Mrs Jessop agreed. 'I've been looking forward to it. When folk admire it, I'll be able to say, "Some of my regulars did it for me," and won't I look like the lucky one?'

The girls started work. They were going to loop chains all around the walls and then use the longest ones to reach from the corners to the centre of the ceiling. Although it was their intention to do the job themselves, much of the work was taken out of their hands as other customers began joining in. Ladies removed the paper chains from the sacks, gently shaking them free of other chains, and men moved the furniture so that the stepladder could be put in position. No end of people cheerfully called 'Up a bit, down a bit,' to make sure every chain hung evenly.

A brass band started playing outside on the concourse. Mrs Jessop propped open the door to let in the strains of 'Once in Royal David's City'.

'It's the Salvation Army band,' she said. 'I love to hear them. They always make me think of my mum. No matter how little money she had, she always had a penny or tuppence to give them. She said they do such good work.'

'You know it's Christmas when you hear them playing carols,' said Dot.

Soon everyone in the buffet was singing along as the rich, mellow tones of the brass instruments poured inside. All work on the paper chains came to a halt as everybody paused to sing 'In the Bleak Midwinter', and then they all commenced their chain-hanging again when the band struck up 'While Shepherds Watched Their Flocks'. Alison grinned when she heard two snowy-haired ladies who were more than old enough to know better belt out, 'While shepherds washed their socks by night,' and then collapse into giggles like a pair of naughty schoolchildren.

When all the paper chains were up and the tables and chairs had been restored to their rightful positions, Alison and her friends looked at Mrs Jessop's face as she gazed around her transformed buffet. She pressed her lips together in a sort of upside-down smile as she tried to hold back her tears.

Dot squeezed her arm. 'Thank you for everything you've done for us, Mrs Jessop.'

'You're very welcome, all of you,' said Mrs Jessop, 'and thank you for this.'

'It's our very great pleasure, I assure you,' said Persephone. She looked around at the others, gathering their attention. 'And now shall we head onto the platform and sing some carols?'

Chapter Forty

On the evening before Christmas Eve, instead of going home on the bus on her own as usual, Alison was surrounded by her bridesmaids and matrons of honour, all of them with bags containing their overnight things and their dresses for tomorrow. Mum and Lydia would both be playing hostess for the night. Alison was delighted that Lydia had offered, not simply because it made things easier, but also because it gave her sister an important role to play in preparing for the Christmas Eve wedding.

Along with Mum and Lydia, they were all due to spend that evening in the church hall, putting up the decorations from Darley Court.

'A lovely way to spend Christmas Eve eve,' said Persephone.

'And Wedding Eve,' Colette added, smiling.

Later, they walked into the foyer of the church hall, taking care not to break the blackout, then entered the darkened hall itself. To Alison's surprise, Lydia gave her a bit of a shove that sent her through the door first. The instant she was inside, Alison stopped dead, her breath catching in her throat.

Christmas trees. Three Christmas trees spaced out along either side of the room. Not just Christmas trees, but Christmas trees with electric fairy lights.

Alison's eyes filled with tears and her breathing went all wavery. She brought her hands up to cover her mouth.

Mum spoke quietly in her ear. 'What do you think?'

What did she think? What did she *think*? Six Christmas trees. All those tiny coloured lights glowing in the darkness.

'It's beautiful,' she managed to say. 'So beautiful.'

'The neighbours lent them for your reception,' Mum told her.

'They have to go back the moment the reception is over,' said Lydia, 'so you're not allowed to let the party run over time.'

'Who'd have thought so many people in our road would have electric fairy lights?' said Mum.

'It's looks magical,' said Alison, still gazing at the scene before her.

Mum laughed. 'I'm happy you think so. The neighbours have been so kind. They'll be along presently to help put up the decorations. They all helped me decorate the church with holly and berries this afternoon.'

'I owe them all a huge thank you,' said Alison.

Dad had driven his van over to Darley Court a day or two earlier to pick up the decorations and holly before popping in at Wilton Close to collect the wedding cake from Mrs Grayson.

Mum switched on the ceiling light and Alison and her friends started to unpack the decorations from boxes, with plenty of appreciative exclamations.

'I like this the best,' said Emily, displaying a long string of tiny silver bells.

'These baubles are my favourites.' Margaret unwrapped a coloured glass ball from its protective tissue and held it up.

Helped by the neighbours she had known all her life, Alison and her friends decorated the hall, transforming its wartime tiredness into a fairyland of colour and sparkles. Over in one corner, some on a trestle table, others beneath it, were all the toys that would be given to local children, who were to be brought into the hall at the end of the reception, just before Alison nipped home to change into her going-away clothes, including the hat that Lydia's clever fingers had turned into a wonderful creation thanks to the petersham band from Ingleby's.

The rest of the toys were stored safely at the hospital, ready to be distributed to the children on Christmas morning, when one of Joel's colleagues was going to dress up as Father Christmas, using the make-do Santa outfit that Cordelia's husband had worn last year.

Alison spent a while looking over the array of toys. Babies' rattles made from tins and boxes with pebbles inside. Yo-yos made from old doorknobs. Necklaces and bracelets made from the coloured beads Auntie Stella had found at the market. A variety of animals knitted by Mrs Grayson and others. Peg dollies, finger puppets, sets of cigarette cards. All the wooden vehicles made by Dad and the men who worked for him, and, of course, the magnificent wooden forts.

Alison felt deeply touched. How generous everyone had been to make these toys as part of her and Joel's Christmas wedding. She thought, too, of little Katharine, the soldier's daughter who was going to receive an embroidered hanky from her absent daddy on Christmas morning. The soldier would be much missed by his family on that special day, but Katharine's gift would let her know that she was uppermost in her father's thoughts.

Mum came and put an arm around Alison's shoulders. 'If you can tear yourself away, it's time to go home.'

'I'd like to stay a few more minutes,' Alison said. 'It all looks so beautiful.'

'I think your friends would like you to come home,' said Mum.

'We need to get them settled in,' Alison said guiltily.

'Yes, we should. It's not like you to be thoughtless about your guests, but we'll forgive you this once.'

When they arrived home, Alison soon discovered the real reason the others had wanted to drag her away from the church hall. Sitting on the furniture and also on the carpet, they wanted to give her a wedding present that was loosely wrapped in brown paper, its creases showing it had already been used multiple times.

Alison could see at once that it was a book. She unwrapped it and found not a novel but a notebook. Turning its pages, she saw that Mrs Grayson and Mrs Mitchell had written out recipes for her, as had Dot and Cordelia and also Mum, Lydia and Mrs Jessop. Mum had done two recipes for scones – wartime scones and peacetime scones.

'And there are recipes for fish pasties and stuffed ox heart signed by *B Foster*.' Alison felt puzzled for a moment, then she twigged. 'Your grandmother,' she said to Joan. 'Oh, and here's one that's been pasted in – it's from Mabel. Oh my goodness – Mabel.'

'We couldn't leave her out, could we?' Cordelia said with a smile.

Alison scanned the recipe. 'It's for devilled herrings and she's written at the bottom, *This is one I learned from Mrs Grayson.*'

'Fay added a couple of recipes at the back,' said Margaret. 'We didn't want her to be left out either.'

Alison exclaimed in delight as she turned the pages. 'This is perfect. Joel will be pleased to know I have such a good stock of recipes. Thank you all.'

'We haven't finished yet,' said Emily with a twinkle in her eyes. 'We've got something else for you.'

This time the parcel was bulky and squashy. Alison opened it to find a bundle of claret-coloured velvet. When she stood up and shook out the fabric, it was a housecoat. She heard Mum's gasp of admiration.

'It's lovely,' said Mum. 'Alison, what good friends you have.'

'It's beautiful,' said Alison. 'I don't think I've used the word beautiful so much in my entire life as I have this evening, but no other words will do.'

'Where did you get it?' Lydia asked, fingering the material.

'It's made from furnishing velvet,' Colette told her.

'Never!' Alison exclaimed.

'Joan made it into a housecoat for you,' said Margaret.

'Once a sewing machinist, always a sewing machinist,' said Joan.

Alison hugged her. 'Thank you. You're so clever.'

'She's even cleverer than that,' said Emily and produced yet another parcel, thin this time but again squashy.

Feeling overwhelmed, Alison opened it to reveal a pair of petticoats.

'They're made from butter muslin,' said Joan.

'Made by you again?' asked Alison.

'Mostly,' said Joan. 'Everyone helped sew on the lace by hand.'

'Thank you all.' Then Alison laughed at herself. 'As well as beautiful, I also keep saying thank you. I mean it from the bottom of my heart.'

'I have one more job for you all,' said Mum, standing up. 'I'd like all of you to decorate our tree for me. Then it won't just be a Christmas tree. It'll be a wedding tree.'

They took their time decorating. Persephone, Lydia and Emily took turns on the Lamberts' upright piano to play a mixture of wartime songs and Christmas carols and they all sang as they worked.

'It's lovely of your mother to ask us to do this,' said Joan.

Alison found a private moment to thank her mum. 'I remember you saying that weddings are for family, so it's extra kind of you to let my friends do this.'

Mum looked at her. 'And I remember you saying that it's important to stand by your friends. I've thought about that a lot – and also about the meaning of family. You claim you're going to be friends with these girls for ever, and maybe you will be. What matters is that they're important to you here and now. That's essential in wartime. It's what gets us through the dark times. It's taken me a long time to see it, Alison, but these friends of yours are your wartime family.'

'Oh, Mum,' Alison breathed.

Together they looked at the Christmas tree with its clip-on candleholders, the string of golden beads, the now almost hairless tinsel, the pre-Great War baubles from Granny's tree – all the decorations that Alison remembered from her childhood.

Then she looked at the dear friends who had helped to decorate her family's tree on this special occasion.

'Christmas is a time for families,' Mum said softly.

Chapter Forty-One

It was here at last. Her wedding day. Alison lay snuggled in bed. It would be cold getting out. There had been frost on the insides of the windows the past few mornings, but she didn't care. All that mattered was that today she was getting married. What a good thing she had never got hitched to Paul. Joel was her one and only true love and their recent difficulties, hard as they had been to navigate, had made them stronger as a couple.

Alison's heart beat harder, but it wasn't just love for Joel that she was feeling. There was resolution too. It was more than the certainty of knowing she was marrying the right man. It was the determination that arose from having survived a storm, coupled with the knowledge that no problem was so great that it couldn't be overcome. Plenty of girls in her position, she was sure, would have been so distraught they would have cast everything away – and those girls would have been wrong, no matter how right they felt at the time.

By weathering the storm and engaging in much heart-searching, and above all by talking things through, Alison had found her way through the problems and emerged on the other side. It hadn't been easy by any means, but she'd done it and she felt more grown-up because of it. She wasn't the eager girl who had longed to marry Paul and devote her life to making him comfortable. She and Joel knew one another far more deeply than she and Paul ever had, and that could only be for the best. They would cherish and support one another and have a lot of fun too. Life was going to be good.

A gentle tap on her bedroom door heralded the arrival of Joan and Colette, their faces wreathed in smiles. They wore their dressing gowns and slippers. They had shared Lydia's old room last night.

Although Mum had pursed her lips at the prospect of having Colette, the separated wife, staying under her roof, she had been nothing but polite to Colette, just as Alison had been confident she would be.

In fact, last night Mum had gone so far as to whisper privately to Alison, 'She seems a very nice girl – and I'm not saying that just because she's handing over her house to you and Joel. She seems sweet-natured and polite.'

'What were you expecting?' Alison asked gently and with a smile.

'Well, not that.'

'I know how iffy you feel about her being separated, but it honestly wasn't her fault. Her husband is a nasty piece of work. He was rotten to her for years while pretending in public to be the best husband in the world. Make up your own mind about Colette, Mum. I think you'll like her.'

Mum hesitated before admitting, 'I already do.'

Understanding that this represented a huge concession on her mother's part, Alison had given her a hug.

Now, as Colette perched on the dressing-table stool and Joan plonked herself on the bed by Alison's feet, Alison

beamed at her two matrons of honour. The bridesmaids –
Lydia, Emily, Persephone and Margaret – had all spent last
night crammed into Lydia's flat.

'Well, Mrs Maitland,' said Joan, 'and how are you this
morning?'

'I'm not Mrs Maitland yet.'

'Not long to wait,' said Colette.

The door opened again and Mum looked in. 'Here you all
are. Alison, put your dressing gown on. I'm getting breakfast
ready. Dad has got the fire going nicely. The others will be
here in a few minutes.'

When Colette stood up to reach for the dressing gown
hanging on the back of the door, Alison immediately said,
'Not that. I'm going to wear my new velvet housecoat.'

'Very grand,' Joan said with a laugh.

It had been arranged that everyone would have breakfast
together. Alison was aware that having her home invaded by
hordes of attendants wasn't exactly the wedding morning
Mum had envisaged; she knew, too, that she had Lydia to
thank for talking Mum into it. And to give credit where it
was due, Mum hadn't merely taken it on the chin, she had
embraced it, for which Alison was thankful.

The doorbell announced the arrival of the bridesmaids,
their hair in rollers beneath coloured headscarves and their
pretty dresses over their arms to change into later. All at once
the house was filled with happy voices and smiling faces.

Alison linked her arm through Dad's. 'Ever felt
outnumbered?'

He laughed. 'Where is everyone going to get changed?'

'Breakfast first,' said Mum. 'Come and sit down, girls.'

'No, you sit down, Mum,' said Lydia. 'The mother of the bride deserves to be waited on.'

Breakfast was simple. There were heaps of toast alongside jars of home-made bramble jelly and carrot jam. Everyone was well aware that there couldn't possibly be anything like enough butter to go round, so only the bride was allowed to have it, which they all joked about.

During breakfast, the doorbell sounded again. Dad answered it and came back with a big box.

He started to say, 'That was Mrs Hanberger from the florist's—' but got no further before being mobbed.

Lydia removed the bridal bouquet from the box and handed it to Alison, whose skin went all tingly. Highlighted by the promised eucalyptus were beautiful white chrysanthemums, which everyone exclaimed over. There were smaller versions of the bouquet for the attendants, as well as a corsage for Mum and a buttonhole for Dad.

'And these buttonholes are for Joel and the best man,' said Lydia.

'I'll take them round to the church,' said Dad, 'while all you young ladies start getting ready.'

It was a busy morning, filled with happy chatter, and Alison was delighted to see that Mum was enjoying it as much as anyone, especially when Persephone and Joan bore her off to help her get dressed.

Alison wanted to be the last one to get ready.

'So that I get all the attention,' she joked, though really it was so she could play a part in helping the others as they did their hair and put on their dresses and the shawls Mrs Grayson had crocheted for them. Persephone's dress was a pretty bronzy shade that complemented her honey-blonde hair. Mrs Grayson had made her a shawl in pale amber. To go with Margaret's lilac was a plum-coloured shawl, and with Joan's rose pink was a shawl of pale pink. Emily's best dress was a sort of peachy-pink and Mrs Grayson had made a warm cream shawl for her, while for Colette's beautiful bluebell-coloured dress she had created one in a soft violet hue. Lydia's dress was light green and her shawl was a toning apple green.

Mum wore her smartest costume, which was a jacket and skirt in dark blue, with a bow of the same colour on the side of her hat. Mum admired all the attendants. To Alison's surprise, she made a point of singling out Colette.

'You look very pretty in that. What do you call that shade?'

'Bluebell,' said Colette.

'Yes, very appropriate. I wanted to say thank you for letting Alison and Joel have your house.'

Colette smiled. 'It's my pleasure.'

Alison got Mum on her own.

'Thanks for what you said to Colette.'

Mum raised her eyebrows. 'You're thanking me for thanking her.'

'Yes. I know you've felt iffy about her all along.'

'I've thought a lot about what you said about standing by your friends. She has certainly stood by you.'

'Even though she's a separated wife,' Alison said gently.

'It's all too easy to see people in a particular way,' Mum conceded. 'I saw her as a failed wife and nothing else, but she's so much more.'

'Actually,' said Alison, 'I'm glad you judged her harshly.'

'That's the last thing I expected you to say,' said Mum, startled.

'It's because of difficult things that have happened to me or that I've seen happen to others that I've been able to become more broad-minded,' said Alison. 'If you were judgemental at first, it's because you haven't had to deal with things of that sort and I'm glad of that. It means you and Dad have had a good marriage.'

'Alison,' called Joan. 'It's high time you got dressed.'

'Unless you're intending to get married in your velvet housecoat,' added Emily.

'Off you go,' Mum whispered.

With a huge smile that she didn't bother trying to restrain, Alison let her friends and Lydia help her into her dress. Then Mum placed the tiara on her head and fluffed the veil around her. Alison gazed at her reflection. Her skin glowed and her eyes sparkled and oh, the dress! It was sheer perfection. Mum's pearls sat nicely at the round neckline. Persephone and Margaret bent to spread the skirt's train behind her.

'You look lovely,' said Mum.

'I feel lovely,' said Alison.

'It's because you feel it that you look it,' said Lydia.

'Go downstairs and show your father,' said Mum.

'Wait,' said Persephone.

She ran downstairs and fetched Alison's bouquet.

Dad had dressed quickly in his suit when he had come back from delivering the buttonholes to the church. Once he was ready, he had stayed downstairs, well out of the way of all the females.

Mum leaned over the bannisters. 'John! Come into the hall.' To Alison she said, 'Now you can go down.'

Smiling at Dad standing at the foot of the stairs, Alison made her way down, her long veil floating behind her.

'My goodness,' said Dad. 'You're so beautiful. Joel is a very lucky man. I'll be proud to walk you down the aisle.'

'Thanks, Dad,' Alison said, feeling tears rising. 'Thanks for everything.'

It was time for Mum and the girls to leave for the church.

'Before we go,' said Mum, 'let's put your cloak on for you, Alison.'

'Don't you trust Dad to do it?' Alison asked, giving Dad a nudge.

'I wouldn't dream of taking on such a complicated task,' he replied.

Once the fur cloak was settled around Alison's shoulders, with the veil settled on top of it, the others put on their coats, which they would leave at the back of the church during the ceremony.

'Have you all got your flowers, girls?' Mum fussed. 'And your shawls?'

Dad was a builder and he had lots of contacts, one of whom had produced a motor car. It took a couple of journeys to get the mother of the bride and the attendants to the church. Then Alison and Dad were alone in the house, waiting for the vehicle to return for them.

'You deserve your special day, Alison,' said Dad. 'You deserve all the fuss and the flowers and what have you, but most of all you deserve to have the best of futures.'

'Joel and I are going to be so happy,' Alison assured him.

'Nobody could ask for more. Shall we go?'

With a flutter of nerves, Alison nodded. Dad opened the front door and she walked outside. The neighbours who had helped decorate the church hall yesterday evening had turned out to see her off and she walked to the motor through a blur of good wishes and admiration. She handed her bouquet to Dad while she took her time settling herself in the car, taking great care with her dress, the veil and the cloak. Then Dad climbed in beside her and they set off.

At the church, the girls crowded round the car door to take her flowers and help her out. Alison crossed the pavement to the church porch.

'Our coats are on the back pew,' said Persephone. 'Let me put your cloak there.'

They all fussed round her, sorting out her train and the veil. Before the short part of the veil was drawn down over her face, she smiled around at her sister and her friends, who all meant so much to her.

'Thank you all,' she whispered emotionally.

'What for?' asked Emily.

'For being my friends,' Alison said simply, and when it looked as if they were waiting for her to say more, she added, 'That's all. Just for being my friends.'

'Good. Here's the photographer,' said Dad. 'Your mother has given him a list of the pictures she wants him to take, but I'm adding one of my own to the list. I want a photograph of me surrounded by all you beautiful girls.'

'Oh, Dad,' said Alison.

'I know how much these girls mean to you,' he answered, 'and that means they are important to me too. Besides, what man could resist being in the middle of a sea of such loveliness?'

The girls laughed and the photographer quickly arranged them into position for the picture.

'Thank you,' he called. 'I'll see you all when you come outside.'

'It's time,' said Joan.

She and Colette slipped the veil into place, casting the world around Alison into a prettily softened focus. Then Dad took her hand and slid it into the crook of his elbow, giving her fingers a loving squeeze.

The church doors opened and the organ sounded, the guests coming to their feet. At the top of the aisle, Joel stood up and turned to look at her, emotion sweeping across his face.

Blinking back tears of joy, Alison walked down the aisle towards Joel and their future.

Acknowledgements

You'd be surprised how many people it takes to write a book. I am grateful to everyone who has supported me through the writing process and who helped polish the book to make it sparkle. My editor Katie Loughnane's input at both the planning and editing stages made the story all the stronger. As a first-time reader, Jess Muscio's contribution was also valuable. Thanks also go to Caroline Johnson, my eagle-eyed copy-editor, and Sally Sargeant, the proofreader, both of whom don't just spot the mistakes but also suggest improvements. And Rose Waddilove, who pulls everything together.

I've also been helped by others. When I needed ideas for flowers for the bride in a winter wedding, I asked my wonderful followers on Facebook for assistance. I am indebted to Sue Hanberger for suggesting eucalyptus as the perfect winter greenery; and also to Margaret Grain, who told me about her parents' wedding. Dora Graves and Kenneth Grain tied the knot on 16 November 1945 and Dora carried white chrysanthemums.

Thank you to my husband, who explained how water columns and water towers work and who also suggested the structural problem with Grundy and Clara's house.

And thanks to everyone who cheers the series along, especially Jen Gilroy, Beverley Ann Hopper and Jane Cable.

Dear Readers,

Here we are with the new Christmas book – the third Christmas title in the Railway Girls series. Some of the early chapters were written while I was in Shropshire on a writers' holiday – oops, sorry! Did I say 'holiday'? I meant a writers' *retreat*, of course – but the fact is that, although we get a lot of work done, we also have so much fun that it feels like being on holiday. The authors I was with were Jane Cable (who also writes as Eva Glyn), Cass Grafton, Kitty Wilson and Kirsten Hesketh (who also writes as Poppy Cooper and Daisy Dougal).

Writing can be a solitary business. For years I thought of this as normal, something I put down to a mixture of two things. Firstly, I am an introvert by nature; and secondly, I was a child writer. When I was at school, a couple of friends had a go at writing because of me, but they didn't stick with it for long, so I grew up thinking of writing as an activity you do on your own.

But then I saw an ad for a writing holiday by the sea in Cornwall, and signed up for it. It was the first time I had ever had the chance to talk about my vocation with people who understood. There, I learned that writers need other writers. Authors are always interested in other authors – in their work, their careers and their experiences. We always share what we know and provide encouragement and support. It is a wonderful profession in that respect.

Friendship is an important part of life and to have that level of kindness and support in the work environment makes a big difference to this aspect of our lives. In the Railway Girls books, it is their jobs on the railways that first bring the girls together, plus of course the wise words of Miss Emery in advising them to stick together. The girls' friendships might have started off at work, but they soon spilled over into their home lives too. I hope that you, as the reader, can feel the warmth and support that are so important to the girls and that help to carry them through, even when, in this book, one friendship is severely tested.

Much love,

Maisie xx

If you loved
Christmas Wishes for the Railway Girls,

Maisie Thomas's next book

Springtime With the Railway Girls

IS AVAILABLE TO PRE-ORDER NOW

Read on for bonus content
from the author and an exclusive
first look at the new book

CHAPTER ONE

January 1944

The loud ring brought Persephone awake and she reached out a hand to bat at the alarm clock on her bedside cabinet, pressing down the button on the top to silence the clamour. She pulled her arm back beneath the covers, sparing a thought for the time when a maid would have crept into her room and got the fire going, returning later with a cup of hot chocolate for Miss Persephone to start the day. How things had changed. Not just for her; for everyone. But, by crikey, they had changed for her. Matt Franklin had changed her life beyond belief.

She had worked until two this morning and then had been called upon to do another hour, so she had slept for much of the morning. She swung out of bed, pushing her feet into her slippers and drawing her dressing gown out from inside the bed. It was much nicer to get into a toasty warm gown than a chilly one that had hung up neatly all night on the back of the door.

Going to the window, she pulled back the thick blackout curtains followed by the lavender silk curtains, which matched the lavender satin bows that held back the white muslin drapes falling prettily to the floor on either side of her half-tester bed. Tying her dressing gown more closely around her, Persephone used the flat of her hand to wipe clear a patch of condensation on the inside of the windowpane. There were even patches of frost there too.

Outside, snow still lay on the ground, several inches deep. The sky was a soft duck-egg blue with wisps of cloud. The light from the sun, though milky, was sufficient to bring forth a smattering of twinkles from the snow, especially where it covered the hedges. Persephone sighed and then smiled at her own reaction to the scene below her window. Even after more than four years of war, of anxiety and rationing and the blackout and every single thing one cared to mention being in frightfully short supply – even after all that, nature could still pull something special out of the bag and take one's breath away.

Tugging the lavender curtains closed, she hurried into the bathroom that was in between her bedroom and the one on the other side. She'd had the bathroom to herself almost the whole time since she had been shunted off to Darley Court by Pa and Ma at the outbreak of war. That had been a huge luxury to start with, because the ancestral pile down in Sussex wasn't exactly over-endowed in the bathroom department. Even so, Persephone now reckoned that her favourite times at Darley Court had been when her friend Colette and later her sister Iphigenia had stayed in the opposite bedroom, and there had been much crossing through the bathroom to sit on one another's beds and talk.

Next to the porcelain enamelled bath, with its black line around the inside showing precisely how much – or rather, how little – water was permitted for wartime ablutions, was a copper gas-geyser on a wood-and-metal stand. From the top of the geyser, a cylindrical flue reached up almost to the blue-painted ceiling before turning and disappearing through the line of flower-decorated tiles that topped the plain white ones below.

Persephone cleaned her teeth and washed her face and hands, using the tiniest possible quantity of soap. It was essential, of course, to ration all kinds of things and Persephone had discovered it was possible to live without many items, but there were others that it was a dratted nuisance to do without. Soap was definitely on the 'dratted' list. To be fair, though, she was fortunate to have a job that didn't involve getting mucky – unlike Margaret, who cleaned locomotives in the engine shed for a living, not to mention Miss Brown's land girls.

Persephone returned to her bedroom. Fond as she was of it, she had to admit that the paint on the window frames, picture rail and door could do with a fresh coat, but nobody had been allowed to have paint for decorative purposes for simply yonks. It couldn't be spared. Besides, if there were to be some paint kicking around, she would far rather see it sprucing up the tired-looking stations and waiting rooms that she saw every day in her work as a ticket inspector.

She hurried into her clothes. Over a long-sleeved silk blouse she wore an olive-green suede top, rather like a long, slimline waistcoat. On top of this went a sweater knitted for her by dear Mrs Grayson.

It had padded shoulders and a high round neckline that hugged her throat. Persephone drew on straight-cut wool trousers, fastening the buttons on the side and pushing her hands into the hip-level pockets on the side seams to make sure they didn't create an unsightly bulge. After putting on two pairs of socks, she stuffed her feet back into her slippers.

She ran downstairs to the cavernous kitchen, where Mrs Mitchell, who had been the housekeeper here since dinosaurs roamed the earth, provided porridge and toast with a scraping of marge. Afterwards, Persephone shoved her feet into her wellies and put on her brown-and-tan tweed jacket with flap pockets, wrapping herself up in the scarf knitted for her by Nanny Trehearn-Hobbs, who had unravelled an old sweater belonging to Persephone's brother Giles, thus making the scarf doubly precious. Pulling on a pair of shabby old gloves, she headed outside to be given a job by the head gardener, a sweet old boy with oodles of knowledge about the land.

Unsurprisingly, there was snow to be shovelled from the stable yard and then – a great honour – she was permitted to help sort through the potting shed, sharpening and oiling the tools, readying everything for the new season,.

Later, she went to Miss Brown's office, where Darley Court's elderly owner spent much of her time. Around the walls, the shelves held books and military helmets from wars of yesteryear. Miss Brown's magnificent desk stood facing the windows, while much of the floor was taken up by a vast table covered by a detailed map of the grounds, showing how they had been arranged for crop rotation for wartime.

Together, Persephone and Miss Brown worked their way through the lists of forthcoming training events Darley Court would be hosting. They checked the dates and put everything in the diary, together with notes about the necessary catering. Even before the war began, back when air-raid shelters were being delivered to houses and sandbags were appearing everywhere, Miss Brown had volunteered her home as a place for meetings and training for all local defence services. She might be in her seventies, but woe betide anyone who made the mistake of imagining that meant she was frail and in need of guidance. She was a strong character with a shrewd mind and sharp eyes. Persephone thought the world of her.

Then, after a helping of Mrs Mitchell's rabbit hotpot, Persephone prepared to set off for work. She was proud to wear her smart uniform, not least because she wore on her lapel the LMS badge, showing its linked emblems of a thistle for Scotland and a rose for England, both of them beneath a wing with the cross of St George. Another reason for loving her uniform and all it represented was that she had her job on the railways to thank for introducing her to Matt. The thought of her handsome boyfriend brought a spontaneous smile to her lips.

Matt was a fireman on the railways and it was his job to keep his train running smoothly. He had to keep the fire stoked inside the engine's massive firebox, shovelling the coal into the right spot at any given moment, always aware of the terrain and the driving conditions and how much energy was being taken from the fire. On top of this, he had to keep an eye on the water gauges and ensure the water never ran low, as well as use his hammer to break up huge lumps of coal and spray water on the footplate to dampen down the dust.

After working at Victoria Station as a ticket collector, Persephone had met Matt once she was promoted to the post of ticket inspector, which required her to travel on the trains. Matt worked very long hours. Everyone did these days, of course, but the engine drivers and their firemen worked longer shifts than anyone. Their shifts might last eighteen or twenty hours. The trains kept running day and night, regardless of weather conditions and regardless of air raids. The railway infrastructure was also a target for Jerry – tracks, bridges, stations, sidings, marshalling yards. The engine drivers and firemen did highly-skilled, dangerous jobs that called for years of experience.

Persephone had heard of one driver who had worked solidly for twenty-two hours, only to go home and find his house had been destroyed by the Luftwaffe and his wife and children had all copped it. She thanked heaven that her lovely Matt had never suffered such a terrible calamity. He still had all his family. He lived with his mother and father, who was a police sergeant, and he had two sisters. Peggy, who, in her thirties, was a similar age to her brother, was married and had her own home – an empty home these days, her children having been evacuated at the outbreak of war. She worked in a home for old soldiers. The other sister, Jill, the youngest by some years, lived with her parents and had a job in a munitions factory.

Persephone was fond of the two girls and Sergeant Franklin, but she had never forgotten what Matt's mother had once said to her. *'I don't want you toying with my son's affections.'*

As if she would! But she could see Mrs Franklin's point of view. The Honourable Miss Trehearn-Hobbs and Matt Franklin, railwayman. It wasn't a conventional combination.

Persephone's family weren't pleased about it either. Pa had given her the most awful wigging.

'You've shown that the pressure of war work has made you lose your respect for your upbringing and everything you've ever learned. Not only have you brought shame on your mother and me and the whole family, but you've also shown that doing a man's job has addled your brains. You've let down every right-minded woman in the country.'

On the other hand, Iphigenia had positively encouraged her to get together with Matt – though only to indulge in a wartime fling.

'The war has given all you single girls this marvellous opportunity to enjoy yourselves. What's wrong with that? Grab it with both hands, little sister, that's what I say. You'll have years and years to be a respectable married lady afterwards. And I promise not to tell tales on you.'

Persephone and Matt were all too aware of the complications their relationship had brought swirling to the surface, yet neither of them had backed away. Their closeness had grown from true friendship. In spite of the social barrier between them, they had much in common, not least the way they had both striven to follow their dreams. Matt had given up a grammar school education in order to join the railways while Persephone had for years wanted to be a journalist. Although her dream of working for a newspaper had no chance of being realised, she had throughout the war produced a steady stream of articles for the local press and women's magazines, in particular *Vera's Voice*. There was a particular knack to writing the sort of thing that the magazines currently wanted and Persephone had worked hard to produce the right mixture of encouragement, compassion and common sense.

Hers and Matt's was a steady, loving relationship. It ought to have everything going for it… but not when the social ramifications were taken into account.

Persephone arrived at Victoria Station to find the concourse busy, as always. She knew the station inside out from her days as a ticket collector: the large clock with Roman numerals hanging from the metal gantry underneath the vast overarching glass canopy; the noticeboards in between the platform entrances; the long line of little windows where passengers queued for tickets; and the small, pale-yellow-tiled buildings grouped together, each with its name above the entrance in elegant capital letters against a background of deep blue – GRILL ROOM, BOOKSTALL, RESTAURANT, BUFFET.

It was towards the buffet that Persephone now headed. She had been there so often that her feet would probably take her there even if she didn't intend to go. This was where she and her friends met up whenever they could, shifts permitting. They couldn't all attend every time, which meant that a full house was extra special.

There was a strict rule that, even if they were off duty, employees in uniform mustn't be seen in public sitting in the buffet, smoking and chatting, in case it looked as if they were slacking. Over her uniform Persephone wore her caramel-coloured wool coat with its over-sized collar and buckle belt, together with a hat that had a rather snazzy curled brim. Her uniform peaked cap was in a bag dangling from her wrist.

A couple of soldiers darted forward, vying with one another to open the door for her. Persephone thanked them with a smile, then insisted they go ahead of her in the queue. Most people gave way to the lads who were fighting to save the country. Indeed, as soon as the people in the queue realised there were Tommies present, they immediately sent the boys to the front, where Mrs Jessop, in common with buffet staff the country over, gave them tea and scones, waving aside their offer of payment.

When her turn came, Persephone purchased a cup of tea, stirring it with the teaspoon that was fastened by a thin chain to a small block of wood. With the shortage of crockery and cutlery, it was a long time since Mrs Jessop had taken any chances with her spoons. She was careful with her crockery too and only handed out the good cups and saucers to her regulars, with strangers having to make do with mugs, old sugar basins or even jam jars.

Making her way between the tables, Persephone approached the one her chums had bagged. When the buffet wasn't too busy, Mrs Jessop didn't mind if they pushed two together, but at this time of day they had to squeeze round a single table. Emily and Fay shared a chair, as did Margaret and Colette.

Joan shifted sideways on her seat. 'Plonk yourself here with me,' she invited Persephone. 'I'll have to go in a few minutes anyway, so then you can have the chair to yourself.'

Persephone smiled. 'Got to get home to Max?'

Joan's blue eyes softened at the mention of her little son. 'Yes. Having the chance to see you all is a real treat and I wouldn't miss it for anything, but I can't be late for Max.'

'What about you, Alison?' asked Cordelia. 'Have you got to hurry home to make Joel's tea?'

Alison looked pleased, her brown eyes sparkling. Each time Persephone had seen her since the day of her December wedding, her skin had been radiant, a clear outward sign of her happiness.

'No, as a matter of fact,' said Alison. 'He's working late today. Our hours won't coincide again until next week, worse luck.'

'Are you enjoying being an old married lady?' asked Fay.

'I've never been happier,' Alison said simply.

'It does me good to see my daughters for the duration settling down in good marriages,' Dot declared. 'Alison and Joel, Joan and Bob.'

'Mabel and Harry,' Joan added.

'I wasn't forgetting them,' said Dot.

She looked at Persephone and Persephone's shoulders tightened, the hairs lifting on her arms. Please don't let Dot say she and Matt would be next.

But Dot merely said, 'And you, love – you're happy with your Matt an' all, aren't you?'

Persephone relaxed. 'Yes, very.' She hesitated. She had never shared this with anyone before, but she could trust these dearest of friends to understand and support her – and quite honestly, some support wouldn't come amiss. 'It's… different for us.' Heaven help her, she had almost said difficult. 'You know, because of the social side of it.'

'The Honourable and the fireman,' said Alison.

Persephone nodded. 'You and Joel, and Joan and Bob, have your happy ever afters.'

Emily sat up straighter. 'But you seem so happy.'

'Oh, I am. We are,' Persephone assured her. 'It's just that we can't have the happy-ever-after part.' She looked around at her friends. Nobody demurred. Of course not. 'It's not like that for us. As Alison says – the Honourable and the fireman.'

'Oh, chick,' Dot said sympathetically.

'The war brought us together,' said Persephone, 'and I'm grateful for that, but I also know – we both know – that once the war is over…'

'Which it will be in the foreseeable future,' said Margaret, 'after the advances the Allies have made.'

'Precisely.' Although her heart felt as though it was cracking open, Persephone kept her tone light and steady. 'We don't have happy ever after to look forward to. What we have is happy for now. When you think about it, that's as much as anyone can truly rely on in wartime.'

Happy for now.

It sounded so simple – so sensible. But it also placed an extra barrier between her and her clever, interesting, kind Matt, because what they had now was all there was and all there could ever be.

Happy for now.

Unsettled for now.

Q&A WITH MAISIE THOMAS

After the Q&A that appeared in the back of *Courage of the Railway Girls*, I asked my Facebook followers if they would like to ask their own questions this time around. I'd like to say a huge thank you to everyone who joined in. I just wish we had room to include every single question.

Paula Davitt asks: *Why did you pick the railways as the war work the girls did?*

The simple answer is that someone else made that decision. Cassandra di Bello, who was a commissioning editor with Penguin, thought up the idea of women working on the railways and then needed an author to write the series for her. She rang my agent, Laura Longrigg, to see if Laura had anyone suitable and Laura suggested me. She sent Cass a pre-publication copy of *The Surplus Girls* (written as Polly Heron). Cass liked my writing style – and I got the job!

I already had a long-standing interest in the Second World War and had several shelves of books on the subject. You won't be surprised to hear that I now have several more shelves. I was especially pleased to be asked to write about the railways as my great-aunt Jessie worked as a railway clerk during the First World War and her father, Thomas, was a railway clerk all his life. If you think back to *The Railway Girls*, where Joan's first job was in the charging office, that is the sort of work Thomas did. He organised the delivery of goods and parcels not just by train but also by road and steamer at the end of each railway journey.

My husband has also been a big help to me, thanks to his love and knowledge of old railways. He quickly got used to answering random questions, such as 'When a steam train is going to pull out of the station, in what order do you hear all the sounds?' and 'How does a water tower work?'. Incidentally, he is also the person who checks that the trains on the book covers are correct.

Pauline Little's question is: *How did you find out what women did on the railways in the war?*

I got lots of information from *Female Railway Workers of World War II* by Susan Major (Pen & Sword Transport, 2018). This book includes masses of oral history, which I found invaluable. It's thanks to this book that Dot became a parcels porter, Cordelia became a lampwoman, Mabel worked as a lengthman and Lizzie and Joan were given jobs as station porters.

Much of the information that enabled me to promote Persephone to the rank of ticket inspector in *Courage of the Railway Girls* came from *How We Lived Then: A History of Everyday Life During the Second World War* by Norman Longmate (Hutchinson & Co Ltd, 1971). Margaret's engine-cleaning experiences came from various sources, mainly *More Tales of the Old Railwaymen* by Tom Quinn (Aurum Press Ltd, 2002) and *Steaming to Victory: How Britain's Railway's Won the War* by Michael Williams (Arrow Books, 2014). And Letitia's work in the munitions factory, double-checking the mathematical calculations for the bomb-making, was what my mother did.

A question from Lynn Dobbins: *How did you choose the girls' names?* **And related questions from Sharon Williams, Jacqueline Frost and Maggie Ramsden, who want to know:** *How do you think of the characters? Are they based on people you know?*

I didn't choose the girls' names – at least, not consciously. When a character appears in my head for the first time, she is almost always fully-formed. I know what she looks like, what sort of personality she has, what her background is, and also her first name. But I do check that the name would have been in current use in the year she was born. All my characters come out of my imagination.

Kirsten Hesketh asks: *Is there something from your research that really surprised or amazed you?*

I don't know about being surprised or amazed, but I do remember laughing out loud at stories of how completely disorienting the blackout could be. There are numerous tales of stone cold sober people leaving buildings and walking outside into surroundings they had known for years and finding themselves wandering around, hopelessly lost in the darkness, or even heading straight into a ditch or a duck pond.

Dawn Wilson wonders: *How often do you write?*

It's my full-time job and I write every day. A lot of people have the idea that authors only write when inspiration strikes, but I can assure you the reality isn't like that at all. As well as writing The Railway Girls series, I also write sagas as Susanna Bavin and Polly Heron, so I have plenty to keep me busy!

And Joanne Bibby's question is: *How long does it take to write a book?*

I set aside three months to write each Railway Girls book, but within that three months, I also have to make the time to work on the edits and copy-edits of the previous book. I don't like having to break off to work on edits, but it doesn't take long to get back into the flow afterwards. For me, writing the first version of the book is the best part of my job. I love it!

HOME FOR CHRISTMAS

As Violet entered the station with Evelyn, her daughter-in-law, the spicy-sharp aroma of steam and smoke caught at something deep inside her. Wasn't smell supposed to be the most powerful sense when it came to stirring memories?

In that moment, it might have been twenty-five years ago. Twenty-five! Violet had been a young lass of nineteen, happy and excited because her darling husband was due home on leave from the army for two whole days over Christmas and she couldn't wait for him to meet his five-month-old son. Baby Hugh was blue-eyed and dark-haired, just like his daddy, right down to the little cleft in his chin. Big Hugh and baby Hugh. That was how she'd thought of them.

'He's the image of his dad,' all the neighbours had said, peering into the baby carriage that was her pride and joy.

Later in the war, she'd used it to carry the local poor bin – filled with peelings, tops and tails of vegetables, plus crusts and bacon rinds – to the soup kitchen to be made into wartime soup for the destitute.

By then, the neighbours were saying, 'You'll always have the little lad to remember his dad by.'

They were right, of course, but Violet had felt annoyed all the same, unbearably hurt by the suggestion that Hugh's death wasn't so bad since she still had their son. Losing Hugh had cut her heart into a thousand pieces. But watching little Hugh grow up had glued her heart back together again.

Now, Evelyn turned to Violet, eyes shining. 'Listen, Mum. There's a band. Doesn't that make it perfect?'

The Sally Army band played 'O Little Town of Bethlehem' near the buffet, the familiar strains lifting up into the station's overarching glass canopy and echoing down again. Bowler-hatted men with rolled-up umbrellas and women with 'stockings' courtesy of Bisto delved in pockets and purses to drop a few coppers into the collecting tin.

There had been a band here twenty-five years ago too – a silver band, with men too old to fight for their country and lads too young to get into the army even if they'd lied about their ages. They had played carols and Violet had sung along softly to little Hugh as she jiggled him in her arms.

Then she had heard the train approaching, white clouds of steam puffing from the funnel. It coasted alongside the platform, brakes shrieking before it stopped. Other waiting women surged forward to meet their husbands, sons and sweethearts, but Violet, not wanting to join the crush with a baby in her arms, had stayed put, lifting herself on her toes, heart thumping as her eager gaze sought her husband's handsome face.

He didn't appear. The platform became emptier and emptier. Violet felt confused and upset. Then, instead of Hugh appearing in front of her, her mum and her auntie appeared from behind her, their eyes filled with anguish. If Violet hadn't set off for the station so ridiculously early, she would have been there to receive the telegram that every wife dreaded. She wasn't a wife any more. She was a war widow.

It was her friends who had seen her through. In a strange way, so had the war. There was so much to do. Bandages to be cut and rolled, socks and balaclavas to be knitted. Charity work, canteen work. The soup kitchen.

Violet worked as a skivvy at the hospital, mopping floors and rinsing bedpans. Her favourite job was pushing the tea trolley and dispensing steaming mugs to men with sightless eyes or bandaged stumps. Hugh wasn't here anymore, but these poor devils were and they needed looking after.

After the war, Bertie came home. He had been Hugh's best friend. He and Violet spent ages together, talking about the old days.

'You could do a lot worse,' said Mum. 'Little Hugh needs a dad.'

Friendship might be a reason for others to marry, but not Violet. She still loved Hugh and that wouldn't have been fair on Bertie even though he said he didn't mind.

He had married another girl in the end and gone on to have six nippers.

'That could have been you,' said Mum.

But Violet was all right as she was. Her friends gave her strength. They were a mixed bunch of wives, widows and women who would now never marry because of how many men had perished in the war. Between them, they looked out for each other and Violet cherished every single one of them.

She was Auntie Violet to more children than you could shake a stick at and little Hugh had umpteen playmates. Mum never quite forgave her for not grabbing Bertie with both hands, but Violet never regretted it. She and her son might not enjoy the material advantages a man's wage could bring, but they had love and laughter and a solid community of friends and neighbours.

When Hugh met Evelyn and they wanted to marry at eighteen, Violet didn't bat an eyelid.

'Too young,' her mum said.

'You're never too young to be happy together,' said Violet.

She thought the world of Evelyn. Some mothers-in-law thought their daughters-in-law weren't good enough, but not Violet. Evelyn was good-natured, funny and loving – a bright star in Violet's life as well as in Hugh's.

Thank goodness Hugh and Evelyn had had those early years together, years that Violet and Hugh's father had been denied. Now war had come again, bringing shortages, rationing, the blackout, fundraising for weapons, fundraising for the Red Cross. Air raids, bombs, destruction. Craters in the street, houses reduced to rubble.

'Here comes the train.' Evelyn clutched Violet's arm.

Even before it stopped, the doors banged open and soldiers jumped out. The waiting crowd pressed forward, but Violet was frozen to the spot. Twenty-five years ago, the most precious moment of her life had ended in despair.

Then she saw him, looking exactly like his father, right down to the cleft in his chin. Tears of joy and gratitude filled Violet's eyes as Evelyn ran forward to meet her husband.